CW00864087

Gather The Children

Gather The Children

Chronicles of the Maca II

Mari Collier

Published 2015 by Creativia

Book design by Creativia (www.creativia.org)

Cover art by http://www.thecovercollection.com/

http://www.maricollier.com/

To my beloved Lanny Dee
Who wanted to see how that young man turned out.

Contents

Prologue

Toma the Justine stared at his controls and the rushing water below in horror and disbelief. What had happened in the intervening one hundred and twenty-four years? He was on the third planet from a star the main civilizations called the Earth and the Sun. When he landed it had been the Year of Our Lord, 1712, in their incorrect reckoning.

When he enlarged the cave to hide his ship, the *Golden One*, the terrain was stable and there were no people to discover it. Homes, small cities, and what the inhabitants called settlements now dotted both sides of a wide, flowing river. All types of river craft plied the water below. He checked and rechecked his coordinates. They were as correct as the first time, second time, third time, and fourth time he had run them.

If he let himself be seen while trying to find his ship capable of carrying him back to his world, someone on this planet would surely see his scouting craft. There was also the unpleasant fact that this exploratory craft did not possess the necessary power to extract the larger vessel, wherever it was. He could dive again, but it would be futile. He had found nothing below the surface but fish, logs, rocks and bits of sunken debris from the river traffic that moved along this great channel called the Mississippi.

He desperately needed to find a place less populated to hide his craft containing information he had gathered about this planet and its various peoples; information encoded on crystals for further study and extrapolation. Toma knew of one other place on this continent that had not shown any evidence of seismic activity. If he fled back to the more civilized continents, the population numbers increased the risk of his craft being discovered long before any rescue ship from his own planet would search for him or find him.

Like many on this continent, he fled to the area known as Texas. He buried his craft far from the sight of man. He would need to live out his life among these primitive beings that valued golden metal, land, and social position above the welfare of their like beings, and many disdained those who sought knowledge. It was a bitter, bitter end to his quest.

Chapter 1

Lorenz

"Hey, Marshal, better come right quick. Some kid's hauling in a dead man." Zeke Cawley stuck his head in the office long enough to yell and then yanked his head back through the door like a turtle retreating into its shell.

Town Marshal Franklin sighed and put down the rattan fan he'd been using to create a futile breeze and shoo the flies. He straightened, brushed the dust from his worsted, brown jacket, and jammed his hat over white locks. At fifty-five he was old for his job in Arles, Texas and he knew it. Eighteen sixty-five had not been a kind year. There had been riots in Houston and Galveston; hungry people fighting for supplies. Once there had been only hardened adventurers passing through his town. Indians and Comancheros might cause concerns, but they remained well outside the town limits. Now he dealt with men who were probably Jayhawkers, Nightriders, or Redlegs. There were bands of hungry, angry men coming home from the War: men coming home to a home no longer there. Not content to let matters alone, Congress was considering a Reconstruction Bill.

Franklin stepped into bright, June sunshine and stood alongside the others gathering around some kid on an old, dapple-grey horse. The kid was leading a gaunt roan with a body wrapped in a tarp and draped over its swayed back. The boy sat rod straight, Henry rifle ready, body tensed, his lips a dead white slash against tan skin. The kid looked ready to shoot if anyone came too close or moved too fast.

To ease matters, Franklin pushed his hat back, stepped slowly forward, and asked softly, "Well, where did y'all find him?"

The boy's weathered hat covered long, curling, black hair that hid most of his features except glowering, grey eyes that raked the crowd. Boy seemed the right term for there wasn't a beard yet and at the distance of four feet it was obvious he hadn't bothered with bathing. Franklin felt that the kid wouldn't bother shaving if he didn't wash.

The boy fixed hard eyes on him, then on the star, and back to Franklin's face. "Ah didn't find him. Ah kilt him. He's Butch Zale, Comanchero. There's a five hundred dollar reward and ah want it." The voice was cold-edged hard.

Franklin was startled. A murmur swelled and flowed through the crowd. "We'll need to take a look. Zeke, pull that body down."

Zeke didn't like the job. His movements were rough and jerky. "Gawd, he's done gut shot him. Somebody give me a hand."

The people were more interested in looking than touching. They watched, but no one moved.

"When did y'all shoot him?" asked Franklin. He had to keep control of the situation.

"Yesterday mornin'. Ah'd been followin' him."

Franklin squinted against the sunshine pelting downward and was thankful he hadn't had to go after Zale if he and his group had truly been that close. The idea of this kid sneaking up and getting away without a scratch was preposterous. Still, it was best to proceed with caution as long as the kid sat there ready to blow away anybody that moved wrong.

"Where did y'all take him?"

"In a gully by the foothills. They tho't they wuz hid." His voice had become a reasonable tenor that wasn't cracking. Franklin

4

revised his estimate. Possibly the kid was about sixteen or seventeen.

"We'll need details for identification. I heard Rolfe is in town. Somebody go find him," commanded Franklin.

"No need to look, Marshal," came an answer.

The crowd parted for two men moving closer. "Ve been vatching." A stream of brown, tobacco liquid erupted from between the lips covered by a blond and graying mustache, expertly missing the bystanders. Rolfe, ex-mountain man, sometimes wolf hunter, now a cattleman, still wore his buckskins and moccasins. A bowie knife hung from the waist of his short, blocky frame. The man beside him towered over Rolfe and the crowd, his huge, lumbering body swaying almost like a bear. He stood more than a foot taller than Rolfe and was equally wide. Unlike Rolfe, he wore boots and duck trousers, his dark blue, collarless shirt was covered at the neck by a blue bandana, and the wide brim hat of a cattleman sat square on the large head.

Franklin nodded at the two. "Take a look and see if it's Zale."

Rolfe walked over and squatted, peering down at the crumpled form while the big man stopped a few feet from the kid and his rifle, seemingly watching the crowd and it's wonderment at the developing tableau with amused, brown eyes.

The kid was grinding his teeth at the delay. "How's he gonna know if'n it's Zale?" He shot the question at Franklin, but kept shifting his glare between the ex-hunter and his waiting friend.

"Believe me," assured Franklin. "He knows."

Rolfe stood and nodded to Franklin. "Dot's him. By damn, poy, I couldn't haf done it better. He died slow." Rolfe's voice was filled with admiration, the blue eyes hard and knowing. Like his friend MacDonald, Rolfe was now studying the young man.

The boy jerked his gaze back to Franklin. "Now, ah want that reward!" His voice was harsh and reward came out like reeward.

Franklin shifted his weight to relieve the pressure on his corns. "It don't happen quite that fast. First there are papers to be filled out, then..." he stopped as the Henry rifle was pointed directly at him.

"You son-of-a-bitch! I killed him. It's mine!"

Franklin stood opened mouth at the authority ringing in the young voice, the sudden change of language, and the rifle pointed straight at his heart. No one saw the huge companion of Rolfe leaping the distance separating them. MacDonald shoved the rifle upward with his right hand and used his left to drag the young body down with a thud. Franklin caught the horse and handed the reins to Zeke. The boy rolled and went for the revolver at his side, flinging it up toward the giant when a knee caught him on the chin. With ease, MacDonald reached down and pulled him upright, turning the body and clamping his left arm around the boy. With his right hand he crunched down on the boy's right hand, extracted the revolver from the boy's suddenly loose grip, and flung it to Rolfe. Then he removed the other revolver, ran his hand over the boy's back and flipped a knife from its hidden sheath. Rolfe caught the knife while MacDonald ran his huge hand over the boy's front pockets and pulled out a pocket knife.

"His boots, Mac, his boots. He's probably got another knife in his left one." Rolfe was watching with professional interest.

"Aye." MacDonald leaned his weight into the skinny body and bent the boy over and tightened his grip. "Be still, damn ye," he said mildly enough. He shifted his hold to the right and fished up the knife from the boot sheath. Only then did he release the boy.

The kid came up with fists clenched, chest heaving. He gauged the size of the man and his strength and knew he had lost, but rage boiled through him, unreasoning and unrelenting. "God damn y'all fuckin' son-of-..."

A huge hand exploded on one side of his face and then on the other, stopping the flow of words. He stood swaying, dazed, the world heaving, but he would not go down. His eyes cleared and he could feel the silence in the crowd, waiting, wanting more violence. He flicked his tongue to the side of his mouth where blood seeped.

"Can ye hear me now?" The voice was low and rumbling with the music of a different tongue.

"Yeah."

"Then ye nay ere say such words to me again; nay ere in the presence of ladies."

The boy stared upward and sucked in his breath, partially to finish clearing his mind and partially in wonderment. Where did this big bastard come up with the right to tell him what to say? God, he thought, look at the size of him. It was wonderment, and he still didn't have his money. The marshal's voice cut into his thoughts.

"Thank y'all, Mr. MacDonald. Zeke, haul the remains over to Doc Huddleson and get Mr. Mallory over here."

"I'm right here, Marshall." Mr. Mallory stepped from the crowd. His Justice of the Peace office was next door, and at the first buzz of excitement, he had joined the rest of the lookers.

"Fine, I need y'all to take a statement from this lad and from Mr. Rolfe."

The boy let out his breath, hardly believing what he was hearing. "Ah get my gold?" he asked.

Franklin gave a wry smile. "I'm afraid the government doesn't work quite that swiftly."

The boy was puzzled. "Why not? Thar's the bank." He pointed across the street in the general direction of the next block.

He doesn't read, thought Franklin to himself, but that was not unusual. "The United States government doesn't keep its gold in some town in Texas. It keeps it up North for the Yankees. We have to send the papers to them."

"Hell, ah need the gold."

Franklin noted the boy's worn jeans, held up by a frayed rope, his ragged shirt, the sloppy, split boots, and sighed inwardly. Damn, young fool. Poverty probably explained the chance the kid took going after Zale, except, there was the full armory MacDonald had stripped off the youth. That didn't make sense. Of course, weapons were cheap now. Men would sell a prized rifle for a bag of flour. "We might as well go inside," he said. "Mr. Rolfe, would y'all write down your reasons for recognizing Zale? If y'all can't, Mr. Mallory will, and then y'all can make your mark."

Rolfe grinned. "Vhat language do du vant, Deutsch or English?"

"English, Mr. Rolfe, English will be fine." He turned to the crowd. "That's all folks. The excitement's over for today." He led the way inside followed by Mallory and Rolfe.

At the door he realized that the boy was still standing in the middle of the street, hands clenched, undecided, his felt hat still in the dirt where it landed when MacDonald had slapped him.

MacDonald solved the problem. He bent down, lifted the hat, and handed it upward, grinning as he did. "Ye might as well learn the ways of townsmen."

The boy slammed the hat on and followed. He could devise no other method to regain the weapons that Rolfe and MacDonald carried. The gold, he decided had somehow been lost, but he needed his guns. He did not like stepping into the building. He had avoided buildings for well over a year and this was certain sure to be another place where people told you what to do and what not to do.

Chapter 2

Frontier Law

The marshal settled himself behind his desk and drew up another chair for Mallory. As Justice of the Peace, Mallory also functioned as the Notary Public and the coroner. The latter was a job that he and Doc Huddleson had been sharing for years. "Now y'all give your details of what happened this morning to Mr. Mallory, who will write them down, read them back, and then y'all make your mark underneath," he said to the boy.

The young man was still defiant, but puzzled by the legalities. "Mark? Hell, iffen y'll mean name, ah can write that." That came out as theat.

Full of surprises, thought Franklin, and turned to Rolfe. "Rolfe, put his guns on the shelf over there for now." He motioned toward the built in cabinet holding the spare shotguns and rifles. "Here's some paper and a pencil. Will that shelf have enough room for y'all to write? We're getting a little crowded for space."

He glared at the young, blond man peering in the door and recognized young Rolfe. Well, no matter, except he didn't like too many people in his office. The space became overheated and stifling. The kid in front of the desk kept shifting his weight, acting like he'd pull some stunt if he dared. So far no words came from his mouth. The kid was watching MacDonald as he deposited the knives on the shelf with the other hardware. MacDonald turned and folded his arms across his chest, his brown eyes glimmering with secret amusement. He knows men, thought Franklin. He knows the kid would gut shoot him as quick as he did Zale if he had the chance.

He turned his attention to the youth. "All right, young man, do y'all have a name?"

"What difference does that make?" The words were sullen, angry, and slurred with some type of border drawl.

"Both Mr. Mallory and I need that for the records. He starts the paper out with 'I, your name, the date', and the rest of what y'all have to say about what happened." Franklin was patient. The boy had his back up, but he did need the information for the county records.

"What for?" The kid was still baffled, and he looked ready to run.

At the cabinet shelf, Rolfe was busy writing, stopping every so often to look at a word, lick at the end of the pencil, and begin again. MacDonald hadn't moved. He was still watching, his face was now intent on the boy's face. Franklin removed his hat and sighed. This was going to take some time. "It is necessary because if the government does acknowledge your claim, they need to know who y'all are and where to send the money."

"What the hell am ah suppose to do fer eats? Ah need it now!" He glared at Franklin.

"Kid," Franklin sighed, "half of the people in Texas are wondering what to do for eats. First things first, state your name and tell Mr. Mallory how y'all killed Zale, that is, if y'all did kill him."

A flush spread over the half-wild face. Franklin noticed the scar that started under the boy's scraggly mane, traversed the length of the right cheek, and slid under the dirty shirt. It was an ugly scar, twisting the mouth upward into a sarcastic grin. Right now the proud flesh was turning purple; the grey eyes were blazing and turning into cold fire. God, thought Franklin, that one kills and probably enjoys it.

"Ah kilt him and his right hand man, Travers. The rest ran like coyotes, but two was limpin' and one sure as hell ain't gonna make it."

"Fine," replied Franklin. "Now just tell Mr. Mallory your name, how y'all came upon them, and exactly what happened out there." He locked his eyes with the boy. "Otherwise I might just throw y'all in jail for disturbing my whole morning."

The kid pondered that for a minute and shrugged. "My name's Lorenz," he gritted out between clenched teeth.

"And?" inquired Franklin.

"Huh?"

"A man generally goes by two names, sometimes more. We need that for the record. First and last name, please."

The gray eyes studied him. It was not slowness that stayed the boy's tongue. Franklin suspected he was hiding something. The boy shrugged. "Some call me Kid Lorenz."

Franklin snapped the fan to hide a smile. Now he recognized the warning twitch in the back of his mind. The name was from an old handbill. What Franklin didn't like was the way Mac-Donald and Rolfe had straightened. The last thing he wanted was trouble from those two. He did not take lightly the tales of MacDonald breaking bones while Rolfe carved away with his bowie knife. Right now, he needed to hear what the youth had to say before he brought up the old handbill. "Fine," he repeated, "tell Mr. Mallory what happened."

MacDonald stepped closer as if to hear the tale, but Franklin suspected he was studying the boy's features. Rolfe seemed to nod and returned to his writing. Franklin slid the bottle of ink over to Mallory and breathed easier as the boy began his recital of following Zale's trail out of Fort Davis down to Juarez and back. Franklin kept his eyes on the big man and on Rolfe. Mac-Donald was still looking intently at the kid and Rolfe was still busy, but, damn it, the boy did bear a resemblance to Kasper Schmidt. Quietly he reached into his bottom drawer to pull out the old handbills, trying to listen and look at the wanted posters without distracting MacDonald. His mind kept worrying about what the big man would do. Should MacDonald decide the kid was his stepson, all hell could break loose.

What kind of man married a woman who had been taken by the Comanche and then goes into court sues for divorce by declaring her husband guilty of desertion, abandonment of wife and children, and attempted murder? To top it off, Rolfe and MacDonald were damn Yankees. They publicly stated to one and all that they had given their oath when entering this country, and by God, they'd not break it. Despised the two might be, but here they remained. The town had tried threats and burning them out. When a trio of townsmen attacked MacDonald while he was recovering from a war wound that crazy woman of his had taken MacDonald's cane and thrashed one assailant as MacDonald dispatched the other two. You'd think the Yankees would have the decency to stay out of town, but Rolfe and Mac-Donald drove in their cattle and sold them to the U. S. Calvary. They walked and rode where they pleased.

Halfway through the handbills, Franklin found what he knew was there. Rolfe interrupted his thoughts by laying the paper on his desk and asking, "Vill dot do it?"

Franklin scanned the writing, still half-listening to the boy's recital. The writing was surprisingly crisp and to the point, a neat up and down slanting script he would not have credited to someone who spoke English as Rolfe spoke it.

"Yes, as soon as Mr. Mallory has time, you can sign in his presence and he'll stamp it," replied Franklin in a low voice.

The kid stopped talking long enough to glance at them. "Ah snuck up on 'em during the night. They didn't know ah was there, and ah waited for dawn's light and gut shot Zale when he was pissing." The thinking of it brought pleasure to his eyes.

"Then ah shot the others and watched Zale finish dyin'. He took some time dyin'," he ended with satisfaction. Then the boy glared at them and clenched his fists as though daring any of them to dispute his version.

In his own drawl, Mallory read back the recital. "Is that right?" he asked when he finished.

"Ah reckon," came the kid's answer.

Mallory brought out his seal, inked it, stamped the page, wrote in the date, and then his name with a Gothic flourish. "All it needs now is your mark right here." He turned the pages and pointed to the correct line where he had applied an X. He handed over the pen and said, "Y'all will need to dip the pen again."

The youth bent over the paper and brushed the hair back behind his ears, took a deep breath, and grasped the pen. The hand was large and bony, a strong hand, showing the strength that would someday come with full growth. He bit at his lip and in printing wrote out LORENZ, scrawling the letters like a four or five-year-old child that has just learned to write. He shoved the paper back to Mallory, straightened and looked at the marshal. "Iffin that's all, ah want my guns."

Franklin smiled. The lad was ready for a fight. He'd lose, but still he intended to fight. "I'm afraid I can't allow that. This handbill says that a Kid Lawrence is wanted for killing one Patrick O'Neal down in Wooden almost two years ago. You're a bit taller, but y'all were only thirteen then. It says y'all ride with Zale. Y'all didn't find his camp, y'all were just there. That's why it was so easy for y'all to shoot him, wasn't it? Y'all just blasted away in camp. Why? Is that reward sounding good in these days of slim pickings?"

"Like shit! Ah kilt him 'cause he did this to me," the kid touched the jagged scar, "an' he kilt the woman that raised me. Ah tried to stop him and he damned near kilt me then. That was most three years back. 'Sides, that O'Neal bastard was alive when ah left."

The kid was getting wild-eyed again, about ready to bolt. MacDonald wasn't helping matters as he had edged forward to occupy the space next to the desk and the kid. Rolfe had casually dropped his hands to his waist. Both men worried Franklin.

"Did y'all ride with Zale?" he asked.

"Hell no!"

"But y'all were at O'Neal's?"

"Yeah."

Franklin knew why MacDonald and Rolfe were ready to fight and he didn't want it; not here. This was to be his last job and he wanted to leave it walking upright. He tried again.

"Y'all said Mr. O'Neal was still alive when y'all left. Do y'all have any proof or anyone to back up your story?

"Yeah, his kin was with me."

"Who would that be?" Franklin asked the question, but he was watching the huge, looming bulk of MacDonald.

"Red, Red O'Neal. His paw's brother to that O'Neal, only his pa's worst."

"Do you know where this Red O'Neal is now?"

"Ah reckon he's in Carson City. That's where he wuz goin'."

"That presents a problem," began Franklin. From the corner of his eye he could see MacDonald straighten.

The deep voice rumbled out, "Marshal, tis that an official handbill or mayhap one put out by the family?"

Small towns rarely covered the cost of printing and distributing wanted posters, but a wealthy family would gladly pay for the printing and shipping. Franklin knew he was losing even though he felt the kid was lying. "It's a family one," he admitted, "but I'm sure the city of Wooden will concur with the charge."

"Hell," broke in Rolfe in disgust, "Wooden and dot whole county belong to O'Neal."

The kid was startled. He wasn't sure why help was coming from two people he considered his enemies, but it calmed him. Maybe there was a chance of getting out of here.

"Mayhap ye could tell the marshal why ye were in Wooden," suggested MacDonald.

"Ah was lookin' for my folks. We used to live thar, out of town a piece."

MacDonald smiled. "Aye, and yere sister, Margareatha, twas she with ye? Do ye ken where she tis now?"

The boy stood open-mouthed and bewildered. He ran his eyes over the six-foot nine, two hundred and ninety-five pound giant in front of him. His questions had so rattled him that he answered without thinking. "She's in Carson City too."

"Good Gar, nay with O'Neal?" The shocked question exploded.

The boy's eyes had hardened again. "Who the hell are y'all? Ah'd sure as hell remember somebody as big..." The voice trailed off and the grey eyes softened for the first time. "There was a big man who useta ride me on his shoulders." He looked at MacDonald, emotions pulling at his face.

"Aye, 'twas yere grandfither. He tis nigh as tall as me." MacDonald turned to the marshal. "As ye can see, he tis one of the laddies we have been looking for. He twill go home with me, and I twill send a telegram to Mr. O'Neal in Nevada. Ye can find out if there are charges against the laddie, and the town twill nay have to bear the expense of his boarding."

"And if the handbill is correct, then what? Are y'all bringing him in?" asked Marshal Franklin. He had considered the costs, but accommodating MacDonald would not endear him with the citizens.

MacDonald regarded the marshal for a moment and then spoke. "Tis the word of MacDonald ye have that I twill be bringing him back."

"Go to hell!" the boy exploded. "Ah ain't goin nowhere with a bastard like y'll, and as far as this shittin' jail..."

A hard hand clamped down on his shoulder and stopped the tirade while propelling the kid toward the back door. "Ye twill excuse us, gentlemen. We twill be back directly," stated Mac-Donald.

Franklin could only nod. Rolfe grinned and spat. Mallory stared at them bug-eyed. "And keep Mr. Mallory here for the signing of any papers if need be." He shoved Lorenz out the backdoor and walked him away from the building.

Lorenz gave up struggling. He had felt the bones move when he resisted. That grip was worse than rawhide cutting into the skin. Survival was his only credo and winning a fight against this man wasn't possible. He noted the flat ground, the lumber yard to the left on the next block, and the backs of the buildings on this street. Everything else was open, exposed, no trees, no boulders, no fit place to hide if he ever got loose. It looked like he was going to listen or get belted again. I'll kill him like I did Zale, he thought.

"Now ye can turn, and we twill speak." The pain left his shoulder and Lorenz turned.

"Weren't no women in there," he protested to MacDonald.

MacDonald chuckled. "Aye, but I'd rather have my say where others are nay hearing, and from now on ye can nay call me those names."

The boy was silent as the dark eyes regarded him, taking in the breadth of his shoulders. His head was held high and proud, grey eyes sparked like flint. The lad had a wide brow, thick, dark eyebrows and eye lashes, a straight nose, the lips were a bit thin set in taunt anger, and the cleft in his chin made him a masculine version of his mother. Except for the scar, he tis a likely looking laddie, thought MacDonald. "Do ye recall yere mither?" he asked.

Lorenz nodded and MacDonald continued speaking, "The Comanche took yere brithers. Have ye seen or heard of them?"

Lorenz simply glared at the big man. Since the big bastard didn't like the way he talked, he was damned if he was going to say anything.

MacDonald sighed. "I twas a scout over at Fort Davis ere the War. Yere mither was at one of the Comanche camps the 2nd Dragoons attacked. She twas nigh starved for she would nay do things their way." He grinned in remembrance. "She tis a stubborn woman."

"Y'all git her out of there?" Curiosity about her well-being forced the words to spill out.

"Aye, that we did. Then I took her to yere eld, er, uncle's place. He twas in Texas searching for her. There tis a bond twixt twins that nay can break."

"She's okay then?" Lorenz felt compelled to ask. Inside he was reeling. Uncle, what uncle? He couldn't remember any uncle. And his ma was double born. Some held that unnatural. "Why cain't ah just go to my ma's and uncle's then?"

The words came softly from the big man. "Ye are going home to yere mither. Nigh seven years hence, Mrs. Anna Lawrence did me the honor of becoming my wife and counselor."

Lorenz felt the sickness rise inside. His ma was married to this lout. Gawd. He looked at MacDonald and knew that within hours he would have the shit beat out of him or worse. No, mustn't think about worse. He had to get away, but to run now was stupid. All he could do was glare at the man and wish him dead.

The voice continued, low words rumbling out of the deep chest. "We have a wee lassie, but nay a laddie. There twas one, but he died within a few minutes of birthing. Yere mither has claimed all these years that ye, Margareatha, and Daniel still lived." He paused to give Lorenz a chance to speak and when no words came, he continued.

"From now on, ye twill call me Mr. MacDonald, and ye twill answer aye, sir, and nay, sir, to my questions. The same holds for when ye speak with Mr. Rolfe or any other man back there."

"Why?" demanded Lorenz.

MacDonald leaned backward and smiled down. "Because tis one of my rules and ye twill nay disgrace me or yere mither with yere tongue."

"What the hell does she have to do with my talkin'?"

"Dear Gar, where have ye been? Did yere sister nay teach ye about civilized behavior?"

The boy looked at him and grinned a quick, sardonic slash. If his ma was like that, it was his ticket out. MacDonald wouldn't dare take him home. "Ah weren't with Rity the whole time. Zale's Comancheros picked me up, and ah lived with them for years. Ah ran away when ah wuz old enough. Y'all cain't take someone like me back. Ma don't want me anyhow. She wants Daniel."

"Ye twere with Zale?" MacDonald was surprised. "What of yere sister? Did they have her too?"

"Naw, some Injun horse came through where we wuz hidin' in the cornfield. Rity always could ride anythin'. Still can. She got on and rode to O'Neal's place for help."

"Damn!" MacDonald exploded, and he eyed the youth in front of him. Which question should he ask first and would he receive an honest response? "Why did they let a wee laddie like ye live? Ye twere nay of any use to them."

"Zale's woman found me. She'd just lost a kid and needed someone to suckle. Zale let her keep me."

"And what happened to Margareatha?"

"She got to O'Neal's okay, but the bastard locked her up and then sent her to some Catholic nunnery down in San Antonio."

"So, O'Neal twas lying. I kenned I should have gone with Rolfe and Kasper." MacDonald clenched his fists. "Damn, all these years wasted."

"Huh?"

"Yere Uncle Kasper and Mr. Rolfe went twice to O'Neal's place trying to find ye and Margareatha. O'Neal insisted that the Indians had taken yere elder brither, yere mither, and young Augustuv and that ye and yere sister twere dead. He claimed to have heard rumors that yere fither had arranged for the attack. He showed them the two graves that supposedly held the dead from the attack." explained MacDonald.

"It did nay make sense to Rolfe and me. Yere fither had red hair. The Comanche twill avoid a man or woman with red hair. Either he did deal with the Comanche or he ran."

MacDonald looked at Lorenz. "Since ye twere with Zale, did ye kill the O'Neal living in Wooden?"

"Naw, I wanted to, but he had me chained up 'cause he and his brother figured out who I was when ah went there looking for ma. Red had followed me from Carson City and made him let me loose, and Red said he wuz taking me back to Rity, but he got drunk one night, and I gave him the slip." Lorenz finished the tale without telling why O'Neal drank too much.

To MacDonald it was an amazement what the lad could tell and what he must have omitted from the telling. "Where twas he takin' ye?"

"Back to Rity in Carson City."

"How did she get there from San Antonio?"

"Red helped her run away from the nunnery. She wound up in Tucson running a bakery." Lorenz figured he'd better leave out the before part about her and Red gambling on the riverboats.

"How did ye get there?"

"Zale was close to there when I ran away, and Rity recognized me when I wuz looking for food."

"Why did ye nay stay there?"

"Zale's woman ran away too and wuz with me in Tucson. She wuz pregnant agin and couldn't take that life no more. Zale followed her and kilt her. I tried to stop him, and he did this." Lorenz touched the scar. "Rity had to pay for the doctor to fix me and to pay for it she started singing in the saloons."

"Ye Gods!"

"Yeah, so y'all cain't tell Mama about Rity and where she is. Women like Mama pull their skirts away and spit at her, if they dast." He looked at MacDonald, his own face flushed with triumph. MacDonald's face showed his words had had their desired effect.

MacDonald took a deep breath and continued his questioning. "Ye still have nay said why ye both left Tucson."

"Red wuz in Carson City, cause of the War. He weren't about to get kilt and the South couldn't make him put on a uniform. He needed help with his cathouses and sent for Rity."

"She works there?" MacDonald's voice sunk to a horrified whisper. If ere his counselor had reason to hate the O'Neal's, she would be in a fury when she heard this tale.

"Naw, she does his books, but she's got her own gambling place."

MacDonald's eyes took on a humorous glint. Somehow it seemed possible. "And why did ye nay stay?" he asked.

"'Cause Rity made me mad by whuppin' me. Ah just left. Ah had to get even with Zale anyway."

"'Tis that why ye went looking for yere mither first?" probed the gentle, rumbling voice. Baffled, the boy clamped his lips shut.

"Now that ye have told yere tale, ye can listen to me. We are going back in there and finish our business. Before we do, ye need to ken the rules for the way ye twill be living."

He paused, his eyes locking with Lorenz, neither giving way. "One, yere name tis Lorenz Adolf Lawrence. Two, ye twill nay be using the vile words to me, yere mither, nay any adult. Three, when I give an order, ye do it, but if any of my orders should puzzle ye, ye have the right to ask why and ye have the right to remind me that I have given ye this right. Ye have the right to learn and to grow the way the good Gar intended, but if ye cross me, I'll drop yere britches where ye stand and use a belt on yere backside."

The boy opened his mouth to protest, but MacDonald cut him off. "The first time ye disobey, twill only be five counts with the belt. Each time ye disobey thereafter, I'll increase the count by one. By the time I reach ten, ye had best learn to count. Any questions?"

By now anger was surging through Lorenz. He swallowed bitter words mixed with bile. This adversary was too large. He needed time to think, to plot, and to run again. He shook his head to indicate no questions.

MacDonald smiled. "Tis welcomed ye are then, in our hearts and our House. Now, let us go back."

Chapter 3

Introduction to Civilization

The office was heat-hot from the extra bodies: everyone sitting or standing and waiting for more excitement. Franklin had half-hoped Rolfe would have taken his grown cub and leave, but, no, the Dutchman just stood there daring any to ask him to leave. Franklin, like most Americans, heard Deutsch as Dutch and rarely made the correct country connection.

The boy came in first, face set and jaw tightened. MacDonald had evidently rough broke him. MacDonald nodded at Rolfe and the assembled audience, but he spoke directly to Franklin.

"Are we in agreement that the laddie goes home with me, and I send the telegram to Mr. O'Neal, sparing the county the expense?"

Franklin would have liked to reject MacDonald's offer. Reality, however, was the small jail he ran had no extra room, and since the South's capitulation, money for rations was nonexistent. If the present United States judge found out the gold taken in the robbery and death of O'Neal involved Confederate gold, the man might not consider it a crime at all.

"All right, MacDonald, but if I find out that there is a valid warrant, I'll be out after him."

"Aye," MacDonald nodded again. "Good day, gentlemen."

"Ah want my guns." Stubbornness slashed through the voice as Lorenz protested.

MacDonald looked at Franklin. "We'll take them with us."

Rolfe picked up the arsenal and moved towards the door. MacDonald clamped his hand down on the boy's shoulder, gently nudging him on his way. "Ye are nay to touch a weapon for a while."

Lorenz breathed deep and looked longingly at his guns and knives, then shrugged. Outside they paused for MacDonald to introduce the young man who had stood at the back. "Lorenz, this tis Young Rolfe. Martin tis his given name. Martin, this tis Lorenz, Anna's laddie."

Martin extended his hand, blue eyes beaming welcome and in a firm, baritone voice said, "Good to finally meet y'all, Lorenz."

Startled, Lorenz shook his hand. Martin appeared to be a couple years older than he, a blond, younger version of Rolfe without the mustache and teeth browned by chewing tobacco.

"My poys und me vill get some eats." Rolfe pointed to Young James up on the wagon seat. The wagon was a sturdy rectangle made of fading, once painted, green slabs of wood, and a solid unimaginative design. Rolfe stored the weapons in a locked box in the back of the wagon and he and Martin climbed aboard. "Meet du in front of Stanley's place."

"Aye, friend Rolfe. Lorenz, we go this way." MacDonald waved toward the section of town where the freight station stood.

"We're gonna walk?" Lorenz couldn't believe it. A cattleman walking instead of riding was not natural. He had seen a huge riding horse; one of the two horses tethered to the wagon, and figured it had to be MacDonald's. It was an animal big enough for him.

"Aye, we twill come back for yere horse."

Lorenz fell in step rather than be dragged or propelled along. There was still no way out as there were far too many people, and why the hell was Martin glad to meet him?

"Ah ain't neveh goin' to see that gold, am ah?"

"Who kens? Mayhap in a few weeks."

"Huh, an' iffen it does come, who gets it, y'all?"

"Nay, twill be yeres."

Lorenz didn't believe him, but didn't argue. They passed people hurrying to be done with their chores before the midday heat. Women would draw away and wrinkle their noses. Lorenz seemed oblivious to their behavior, but he knew they were afraid of him. Afraid, just like his ma would be when she saw him again. Why the hell was this big bastard taking him there? For Lorenz, it was enough to know that she was alive and safe. Then again, maybe she wasn't safe; not with this big bastard beating on her. Maybe he should swing by there once he got away.

A huge blue star hung over the freighting office, proclaiming to one and all that this was the Blue Star line. The blue star identified the office as the town's reason for being. Men were constantly going in and out with orders to be filled, teams to be tended, harnesses repaired, the shifting, stacking, and rerouting of trade goods. This part of the country's network of merchandise distribution was as yet undisturbed by railroads. Freight was hauled in from every major point by wagons, mules, and men. The building housed the merchandise, wagons, loading docks, separate quarters for the teams and men, and in the office, the indispensable telegraph. Town women had agitated for the telegraph to be moved to a more genteel location, but economics kept the telegraph were it was needed.

"Hallo, Mac," said the man at the desk. He was long, lanky, dark haired, and mustached. Whatever animosity the town felt towards Yankees, this man didn't. Business was business. "Y'all planning to carry your goods home now?"

"Nay now, but in a bit, Andrew, it tis your communications I'm needing this time."

"My what?"

"The telegraph," explained MacDonald. "I find it tis necessary to send two. Ye can get messages to Carson City, Nevada, aye?"

"Sure thing. I heard y'all and Rolfe had brought in a herd. Prices any better for beef?"

"Bah!" A deep rumble issued from the throat. "If we nay had the contract, they would have screwed us as badly as any that wore the grey. As tis the money twill buy beans. Andrew, this tis Lorenz. Lorenz, Mr. Andrew."

Andrew nodded at Lorenz and shoved a piece of paper to Mac-Donald. "Howdy, young man."

Lorenz nodded and watched MacDonald bend and scrawl lines across the sheet. He finished with a flourish and looked at Lorenz. "Does yere sister have an address?"

Lorenz shook his head. "Then what about O'Neal? Does he have an address?"

"He owns the Sportin' Palace, or did when ah left."

MacDonald sighed and shook his head. "Andrew, the first goes to Miss Margareatha Lawrence, General Delivery, the other to Mr. Red O'Neal, owner, Sporting Palace."

"I'll read them back just to make sure there's no error." Andrew's face showed no emotion as he read. "Miss Margareatha Lawrence. Stop. Lorenz is safe with us. Stop. A letter from your mother, Mrs. Anna MacDonald, nee Schmidt will follow. Stop. Mother rescued eight years ago. Stop. Zebediah L. MacDonald."

"Next one," continued Andrew. "Mr. Red O'Neal, Sporting Palace. Stop. Marshal Franklin of Arles, Texas needs your confirmation that Patrick O'Neal was alive when Lorenz left with you two years ago. Stop. Marshal has family poster. Stop. Speed is important. Stop. Zebediah L. etc." Andrew looked at MacDonald.

"Aye, twill do."

"That'll be five dollars for the two."

"Tis dear." MacDonald dug down in his trousers and extracted a coin.

"At least it gets there," replied Andrew. "Y'all going to pick up everything for Schmidt's Corner?"

"Nay, just the liquor barrels for friend Rolfe and myself. Twill be another hour or so ere we're back," answered MacDonald and tipped his hat at Andrew. He and Lorenz stepped outside and walked back towards the Marshal's office.

Lorenz was trying to devise an escape plan. Maybe he could race the man and jump on Dandy and be gone. He tensed. The crowd wasn't much and big man probably couldn't move too fast.

"If ye are thinking of bolting, dinna. And when we are at the wagon, ye dinna touch yere mount."

"Why?"

"Tis another of my rules."

Lorenz sulked. The man's rules were becoming tedious. This was just like being with his sister. And how the hell did he know what he had been planning?

MacDonald untied the reins and led the way to the wagon now parked in front of the general store called Stanley's Dry Goods and Sundries. The wagon's faded green slabs were hung with water barrels and nose bags. The team of part Morgan and some other lineage stood with heads bowed and tails swishing at the gathering flies. MacDonald tied Dandy's reins to one of the hoops at the back and pulled down the tailgate revealing an interior lined with boxes. "Now we'll have a look at yere stash. Ye can take off yere saddle and bags as they'll go in the wagon. Ye'll be riding with Martin on the seat."

"Like hell!"

"Laddie, I am being patient. Take off that saddle," MacDonald commanded.

Lorenz stared at him. "Why cain't ah ride?"

"Lorenz, if ye dinna wish yere britches down now in front of all of these people, ye twill do as I have said." MacDonald's r was rolled into three in his pronunciation.

Lorenz yanked at the cinches. Outright rebellion was futile. He would wait for a better time. He half-threw, half-slammed the saddle onto the wagon bed. MacDonald's eyes glinted, but he knew he had won.

"Now, let's see what ye have."

The contents of the saddlebags were slim. There was no food and no tobacco. MacDonald held up a pair of canvass jeans and critically eyed the lad before him.

Lorenz flushed. "Ah grew. Ah would have traded 'em, but no time."

"Tis this all the clothes that ye have?"

"That's it."

MacDonald shook his head and extracted the remaining items: a thin blanket, a tin plate and a spoon. The implements he put into the chuck box and left the blanket in the saddle bags. Then he shoved the saddle against the sidewall.

"Since all the clothes that ye have are on ye, we twill go shopping."

"Why?"

"I canna take ye back to your mither with nay but those clothes."

Lorenz was puzzled, but then realized that his mother was going to have opinions about what he wore similar to Rity's ideas. MacDonald's voice rumbled on.

"Walk." He pointed to the doorway in front of them.

"We ain't eatin'?" There was real regret in Lorenz's voice.

"Aye, ere long."

The inside of the store offered relief from the sun's gathering strength, but there was no breeze and the air was beginning to resemble a modern sauna. The smells of pickles, brown earth still clinging to potatoes, coffee, spices, dyes from the few new clothes and polished boots assailed the nose. A slender, balding man of about forty nodded at them. Stanley would have preferred to ignore the huge man, but like the rest of the town, he knew that the damn Yankees had delivered a herd to the cavalry stationed outside the town. If necessary, Captain Richards would enforce the sale.

The bile rose in Stanley at the thought of MacDonald and Rolfe, two of the few people with cash money in their pockets in June of 1865, walking around and not hung or tarred and feathered. The soothing proclamations of the provisional governor notwithstanding, the War had left the South bereft of valid currency. He knew that both men would buy most of their goods from MacDonald's brother-in-law at Schmidt's Corner. "Anything ah can do for y'all?" His offer was perfunctory, his voice cool and aloof.

Amusement lurked in MacDonald's voice as he answered, "Aye, the laddie needs a pair of boots." Inside, the big man was shaking with laughter as Stanley's eyes lit up. "Plus two pair of socks as the missus twill knit more." No need to raise the man's expectations too high. "And a pair of britches," he concluded.

To Lorenz he asked, "Do ye have a slicker?"

Lorenz shook his head. "Answer and say it right," MacDonald's voice rumbled out at him.

Lorenz quit gawking at the meager goods laid out on the table, flushed, threw a baleful glance at the big man and spat out, "No, suh."

"Mayhap that can wait. It does nay seem ready to rain for a while, but twill need a shirt."

"Will Mrs. MacDonald be needing any material for new shirts?" asked Stanley, a note of expectation crept into his voice.

"Nay, she still has a bolt from her last shopping trip, howe'er, once we have selected a pair of boots and some clothes, twill need a few supplies for the extra mouth." He turned toward the end wall and the rack of boots. They were all crudely made, and all the same color: black. The boots were made to fit either foot and so fit neither. MacDonald had his own boots cobbled as none such as these would fit him. He longed for the day when they could afford a tailor, and his wife would no longer need to make all of his clothes.

Stanley, ever the salesman, selected two of the boots and handed them to MacDonald with a flourish. "Finest pair in town."

MacDonald held them alongside one of Lorenz's feet. It was impossible to tell if they would fit or not. Lorenz's current boots were slashed at the side to allow for feet that had outgrown the pair he wore.

"Lorenz, take off yere boots and try these on."

He turned to Stanley. "Ye might as well give us a pair of those socks so that he twill have them on when we buy the boots. I dinna want the boots to fit without the socks."

Stanley raised his eyebrows. "Why not, is he still growing?" He was curious as to which of the lost children this one would be.

"Nay doubt he twill. He tis but fifteen, and already he tis as tall as his mither."

Lorenz looked at his stepfather with a puzzled frown. No woman he'd ever seen was that tall except Rity. He took the socks from Stanley and slowly dragged them on while searching in his mind for some remembrance of his ma.

He remembered her towering over him enraged, grey eyes flashing, her lips drawn in a tight line, "Nein, nein. Du must not!" He must have always had the ability to make people mad. He looked up to see MacDonald ruefully regarding the unclad foot. At least the big bastard didn't say anything about the toe-nails and dirt clinging everywhere and he hurriedly pulled on the other sock.

After comparing the new boots with the old pair, MacDonald asked, "Have ye grown in the last few months?"

Lorenz shrugged. "Some, ah reckon. My shirt got too small and had to..." He stopped short and began tugging vigorously on the new boot. No need to tell MacDonald that he'd taken the shirt from someone's clothes line. Instinct told him that Mac-Donald would want to pay somebody for it even if the price came out of his own hide.

MacDonald watched the fight with the boot and said to Stanley, "We best see the next size."

This pair proved to be a tad wide, but the selection of sizes had ended. "Twill do," sighed MacDonald. "Now we need a shirt and a pair of summer drawers and vest."

Lorenz was horrified. "Ah gotta put those on? Hell, it's hot out there."

"Ye need nay wear them right now." The voice was patient, half amused at his distress.

The shirt was blue, rough, and collarless. The cotton drawers and vest were bought a size too large to allow for any growing Lorenz might do. MacDonald added a couple of handkerchiefs, a belt, and then moved toward the counter.

Stanley rapidly positioned himself in line with the counter and the shelves to be able to retrieve any item that was ordered. If the man bought enough, Stanley would be able to pay on his account at the Blue Star. Maybe he could even stay in business.

On his way to the main counter, MacDonald picked up a doll with brown hair and a fixed smile. "And how much tis this," he asked holding it aloft.

The doll, like many items in his store, had lain there since the second year of the War. Stanley licked his lips. "Two dollars."

"One." MacDonald's eyes hardened.

Stanley nodded. "One dollar it is." Damn the man. He always seemed to know what a body would accept in payment. At the counter, Stanley took out his pad to jot down the purchases.

"We need a pad of paper, lined, and a pencil." MacDonald was consulting a list. "And do ye happen to have some colored chalk for a wee lassie to do some drawing?"

Stanley retrieved the items from their respective shelves. "Come fall, we'll have some of those nice wax crayons," he volunteered.

"Nay. Kap twill get them for us." MacDonald could not resist shooting an arrow into the Stanley's pocket of hopes.

"Now as to the food," he continued. "Twill be needing an extra pound of beans." He eyed Lorenz critically. "Mayhap ye best make that two pounds, two pounds of flour, and five pounds of potatoes. Do ye have any canned tomatoes left?"

"Not a one," came Stanley's bitter reply. "There are a couple of cans of peaches left though."

"Aye, we'll take them. Do ye have any condensed milk? Twill go well with the peaches."

"Certainly," Stanley's voice became brisk and businesslike and his movements quickened. As he brought the canned goods to the counter, he noticed the boy eyeing the loaves of bread and rolls. "Maybe he'd like a roll while we're conducting our transactions," he suggested.

MacDonald nodded glumly. He suspected a hollow stomach in that skinny body. "Aye, add it to the bill." Lorenz snagged a roll and stuffed it into his mouth.

"We are nay sure if the dried apples twill be on this shipment to Schmidt's Corner," continued MacDonald. "Do ye have any?"

"No, we're completely out, but here, try some of these. Brand new this year, just in from California." He removed a saucer from the top of a cup and handed the cup to MacDonald. "I can't keep the flies out of them else," he said to explain the saucer. "They're called raisins, dried grapes, and just as sweet as can be." He didn't add that they were on consignment from growers in California desperate to get rid of two years' worth of agricultural products.

MacDonald's huge fingers barely fit into the cup. He extracted a few of the raisins and warily rolled one on his tongue and bit down. Surprise flooded his face. "Tasty. Here, laddie, try some."

He dumped the remaining fruit onto the quickly outstretched hand. The raisins went the way of the roll.

"How do ye use them?" he asked Stanley.

"Just like any dried fruit; cakes, breads, and pies," answered Stanley.

"Then twill take a pound. Mrs. MacDonald twill be pleased. Now, do ye have any ladies' gloves?"

Anger reddened Stanley's face. MacDonald knew he did not carry finery. Stanley also knew MacDonald would take his money down to the French seamstress. He considered the woman an insult to the town. A former prostitute, she did the sewing for the whorehouse floozies, and kept a supply of cheap doodads for their costumes, plus an assortment of ribbons and leather items that cut into Stanley's business. For some reason, the women from the saloons and brothels preferred her establishment. That MacDonald would even acknowledge his wife in public was another insult. Whoever heard of any other white woman living with the Comanche for two years and coming out in public places? Why couldn't she stay hid like a decent woman? "None," he said as smoothly as possible.

"Ah, very well, then I twill need a pouch of tobacco." He turned to Lorenz and asked, "Do ye smoke, laddie?"

For once Lorenz was polite, "Yus, suh."

"Make that two bags of tobacco and some papers for the laddie. We twill also need a loaf of that bread and a pound of cheese." He looked around, "And do ye have some pickles left?"

"Yes, suh, we do. They're in the bottom of the right barrel. Y'all can fish out what you all want."

Lorenz retrieved the pickles while Stanley removed the cheesecloth from the cheese and positioned the wheel over the round to hit the mark for one pound. The cleaver moved downward in one deft stroke. "Will that be all?"

"Aye, tis enough."

Stanley totaled the sums, frowning and wetting his pencil stub. "That comes to twenty-five dollars."

"'Tis dear," muttered MacDonald and reluctantly counted out the money.

"The price of flour just keeps going up. Sugar too. Even if folks had jobs they couldn't afford either one." Bitterness was back in Stanley's voice. "How's Schmidt doing way out there?" Not that he cared. He just wanted confirmation that the damn Yankees were caught in the same unnatural way of things since the War's end.

"Nay well. He has carried too many on his books too long."

Stanley nodded. Somehow he couldn't gloat. What's a man to do when kids and women were hungry? He wrapped the purchases in brown paper, tied them with twine, and handed the bundles to MacDonald.

Outside the sun hit full force. Dust rose in puffs and streams with every passing horse and vehicle. An undersized eight-year-old boy with snotty nose and cut down trousers was hustling down the street paused and asked, "Beer, mister?" He held up an almost clean lard bucket.

"Aye." MacDonald tossed the boy a nickel. The brown hand shot out and clutched the coin while the boy spun on his heels and lifted them in a dead run to the saloon down the street.

MacDonald handed Lorenz the packages and put down the wagon gate. He shoved the clothing and sundry items back and opened the bread and cheese, cutting both in huge slabs. Lorenz waited, his stomach lurching with the anticipation of food. He took the sandwich MacDonald made and swallowed it in huge gulps. MacDonald eyed him, sighed, and built two more sandwiches before hoisting himself up on the wagon.

"We might as well sit. And chew that damn thing. There tis more." He took one of the pickles and halved it neatly with his broad teeth.

Lorenz flushed. The bread and cheese were hitting his stomach like lumps, but it had been a long time since he had eaten more than a mouthful of jerky. The last two days he hadn't hunted. He had not wanted Zale to know that he was near. Money he had run out of months ago.

The boy came dashing back with a full bucket of beer, neatly avoiding the woman on the sidewalk. MacDonald handed down his own lard bucket and the contents of the first was transferred. "Here, laddie, have a bite of cheese." MacDonald cut off a generous chunk and handed it to the child.

Saliva drooled out of the boy's mouth. "Thank y'all, suh!" He snatched the cheese with the same alacrity as he had the coin and ran towards the freight office. Someone there might be thirsty.

Lorenz took another sandwich and a pickle. This one he chewed. "Don't that Stanley fellow like y'll?" He looked at MacDonald warily, but the man had said he had a right to ask questions.

"To most in this town, we are nay but damn Yankees. They tried to burn us out during the war and failed. Now they can do nay." Laughter edged in MacDonald's speech, then vanished. "Then too, they are nay happy with yere mither." He paused and Lorenz looked at him.

"She twas with the Comanche for two years, laddie. The townspeople think she should hide away like some dirty thing." The r's rolled more thickly on his tongue again. "Fortunately, yere mither has more sense and pride than that. Howe'er, any slurs that may be said against her in this town are my business, nay yeres."

Anger shook Lorenz and he forgot to use his dialect. "They wouldn't dare."

"They have nay openly dared since the first time I brought her back," said MacDonald complacently. "That does nay keep them from thinking." He took another hunk of cheese. "Do ye wish another sandwich?"

"Ah reckon." A man could travel far on a full belly. They split the last of the pickles.

"Do ye wish some brew?" MacDonald hefted the beer bucket.

"Nah, ah don't like it."

MacDonald tipped back his head and drank heavily and then wiped his mouth. "That seems strange when yere mither makes some of the best brew around."

"Mama makes beer?"

"Aye, tis a receipt she and Kap have from yere grandfither."

Lorenz shook his head. Who the hell was Cap? There was still a lot he had to put together. "Why din't we eat at the restaurant like Rolfe and his kids?"

"Tis Mr. Rolfe, laddie," reminded MacDonald. "He spends his money his way, and I spend mine my way."

"What's laddie mean?"

"'Tis my way of boy, kid, or son." MacDonald's voice was low and gruff, but sounded kind. Lorenz was beginning to think the man a fraud. People feared him because he was huge. Sheer meanness probably wasn't in him. The problem was his size. If the man got aholt of somebody, he would do damage, mean or not. Worse, it was possible he was someone that Lorenz had heard about.

"You and Mr. Rolfe," Lorenz emphasized Mister to see if MacDonald took offense and didn't see the warning glint in MacDonald's eyes. When no verbal warning came, he continued, "are you all called the Bear and the Wolf?"

MacDonald chuckled. "Aye, the Comanche have called us that. Where did ye hear it?"

"In Zale's camp. Wolf, Mr. Rolfe wuz after 'em. Ah saw him once. He was slow skinnin' a man. Scared the shit out o' me.

MacDonald lowered the beer and looked at him, not sure that he had heard the mangled English correctly. "When was this?"

"Ah wuz about seven." Seeing the puzzled look on MacDonald's face, he kept on talking. "Mamacita, that's what ah called Zale's woman, kept a countin' stick." At MacDonald's nod of understanding, Lorenz launched into a recital with his own brand of English.

"Somebody came into camp claiming a whole passel of folks was after Zale, and they all broke like crazy. Ah wuz off doin' somethin', ah doan recollect what, and snuck out of there. Ah thought ah got clean away when ah looked down over a bluff. Figured somebody wuz down there, cuz ah heard a horse. Iffen they wuz after Zale, ah tho't they might take me home. Anyways, ah looked over and there wuz one dead horse and two of Zale's men jist as dead. Another of his men wuz tied down oveh the dead horse and the Wolf, ah means Mr. Rolfe, wuz parin' away; real slow like." Like came out as liake.

"The man was part Injun so he warn't screamin', but ah ran back towards where camp had been. Rolfe didn't seem no different from Zale and his men. At least ah knowed them. Mamacita wuz lookin' for me and took me back with her. We both got a beatin' that night."

MacDonald set the empty lard bucket down. "'Tis a shame ye ran. Friend Rolfe would nay have harmed ye as he kenned yere mither and uncle even then. Ye would have been safely home within the week." He reached for the cans of peaches and milk. The laddie's face showed nay emotion. "However, dinna mention the skinnin' to Young James."

He held up the two cans. "Have ye tried these?" Deftly, he used his knife to saw open the peaches and put two slits into the canned milk.

Lorenz shook his head no. The sudden spurt of confidence had spurred him into gabbing like a jaybird. He was confused, but this time with himself. He watched MacDonald slap two peach halves each on two slices of bread, and then empty the milk into the juice of the peach can. What the hell does kenned mean, he

36

thought. Knowed? He accepted a peach crowned slice of bread, used his hands to keep the fruit from sliding off, and gulped half of the bread. The jolt of sugar hit his taste buds. God, that was good! He took a swig of the milk sweetened juice and nearly gagged. He hadn't tasted milk since he was what? Seven? Eight?

MacDonald's huge paw grasped the can before it dropped from his hand. "Nay so fast to be rid of it, laddie." Laughter skirted the edge of his voice and Lorenz flushed.

"I wish some too." He tilted his head and downed half the liquid, finished chewing the crust in his mouth, offered the can to Lorenz, and at his refusal, downed the last of can. "It makes a tolerable pudding," he said with a grin.

"Milk's for babies," Lorenz protested.

MacDonald's shoulders shook, the breadth of them straining against his shirt.

"Laddie, the Union men thanked the good Gar for that invention," he said as he pointed to the empty milk can.

Lorenz ignored him and watched the stragglers moving on the plank sidewalk. The Rolfe family approached, ten-year-old James scooting in front, then dropping back, his head working like a swivel under his brown hat, gooseberry eyes taking in everything, his nose working almost as fast as a hound dog on a trail, and his legs jerking like sticks as he skittered in one direction then another, never far enough to provoke Papa Rolfe to wrath. Martin lifted a hand in greeting and disappeared into the dry goods store. Rolfe handed James a coin and watched his youngest charge after the older.

"Und mind your manners." With that bit of fatherly advice, Rolfe walked to the wagon. "I sent the poy for some beer. I'll buy du a drink, friend Mac."

"Thank ye, friend Rolfe." It was the easy banter of men who spent long hours in each other's company.

To Lorenz he said, "Laddie, I need to purchase yere mither a gift. Ye twill remain here."

He grinned at Lorenz and then at Rolfe. "Try nay to hurt him if he bolts. I would like to take him to his mither in one piece."

Cold blue eyes swept over Lorenz. "Don't vorry." Rolfe spat. "I may drink your beer if du take too damn long." He leaned against the tailgate and folded his arms across his chest.

Lorenz remained where he was. He knew Rolfe would nail him with the bowie knife if he were dumb enough to run. He watched MacDonald's wide form rock down the planks and enter a small store at the end of the block. He was puzzled again. What kind of man bought a gift for his woman? Zale hadn't ever given his woman anything but a bunch of still-birthed kids and beatings. Red never gave the women that worked in his brothels anything, and that fellow he worked for when he was twelve and swamping out the livery stable in Tucson never said anything about buying his woman a gift.

The snot-nosed kid dashed up with another pail of beer and Rolfe held the empty for filling. Then the kid ran off for the freight depot again. He knows where his customers are in the heat of the day, thought Lorenz. He could see James hopping up and down inside the store, impatiently waiting for Martin to make his selection and pay Stanley. The guy in the store sure knew where the money was and it weren't no kid.

Rolfe swigged at his beer and shot Lorenz a glance. "Du thirsty?" he offered.

Lorenz shook his head. That Baptist preacher he heard once must have been right. The Dutch could drink all day and think nothing of giving it to their kids. He wondered if he should say anything about the slow skinning and thought the better of it.

Martin stepped out of the store, a grin cutting across his face. He swaggered over to the wagon and opened his package for them to see. "Now by golly, I've got a good shirt for when the Pastor comes, or we have doings in town." The white, collarless shirt lay on the brown wrapping, stiff and unnatural in its folded pleats. "The next time we come here, I'll buy the collar to go with it," he finished.

"Vat's vrong mitt the shirts Olga sews?" asked his father.

"They're always the same, either blue like this one, or red flannel for winter. I get tired of it." Martin grinned at Lorenz. "Olga sews real good, she just don't know what a young man needs. She still thinks I'm ten years old." He rewrapped the shirt and scooted up on the wagon bed to put the package in the same box MacDonald had dropped his goods in. "Olga's my sister." He finished by slamming the lid down and dropping to the ground by his father.

Young James came flying out of the store, a paper bag firmly clenched in one sun-tanned hand and the other hand holding his hat against a sudden breeze. He clambered up beside Lorenz, his jaws furiously working a taffy ball inside his mouth. He made a show of setting the bag between himself and the wagon. Rolfe ignored them and continued drinking.

"What 'cha got, James?" asked Martin with a wink at Lorenz.

"It ain't..." started James.

"Don't say ain't," admonished Rolfe.

"Isn't for you," finished James. "It's all mine."

"Hoo, what a fine Christian y'all are! Y'all won't even share with your brother," taunted Martin. "I'll bet y'all don't even save one for Olga."

James flushed. The taunt about not being a Christian upset him. "I saved a penny for the collection plate when Pastor comes, and maybe I'll save a candy for Olga, but just her. Besides, you still got money."

Lorenz picked up the empty peach can with the drops of the juice and milk puddling in the bottom. He knew James was being teased, but he couldn't figure who the Pastor fellow was. He sounded important to these people. And why wasn't James supposed to say ain't? He figured they were talking English, but the elder Rolfe's English wasn't making much more sense than Mac-

Donald's brand of speech. He made a show of drinking the liquid and smacking his lips. "Y'all want some?" he asked Martin.

Martin's blue eyes lit up. He made sure James saw the peaches stamped on the can, threw back his head, and pretended to drink. "By damn that's good!" He too smacked his lips. "Uncle went and put some milk in it." He grinned at James. "I'll bet Lorenz will trade you for some of the candy."

Green envy fought on James's face, twisting the features and lighting up his eyes with hope. Then determination stilled the desire. "I'm not drinking after you two," he declared. He popped a red ball in his mouth and worked it as deliberately as he had the taffy. "Besides, if Uncle Mac had any, it's all gone."

Rolfe was laughing in short snorts. "Und that's vhy he'll be a Pastor someday. Du can tempt him, but by golly he's got brains."

Martin shrugged, totally unconcerned that a ten-year-old had refused the bait. MacDonald appeared and handed a dainty package to Martin. For Lorenz, it was the beginning of an active dislike of the younger Rolfe.

"Would ye put that in the box, Martin?"

"Ja sure," said Martin. He stood and placed the package with the others.

"And ye, laddie," continued MacDonald, "can join Martin up on the seat."

Lorenz set his jaw, looked up at the man and shrugged. He had lost the argument about riding Dandy earlier. He followed Martin, not noticing the disappointment on young James's face.

"Do I have to ride back here, Papa?" asked James.

"Ja," replied Rolfe as he and MacDonald pushed up the wagon gate and secured it.

"Mayhap ye can ride with me later." MacDonald smiled at the boy.

"Where to first?" Martin yelled down. "The lumber yard?"

"Aye." MacDonald and Rolfe mounted their horses, swinging out on either side of the wagon.

Martin gathered the reins and snapped them. "Hi-yi-yup," he shouted to the horses and as a warning to any coming behind them.

Lorenz wondered whether the two men were guarding him or the wagon. Hell, they had just sold a herd. One or both of them had money, or maybe it was in the wagon. Maybe he shouldn't be in such a hurry to leave. Martin or James ought to know where it was hid. He glanced back at James who promptly stuck out his tongue. Gonna get you, boy, thought Lorenz.

"What ails him?" he asked Martin, jerking his thumb back at James.

"Ach, he's mad because y'all have got his seat." Martin's speech would forever be a cross between the German utterances of his parents and the drawl of Texas.

"Hell, he can have it for all ah care."

"He don't know that." Martin threw a quick glance at Lorenz. "It's his first time to town, and the first time working with us. He was helping with the driving and cooking. He wants to be real important and ride up on the seat, not in the back like the baby. Y'all spoiled that."

"How many head y'all drive in?"

"Three hundred."

Lorenz whistled. "Just the three of y'all drive that many?"

"Yeah, that's all it takes. We're just in town now to pick up supplies." He turned the team to the left.

The right side of the street was occupied by two sporting houses. A few of the women were leaning out of the windows for air and to hustle business for later. Like the buildings, they badly needed paint to make their pale faces attractive. Usually the whores moved from town to town, or state to state, but the war had interfered with movement, and now there was no place to go, and no one to send them.

One buxom blonde leaned way out and waved before yelling, "Hey, big man, we ain't seen y'all in years. Why y'all been staying away and depriving us of your charms?"

MacDonald was riding easily; one hand gripped the reins, his left arm akimbo as the hand rested on his hip. He looked up, white teeth showing, "Ye twill have to forget me, darling. I'm a wedded man with a wee bairn."

The blonde hooted. "Hell, that didn't stop your friend. He was in last night."

MacDonald roared. Martin's face flushed. Rolfe grinned and spat. Lorenz looked to see how young James was reacting. The kid was busy praying while he choked back tears.

"That ain't true," Martin muttered. "Mama's dead. When she was alive, it did stop him." That his father would keep an Indian woman for a season of trapping whether his wife lived or no never occurred to Martin.

"Then why's he praying?" Lorenz was curious.

"Because he's going to be a pastor." Martin slapped the reins to keep the horses moving. Lorenz knew he'd been given an explanation, and obviously a pastor was like a job that had something to do with praying. The idea of marriage keeping men out of a whorehouse, however, sure didn't fit with anything he knew.

"Well, iffin yore Ma's dead, what's wrong with yore Pa goin' there?" he asked.

"It's still a sin." Martin's voice implied amazement at his ignorance. He swung the horse to the left to enter the lumberyard.

MacDonald dismounted, tied his horse and walked over. "Ye come with me, laddie."

Curious, Lorenz clambered down and followed MacDonald inside. The one-story building and its fence ran almost the length of the block. After the glare of the sun, it took awhile for his eyes to adjust. Stacked lumber and the remnants of spilled varnish fought with dust to overpower the nose. The man that greeted them had a full head of hair and jowls that should have been full. Instead the jowls had become skin that hung at the sides waiting for better times to flush them out again. Where Stanley had been aloof, this man was openly hostile, resentment edging his voice and manner.

"Your materials are ready for you all to pick up," he said stiffly.

"There tis now a need to change my plans, but I still need the lumber. I also need a door handle to finish one of the upstairs' rooms for the laddie. The shed twill wait another season," said MacDonald.

"Do you need Bailey?" asked the slack jowled man. "I can send him out for a day or two. Y'all would pay me by the day."

"And how can that be legal now?" asked MacDonald.

"Bailey works for me." The answer was given in flat, final tones.

A small smile worked at MacDonald's mouth. "And did he nay before?"

Clifford flushed, his eyes locking with MacDonald's. "Do y'all want him out there or not?"

"No, thank ye, we twill manage. How much do I owe ye?"

Lorenz watched the money exchange hands and followed MacDonald out the side entrance where Rolfe and Martin were busy loading the lumber in the wagon. An overly thin, black man was helping.

"Bailey, go fetch Mr. MacDonald enough material for an interior door and jambs," commanded Clifford. He looked at MacDonald wondering what the man would do when it came to installing the lock plate, but didn't ask. He didn't want to hear that someone from Germantown would be summoned. Damn Yankees. They wouldn't use a black before the War and wouldn't use one after. What good was freedom to a man starving to death? He turned and walked back inside, praying for the day when he could refuse to sell to the likes of MacDonald.

Bailey returned with a stack of lumber and added it to the boards on the wagon and handed him a small sack. "That's the handle, latch, and plate, suh."

MacDonald eyed the man who was no better clad than Lorenz or the laddie carrying the brew for the saloon. He felt a certain kinship, for this man was as trapped as he.

"Aye, thank ye." He motioned Lorenz to the front, watched him climb up, put the sack in his saddlebag, and mounted his horse. He gave a nod to Martin and the wagon started to roll.

Lorenz settled himself. "Now where we goin'?"

"To the Blue Star," replied Martin. "Papa and Uncle Mac had the liquor ordered last year, but they couldn't get it through with the war on."

The blonde was still hustling up business and tried a new angle. "Hey, why don't you all bring your boys in. They look big enough to learn."

Lorenz grinned and waved his hat. He shot a quick look at MacDonald who had a frown on his face, but he said nothing.

"Any chance of that happening?" he asked Martin.

"Naw."

"Y'all ever had a woman?"

"Naw, it costs too much. I spent my money on the shirt. It's going to last a lot longer."

Lorenz twisted to get a better look at Martin. His tanned face was not flushed. In fact, it was downright complacent.

"Besides," Martin continued, "if things go right, in a couple of years I'll send for a bride. I can wait until then."

Lorenz sat back to consider that statement. What kind of people was he riding with? Every man he ever knew had considered it natural to go to a whore. Right now he had a hardness between his legs just thinking about it. Was he unnatural?

One of the freighters was ahead of them when Martin pulled to a stop at the loading dock. Lorenz scrambled down. The hardness had evaporated and something more urgent was necessary.

He was about to open his fly when MacDonald's big hand closed on his shoulder again.

"Nay here!" the angry roar sounded in his ear. "Have ye nay sense?"

"Why the hell not?" Protest was useless as MacDonald marched him behind the nearest building.

"Ye dinna expose yere privates when there may be ladies or young lassies about. Yere mither would have both of our ears. And dinna piss on the boards, use the ground."

Lorenz finished and buttoned up the canvas flap. "Others do it that way," he grumbled.

"Aye, but ye are now part of my House, and ye dinna."

It was, Lorenz decided, going to be a long ride to wherever they were going. They walked back to the wagon where Martin was pulling up to the dock. Rolfe had a shit-eating grin etched across his face, but Lorenz knew he could do nothing about it.

"Friend Mac, du are learning how much nicer daughters can be." Rolfe punctuated his remark with another blob of juice.

"Aye," the word eased out, slow and thoughtful.

Andrew was waiting for them. "I got your papers right here. Y'all want to prove a point?"

MacDonald eyed the man warily. "What have ye in mind?"

"I bet these buggers y'all could carry that barrel of booze with no help."

"Aye, I do the work, and ye collect the money. I have waited too long for the goods. I twill nay chance breaking the bottles now," replied MacDonald.

"We'll split it half and half," cajoled Andrew. Personally, he was glad the war was over. Now a man could earn money again.

Light gleamed in MacDonald's dark eyes. "How much?" came the terse question.

"It's five for y'all and five for me. That makes your telegrams free."

"Laddie, ye wait here with Mr. Rolfe." MacDonald rolled after Andrew and soon reappeared, the barrel resting on one shoulder, propped by his hand at the top. Lorenz, like the others, was awed. The man wasn't straining or breathing hard. To him it was child's play. MacDonald's stance once again convinced Lorenz that this man was built somehow different. The body was thicker, the arms and legs sturdier, heavier, wider, the arms looking as if set just a tad too forward, or was it simply they, like the rest of the man, exceeded all normal proportions? MacDonald walked to the wagon and without missing a step walked up the plank, over the lumber, and set the barrel gently against the front. Two other men appeared carrying Rolfe's barrel and placed it beside the first. MacDonald lashed them down with a rope that Rolfe tossed to him.

"Up ye go, laddie." MacDonald jerked his thumb towards Martin and went to collect from Andrew, a satisfied grin on his face.

Chapter 4

Lorenz Takes A Chance

Lorenz rolled his cigarette and looked at Martin. "Y'all want some?" he offered. He was bored with the silence and the jolting of the wagon was sure to do damage to his backside.

"Naw, thanks, but I don't smoke or chew. Both cost too much money."

"That's a fact," muttered Lorenz, glad of the refusal. He didn't know when he would get more. Red had kept him supplied in Carson City. 'Course Rity didn't know nothing about it. "How long's this trip gonna take?"

"We're getting a late start so it'll be four nights on the trail, then close to another half-a-day before we reach your place."

"Ain't my place," protested Lorenz.

"Sure it is, now. Uncle Mac ain't got any sons, just Mina, and in Texas, girls can't own land." To Martin, this fact was ir-refutable; therefore, Lorenz would inherit.

"How much land?" asked Lorenz.

"Papa and Uncle Mac each own a couple of thousand acres and all around us is more land and wild cattle that nobody owns. We use the land and brand all the cattle we can catch."

"Why bother if prices are so bad?" Lorenz began to see why MacDonald wanted a hand.

"Because the prices are going to get better," replied Martin. "We got a contract with the U.S. Cavalry for another three hundred head this fall and again come spring. That's six hundred dollars split two ways each trip, but prices are better up North." His voice became excited. "Do y'all know what they get for each head up there?"

"Nope." He took a deep drag on the cigarette, sure that Martin was about to tell him.

"Thirty dollars a head, that's vat!" In his excitement, Martin lapsed into the accent of his father. "Do y'all know vhat that comes to?"

Lorenz shook his head no while Martin explained.

Like most men, Martin would plod through life, secure in his own lot, thanking God for his blessings and asking help from above when needed. This, however, was his idea, one of the few original ideas that he would ever conceive. He had gone over and over the details in his mind and now there was an opportunity to execute it. From this one thought would come riches and security for him and for his yet to be conceived children. When he first mentioned it to his father and MacDonald, Rolfe started to laugh, but the interest on MacDonald's face stilled the mirth. After much discussion the two older men had agreed.

Martin warmed to his subject and the chance to explain it again. "Say we each drive three hundred, maybe five hundred head north. That's nine, fifteen thousand for each family. It's more money than this whole county has seen in four years. Even with paying the men and other expenses, it will leave seven or ten thousand each. Every year we can drive another herd. Prices are sure to get better and the herds bigger, if we cull them right and hire the right men to drive them."

"Who the hell ever heard of driving cattle that far?" Lorenz was skeptical.

Martin's voice was stubborn as he said, "Papa used to drive herds to New Orleans before the war, and he was paid good money. That was after trapping went to hell and Uncle Mac was scouting for the 2nd Dragoons. He helped on the first drive though."

"Ah still don't see how y'all will get through Injun country. Where's the water and feed y'all need for that many cows?"

"Papa and Uncle Mac know how to get through," Martin replied. "Papa still goes to see Old Chisholm on the Cherokee Reservation."

"What's that got to do with anything?"

"Chisholm is still a trader in the Cherokee lands. Papa and Uncle Mac know him from their fur trapping days. His wagons made trails carrying the freight in for the Indians. We can drive a herd through Cherokee territory and not worry about being attacked. There's probably some Jay Hawkers left from the war, but we'll get enough men for any fighting. We just need extra horses and plenty of grub. Cattle, even longhorns, trail good. We can sell the extra horses there too, just like we do in Arles. They're just wild mustangs that we rough break for herding."

"Yeah, but iffen y'all can drive cattle, others will too. Then who buys that many beeves?"

"Meat packers or brokers back east, that's who. There's lots of people pouring into this country, thousands every year! The North needs our beef." Martin had heard these arguments before and he had an answer for everyone.

Lorenz considered the possibilities and the reasons. "Why so many people coming here?"

"Because things in the old country are bad. It's much better here. Here a man can get land and try to get rich."

"Why not do that where they are?" Things weren't really that great in Texas as far as Lorenz could see. People were starving, empty houses dotted the landscape, the Comanche were acting like they owned the western part of the state, and the men coming home from the war were gaunt, tattered clad skeletons that rode mules and horses equally ill fed, if they had horses or mules.

Martin looked at Lorenz in wonderment. "In the old country," he said firmly, "men like us can't get rich. Some places, we can't even get schooling. Men are expected to do what their papas did, and they sure can't vote. All the land is owned by the rich, and that's who y'all work for. Y'all can't even worship God like y'all want, and if y'all catch so much as a rabbit for food they hang y'all."

Lorenz had never heard such things. Maybe other places were different. He didn't know. It was safer to go back to talking about selling beef and horses. "What do y'all mean about sellin' horses? Ah thought y'all wuz trailin' beef."

"We needed the extra horses for the trail. One horse gets tired if y'all use it all the time. So we each have an extra horse and then sell it. That's how I got the money for the shirt. Papa gave it to me."

"Why wouldn't he? Sounds like y'all earned it."

"That's how it is in families. It ain't your money until y'all are twenty-one, the legal age." A quick glance was enough to see disbelief written on Lorenz's face and Martin elaborated. "After y'all turn twenty-one, anything y'all earn is all yours. Papa is right good about money though. He lets me keep anything Uncle Mac or Uncle Kap pay me for haying or helping. It ain't much, but it makes a difference. Papa left home when he was sixteen because his papa beat him and always kept the money from Papa's job. Papa figured he was better off on his own."

"Damn right," agreed Lorenz. "Does yore pa beat on y'all?"

"Only when I needed it." Martin threw a quick smile over the reins. "It seems a boy can always get into trouble. He only laid me out once, and it was my own fault. I got into the last of his whiskey and what I didn't drink I broke when I fell down."

Lorenz gave a half-way chuckle, but he was wondering how Martin could be so free of any hatred towards his sire. "Was it worth it?" he asked.

"Naw, whiskey don't taste half as good as beer or wine."

There was another matter that didn't fit in with life as Lorenz knew it. "How come y'all got all that booze if y'll are Christian?"

"Huh, y'all must have been listening to some Baptist or Methodist preacher. Jews drink wine, and Jesus was a Jew. He made wine. Not that booze has anything to do with salvation." Martin liked being the knowledgeable one.

Lorenz tried sorting the words out. The words Martin used had no meaning to him; yet, Martin's voice and words had a familiarity to them like some long ago echo of family conversations and word patterns that moved in his head and visited his dreams: Voices from far away calling him home to safety and sanity. He didn't want Martin to stop talking. He wasn't sure what salvation meant either. Rity had said it meant to be saved, but right now the only thing he needed saved from was MacDonald. Rolfe and MacDonald were still on either side of the wagon. Sometimes one would go to point and one to drag, but never far enough away for Lorenz to bound over the side and loosen Dandy for a quick exit.

"I don't know who I was listening to," said Lorenz, unaware that he was picking up the speech of Martin, "but them camp meeting ladies sure didn't hold with drinking. And the preacher man doing all the shouting was sure agin it."

"Ja," agreed Martin, "and he was probably ignorant too. Them kind don't have any education. They can't read much English, let alone Greek or Hebrew." Martin slapped the reins over the backs of the horse in disgust.

Lorenz listened in amazement at the words. He didn't realize that Martin was iterating the standard Lutheran argument against any uneducated preacher. "What's reading got to do with it?" he asked.

"Y'all can't preach the word of God if y'all can't read it."

Lorenz was sure that that didn't keep any number of people from preaching, but at least this opened a new line of thought as Martin was becoming irate about something. It would be best to stick to subjects where Martin wasn't watching and alert.

"Can y'all read all those languages," asked Lorenz.

Martin relaxed and smiled. "Well, not Greek or Hebrew, but I ain't a Pastor. I can read and write Deutsch and English though, and your Uncle Kap is teaching James Latin. In a few years, he'll be learning Greek."

Lorenz was awed. "Why Dutch in this country?"

"Not Dutch, Deutsch. It's pronounced German in English."

Then why didn't he say German in the first place, Lorenz wondered. "Can y'all cipher too?"

"Sure, pretty good at numbers. Least ways, I'm good enough so nobody's going to cheat me." Martin wasn't bragging. He was just stating a fact.

"Where'd y'all go to school?"

"Right in Schmidt's Corner. Your uncle, he was the teacher, and he taught everybody."

There was the reference to his uncle again. He sure as hell couldn't remember him. Lorenz stayed on the subject. "Who's everybody?"

"My sister, Olga, some of Tillman's relatives, and Tillman's oldest girl. The Tillman's relatives have moved out. They didn't have anything to eat after the men joined the Rebs. Now Young James is his only student. Tillman won't send his girls if he can't pay. Y'all ever been to school, Lorenz?"

"Naw, never no time." He wondered what Martin would say if he told him about Comancheros, or Rity singing in saloons. Probably best not to. Aloud he said, "Rity taught me some ciphering. Ah didn't do much learning to read though."

"I'll bet Uncle Mac and Tante Anna teach y'all."

"Mama reads and writes?" burst out of Lorenz's mouth.

"Ja, sure, the same as me: Deutsch and English."

Lorenz pondered the information. Most men he'd known couldn't much more than sign their name. What the hell was a woman doing reading and writing? Of course, Rity did both, but that didn't count. There wasn't much of a woman about Rity except her figure and clothes. "What does Tante mean?" he asked.

"In English it means Aunt. As much as she helped to raise us after Mama died, it seemed silly to call her Mrs. MacDonald."

"Is yore sister older or younger than y'all?"

"Older, by a year."

"Is she pretty?"

Martin hooted. "She's okay, I guess. She's sister. Besides, she's sweet on Tom Jackson."

Lorenz didn't know who Jackson was and didn't care. MacDonald and Rolfe were hanging too close to the wagon. He might as well jaw some more.

Young James had tired of sitting in the back and was now hanging over the boards waiting for a chance to break in on their conversation. He hated the interloper on his seat. The light breeze kept swirling the dust up and around. If he was up high, he wouldn't have to breathe any dust. He was tired of watching clouds half-form and dissolve in the blue sky. How he longed to be up there beside Martin.

"Is your sister pretty," asked Martin.

"Ah reckon. Some say so. She's too tall for most men," Lorenz added.

"How tall is she?"

"Ah reckon about six foot."

Martin whistled and looked at Lorenz. "I didn't think any woman would be taller than Tante Anna." He was impressed. "Is she married?"

"Naw, she won't even look at a man. She beat the hell out of one fellow that tried to kiss her."

Young James gasped. "Your Mama will wash your mouth out with soap if you talk like that," he declared.

"Sez who?"

Martin laughed. "Young James should know. She's washed out his mouth enough times."

Lorenz raised his eyebrows. The notion of anyone washing out his mouth went against the grain.

James would not retreat. "She has not! Only twice, and besides, it was your fault, Martin."

"Young James, shut up!" Martin was not the older for nothing. "We are talking." He turned his attention Lorenz. "Did y'all live in Carson City for long?"

"Only a few months."

"I've heard it's a real big place, plenty of businesses, and lots of people pouring in. Did y'all ever go into the mines?"

"Naw. Red knew some of the owners, but he wasn't about much during the day."

"Is that the fellow that knows y'all didn't kill his uncle?"

"Yeah."

"What's he do for a living?"

Lorenz hesitated before answering and then decided it wasn't worth lying about. "He owns two cathouses."

Young James covered his ears at this sinfulness and then had to scramble to regain his balance as the wagon bounced over a rock. Martin turned to look at Lorenz, his blue eyes wide with interest.

Honest? Did y'all go in there?"

Lorenz decided to lie. Rity's arrival and retrieval of his one time visit to the whores was too shameful for the recounting. "Naw, ah didn't. Ah didn't have no money."

"Are they fancy places?"

"Just the one is all gussied up for the mine owners. The other's for the miners and it's just a long shack."

"I thought y'all weren't inside."

"Ah wasn't," Lorenz protested. "Ah just walked by the outside."

"I thought the O'Neals were big planters down in south Texas," Martin prodded.

"The old man is, but Red didn't much fancy fighting in a war that the South was going to lose."

Martin was dubious. "Are y'all sure he just didn't want to be shot at?" He had a low opinion of men that sold women.

"Hell, no! He's a damn good fighter and one of the best shots around. He just don't care shit for fighting in wars."

"Uh, uh, Lorenz, y'all keep talking like that and I'm going to tell," sang Young James.

Lorenz turned around to glare at him. "Just who the hell yu'll gonna tell?"

James edged backwards and pulled himself up over the sideboards. "Hey, Uncle Mac!" he called.

"Little shit," muttered Lorenz watching the big man draw closer. "Ah'll get yu'll."

"Lorenz, shut up and sit quiet," advised Martin. Young James ain't going to tattle."

"What makes yu'll so sure?"

"If he tattles, Papa will whip him. He's just egging y'all on."

MacDonald trotted alongside of the wagon. "And what do ye want, Young James?"

"Can I have that ride now, Uncle Mac? You promised."

"Aye, that ye may. Martin, ho up."

Martin pulled the team to a stop. Lorenz clenched his fists. If the big man came toward him at least he'd have one swing.

MacDonald's long arms swung out, lifted James up and over the wagon, and then settled James in front of him. "Ye can guide Zark for a while, Young James." James threw a triumphant grin at the two left on the wagon.

Martin lifted the reins and smacked them down. "Hi-yo-up!" He smiled at Lorenz. "See, I told y'all. Young James knows better than to tattle."

Lorenz let out his breath. "Ah swear ah'll kill that big son-of-a-bitch iffen he lays another hand on me." His voice was flat and vicious.

"Y'all crazy? Besides, y'all ain't got no right to talk like that about Uncle."

"Ah'll kill him just like ah did Zale." The words ground out.

"Lorenz, he's a damn good man, and married to your mama. What would she do without him?"

"She'd probably be better off without that big bastard." Lorenz was certain of it.

Martin shook his head. "Y'all can't talk about Uncle like that." His voice was becoming set.

"What are y'all going to do, tell?"

"No, but by God, I can make y'all take back those words." Contempt laced through his voice. "Guess I made a mistake about y'all." He retreated into silence, his eyes fixed on the horses and the road.

Lorenz was glad to sit there and think. Martin must be like all the others: full of nothing but horseshit. He knew how men treated women. There hadn't been any privacy in Zale's camp. What little he'd seen of men being polite to women was in town among a group of people to avoid talk. Rity was just bigger and smarter than other women. She didn't need a man. Maybe she could get Mama away from the big bastard. Nobody ever stopped Rity from doing what she wanted; not even Red. He watched Rolfe swing his horse towards MacDonald. They were probably going to confab. The two men had dropped farther behind, but were still too close to make a break. Dandy was tied to the back and it would take time to untie the reins. He didn't need a saddle as he could always steal one later. He settled back. He had four days. In a way it had been fun talking with Martin. It was the first time he'd ever really talked with anyone near his own age. If things had been different, maybe Martin would be his friend. Lorenz considered that. Other people had friends, but he never knew how. Maybe he could mollify Martin. Trouble was, he didn't know how to do that either. The wagon jolted to a stop.

"Piss call," said Martin and stepped down.

Lorenz swung around in the seat. Rolfe was relieving himself, and the big bastard had turned his horse to show Young James something in the distance. "Good idea," he said to Martin and left the seat with a leap.

He'd be in plain view, but neither man had a rifle in hand. Damn careless. He slipped the hitch and jumped on Dandy. He could hear them yelling as he dug his heels in. First they would have to get Young James off MacDonald's horse. He figured they wouldn't shoot him, just yet. He had no rope, no saddle, no gun, no knife, but by God he had his freedom, and he knew just how to run with another chasing. So hi-ya, Dandy, lift them legs. Big Bastard was too big and too heavy. He couldn't catch him on Dandy even if Dandy was past his prime. He stretched out and let Dandy run, automatically calculating the distance. One mile at a hard run, then trot, then run, then trot, and then worry about hiding your tracks.

When he pulled Dandy up to look back, his jaw dropped. Mac-Donald was still in sight. That big horse of his was cutting away at the distance. He gauged how much time separated them. Naw, let Dandy walk for a while. He had time.

He kept Dandy at a trot. His eyes raked the landscape near the road and towards the hills to the northeast. He reckoned the distance to the hills, but it was too far with the land so flat and open. The other side of the road wasn't any better as it was cut by the river the road more or less followed. The banks here were too steep for Dandy to go over and it might spook him to push it. If he knew the country, where the river turned, or where a ford was, he'd cross. Right now, it was best to wait for better terrain. He twisted in the saddle for another look. MacDonald was walking his horse now. Lorenz half-hoped the big bastard would have pushed his mount into a punishing gallop, but then in this heat it might wear Dandy something fierce, and he did not want to steal a horse. The law might look the other way at swiping food or a pair of britches, but a horse was a definite ticket to hell. Lorenz kept a firm hand on Dandy and when time and distance demanded, he kicked him into another run.

He had but one advantage: weight. He kept the run, trot, walk sequence going twice more. When he pulled Dandy to a walk and looked again, a curse burst from him. MacDonald was rapidly closing the distance, not bothering to slow his brute of a horse, cutting the remaining ground to yards. Lorenz kicked his heels into Dandy's sweating flanks and headed for the river. It was now or never, and never wasn't looking too good.

He chose a spot where the bank seemed to flatten and slid off to lead Dandy down the loose incline. Once on the level ground, he realized his mistake. The bank on the other side was too steep and too sandy. He glanced up river and saw the cut on both sides where there was a natural fording area. He threw himself on Dandy and headed towards it. He was too late.

MacDonald rode down the cut and met him at the ford. Lorenz glared at MacDonald to cover the sick feeling rising in his stomach. The man's face was set and grim; all humor was gone from the wide mouth and dark eyes.

"Ye twill dismount," came the command.

Lorenz remained seated on Dandy.

"Dismount or I'll knock ye down."

Lorenz hit the ground on the general theory that since he had survived Zale's beatings, he would survive this one too. He stood beside Dandy, slackening the reins and letting him drink. He could hear MacDonald remove his saddle and talk soothingly to his horse while he did so. Why didn't the big bastard say something to him?

MacDonald let his reins drop and emerged on the other side of Dandy toting his saddle on his shoulder. The saddle must have been crafted for him alone as no other man would sit in it comfortably. "Tis yere horse trained to ground reins?" he asked.

Lorenz kept his back turned and refused to answer. A big hand grasped him by the neck and shook him like a puppy dog. "Answer me aye or nay with a sir after it."

He spat the words out, "Yes, suh." His neck was burning and his head felt like his brains had shifted.

"Goodie, now ye walk towards that downed log resting on that boulder."

They tromped towards the log, MacDonald's one hand gripping his shoulder, the other steadying the saddle. After placing the saddle on the log, MacDonald addressed the stiff figure. "Do ye remember what I said would occur when ye broke the rules?"

"Huh?"

"What did I say I would do if ye broke my rules?"

Lorenz began to breathe easier. "Yu'll said yu'll would use a belt." At least the man might not use his fists.

"And how many times?"

Lorenz began to think the man crazed. "Five," he answered.

"Aye. So ye did listen. Now, yere belt or mine? Bear in mind that mine measures a good two inches across."

Lorenz took a deep breath. "Mine."

"Take it off and hand it to me."

"Mr. MacDonald, go to hell."

He heard the man yank his belt off. "Drop yere britches and bend."

Lorenz stood where he was. The hell if he'd help the man. A hard arm wrapped around him, the free hand unbuckled the belt, worked the buttons, and then slipped the trouser down the skinny flanks.

"Now bend."

Lorenz felt his knees give where MacDonald dropped his weight against them and at the same time gave a not-so-gentle shove to the back of his head. Like it or not, he wound up sprawled over the log, his hands grasping at the rough bark to pull himself up as he heard MacDonald's voice.

"One," and the belt bit into his butt. "Two, three, four, five. Stand."

Stunned, it took Lorenz a second to gather his wits and comply. He yanked the britches up to cover himself. As he was stuffing the shirt into the pants MacDonald continued to speak, his voice steady, broking no interruption. "That twas for disobeying me, for touching yere beastie, and for running. The next time ye break the rules, I twill ask ye what ye have done wrong and I twill have an answer from ye. And remember, when ye break the rules, ye have disobeyed."

MacDonald finished buckling up and looked at Lorenz. "Do ye have any questions?"

"Yeah, why the hell did yu'll bother with pulling my pants down for that? Yu'll just want to see my butt?"

The blow set him down on the log. "I said questions, laddie, nay insults. And the next time it twill be six, then seven, till we reach ten."

Lorenz retrieved his hat. "Yu'll figure ah'm gonna run agin?"

"Oh, aye, since ye ran from yere sister and O'Neal, ye twill try running from me." MacDonald gave a slight smile at the surprise on Lorenz's face. "Next time ye may plot a bit more carefully now that ye ken extemporaneous flight twill get ye nay."

Lorenz's face and grey eyes went blank.

"Ye dinna ken my words?" MacDonald sighed. "Laddie, do ye have any idea of what I have just said?"

"Hell, no! Not yu'll, not Martin, not anythin' that's been said or happened since ah rode into town."

MacDonald's sternness faded, his dark eyes softening. "The word I used, it means spur of the moment. Ken means to understand."

"The why don't yu'll all use them words?"

"'Tis the way my people speak. Ye twill have to adapt; become use to my ways. Now we twill rest awhile." He led the way to a stand of willows, his hand propelling Lorenz in the direction of the shade. Out of the sun's glare, he released Lorenz, pulled his rifle from the scabbard, put the saddle down, and sat, crossing his legs Indian style.

"Sit, laddie. Tis shady here and the horses need to cool down."

When Lorenz remained standing, a long arm swung out and caught him behind the knees, dumping him on the ground. The man extracted a pipe and makings and became busy tamping the tobacco.

Lorenz tucked his legs and asked, "What kind of horse yu'll all got anyways?"

"Tis part Morgan and part Thorough Bred. He tis nay cut and hopefully with the right mare twill breed me another like him."

Lorenz picked a willow branch and chewed on it, contenting himself with smelling the aromatic smoke rising from the pipe. He watched the coots that were flocking back to the river bank now that the horses had drunk their fill and he eyed the big, black stallion. Like its owner, it seemed a brute apart. How in the hell was he supposed to know something that big could move so fast? "Yu'll name him?"

It was as if the months of no human contact now compelled him to talk, to once again be part of the human community. Besides, he had to figure this man out: To probe for his weaknesses, his blind side. Even when he considered everything that had happened, MacDonald's voice held a kindness that he had not heard in Red's voice. Red's voice and actions always implied there would be a reckoning, a calling in of favors owed. Lorenz doubted that there would ever be a way he would be of any use to MacDonald. It didn't seem possible that the man even wanted him around, let alone take him home. Lorenz had enough savvy to know that white men and women were peculiar about who came into their houses: peculiar to the point of being picky.

"Aye, he tis my Zark," answered MacDonald.

Once again, Lorenz was hearing a word that meant absolutely nothing. What the hell kind of name was that? His eyes tightened against the sun and he idly rolled some pebbles in his hand. Two canvasback ducks had jostled the coots away from the bank with a great deal of squawking and ruffled feathers. "Yu'll gonna take those for eatin'?" He was hungry for meat, any kind.

"Nay, friend Rolfe does the hunting when we travel together."

"Why?"

"Because he tis a better hunter than I." Like Martin's speech, the words were calm and factual, showing no jealousy that a small man would be more proficient. "We nay e'er kill more than we can eat."

Lorenz turned to look at the huge bulk sitting so contentedly. He thought of the times he'd come across some bank where below mounds of rotted buffalo remained from an Indian kill or the birds lying on the ground where some sharpshooting man had proven his aim. There had been times when Zale's gang had simply shot and shot at cranes going through their wild dance. What difference did a few birds make? But he had no words to form his questions about a difference in philosophy. He wasn't even sure he wanted to hear the answers. The man might tack another rule onto the others. He gave up on talking and watched the river, listening for any sound that would tell him that things were changing.

MacDonald stretched out on the ground, his rifle across his chest lengthwise, his finger on the trigger, trapper like. "I'm going to rest a wee deeper. Dinna move while I do," he suggested and pulled his hat down over his eyes, effectively blocking out the light.

Lorenz looked at the man. Had he heard right? The big bastard was going to take a nap. Shit, it was a test to see if he stayed put. The man's sweat soaked shirt was drying in patches, leaving salt-stained rings in odd patterns. An odor exuded from the man different from any Lorenz had ever smelled. It wasn't white, Indian, Mexican, or black. What was it? It invaded the senses and sent warning signals like, like something so different it began to raise the neck hairs. Lorenz jerked, drew his breath in. Damn, he was getting jumpy. Bad as a dog or a horse that smells a panther for the first time.

He eyed the horses. They were standing there, waiting, and swishing their tails against the heat and the flies. If he could get to them, take both, he wouldn't have to worry about pursuit for days. Rolfe wouldn't leave his sons and money, and MacDonald was sure as hell too big for Rolfe's horse. That wagon was back there somewhere, getting closer. MacDonald's chest was moving slow and easy. He'd wait awhile and then stand real cautious like. All he needed was a few feet to be away. Maybe he'd even look in on Mama. Nobody would think he'd do that. He sat very still and listened to a scrub jay screeching and scolding. A light breeze stirred the willow leaves and a low snore escaped from under MacDonald's hat. Lorenz waited for his breath to even out again.

Very slowly he bunched his legs, glanced at the prone body, and straightened in one easy motion. He studied the ground, deliberately uncrossed his feet, and placed one foot slightly in front of the other. Then he glanced at MacDonald again. The man hadn't moved. He started to inch forward when unspoken words pounded inside his mind. 'Dinna be so foolish, laddie.' Lorenz sat his grey eyes wide in amazement. He took another look at MacDonald.

This time the hat was tipped back to show one brown eye and a smile on the man's lips. "'Tis glad I am ye dinna try that."

"Ah got stiff. Had to stretch." His lips tightened and he looked straight ahead.

MacDonald grunted. "'Tis time to be leaving." He stood and brushed the dirt from his backside.

"Remember, ye dinna touch yere beastie." He kept his rifle in his right hand and swung the saddle to his shoulder. Lorenz stood and watched.

He was puzzled. Was the Big Bastard going to make him walk? He savored his renaming of MacDonald in his mind. Whenever he thought of him it would be Big Bastard. Once more unspoken words pounded inside his head. 'And ye are nay punished for thoughts.' Lorenz could swear he heard a chuckle on that one, but MacDonald's face was smooth, mouth closed, unsmiling. He watched the Big Bastard saddle his horse, making soft, soothing noises as he cinched the saddle down and returned the rifle to the scabbard.

MacDonald gathered the reins of both horses and pointed at the incline where he had ridden down. "Walk," he commanded.

Lorenz saw no gain in refusing and began walking, the stiff leather of the new boots protesting against his heel and instep. He'd druther have his old boots for this hike, for hike it would be he realized when they reached the road. They'd ridden a fair piece and only dust wavering in the distance showed there was anything nearing them. He glanced at the Big Bastard to see why he had stopped.

The Big Bastard was tying Dandy's reins to his saddle horn. He smiled at Lorenz and said, "Ye twill ride behind me."

By the time Lorenz was ready to protest, MacDonald had his left foot kicked out of the stirrup and his hand down. Lorenz stood rock still, his eyes screaming hatred. MacDonald sighed, "Laddie, either ye ride behind me or I twill truss ye up like a pig going to market and hang ye over the back."

Lorenz took the extended hand and swung up. MacDonald kept his big hand securely wrapped around Lorenz's left hand. "Now put yere right arm around my waist and yere right hand over yere left hand."

Lorenz hesitated and the huge hand began to crumble his. Son-of-a-bitch, he thought, and rapidly put his arm around

MacDonald as directed. In an instant, MacDonald had both of Lorenz's hands clamped firmly against his belt. "I want nay tricks on this ride." He clucked his tongue and Zark began a slow trot.

It was downright humiliatin'. Lorenz sat with his back as straight as possible, but the gait was uncomfortable, and the almost musky smell exuding from the sweat stained shirt in front of him was bewildering. It flat was no human smell he could recognize. There was no seeing around the man's bulk so he contented himself with searching to the side, committing the terrain to memory.

Within one-half an hour they met the approaching wagon. "Whoa up, twill ye, Martin?" asked MacDonald and trotted to the back of the wagon.

"Dismount." His hands released their grip and Lorenz slid down. MacDonald followed and tied Dandy to one of the back hoops. "Now walk to the front."

As they moved to the front, James glared at Lorenz as MacDonald gave a rueful grin and said, "Sorry, Young James, but ye twill need to ride in the back again."

James looked longingly at his father, then at MacDonald, but decided that begging for a ride at this point would not be in his favor. He climbed over the seat and settled for a position at the sidewall.

Lorenz looked at MacDonald and the big man pointed to the seat. Red faced, he swung up over the wheels, plunked his butt on the hard seat, and folded his arms across his chest. Martin didn't even bother to look at him. He had his face set, eyes forward with no welcoming smile as he snapped the reins over the team's back to start their journey again. That was fine with Lorenz. He didn't want to talk anyway. He sure as hell had lost that round. He watched the back muscles of the horses move with easy ripples, dust raising and swirling around the hooves with every step. A light breeze shifted the smell of spring into dry summer.

When they passed the point of his debacle, he looked the other way. Flat, gently undulating prairie stretched over the horizon, studded with an occasional oak or boulder. Sometimes you could see a column of smoke in the distance where some rancher was holding onto the land for a reason that only God could know or see why. He looked over at Martin. The young man still had his jaw set in a stubborn line while staring straight ahead.

Young James had hung his arms over the wagon lip and was standing on the possible box. He was clearly bored with the scenery and was watching the clouds. Every so often he would turn and stick his tongue out at Lorenz. Lorenz half laughed to himself. Crazy little kid! Hell, he didn't want his seat.

He looked again at Martin. "What's got yore back up? Ah'm the one who took the lickin'."

"Ja, and I'm the one who's a jackass."

"Hell, didn't yu'll figure ah wuz going to hightail it?"

Martin shifted uncomfortably. "Never even thought about it, but Papa did. It seems I should a little smarter be." His speech had slid back into the German syntax. "Besides, I figured y'all would be glad your Mama to see."

"Ah doan even remember her." The lie slid out easily. "Ah might have swung by there iffen ah got away just to see iffen she wuz all right." He spat over the wheel. "Nobody would figure ah go that way. Besides," he added, "she doan want me, hit's Daniel she'd be waiting for."

"Y'all know what, Lorenz," said Martin, "I think y'all are half-crazed on loco weed. Tante Anna wants all of her children back. If y'all don't really remember anything, why do y'all think she wants only Daniel?"

"Yeah, and if Tante doesn't want you, how come we had to put your name in all of our prayers?" Young James had been waiting for his chance to talk again.

Lorenz straightened. "Prayers?" He laughed, forgetting to use his broken language. "Y'all have been saying prayers for me? That's funny. Y'all don't really believe there's a God listening to that?"

"You're here, aren't you?" shot back James. "And Papa says your sister's alive too."

Lorenz shifted his position. The strapping had been nothing, but the wagon seat was tolerably hard as it jolted from rock to rut, and his backside bruised from when MacDonald knocked him on the log. James's logic worried him. He didn't like it that Martin had seen through the fact that he did remember Mama. That adults labeled his words lies was natural, but he was unaccustomed to give and take with someone his own age. Now these two had called his bluff. He drifted into silence.

The day's heat was retreating when Martin pulled off the road under a shaded spot guarded by tall cottonwood trees. The bank, pebbled with stones and grass, spilled down towards the river where willows clustered and covered the bank at the turn where water pooled. Cottonwoods sprouting up from the roots provided a natural fence. The blackened stones around the cooking area gave testimony to the fact that here was a spot favored by travelers.

Young James scooted from the wagon, glad to be free of its confines and began a mad search for firewood. He caught the bundle MacDonald tossed to him.

"There were plenty of cow chips from our passing." MacDonald grinned at Lorenz. "Ye have yere choice: work and eat. If nay work, ye hunger."

Martin had already swung down and was busy unhitching the horses. Rolfe was working at the wagon gate, obviously going for the camp gear. "Ah'll work, ah reckon." He climbed down, his legs stiff from bracing against the jolting ride.

MacDonald dismounted and unhooked the cobbles. "Then take the nosebags from the side. When we get to where the beasties are to be bedded, use a portion from each and put that into yere hat for yere own horse, but dinna touch him. I'll attend."

Inside, Lorenz fumed, but did as he was told. At least they had given the squaw's work of wood gathering to Young James. MacDonald walked beside him as he led both Zark and Dandy over to where Martin was removing the harnesses and bridles. Martin took two of the hobbles from MacDonald and carefully clamped one pair on each horse while Lorenz apportioned part of the grain for Dandy. MacDonald slid his saddle off while Martin finished hobbling the last two horses and then loped down to the river, lay prone, and gulped the fresh water. He half-rose, rinsed his hands and came back grinning. "By God, I was dry I'll have supper on before long, Uncle Mac."

Lorenz watched him stride off. "He do the cooking?" he asked. Dandy was making a mess of what was left of his hat. He wondered if maybe he could convince the Big Bastard to replace it before he left for good. Probably not.

"Aye," came the reply to his question.

Rolfe joined them, unsaddled, and attached the last nose bag "I think ve should get wasser here, Mac."

"Aye, twill nay be as clear nearer to House." To Lorenz, he added, "We twill be the last two days with but a trickle of water." He and Rolfe headed back to the wagon carrying their saddles and guns.

Should he run now? Naw, either one could drop him. He watched MacDonald take both saddles and walk to the back of the wagon where he deposited them. Rolfe took down the barrel on the passenger side and slung it over his shoulder and hiked back to the river. MacDonald appeared on the side with a second barrel. By now Dandy had finished his grain, and Lorenz wiped out his hat and set it back on his head. The sun was slowly meandering toward the back of the low foothills while the leaves rustled in tune with the singing river.

"Ye can give a hand, laddie, with the filling of the barrels," said MacDonald.

When both barrels were filled, Lorenz helped Rolfe carry the one and MacDonald took the other. Big Bastard, thought Lorenz. Damn, the man was strong.

Rolfe finished lashing their barrel and bit off a chew. He grinned at Lorenz. "Gut day for a swim." He swaggered off while Lorenz tried to puzzle if Rolfe had meant good when saying goot.

Once more MacDonald emerged from the back of the wagon. This time he carried one of the bundles from the store and a towel wrapped around it. He too was grinning.

Lorenz considered running, but the man was beside him with the huge hand clamping down on his shoulder, brooking no opposition. They marched back to the river. He could hear potatoes plopping into the hot grease and wished he was helping Martin.

MacDonald released him and began to undress. "Take yere clothes off."

"The hell!"

The next thing Lorenz knew his britches were down around his ankles, his shirt and hat removed, and his butt hit the ground. MacDonald yanked his boots off and pointed his finger at him.

"Dinna move." He then continued to disrobe.

Lorenz sat with his knees up to his chin, once again thoroughly humiliated. He hoped like hell Martin and James hadn't been watching. He sensed MacDonald folding his clothes and was rudely raised from the ground by the hand under his arm.

"This, laddie, tis called soap. Yere mither has spent long hours preparing it. If ye drop or lose this in the water, I twill consider it open rebellion. Do ye ken?" The bar was but three inches from his eyes.

"Reckon," he muttered sullenly while half looking at the man and stopped to gape. Never, never in his life had he seen such a build. The man was solid, corded muscle. Normally a man of such girth had flab for a stomach or was stocky fat: not MacDonald. He had rope cords for an abdominal wall, biceps ran into triceps, even the calves of his legs were hard, rolled muscle, and unlike most white men, the body was practically devoid of hair, even in the genital area. "My God, y'all ain't fat nowhere," slumped out of his slackened jaw.

"Thank ye, laddie." The man's eyes twinkled in amusement. "Now 'tis time ye joined the ranks of civilization. Walk." He pointed towards the river.

Defiance snapped back into Lorenz's eyes. "The hell!"

MacDonald's hand was on his shoulder again and he thought the better of saying more obscenities. He walked. When the water was up to his thighs, the pressure stopped. Once more the soap was held directly in front of his face, a faint whiff of lavender greeting his nose.

"Now, ye are to wet yere hair and rub this into it and soap yere body. Remember what I said about the hours it took to make."

Lorenz remained standing. The huge hand went around his neck and a knee hit behind his. His face and upper torso were completely immersed and he was shaken like a rag flapping in the breeze He came up sputtering, water running from his long hair into his eyes and mouth.

"Now, ye take the soap and begin at the top of yere head and finish with yere toes, or by Gar, I'll do it for ye, and nay too gently."

Lorenz did as he was ordered. He hoped the Rolfe's were all busy elsewhere and not watching his final humiliation. He thought seriously about pounding on Martin if there was so much as a snicker when they got back. He fought desperately to hold onto the soap. He figured MacDonald was just waiting for the chance to belt him again, and this time there would be an audience. He was about to hand the soap back when MacDonald checked him.

"Ye have nay finished. Ye move the skin back like this," he said as he demonstrated with his own dick. "Or ye twill nay be able to make bairns when ye are a man."

Lorenz gazed at him dumbfounded and wondered what the hell the man was talking about this time.

MacDonald grinned. "Bairns are babies, wee ones. Wash."

Lorenz half-way choked, turned his back, and half did as he was told. He was afraid that MacDonald might carry out his threat to wash him personally, and he wasn't giving that Big Bastard any excuse to touch him. Stiffly he held the soap out.

MacDonald extracted the soap. "Rinse off while I do myself."

Lorenz slipped into the river and dog paddled furiously. The water was warm and soft, and it floated away the soap on his body and part of his agitation. Could he out swim the man? For what? He was naked and weaponless. Did he have time to get back to the bank and unhobble a horse? Rolfe was already out of the water and had a rifle. Would the man shoot? Probably. He stopped and stood while the water swirled chest high. He saw MacDonald throw the soap up on the bank and slide easily into the water. The man slipped through the water like a knife through bear fat. With less effort and fewer strokes, he was suddenly beside Lorenz. The Big Bastard was a wonderment. Lorenz didn't know people could swim like that.

The man was smiling down at him, the dark hair plastered to his head. "Ye have nay learned the rudiments of proper swimming. Ye lay yere body out flat and move yere arms and legs in smooth strokes like this." Once more the huge body propelled itself through the water, moving as smooth as a fish. He stood. "Try it."

71

Lorenz was dubious, but if the Big Bastard could do it, so could he, and he shoved into the water. His body betrayed him and became tense. He was dog paddling by the time he reached MacDonald.

"Better," grunted MacDonald. "Now try again, but remember to move yere head from side to side for the breathing." He took off for the bank and Lorenz followed.

The strokes were smoother this time and Lorenz floundered up on the ground without reverting to dog paddling. If there was anything he could out do the Big Bastard on, he hadn't discovered it yet. He moved to put on his clothes when the deep voice stopped him.

"Ye dry off with this." MacDonald handed Lorenz a towel. "Then ye put on these," and he held up the summer drawers and vest, an abbreviated, cotton version of winter underclothes by being shortened to mid-calf and upper arm.

Lorenz took the towel and swiped at parts of his anatomy while eying the underwear with distaste. "Hit's too hot!" he protested.

"Aye," agreed MacDonald, "but if I must wear the damn things, so twill ye."

Lorenz ground his teeth. Rity had made him wear the itching, confining clothing and he detested them. He glared at the big man. "An' iffen ah doan put 'em on?"

"Laddie, I took yere clothes off, and I can put others on ye."

The spoken fact was irrefutable. Lorenz grudgingly donned the underwear. MacDonald handed him the new shirt and trousers.

"Hell, they'll just be dirty by the time we reach Mama." Lorenz searched for a way to avoid the stiff, new clothing.

"Twill be better than what ye are wearing." MacDonald pulled his boots on and handed Lorenz a jackknife already opened. "Tis for the paring of the toenails ere ye put on the socks," he explained.

While Lorenz worked the knife, MacDonald eyed the long hair as he waited, but decided to let Anna attend to the barbering. Gar kenned he had subjected the laddie to enough indignities in one day. He reclaimed the knife, rolled up the dirty clothes, adjusted his hat, and picked up the towel and soap. The smell of potatoes and bacon frying, coffee boiling, and beans filled the air.

Lorenz felt his mouth watering. No help for it. It seemed best to follow MacDonald back to the wagon and eat before plotting another escape. Maybe there'd be an opportunity tonight or tomorrow to slip away.

Rolfe grinned at them and waved a bottle as they approached the back of the wagon. "By Gott, we're a clean camp tonight! Have a drink, friend Mac. It's been too damn long."

MacDonald deposited the items and took the proffered bottle and drank well. "Thank ye, friend Rolfe." He did not offer the bottle to Lorenz, but returned it to Rolfe. Lorenz had not really expected it, but the man had offered him beer.

MacDonald shoved all of the bathing paraphernalia into the possible box and handed Lorenz a cup. "Help yereself to some of the coffee if ye like."

Lorenz did like. It had been weeks since he'd had any. He watched Martin stirring at the gravy and checking the coals under the Dutch oven. He wondered if those other two would drink themselves pie-eyed. Getting away would be no problem then, but he doubted if they would. Still, they were getting older, and Lorenz had noticed that older men often had a problem holding their booze. Rolfe he judged to be between forty or fifty. MacDonald sure looked younger, but it was hard to say. Rity said Mama would be about forty now. That meant MacDonald had to be older, but he didn't look it. He quit trying to ponder their ages and decided to make his peace with Martin, or he'd have the whole camp watching him for just one wrong move. MacDonald and Rolfe were now talking about everyday things:

weather and cows, men in town. Easy they were with each other, not bothering the bottle at all. Weren't they like other men and drank until every drop gone? He sipped at the hot coffee and said, "Yu'll make a good pot." Would that mollify Martin? He'd better not say anything about the bath though.

Martin grunted a reluctant, "Thanks."

"How'd yu'll get the beans cooked so fast?"

Martin pointed to a hefty box sitting to the side. "It's an old country method. Y'all take a box lined with bricks, straw, or hay. Then start your beans in the morning and put pot and all in the box, put the lid on, cover it with more hay or straw, then the box top, and let it ride all day. The heat stays inside and keeps right on cooking. I'll show y'all in the morning." Martin's voice became authoritative as he demonstrated his superior knowledge.

Lorenz examined the box built of wood and bricks. Could something so simple serve as a stove? He would have preferred meat, but right now he was so hungry he didn't care. "Didn't wimen in the old country stay in the house and cook?" he asked.

"Ja sure, but the peasants, the ones who work the land for the rich, would have to be out in the fields all day, them and their kids. They would use a box like that to have something cooked when they came in from the fields." Martin kept stirring the gravy while he talked. "Hand me some water," he said to Lorenz.

Lorenz obliged and wondered where Young James was. Dusk was rapidly splashing the ground with lengthening shadows and the sky with quiet pinks and golden grays. The breeze cooled the body and quickened the flames.

"Too damn much smoke," came from the elder Rolfe. He walked over and pushed the coals and burning materials together. "Like dat." He shook his head and wondered if his eldest son would ever learn.

James returned carrying more cow chips piled on a few dead pieces of wood and didn't notice Martin's red face and set lips.

"Chow's on," called Martin as James added to the fuel pile. James then darted between everyone and grabbed his plate and fork to be first in line. Lorenz waited to see retribution descend, but none came.

MacDonald handed him a plate and fork. "Ye are second." A slight smile played over his lips at the amazement on Lorenz's face. "We feed the wee ones first."

Lorenz snapped his lips together, but decided this was no time for anger. He was too hungry. He waited while Martin filled James's plate and then his. After Lorenz came MacDonald and Rolfe. Martin filled his plate last, first positioning the beans and gravy to a place where they would stay warm. Before eating, he hung a pot of water directly over the coals.

By mutual consent they sat Indian style, and Lorenz devoured the contents of his plate.

MacDonald nodded toward the pots. "Tis plenty. Help yere-self."

Lorenz needed no second invitation.

The pots were empty when MacDonald brought out the last cans of peaches and milk. He divided the contents onto each plate. Everyone but Lorenz poured the evaporative milk over the fruit. Lorenz still couldn't see grown men willingly drink milk, but held his tongue. After they finished Lorenz learned that he was expected to scrape the plates and wash the gear while Martin tidied the cook area and put the washed utensils away.

When the last pot was stowed, Lorenz started off towards the willows and MacDonald followed. "Yu'll doan need to worry. Jest somethin' ah need to get rid of." He spoke through clenched teeth.

"Face it, laddie, I am yere nursemaid for the next few days. I dinna trust yere wanderings."

Once again there was no avoiding the humiliation as Lorenz could think of no way to stop the man. He used the willow and cottonwood leaves when he had finished and MacDonald pointed towards the river.

"We twill walk down there and ye twill rinse yere hands."

"Why?"

"'Tis another of Mrs. MacDonald's and my rules."

"The Rolfe's do that too?" Lorenz couldn't help but ask.

"I am nay responsible for the Rolfes."

Lorenz gauged the bulk blocking his way back to camp and walked to the river. "How come yu'll all feed kids first?" he asked.

"'Tis my way, and tis the German-Lutheran way of yere mither. We all consider children treasures from Gar."

Lorenz knelt and rinsed his hands. What the hell was German-Lutheran? Every time he got an answer, it meant another question. "Injuns feed the man first," he stated. "That's fer the huntin' and then they feed the boys. After that, the women and girls can have what's left. When do women folk eat yore way?" He remembered sitting with Rity at the table while Theresa served them.

"My way tis the same as yere mither's. We are adults and when together, we eat together."

Lorenz decided that white men's ways were pretty much the same on that score except for feeding the kids. He'd seen men eat while their kids stood there skinny as a hound dog after a chase and their eyes begging the same way for a crumb. MacDonald pointed back at the camp and he matched the big man's pace.

"The first watch tis mine," said MacDonald as they neared the wagon. "We twill set up our sleeping equipment now."

He brought out Lorenz's blanket and his own roll. Lorenz seethed inside. The Rolfes were in different stages of bedding down, their rolls spread away from the light of the dying fire. Darkness was bold in its coming and covered the area. Lorenz flopped out his one blanket and MacDonald handed him another. "Ye may need this," came the gruff voice.

"Not in this heat and with these damn clothes on," Lorenz shot back.

"Keep your voice down. Young James tis already abed. Now, front side or back side?"

"Huh?" Lorenz turned and saw the rope swinging in MacDonald's hand.

"When ye sleep, ye twill be tied, but the hands can be either in front or in back."

"Front," muttered Lorenz, then louder, he said, "but ah ain't tired yet. Why cain't ah jest walk around with yu'll? Ain't nobody out there."

MacDonald considered and then rolled and tucked the rope under his belt. "Aye." He motioned towards the horses with his rifle, and they walked softly out of camp. After a quick check on the horses, MacDonald settled on a rock and filled his pipe. "Do ye ken the name of that star?" he asked, pointing to the end of the Little Dipper.

"Ah reckon. Ah heered it called the North Star."

"Aye, or the Polar Star. Do ye ken any of the other constellations?"

Darkness hid the blankness of Lorenz's face and the big man's voice rumbled on. "There are spiders, twins, a crab, and a flying horse among them. Do ye ken?"

Only a cricket answered and MacDonald sighed. "Sit down," he invited, "and I twill show ye as they appear."

It was better than being tied, so Lorenz sat. For the first time he heard the tales of the Twins, Orion's Belt, and Pegasus. Every so often, MacDonald's arm would sweep skyward as he recited the legends while star-shine and moonlight brightened the night. Lorenz was slow to realize that he had been snookered, hooked on the tales, and kept asking what happened next. Sometimes he snorted at the foolishness of it all, but still he wanted more.

When MacDonald finally banged the last dregs from the pipe bowl and stood, Lorenz knew he didn't want it to end: this feeling that somehow, someone, thought he was worth the spinning of tales. He was tired, too tired to realize that MacDonald's syntax and vocabulary were being imprinted on his brain. "How did y'all learn all that?"

"In truth, yere Uncle taught me the lore of this, ah, ancient Greece."

"How'd he learn it?"

"He attended school."

"They teach that in school?" Lorenz found it strange as it certainly wasn't ciphering or reading.

"Aye, tis called mythology," explained MacDonald as he started back to camp, but Lorenz was desperate to delay the inevitable.

"Didn't y'all go to school?"

"Oh, aye, but twas a different lore that I twas taught."

"What lore? What's lore anyways?"

"Laddie, ye nay fool me. 'Tis yere bedtime. Walk."

Lorenz tried to stand his ground and slipped back into his usual way of talking. "Ah don't like bein' tied. Why can't ah just stay out here with yu'll?"

MacDonald clamped his hand down Lorenz's shoulder, but more gently than the last time. "Walk, and ken ye, I dinna like tying ye, but ye are going to House. If, per chance there tis trouble, I twill nay worry about yere whereabouts; nay twill Mr. Rolfe. Nay can I allow ye to cause a disturbance while we are in camp. Mr. Rolfe twill relieve me later, and he needs his rest."

Lorenz was wise enough to know that if he fought now, he would be tied sooner tomorrow night, nor would the Big Bastard bother being gentle again. Somehow he had to convince the man that it wasn't necessary to tie him. Maybe the man would knot the rope wrong, and he could get loose. He remembered that he had answered "front." Maybe he'd be able to use his hands.

It was a wrong assumption. Dark as the night was MacDonald skillfully tied the cord around his wrists, lapped it under his belt, and finished by tying his ankles. He stuffed Lorenz's hat under his head and gently laid the blanket over him before melting away. Damn, thought Lorenz, someone that big shouldn't be able to move that quietly. And don't think about the Big Bastard being kind. It's a trick, he reminded himself. He closed his eyes against the stars and the slowly moving moon.

Later he heard MacDonald roll into the bedding beside him. He knew Rolfe was now on guard, but he hadn't heard Mac-Donald wake him, or heard Rolfe leave. I must be getting soft, he thought, and stillness closed his mind again. It was safe here and now was the time to rest.

Chapter 5

The Journey Home

He rested so deeply the soft light of dawn failed to rouse him as it did the others. It was Rolfe banging the coffee pot and building the fire that nudged him awake. MacDonald was pulling on his boots, a grin cutting across the wide face, "Good morrow, laddie, and did ye sleep well?"

Lorenz blinked his eyes against the rapidly expanding light, but did not answer. He forced himself upward and shook his head, clasping and unclasping his hands. MacDonald reached over and undid the rope. Lorenz rubbed his wrists to restore the circulation and tugged his boots on. Young James roared away in the direction of the willows while Martin mumbled, "Guten morgen," and followed James. Lorenz stood. Except for the needles exploding in his feet, he felt fine. He and MacDonald headed in the same direction as James and Martin. He had to figure out a plan to prevent being tied tonight.

After rinsing their hands in the river, Martin headed towards the camp to fix breakfast, and MacDonald led the way back to the sleeping area. "We twill pack up the sleeping gear," he commanded.

When they finished storing the articles, Lorenz noticed that Young James was once again searching for cow chips and any dry wood. Martin was busy at breakfast, and Rolfe was resting against one of the wagon wheels. MacDonald indicated a spot for him to sit and Lorenz decided it was time to try his plan.

"What am ah supposed to do, just twiddle my thumbs?" he asked. He hadn't meant for it to sound sassy, but he didn't know how else to start out. Sass wasn't going to get him anywhere with the Big Bastard. "Didn't mean it like that," he mumbled as MacDonald looked at him. "Ah doan like just sittin' around." It sounded lame, but it was the best he fish out. "Ah just meant, maybe ah could do somethin' and maybe not cause so much trouble. Hit's been a long time since ah saw Mama," he finished.

MacDonald's eyes were surprisingly hard. "Are ye tellin' me that ye have had a change of heart?"

Lorenz lifted his chin. "Ah was just wonderin'. Iffen ah did, would things be different?"

"Twould what be different?"

"That's what ah'm askin'. How'd it be different iffen ah follow all of yore rules?"

MacDonald pushed his hat back. "And, of course, ye twill be giving me yere word on this behavior?" he asked softly, the rolling r more pronounced than usual.

"Ah ain't givin' nothin'." No point in lying when he wasn't going to be believed anyways. "Just wanted to know iffen it would be different. Would there be as many rules?"

"As to different, I canna say. The rules would be the same as tis the way we live. Mayhap ye would even begin to ken why."

As usual, the Big Bastard wasn't making sense. "Ah mean are yu'll goin' stand over me every time ah fart or take a piss?"

"Ye have such a novel way of putting words together, laddie."

Lorenz flushed. "Forget it."

"Nay, bide a moment. Are ye saying ye wish to try being part of this group? Mayhap ye are even glad to be going to the House of yere mither?"

"Well, ah was just, uh, uh, ah mean, just wonderin'." Lorenz let the words hang. Sometimes it was better to let people put words in your mouth. That way they believed you had said what they wanted to hear.

"And what do ye expect out of this behavior?" The Big Bastard wasn't giving him credit for anything.

"Ah could at least scratch Dandy's nose when he wants me to without being whomped on. Dandy doan know nothin' about rules."

MacDonald chuckled. "Ye twill push, won't ye, laddie? Very well, go help Martin with breakfast, and I twill dwell on what ye have asked."

Lorenz let out his breath. He was going to be at his best and by tomorrow night, no one would pay him any heed. He smiled at Martin when he reached the cooking area. "Ah'm supposed to help. What do yu'll want done?"

Martin was shaping biscuits and slapping them in the Dutch oven. "Them spuds need peeled and cut up for fries. We need at least eight or ten." He pointed to the tailboard let down to serve as a table.

"Right," responded Lorenz and began carving away. He was on the third one when he heard the heavy footfalls and dropped the knife. Damn, he'd forgotten the stupid rule about weapons, and Big Bastard was sure to consider the knife a weapon.

"Turn and face me," came the command.

Lorenz took a deep breath and turned, defiance settling into his eyes and mouth. "Ah wuz only doin' what Martin tole me to do," he protested.

"Walk." MacDonald pointed toward the wagon.

"That knife wuz part of the gear ah helped clean up last night."

MacDonald's face remained stern, but something changed in his demeanor. "Then the whiskey dulled my brain more than I thought; however, twas nay my intent to set ye up for a burning. Stand away from the knife now."

Lorenz moved to the side waiting for the huge fist to lash out at him, not really believing the man would not do something to settle the 'rules' more firmly in his mind. To his amazement, MacDonald picked up the knife and continued to pare the potatoes.

"Martin," asked MacDonald, "tis there nay else that Lorenz can do?"

Martin had heaped coals over and under the Dutch oven and was busy tending the bacon. "Ja, he can pour off the water on the beans for tonight and fill it with fresh water. I'll put it on when we finish frying the potatoes. Let me know when the spuds are ready."

The next three days blended into a repeat of the first with Lorenz seated beside Martin and Young James despairing over his demoted status on the long, dusty way toward the ranches. Lorenz knew that Martin once again trusted him, but the Big Bastard continued to watch his every move, nor was he left untied at night. Lorenz planned to make his move on this, the fourth night, and carefully memorized their movements. He knew when and where the two men might put down their rifles or relax their eyes just for a moment. Lorenz didn't worry about Martin and Young James. Martin was not a fighter, and James was like his nickname: young. On the second night they had camped early, giving Martin and Lorenz an opportunity to romp in the water. Later they lazed on the bank before starting supper. Lorenz had expressed surprise that MacDonald was using the soap again. Martin merely laughed. It was then Lorenz realized that Martin didn't bother to figure out other men. Martin would never be a hunter or dangerous man like his father. It would make tonight all that much easier.

Since they had gone through the bacon and eggs, Rolfe would disappear in the late afternoon and return with his kill. Lorenz couldn't figure out how the man could bag an elusive deer or antelope so easily at the wrong time of day. MacDonald, however, seemed to think it natural. After three days of filling his belly, Lorenz knew he was fit to travel.

Lorenz waited until he and Martin were cleaning up from the evening meal. They had stopped later in the day with the thought of reaching their homes tomorrow. Night had blanketed the earth and the moon and stars competed to give light to the shadow time. Rolfe had headed up the small rise of ground towards the road to start his first patrol, and the Big Bastard was busy putting away the improvised oven. As usual Martin had left his rifle wedged by the wagon seat.

Lorenz stacked the tin plates into the Dutch oven to carry them to what was left of the river and use the sand creeping up to the edge as a scouring agent. As he drew even with the wagon wheel, he used his free right hand to pull himself upward, turned, and balanced the Dutch oven on the top of the wheel as he leaned against the wagon and pulled Martin's rifle free.

He dropped to the ground as the Dutch oven and contents clattered down and broke into a run for the horses. Lorenz figured he had less than two minutes to remove the hobbles and bolt.

He figured wrong. Just as he removed the hobbles from Dandy, MacDonald charged into view, a rifle clutched in his right hand. Lorenz scooped up the rifle he had placed at his feet and stood aiming the rifle at the big man's middle.

"Hold it, big man, or y'all are dead!"

MacDonald halted his advance and did not raise his rifle. "Nay, laddie, if ye twere going to shoot me, ye twould have done so from the ground." He walked at a slow pace toward Lorenz, his voice a low gruff tone as he said, "Ye are going to yere mither and to House just as I told ye."

Lorenz stood stunned. How could the Big Bastard know he wouldn't kill him? His breathing became intakes of short gulps of air, and the big man reached out and removed the rifle.

"Mac, du should have let me ving him," Rolfe protested from the darkness.

"Nay, friend Rolfe, he tis my responsibility." To Lorenz he said, "Replace the hobbles and walk to the front of the wagon."

Lorenz's stomach lurched downward. That small nagging worry about Rolfe had been right. The man would have shot him as coolly as he killed an animal for meat. Lorenz knew what type of beating MacDonald would administer and the urge to run built again, but at the moment he could think of nothing to do except obey.

As they approached the wagon, Martin hurried towards the river carrying the Dutch oven reloaded with the spilled plates and utensils. "Twill ye need a hand later, laddie?" asked MacDonald.

"No, thanks, Uncle Mac. He'd just make more work." A tight lipped Martin glared at Lorenz.

On the dark side of the wagon, the two halted their walk. "My belt or yere's?" came MacDonald's gentle inquiry.

Lorenz had his back to the man as he had walked a half-step ahead, certain in his own mind that a fist would send him to the ground at any time. The question left him blank. Belt? Wasn't the man going to use his fists?

When no answer came, he heard MacDonald remove his own belt, and he was pushed against the wagon wheel. "Drop yere britches," rang in his ears.

His frustration and anger welled to the forefront and he whirled screaming, "No, yu'll are supposed to use your fists and beat me. Ah jest broke yore damn rules and ran, and had a rifle pointed right at yore belly."

MacDonald looked at the angry youth and shook his head. "Laddie, I canna use my fists on ye. I would damage ye for life as ye are still but a wee one. The burning is to get yere attention, nay harm ye. Ye had the rifle pointed at me and yet ye dinna pull the trigger. Why?"

The anger subsided as Lorenz closed his eyes and reopened them and locked them onto MacDonald's face. "Because it would have been one of the dumbest things ah've ever did." He swallowed. God, what was this man going to do to him?

MacDonald's face softened. He was looking at a face with eyes so like his Anna's. A half-smile flitted across his face.

"So, I did get yere attention, and ye have been thinking. Laddie, do ye ken ye have just told me what ye did wrong?"

Lorenz felt his world turn over. The man was as crazed as he was, and he still couldn't figure out what was going on. He watched MacDonald put his belt back on. That would mean no whipping. Why wasn't this man like the others he had known?

When no words came from Lorenz, MacDonald tried again. "Laddie, ye are nay a cold-blooded killer. Ye are Anna's laddie, and so much like her. I dinna ken why ye have nay wish to see her.

"Ah kilt Zale and one of his men," Lorenz forced out.

"Twas a deed needing done. That does nay make ye a killer enjoying the hunt and the ending of another's life."

Lorenz could think of no response, but he realized the danger of being beat to the ground was over. His mind, his body, however, refused to believe it.

MacDonald kept probing. "Why are ye so set on running rather than return to yere mither?"

The anger came roiling up again, transforming his eyes into two blazing points of grey. "Ah cain't go back," he screamed at MacDonald. "Y'all don't know the things that happened in that Comanchero camp."

MacDonald shook his head. "Laddie, Mr. Rolfe and I twere fur trappers. We lived in the wilds with men alone or sometimes with the native peoples in their camps around the trading forts. I ken the depravity that runs in some men's doings. That, however, does nay make ye like them, nay does it prevent ye from returning home."

"Mama don't want someone like that in her home," Lorenz grated through his teeth. "She was a praying woman, probably still is."

"Oh, aye, that she tis, and one of her prayers tis for yere safe return. I canna return without ye."

Lorenz was staring at the man. Was he crazy? No white woman would let someone like him in their house. He had one last argument. "Mr. MacDonald, ah doan know how to live with people like Mama."

"Then ye can learn. Twill be like going to a new country, but ye are a clever laddie." He put his hand out to start Lorenz back to the camp area when Lorenz began slamming his fist into the wagon wheel in frustration. The sheer viciousness of the blows surprised MacDonald as the wheel began to shudder. Instinctively, he grabbed the boy's upheld fist and wrapped his other arm around the shoulders. He stepped in closer and held the shaking body.

For the first time in years Lorenz felt protected and cared for. He almost relaxed and then his body snapped straight and a strangled voice demanded, "Let go of me!"

As MacDonald stepped away the almost disemboweled voice continued. "Don't y'all understand? I killed another one of them bastards. Zale's men had made a big raid, and they had lots of women and booze. Everybody had a woman, but the damn runty half-breed. I was only twelve and he drug me off in the bushes, but I had my knife and I slit his damn throat. It was night and no one was watching. I just stayed hid while the rest of them kept drinking and using the women they had until they passed out."

"Then I went and got some grub, and some of the money they stole, and took two horses, and skedaddled the rest of the stock, and lit out for anywhere else. That's when all the rest happened I told y'all about. I ended up in Tucson, and after I moved in with Rity, I worked at a livery stable and thought everything was going okay. That's when Mamacita showed up, and Rity let her stay. Then Zale found us. That's when he killed Mamacita and did this to me." Lorenz ran his finger along the scar. "I don't know how Rity got him out of there, 'cause I don't think her shotgun was loaded. She'd have blasted him if it was."

Lorenz stopped his recital long enough to take a deep breath and remembered to use his border drawl. "That's when Rity started singin' in saloons for money to pay for doctors. When ah got better, she took me along to Carson City and went to work there for Red keepin' books and as a partner in his card place. Still think ah can fit in a real home with a decent woman," he jeered at the finish.

MacDonald loomed over him, silent for a moment and then said, "Aye, but when that anger comes on ye again, I suggest ye take it out on stones and rocks, or mayhap, the woodpile."

Lorenz closed his eyes and shook his head. The telling of it all had been hurtful, but he had been so sure that MacDonald would not consider letting someone like him near his wife and daughter that he risked it. Maybe MacDonald thought it was all right, but Lorenz knew he wasn't fit.

He looked at the big man standing there like a rock and his real reason for running came blurting out of his despair and his mouth. "Mr. MacDonald, I can't go where Mama is. I don't know what I'll do when she tells me to get out."

MacDonald felt rocked by the revelations, but knew he must go gently. "Lorenz, I have been wed to yere mither for almost seven years. That tis more than the time ye had with her. I ken her ways and her thinking. She twill nay throw ye out."

From the time of Lorenz's outburst, they had been moving further and further away from the wagon and the path to the edge of the barely running water. They were south of Martin, but at the banks of the small river. "To me, it sounds like ye are saying that yere perception, way of thinking, of yere mither tis why ye keep trying to run. Since ye kenned that yere sister had nay but yere welfare, wellbeing," MacDonald took pains to make sure Lorenz understood his words, "upper most in her mind, why did ye run from her? Yere actions make some of yere words hard to believe."

Lorenz clenched his hands and half turned to him. "Cause she whupped me right in front of the whole town."

Not really surprised that Lorenz could drive someone to that point, MacDonald asked, "And what had ye done that brought it on?"

"Nothin'!"

"That too tis hard to believe as once more yere actions make yere words hollow. What twas it that she thought ye had done?"

"I was with Red, and he stopped in at the fancy whorehouse to talk with the Madam. The girls were all clucking over me while Red and the Madam went in another room for a drink when Rity came busting in screaming her head off. She used her parasol on the girls and on anyone that was handy. The Madam and Red came running out to protect the girls, and Rity knocked the Madam down and slammed the point of the parasol into Red's belly. Then she grabbed me and pushed and pulled me out the door using that damned parasol on me, and everybody in town getting an eyeful. She kept swinging it like a cane until we got home and then she really laid into me with a belt. After that she said I had to go my room and stay there without anything to eat 'cause I had cussed at her. She slammed the door on me and then she went to work at her gambling place. I just grabbed my gun and some food, and high tailed it to the stable were Dandy was, and left. I knew nobody would be looking for me until morning and by that time I'd be long gone, and I was."

At the end of this recital, MacDonald was thankful for the darkness that hid his smile. "Did ye, ah, actually bed one of the whores?"

"Nah, there wasn't time, and Red had only said maybe 'cause I was pretty young. He said he'd see how I do just talking with them."

"Good, tis nay the way of a first bedding."

"Huh?"

"Oh, another subject that I am sure yere mither and I twill nay agree upon when the time comes." He shrugged. "It seems yere sister also has yere mither's temper."

They paced along the water's edge, staying away from the camp area. "Mama cain't have one that bad," Lorenz insisted.

MacDonald chuckled. "Oh, aye, that she can. If there had been but two Indians that attacked yere cabin that day, they would have lost. Yere fither must have kenned they would be attacked for he had taken both guns with him. Daniel had been sent to the field to help him ere the attack came. She ran out of the house with a broom as her club and used it on the first one to dismount. She downed him and knocked the wind from him, and nigh had another down when the third emerged from the cabin swinging the babe by one leg. Of course, yere mither dropped the broom and grabbed yere brither. They may have thought her mad for nay running as an Indian woman would have done and let her live. I dinna. Then too, such a woman would breed brave laddies, and they had two of hers already."

"By the time I rescued her, she twas a skinny body of bone and her hair had turned completely white. The Comanche were sure she twas mad indeed. They had cut off the ends of her little fingers as their way to show her grief over losing two of her wee ones to members of the tribe, but she kept trying to tempt Daniel back to her. They tried cutting off her ears since she did nay listen to their commands, nay to their reasons as she would nay bide by their rules. She may have kenned their ways more than they kenned as she kept behaving as though she twere mad. Mayhap she did become a bit mad when the babe twas given to a different tribe. Since they were nay certain of her sanity, they fed her very little. Starvation usually brings a sane person to heel. Nay her. She defied them to the day we hit their camp."

"Y'all married her anyways?" To Lorenz this seemed as mad as the tale of his mother.

"Of course, I did. She tis a brave, magnificent lassie. Who else would have the courage to attack me with fists and tongue because I rescued her and nay her laddie? She kept screaming at me to go find Daniel. She did nay calm down till I went to look for him."

MacDonald changed the subject. "It grows late, and I must rest. As much as I would nay, I must bed ye down with the ropes, and in the morrow, ye have the task of apologizing to Martin."

"Why?" Lorenz stopped. He felt beaten and drained. It was one more thing that he could not understand.

"Ye took his rifle. Tis almost as serious as taking his horse in this country."

"Mr. MacDonald, I don't know how to do that," Lorenz admitted.

"Ye use such words as 'I took yere rifle and I should have nay and I sorrow'; nay, yere way is to say 'I'm sorry.' Any of those words should do nicely." He prodded Lorenz towards the wagon.

Lorenz reverted to his usual way of speaking. "And iffen ah don't, yu'll ain't going to let me ride Dandy into yore place, right?"

MacDonald grinned into the darkness. "Aye, that tis correct. Yere actions and the doing of what tis right twill determine how much freedom ye have."

Lorenz kept walking as he continued protesting. "Hit won't do no good. Martin ain't goin' to believe me."

"That does nay matter. What matters is that ye do apologize."

As usual, MacDonald was proficient in tying Lorenz, who stretched at the ropes in the hopes that just once the big man would relax or make an error. Nothing had gone the way he had planned. He had thought the act of killing Zale and watching him die would silence the rage inside him. It had not. Instead, he was physically confined, going where he did not want to go, and for some reason he was calling the big man Mr. MacDonald.

When he came in from his night watch, MacDonald started the coffee. As usual, the noise roused the rest of the camp. Martin didn't bother to glance at Lorenz, or give his usual greeting on his way to the latrine area.

Lorenz tried once more to convince MacDonald that Martin was in no mood to talk to him, but MacDonald simply raised his eyebrows and pointed. Lumps stuck in Lorenz's throat as he approached Martin slapping the biscuits into the Dutch oven.

He squatted down by the older youth and tried. "Uh, Martin, I took your rifle last night, but, well, ah…"

"Lorenz, shut up. I ain't interested and y'all are saying words that Uncle put into your mouth." Martin clamped the lid on the Dutch oven and set it in the coals. "I've got work to do." He turned his back on Lorenz and started heating the pan for gravy made with flour and water.

The words stung deeper than he believed they could. Lorenz stood and walked back to MacDonald, heartsick and breathing heavier. A week ago, he would not have cared, but for awhile there had been a comradeship with Martin that he wanted to keep. He could find no one to blame but himself. Martin was the one person who really believed that he, Lorenz, was worth trusting, and he hadn't proved out. It was a bitter realization. Lorenz was under no illusion that MacDonald trusted him, or did he? Why hadn't he pulled that trigger? How did MacDonald know he wouldn't? He stuck his hands in his pocket and mouthed the bitter words. "He won't let me finish."

"Try again after breakfast," suggested MacDonald. "Meanwhile, we twill wait for the coffee."

Lorenz considered and took a deep breath. He would try again and this time Martin would believe him. Hell, he always could make people believe him, but this time, he decided, he wouldn't try any of his mind tricks.

After breakfast, Lorenz grabbed the coffee pot as Martin loaded the Dutch oven with items to be cleaned. "Ah have to work, or else ah'm in trouble," he announced.

Martin raised his eyebrows and continued to pack the rest of the eating gear. They both carried their load over to the slow, running water. As Martin rinsed and scoured the plates and utensils, he ignored Lorenz's clumsy attempts to apologize again.

Lorenz set his lips, and continued to try to find the right words to break through Martin's resolve when James broke in. "Thus sayeth the Lord: Seven times seventy."

Martin's head snapped up. "What's that got to do with him?"

"You know, you studied the catechism. Jesus meant you can't decide whether he means it or not." James was quite pleased with himself. He could quote scripture and not be in any danger of retaliation from Martin; not without Martin being in trouble. Maybe he could even make Martin squirm while he practiced doing what a real Pastor would do.

It was almost possible to see Martin thinking. Guile wasn't in him and he knew James was right. That was the maddening part. Both young men stood and faced each other. "Why should I believe y'all? Are y'all telling me y'all ain't going to try to run again?"

Lorenz shook his head. "Ah ain't going anywhere but home today. Ah'm just sayin' if ah try anything again, ah won't touch nothing of yours, and ah'll do it when ah can't get y'all in trouble." He stuck out his right hand as a peace offering hardly daring to believe whatever it was that James said had worked this change in Martin.

Martin looked down at the hand and reluctantly shook it. "All right, I'll accept your apology, but I ain't going to trust y'all to keep it."

"That's not what God meant," intoned the younger Rolfe. He had his hands behind his back and was rocking back and forth on his heels. He was quite pleased with his efforts. He had made Martin do his bidding.

Martin made ready to go after his younger sibling, and Lorenz stepped in front of him. "Blame me, not him."

"Y'all are sticking up for him?" Martin was struck by the unbelievable situation.

"Well, he helped me. Seems fair."

Martin looked at Lorenz and smiled. He then put out his hand and they shook again. "Okay, maybe y'all mean it this time."

Chapter 6

Anna's and MacDonald's Way

As MacDonald and Rolfe saddled their horses, Lorenz moved toward Dandy. MacDonald shook his head. "First ye ride the wagon. Twill be a couple of hours ere we ride ahead."

Lorenz swallowed, but accepted the dictum. "How long does it take before we get there?" he asked Martin.

"We'll be there about noon. Tante Anna will feed us. A good thing. I'm damned tired of my cooking." He clucked at the horses once James was in the wagon.

"How would she know to have enough food for all of us?" asked Lorenz. To him it was another puzzle.

"Y'all would be surprised. Women whose men are gone out here always seem to know when they are coming back in. Besides, we've made the trip before. She knows how long it takes."

Morning slid by in a haze of dusty, jolting minutes. Martin ventured few subjects as Lorenz sat huddled with half-true memories and perceptions. At times, he felt an unbelievable elation and next he felt completely lost. He knew his homecoming would be a complete debacle. MacDonald, however, had won and he would soon see his mother. Lorenz harbored a grudging admiration for the man as they traveled over a land covered with prairie grass, some still green with new growth, some of it starting to yellow at the tips, and clumps of waving blue flowers nestled among the green. Gradually, the sun swung higher as it moved to a late morning position.

MacDonald brought Zark alongside and signaled for Martin to rein in. Lorenz bailed over the seat and grabbed his saddle. He told himself that it was the excitement of actually riding again impelling his haste, not the possibility of seeing his mother after so many years. Within minutes he had cinched down his saddle and bolted into it. MacDonald nodded at him and waved at the others. Lorenz lifted his chin and even smiled at Young James ensconced on the wagon seat.

Twenty minutes later, they topped the rise and looked down at the ranch quarters. To their left, about a quarter of a mile from the two-story ranch house, a rock formation jutted skyward creating a sculpture by nature. It flared upward and then about three quarters of the way to the top the rock flattened out in front of a small cave. Behind the cave, rocks reared again and flowed upward into a caricature of a monk's head. Below them, the prairie grass spread out towards the house, the springhouse, barn, washhouse, outhouse, and small shed. Corrals circled three-fourths of the barn and extended back by almost two acres. It looked like there were three sections to the corrals. The smallest fenced section held a lonely milch cow that lowed a greeting. The headquarter buildings of the Rearing Bear ranch, unlike most of the ranch buildings Lorenz had seen, were painted and not faded wood.

"Ah didn't know yu'all was rich," he said as they drew up to look.

"Nay rich, laddie, but someday, mayhap. Look, there stands yere mither and the wee one. He took off his hat and waved at the two distant figures on the porch. "Let's ride."

"How'd she know?" asked Lorenz, keeping Dandy at the pace set by the larger horse.

MacDonald barely glanced at him. "She tis a Kenning Woman. Oh, and ye are to remove yere hat when ye greet her."

Lorenz swallowed. More damn rules. He kept looking at the woman holding the small figure by the hand. She wore a simple, straight grey skirt and white blouse covered by an apron. The hand that had been guarding her eyes against the noon sun was now clutching at the hitching rail, the knuckles as white as her hair. As MacDonald had said her hair was completely white, parted in the middle and drawn back into a bun to better cover the missing ears, the severity softened by the escaped curls framing her face. The eyebrows were still dark, arched over grey eyes lighted by quick intelligence. Her body was no longer skinny as MacDonald had termed it, but filled out to match her tall frame. Her movements were decisive and controlled. The little girl at her side was jumping up and down, waving at them, and screaming, "Papa, papa."

As they reined in, MacDonald reached over and grabbed Dandy's reins and dismounted. He lapped the reins over the post and picked up the "Papa, papa," screaming child. Lorenz found his face and body frozen, unable to smile or move. He stared straight ahead; afraid to look at his mother should she recognize him and reject him once she realized he was not Daniel.

"Lorenz, dismount!"

No help for it. He had to move or be pulled down. As he swung down, the woman was on him; her arms around his body, squeezing hard and then she removed one hand using it to touch his face, his hands, and his hair. "Mein sohn, mein sohn, mein liebe, mein herzen," she kept repeating. Finally, she stopped long enough to touch the scar and he tried stepping back, but she retained her hold on him and her grey eyes opened wider, "They hurt du!" she exclaimed in English and turned to MacDonald.

"Mr. MacDonald, they have hurt him. Who did this? Du must run them down!" Her English was almost as accented as Rolfe's, the German idioms and words as frequent.

"Mrs. MacDonald, the man who did that tis nay longer with us."

"Good!" She turned her attention back to Lorenz. "Vhere is Margareatha? She vas mitt du when ve vere attacked. Vhy is she not mitt du?"

Lorenz was staring at her, his mind reeling, the German words too much for him to process, but somehow he knew they were endearments. Then suddenly everything she was saying made sense; even the German and accented words he had not heard in eleven years; vhere became where and vhy became why. How could he tell her about Rity?

MacDonald answered for him. "It seems she tis in Carson City, Nevada. We have sent yere lassie a telegram and told her a letter twill follow."

The grey eyes snapped at MacDonald. "Du did not tell her to home immediately come?"

Lorenz took some satisfaction in watching MacDonald's face become a bit blank. "I did nay think to do so," he admitted. "I did tell her that Lorenz was safe with us."

"Ach, gut," she turned to Lorenz again, "have du seen Daniel or August?"

Lorenz was still dazed from her greeting and shook his head, unable to form words. She was still touching him, stroking his hair, his face, his arm as though he would evaporate like smoke and suddenly she was holding him tight again, strange choking noises coming from her throat. The warm smells came up from her body, smells no longer just lingerings in his mind, but smells of vinegar, sugar, flour, vanilla, and her own individual scent. He couldn't stop his arms and they wrapped around her, his voice choking out, "Mama, Mama." Now it was his turn to fear this was a dream and she would disappear and a world filled with hate and hurt would return.

MacDonald watched them sway together for a moment as he explained to Mina that her brother was as happy as she would be if she had not seen Mama for a very long time, then he stepped closer and wrapped one arm around his wife. Gradually her choking sounds stopped and she lifted her head.

"Mr. MacDonald, I thank du."

He smiled down at her. "Mrs. MacDonald, ye are welcome."

Lorenz and his mother stepped slightly apart, his breath coming in heavy, rapid gasps as he fought down the urge to cry. He couldn't let the big man see tears, not now. He set his teeth as he realized MacDonald had bent and kissed his wife.

To his dismay, his mother did not protest, nor did she seem flustered as MacDonald lifted his head to smile down at her. Her face had grown pinker, but her eyes were sparkling as she stood on her tiptoes and kissed MacDonald on the cheek. "Velcome home, Mr. MacDonald."

MacDonald's smile grew wider, "'Tis good to be back," he said. Then he turned to Lorenz. "And this wee mite tis yere sister, Wilhelmina LouElla MacDonald. We call her Mina as tis much easier." He turned to the child riding on his arm; her arms were firmly clamped around his neck. "Can ye nay say 'hello' to yere brither?"

Mina turned solemn, amber eyes on Lorenz and her face reddened. She looked back at her father. "Is he really mein bruder?" Like her mother and the Rolfes, she spoke a mixture of English and German, freely mixing the words and meanings.

"Aye, that he tis, and he tis called Lorenz."

Mina turned back to Lorenz with puzzlement in her eyes. "But he is big," she protested stressing the word big. She had heard the tale of children taken and could not understand how Lorenz could be the same height as her mother.

Lorenz grinned. At least someone conceded he was not a child. "Hi, Mina."

In response, Mina leaned forward and put her arms around his neck and hugged. Once again Lorenz went into shock. The child was warm and smelled of youth and innocence. He waited for MacDonald or Mama to scream at Mina not to get so close to him.

Instead, MacDonald addressed his wife. "Anna, the Rolfe menfolk will soon be here with our purchases. Tis there enough for all?"

"Ja, of course. Ach, the food!" She grabbed Mina and ran for the door.

MacDonald stood with a smile playing at the corners of his mouth. "She can become excited." He looked at Lorenz. "We need to put up our beasties." He took both of the lead reins and led the way to the barn. Lorenz still in a daze stumbled along. As usual nothing had gone the way he had said it would. Why had Mama made such a fuss over him?

He stayed in his dazed world, scarcely able to breathe or think while they removed the saddles, turned the horses into the holding pen, and placed the saddles inside the barn. MacDonald's went on a saddletree while his was placed up on the shelf. "We twill build one for ye later."

Lorenz barely noticed the long area between the two sets of stalls running on either side of the barn. One set of three stalls was for horses with a high manger and separate grain box. The two mangers on the other side were lower and open, each with a moveable bar in the rear, and another up and down one that moved in front. Tools and saddles were stored against the entry wall and a work table set under a small window. Various tools for ranch and farm hung neatly on the wall. Lorenz decided that he was going to be a free hand for this ranch and his mind returned to reality. He heard the wagon roll into the yard, looked out, saw the Rolfes, and realized there was a fence with some sort of tree in front covered with small pellets of growing fruit.

"Mr. Rolfe, du and your boys vill for dinner stay, ja?" his mother greeted the new arrivals. "There's fresh beer in the springhouse. Help yourself."

"Ja wohl, Frau MacDonald, ve'll be glad to eat here. Danke schon." Rolfe dismounted and went through the side gate, heading for the springhouse and his beer. "Du vant one, Mac?" he yelled as Martin pulled up the team slightly pass the tree and applied the brake.

"Aye, friend Rolfe," boomed MacDonald's reply, "right after the laddie and I have unloaded our purchases."

The barrel of liquor was set in the washhouse with the parcels from the store on top, the lumber stacked alongside of the fence, and their camp gear set out by the back door. "We'll take it inside when Mrs. MacDonald is out of the kitchen," explained Mac-Donald. "We'll nay be in her way while she tis setting the table." Somehow he made it sound like a sin to be in Mama's way.

Lorenz looked around. Young James had helped Martin with the horses and then both made a beeline for the outhouse. Mac-Donald accepted the bottle from Rolfe and sipped away with satisfaction. His mother emerged from the springhouse carrying a pitcher of milk.

Rolfe then proceeded to wash his hands and face at the improvised stand near the back door. A wavy mirror was set over the enameled, white basin and a shelf with a dowel holding a towel underneath completed a place for a quick toiletry. Rolfe removed his hat and used the comb, and as they reappeared, his two male heirs followed his example. Then it was MacDonald's turn. He handed the bottle to Lorenz and generously splashed water on his face and hands before combing his hair. He reclaimed his bottle and said, "Now tis your turn."

Lorenz could not believe he was home and welcomed. This was contrary to the world he knew existed. Since he had not yet stepped into the house, freedom was still his. He knew once inside there would be no escape. Even if he escaped, his mother and her voice would imprison him forever. MacDonald's command made him blink his eyes and he shook his head, "Ah ain't dirty."

Martin guffawed. "Lorenz, Tante Anna ain't going to let y'all to the table unless y'all wash up."

Lorenz felt the blood rise in his face. Everyone was grinning at him now. It was no longer him against the big man. It was him against all of them and there was nowhere to run. His mother appeared at the door, smiling at them all.

"Dinner is ready. Von't du come in?"

"As soon as Lorenz washes his hands and face," the words rumbled out of MacDonald, amusement flickering in his brown eyes.

Anna moved outside and fixed her large, grey eyes on him. "Vash your face and hands, und use that comb." Her words, simple and direct, burned into him. Weren't mothers supposed to be on your side? He stood looking at her.

A puzzled look came into her eyes and MacDonald added an explanation. "I dinna think yere lassie had time to re-teach him the ways of civilized mankind during the brief time he twas with her. All that twill be explained later," he added as a closing.

His mother's eyes were still puzzled, but a more determined look came into them. "Lorenz, du are the food letting get cold. Vash now und use the comb." Her voice was stern, broking no argument.

Somewhere in the recesses of his mind, Lorenz remembered that look. This was not the time to defy her with everyone else standing around with smirks on their faces. He bent and hurriedly splashed water on his face and hands and used the towel. He heard the door close and he started to turn and realized MacDonald blocked his way, standing there with comb in hand. The big man didn't say anything. He was just smiling a closed mouth smile, but the eyes were hard and the amusement gone. Lorenz yanked his hat off and grabbed the comb. It stuck almost half way down when MacDonald caught his wrist.

"Nay so hard, laddie, twill break the comb, and then yere mither twill fuss."

Rolfe laughed. "Dot's the last thing du vant. She is a formidable voman." Still chuckling he led his sons into the house.

Lorenz looked helplessly at MacDonald after trying twice more to run the comb through his tangled mass, MacDonald took the offensive implement and said, "For now, just tuck the hair behind the ears." He opened the door and motioned Lorenz in.

The humid heat from the black woodstove nearly knocked Lorenz to his knees. How did his mother stand it? MacDonald pointed to the hat rack inside the doorway. "Put yere's there with the rest." He kept behind Lorenz and half pushed him towards the door at the far end. The smells from the food were now vying with the heat to win Lorenz's attention. "And remember, we say grace ere we eat."

"Huh?"

"Tis a way of thanking the Maker for our food. Just do as the others do ere ye start to pile the food on your plate." Mercifully they were through the narrow, stifling kitchen and into the dining room where the open front door and windows let in the breezes and flies, effectively taking most of the heat from the room.

It clearly was the main room with a huge table in the middle, but Lorenz was back in his emotional daze and didn't see the sewing machine set by the east window looking out onto the porch, nor the dark wainscot underneath the flowery wallpaper. The blue curtains outlining the windows escaped his eyes. Everyone was seated, and Anna called gaily, "Du sit here at my right, mein sohn."

It looked like Martin would be in the chair next to him. Lorenz walked stiff legged to the table and collapsed in the seat. All the aromas mixed and settled into his stomach, and he stared straight ahead. He did not see Martin smile and nod his head in greeting. Mina sat in a higher chair at her mother's left. Young

James was next to Mina and then Rolfe. MacDonald took the chair at the head of the table opposite his wife at the other end.

"Mr. Rolfe, will you please ask the blessing?" Anna spoke in German.

Lorenz watched in amazement as they all bowed their heads and evidently did something with their hands under the table. Then Rolfe began to speak, the guttural tones sweeping out with authority and ending with "Gott der Vater, Gott der Sohn, und Gott der Heilig Geist".

It was unbelievable. The man he watched slow-skin another human being was sitting there reverently asking a blessing and the rest complied silently. Were they all crazy? A booming, "Amen," from MacDonald brought everyone's attention back to the table.

His mother began by slicing the roast, placing a slab of meat on her plate, and then asking James for his. Once she had given James the meat, she passed the platter to Lorenz. "Take vhat du vant and then hand it to Martin. Everything vill be passed to your right."

Lorenz grasped the heavy platter, the aroma from it bringing water into his mouth. He grabbed a slab with the large fork, flopped it on his plate while the juices ran in his mouth. After he passed the plate, he used his hand to raise the slab of meat to his mouth and the babble around the table ceased. Lorenz looked up and realized that six pairs of eyes were looking at him.

Anna reached over and from the left side of his plate lifted a smaller fork than the one on the platter. "Du use the fork und knife to eat with here."

For the first time, Lorenz saw the eating utensils at the side of everyone's plate. Even little Mina had a mini fork in her fist. His face reddened, but he grasped the knife and tested the edge. "It ain't sharp," he protested.

"It does nay need to be." MacDonald's eyes were laughing again, laughing at him, he thought bitterly.

Lorenz slashed at the meat. To his surprise, the meat parted instantly, almost falling apart. His eyes widened. What sort of meat was this? It smelled like beef. He took a bite and the succulent, savory smell proved to be true. That food could be more than something to fuel his body was a new concept, and he savored the thought and the meat. "Hit's good, Mama."

Anna smiled and for a moment she became a woman transformed as her face and eyes lighted. Lorenz realized that many men would find her as beautiful as her cooking. It was disturbing. He lowered his head again as ordered confusion returned with every one passing a dish or asking for a platter or condiment to be passed to them.

Anna and Martin both watched and assisted him as the dishes went around the table. Martin, puffing with importance, showed Lorenz the superiority of boiled potatoes being mashed with the fork before ladling the gravy over the top. Lorenz couldn't see the difference: they were still potatoes and they still had gravy over them.

Somehow everyone was served: Potatoes, gravy, fresh pickled onions and cucumbers, fresh greens coated with some sort of sweet-sour dressing, dark bread, butter, homemade apple butter, with beer for the adults, and milk for the children. Martin, like the younger children, drank milk, grinning at Lorenz as he poured from the pitcher. Lorenz in his bewilderment forgot that he didn't drink milk, let Martin fill his glass. Rather than insult his mother, he drank it, almost choking on the amount of cream still in it.

He couldn't remember eating like this. The time with the Comancheros had seen mostly beans, wild game, and biscuits. While he was with Rity, the food had been pretty much the same with the baked goods as extras, although there had been the occasional eggs, bacon, and potatoes. Later Rity's maid had cooked mostly Mexican dishes. This food was overwhelming and rich.

His stomach stretched to the limit, and he knew he couldn't eat another bite.

"Vould anyone like dessert?" came his mother's voice. "I have a nice cottage pudding with a hard sauce."

"Me, please," shouted Young James.

"Me, me," added Mina.

The older men agreed to desert as did Martin. Lorenz looked helplessly at his mother, and she smiled again. "It's all right. I'll save yours for later." She rose and went to the kitchen. MacDonald followed to retrieve the coffee.

Lorenz sat back stunned. How had she known? He had been away for years; yet she had known what he was thinking. Was it possible?

The conversation resumed with the desert and coffee. Once everyone was served, Anna stated, "The hay has been cut and is ready to be brought in."

The spoon stopped on its way to MacDonald's mouth. "Anna, ye dinna do that by yereself, did ye?"

She laughed. "Almost. Kasper helped me one day. He and Gerde vere here since business is so slow. Ve also need to arrange a day to go in and celebrate that mein sohn is home."

MacDonald raised his eyebrows as Rolfe cut in. "Ja, gut idea. Ve need to relax before ve go after more horses. Ve'll need them before ve start branding again. Martin can ride in tomorrow and tell everybody. Vhat day du vant to do this? Du got a gut, strong poy now to help mitt der haying. Shouldn't take more than a day, ja?"

Anna smiled happily and then considered. "Ve can go in day after tomorrow. That gives everyone a chance ready to be."

MacDonald looked askance at his wife. He knew she would be washing clothes and baking, plus cooking for all of them. "Are ye nay sure it wouldn't be better to make that two days after tomorrow?"

"Ja, I'm sure. I vant Kasper and Gerde to see how much Lorenz has grown." She smiled at MacDonald. "It vill be fine."

"Time to go den," said Rolfe. "The meal vas delicious. Poys, tell Tante Anna, danke."

Everyone rose amid a clatter of thank yous and compliments on the food while they trooped outside. "Y'all want some help?" Lorenz asked Martin. He was desperate to walk away from the hubbub and begin to think out his plans. Somehow it had sounded like he was going to be working, and working hard, at something he had never done.

"Naw, but glad for the company. I told y'all that my extra money would disappear now. Y'all will be helping Uncle Mac, and he won't need to hire an extra hand." He jokingly aimed a blow at Lorenz's arm.

Lorenz grinned and danced away from the half-blow. He knew Martin was just horsing around. He did not doubt that he would be put to work, and he knew he wasn't going to be paid. Out of the corner of his eye, he could see both Rolfe and Mac-Donald talking. They were watching him, waiting to see what he would do. This was no time to run. He helped Martin harness the animals and lead them to the wagon.

MacDonald held Mina as the horses were backed between the wagon tongue and secured. The wagon drove off as everyone waved furiously and promised to see each other in another two days. You would have thought they hadn't spent the last few days and hours together. As the dust settled down, Mina asked her father, "Can I haff mein present now?"

A huge smile greeted her request. "Aye, my wee one." He handed her to Anna. "Lorenz twill help me bring in the purchases and eating gear. Did ye wish the dirty clothes left there?"

"Ja."

"There may be a slight problem. The clothes Lorenz had on are filthier than those he's wearing, and he nay has any other clothes. I dinna ken ye would be in such a rush to see yere brither, and I had hoped to buy more from Kasper as tis a rough time they've had carrying those who canna pay."

Anna took Mina and looked at her husband. "I can cut off the pants and the sleeves of some of your old clothes I have in the trunk. They are too small for du now."

The big man smiled. "My love, even so, they twill wrap around his skinny body."

"It vill vork for a day," retorted his wife and walked off.

MacDonald looked down at Lorenz. "Well, I tried. Come, we'll take in the gear and the gifts.

The washhouse was stuffier than the house and almost as hot. Lorenz wondered how anyone could work inside of it. Mac-Donald unceremoniously dumped the clothes into a basket and handed the bags and packages to Lorenz. Then he opened the liquor barrel and pulled out a bottle of wine. "She twill be wanting to cool this in the spring."

Anna smiled at them as they walked in and hung their hats on the pegs. She was putting plates over the bowls that contained (to her eye) sufficient leftovers and scraping the food remnants into a tin.

Mina leaped at her father, certain that he would catch her. She squealed happily as he swung her up into the air. He turned and pointed to the small, kitchen table, and Lorenz deposited the packages where indicated.

The big man moved over and began to distribute his gifts. "Ah, what have we here?" MacDonald handed the doll to Mina. She began her squealing again. He set Mina down and handed the paper tablet to his wife. Then he proceeded to unpack the rest of the items. "They dinna have any dried apples, but these are dried grapes and quite tasty. Mayhap ye can do something with them."

He turned from Anna and handed Lorenz another small bundle of tobacco. "Ye dinna see me get that did ye?" Lorenz took the tobacco in amazement. Then out came the colored chalk and the wrapped gloves. The latter he handed to Anna with a smile.

She was shaking her head at him. "Mr. MacDonald, du have spent more than du should. Ve may need that money later this year."

"Bah, what good tis the working if I canna give ye what ye deserve? As tis, there should be more."

She knew from past arguments, he would not change, and she smiled at him while she continued to shake her head. While Anna un-wrapped her gloves, MacDonald pulled out a letter and a newspaper. Lorenz blinked his eyes. Whatever printing was on that newspaper, it was nothing he'd seen before. Anna gasped when she saw them. "From Papa?" she asked.

"Aye, and Der Lutheraner. Anderson let me have them for early delivery ere I won his bet for him."

Anna hugged him, tore open the letter, and began reading. "They are all vell. Tante Berta is with Christ." She scanned the letter. "He asks vhen vill ve come for a visit again. Cattle and hog prices are good. I'll read it better later." She put the letter with the periodical. "Du and Lorenz vill be a bath vanting tonight?" she asked her husband.

"Aye."

"We just had one." Lorenz wasn't sure he had heard right.

His mother turned grey eyes on him. "Du both smell of horses and camping, and your hair needs trimming. Du are not a girl." She turned to MacDonald. "I vill vater need for the dishes and for the vash tomorrow. Vill du a bed for Lorenz be making?"

Lorenz felt his head swimming. He was determined to run for it when the chances were good, but until then it looked like he was going to be told how to look, how to act, and he damned well knew in the meantime, he was going to be put to work. He pocketed the extra tobacco as something he should keep with him.

His intuitions were correct. As soon as he and MacDonald walked out the door, he was set to work at the pump that somehow hooked to the spring and springhouse. It took pails of water to fill the huge copper kettle in the washhouse, the extra tubs, the buckets for household water, and the troughs circling the stone enclosed garden. MacDonald set to work using the lumber to build a plain, sturdy bed frame: four posts and wooden rails on the side. Meanwhile his mother was heating a smaller pan of water and working in that impossible kitchen. By the time MacDonald started tying the rope to the frame length ways, Lorenz felt his hands burning. This was harder than forking hay in the livery stable.

"Come give me a hand, laddie. I need the rope held steady as I do the cross tying."

Lorenz gladly set the pail down and joined the big man. "Is she trying to drain all of Texas dry?" he asked.

MacDonald looked up and chuckled. "Nay, but it does seem so at times."

When the ropes were knotted, they carried the bed inside as Mama held the door for them. Then she held open the stairway door in the living area and they carried it up a narrow flight of steps after much twisting and edging. Lorenz had thought MacDonald had made the bed cot size because of thrift. Now he knew the man simply hadn't wanted to do the work upstairs. A couple of windows were open on each side to let air through and the doorless, unfinished rooms were open, but it was still hotter up here than below. They set the bed in the northeast bedroom. "'Tis smaller, but twill be cooler at night once we have a mattress. Some day there twill be a real bed up here and the rest of the rooms finished."

Lorenz looked out the window over the bed and looked down at the back part of the washhouse where two filled washtubs were set to catch the sun. The garden, pastures, and the foothills stretched into the distance. He could see enough greenery on the rock-rising hills to realize there must be a stand of oak and pine trees on them. MacDonald mopped his forehead. "Tis back in those hills the wild horses run in the summer months. They like the coolness and there tis a small stream with meadows for grazing."

Mama was waiting for them as they came down the stairs. She had a shirt and pair of trousers, both of which had seen better days, and a scissors. "Lorenz, stretch out your arms so I can measure."

Lorenz looked at the size of the clothes and knew no matter how much cutting she did, they would flap around him. He looked at MacDonald. The big man's expression was completely bland and the twinkling far back in the brown eyes. He gritted his teeth and stretched out his arms.

"Mr. MacDonald, please hold the material at the shoulders." Her words were more of a command rather than a polite request.

She snipped one sleeve, then the other. "Now the trousers" she muttered draping them against his waist. "Hold still," she added to Lorenz. The pants she marked off with some of the chalk. "I'll cut these vhile du take your bath. Then ve'll do your hair."

Lorenz stalked out the door with MacDonald. In his rush, he forgot his hat and turned to reenter the house, but MacDonald blocked his way. "The tub tis that way."

"Ah know where it is. Ah put water in it." He looked at the big man "No way out? he asked.

"Nay that I ken. Yere mither believes that cleanliness is next to Godliness. She twill brook nay argument, and nay twill I."

Once Lorenz was in the tub, MacDonald collected his clothes. "I twill bring the others in a bit. I suggest ye wash the hair first ere the soap gets too thick in the water and twill nay rinse clean."

At least he had privacy for the first time in a week. He tried sorting out everything, but nothing fit. Going against the big man was like ramming your head into a boulder. He couldn't beat him physically or mentally. No matter what he did, he would lose. His mother, it seemed, was more demanding, and MacDonald was backing her every play. Lorenz had tried to influence her mind once and a wall had slammed down. There were no words from her, yet she had known. He felt the sun burning at his skin and wondered where the hell MacDonald was. He grabbed at the towel. He had had enough water.

MacDonald appeared with the cut off clothing. "Well, ye have one benefit from all of this. There are nay of my drawers to cut down for ye."

His new belt was barely long enough to hold the extra material and he felt like a fool. He slipped the boots over the last pair of clean socks that MacDonald had bought a few days before. They walked back, pass the kitchen door to the shade of the crabapple tree where one of the kitchen chairs sat. Mama was standing there with some sort of material draped over her arm, a pair of scissors, and a comb in her hands. Mina was playing with the doll at the side of the springhouse where there was shade from the western sun.

Lorenz thought about arguing again, looked at his mother's set lips, and gave up any thought of talking his way out of the haircut. He sat down. Mama flicked the material around him like a cape and stuffed the ends down inside his collar. He clenched his teeth. The scar would soon be out for the whole world to see as he heard and felt the scissors snip across the sides and back. She hadn't even tried to comb the tangles out first.

Mama stopped long enough to ask, "Do du vant a side part, or one down the middle?"

"Side part, ah reckon. Hit curls anyways it wants to."

Now she vigorously applied the heavy comb to the snarls in his hair. "Ow!" he started to raise up and realized that MacDonald was beside him. He plopped back into the chair, and Mama continued with the comb and the scissors.

Finally she was satisfied and she handed Lorenz a mirror. "See, is gut?"

He barely bothered to glance at the wavy mirror. He didn't want to see. "Hit's fine," he muttered and stood. The accumulation of hair slid downward to join the black nest on the ground.

Anna pulled off the cape and announced, "Du look so handsome. Just like your Uncle Kasper!"

Lorenz could only stare at her. Handsome? Him? With that scar? He looked at MacDonald lounging against the tree with that damned half-smile still on his face. Meanwhile Mama was using some sort of small brush on his neck. He almost yanked away and then thought the better of it. He could see MacDonald relax. The man was just waiting for him to do something stupid.

Mama began shaking the cape in noisy, flapping snaps. With another flick, she folded it and draped it over her arm. From her pocket she extracted a small jar and removed the lid revealing a golden wax. She dipped in her index finger, creating a slight film on her finger, and applied it to the scar. He stepped back to avoid her and slammed into MacDonald's bulk. He'd forgotten how quickly the man could move and how hard he was. Instantly MacDonald grasped him by the biceps, not really squeezing, just letting him know he could. "Stand," came the command.

Lorenz felt his jaw muscles tightened, but held still for the final indignity as Mama proclaimed, "Mr. MacDonald brought this salve. It vill take avay the proud flesh. That vill take some time, but in a few months, I promise, the scar vill almost disappear. See how much it has helped." She drew away the hair covering her missing ears.

The sudden revealing of his mother's physical suffering was almost too much. He had been so wrapped in his own troubles, he'd never thought about anyone else and what they endured. Zale's death had not been the release for him that he had felt it would. Now who did he punish? He couldn't kill every Comanche that lived. Where was the salve for the heart? And how could his mother be so content and keep living as though life was something worth living?

It was a relief to be put to work again with MacDonald in the barn. MacDonald had grabbed a pail from the springhouse. "Tis time ye learned some of the chores around here."

Lorenz paid scant attention to the milking and putting up of the milk. He was reeling from the week's events: mind and body became separate items. His brain was wandering, lost in memories and envisioning a life that should have been; his body moving only to fulfill the necessary commands, and somehow there was more water to be pumped for the evening wash-up, for dishes, and for drinking.

Supper was served in the dining room. A simple meal of hash made from the leftovers and more bread and gravy. The dessert Mama had promised was waiting for him. The others dipped some sort of white stuff into their bowls and placed the crabapple butter over it. He looked at it questioningly. "It's clabbered milk mitt apple butter for sweetening," Mama explained.

Mina rubbed her tummy and exclaimed, "Und it's yummy." She giggled.

He still couldn't get used to the way children were treated at the table and afterward was even more puzzling. MacDonald made him help carry out the dirty dishes. "We eat, we help, just as we did in camp," was his explanation. He grinned at Lorenz, "After we've helped yere mither, we begin yere lessons."

Lorenz was soon seated at the table with a sheet of blank, lined paper in front of him. MacDonald sat next to him with Mina balanced on one knee. It was MacDonald's turn to become Lorenz's teacher. "Reading and writing are based on symbols called letters. Each letter stands for a sound, sometimes two different sounds. The letters, or symbols, we use are called the alphabet, and it goes like this. Mina will help me as she is learning them too."

Mina's little girl voice crooned with her father's each time he wrote a letter. Soon he had Lorenz tracing them and then

MacDonald smiled deeply. "Tis now time for ye to practice till the letters are as neat as mine."

Lorenz's fingers became cramped from holding the pencil and his frustration grew. It seemed impossible that a three-year-old child could make some of the letters on paper as well as he, but he kept at it and the letters gradually became evenly shaped symbols.

Mama appeared and collected Mina for their bath, and MacDonald sat back. "Ye twill be sleeping on the daybed this evening. Since ye have nay underwear, ye'll need to sleep in yere clothes. We twill head out the front way to the back of the barn and ye can relieve yereself ere I bed ye down."

Lorenz looked at him. "Ah thought that warn't allowed."

"Tisn't usually, but we canna go to the back since yere mither and sister are bathing." Outside the sun was bidding the world goodbye with fruit-stained smears of gold, rose, and purple against a blue-grey sky. The air felt soft from the light breeze, and the foothills to the east were splashed with an improbable rosy purple. It was, thought Lorenz, a place he could spend his whole life. Why hadn't he found this place alone and unpeopled? He couldn't stay here. He couldn't bear the pain of losing his ma again. He absently rubbed Dandy's nose as they threw extra hay over to the horses and didn't really remember walking back to the house.

As usual MacDonald was efficient with the rope. As an extra precaution, he looped the rope behind Lorenz on the daybed's iron headboard before tying the hands and then around the iron footboard before tying the ankles. Lorenz stared stony-eyed at the ceiling. He wasn't falling asleep. He needed to know how bad Mama was treated before he made his plans. Mama was in the bedroom with Mina, and MacDonald had disappeared through the kitchen carrying his towel.

His mother appeared with her letter and newspaper. She was dressed in some sort of dark blue belted robe that swept down to the floor. With her white hair and grey eyes, she seemed to float into the room. Lorenz tried not to look. It was his ma, for Pete's sake.

She pulled out a chair and then realized her son was tied. "Vhat is this? Vhy are du tied?"

Lorenz turned his head to answer her. Her eyes were large and bewildered, her mouth slightly parted, complete wonderment on her face. "Because ah'll run," he answered.

"But vhy?"

He looked at the ceiling again and gritted out his answer, "'Cause y'all ain't going to want me heah very long."

Suddenly she was gripping his shoulders with a strength he hadn't dreamed a woman would possess. "Vhat nonsense is that?"

He had no answer, and she shook his shoulders. "Du are mein sohn! I vanted du as a baby and all of those long years du vere gone. Did Margaretha tell du such a thing?"

Lorenz closed his eyes against the hurt in her face and in her voice; and yet her hard, screaming voice from long ago kept echoing in his mind. "Du cannot do such things. Du cannot ever, ever get so angry again. Do du hear me?" If he could cause that reaction when he was four, he knew he would do it again.

His mother suddenly released him and went flying out the door to where MacDonald was bathing, and he eased his shoulders. God, the woman had a grip like a man. From outside their voices floated in: her voice excited, MacDonald's low and steady. They were probably quarreling about him. Good, that meant he would be leaving soon. He knew MacDonald wasn't a man to allow feuding in his own home.

He heard the kitchen door close behind the couple as they walked in and heard them move across the floor. He looked at MacDonald and gaped. The man was in his summer underwear and boots, the hard muscles bulging underneath the cream-colored linen. Lorenz blinked and looked away. Damn. The man left no doubt as to what his intentions were that night.

His mother stood over him. "Lorenz, tell me vhy du vould run away from here, from me, from this home." Her voice was demanding, yet edged with desperation.

He shrugged. "It ain't natural for me to be cooped up in a house. 'Sides ah don't belong heah." It was words he wanted to disbelieve, but couldn't.

Anna gasped and stepped back. He realized his words had hurt his mother. Damn. That was the last thing he wanted to do. Why couldn't he say things right? "I mean, I don't think I know how to live your way. I'll make everyone glad to be rid of me."

Anna stared at her son. "That is nonsense," she stated. "Du have things confused in your mind because du vere so young. Du vill see in a few days how wrong du are." She turned to Mac-Donald.

"Zeb, du finish your bath, and I vill write to Margaretha and read my letter and paper."

MacDonald looked down, smiled, and hugged her. "Aye, that I twill." He looked at Lorenz and almost snapped his words out. "Ye twill nay cause another disturbance." He then stomped out of the house.

Lorenz relaxed as his mother took her seat and opened the letter. Damn. How did he get blamed again? He hadn't started the ruckus, if that was one. His mother had been the one upset.

Anna began reading the letter aloud in German, laughing softly to herself, then in English she said, "Hans, the baby just turned two. He has learned the vord, no, and says it to every-thing they say. He does this even vhen it is pie."

Lorenz puzzled on that one and asked, "Y'all have a brother that's two?"

"Oh, ja, Pappa's wife is just three years older than I. He vas a very handsome catch at forty when they married. I did not vant to live at home with them. I had been running the household, du

117

see." She sighed and put the letter down and took up the paper. From outside came strange, deep, booming sounds exploding in a rhythmic pattern.

"What's that noise," he asked.

"Ach, that is Mr. MacDonald singing. He does enjoy his bath." She smiled complacently and continued to read.

Lorenz sank back. How could she be so content? Wasn't she worried about what would happen? It made no sense. He tried to remember what it had been in camp and hurriedly shut the screams out of his mind. He could wait until tomorrow. For some reason, MacDonald had left the shotgun hanging over the front door. Was it carelessness?

Quiet slipped over the household as Anna read. Occasionally, she murmured in German, usually a "Ja, das ist recht." Finally she set the paper aside and began to use the pencil on a very, thin sheet of paper. "Do du have any greetings for your sister, Margaretha," she asked.

Lorenz was almost asleep, but he roused long enough to say, "Ah don't think she wants to hear from me."

Anna raised her eyebrows at her son. "Du are wrong. She vill be vorried about du. I vill tell her that du say, 'hello,'" and she returned to her writing.

MacDonald stomped back into the house, the outside door banging behind him. Lorenz gritted his teeth at the sound and looked at his mother. She was calmly folding the letter, a slight smile on her lips. As MacDonald came into the dining room, she looked up and patted the paper, "Pastor Walther writes with such clarity. Du must read his article." It was as though she did not notice that he had not bothered to put on a shirt, nor the top of his summer johns. His hair glistened, wet from the water, his skin, almost a milk white, looked damp as though the small, rough towel was inadequate for his massive body. As usual, a half-smile lit his face and eyes.

"Aye, that I twill do." He widened his smile for her and added, "in the morrow."

Lorenz gritted his teeth at his helplessness, when his mother stood and said, "I must bid him goodnight," and suddenly she was beside him, bending down and kissing his forehead.

"Schlafen sie gut, mein sohn." Her words were husky and low, charged with emotion. In English she added, "Do du remember the prayer ve said at night?"

Her words, so familiar, cut into his very being and he felt his throat tighten. There was no way he could push words out of the constricted area and he dumbly shook his head.

"It goes, 'Wohl einem haus, da Jesu Christ'." She saw the blankness in his eyes, the sudden illumination, and the anguish on his face, and she finished in English, "and all who dwell within." She kissed his head one more time, straightened, and walked to her husband. Lorenz could not see the smile on her face, or the brightness in her eyes.

MacDonald wrapped his arm around her waist, nodded at Lorenz, dipped and blew out the lamp. Moonlight fell through the windows and lighted their way. The two walked to the doorway leading into the short hall and softly they closed the door behind them.

Lorenz heard the door to their bedroom close and he tensed his muscles, trying to pull at the ropes that bound him. The ropes tightened and bit into his flesh, he relaxed, and then pulled again. After the sixth try of pulling and relaxing, he gave it up. He was helpless until morning.

He closed his eyes and listened, listened for the sound of his mother in pain. He had to know. For the longest time, he heard nothing. There was silence, or had he imagined something like a woman's laughter. Impossible. He tried finding his mother's mind, and it was like a door slammed. When he tried MacDonald's, a black curtain fell: a curtain heavy with a darkness he could not penetrate. He strained at the ropes again and tried futilely to turn.

His mother, however, was not enduring the agony Lorenz imagined. Once the door had shut behind them, MacDonald's hands had swept away her robe and unbuttoned the nightgown, loosening it, and then sliding the material downward to the floor. He bent his head to her shoulder and ran his hands over her sides, her buttocks, and every inch of her he could find. "My sweet one, how I have missed ye." She giggled as his tongue licked at her neck. He lifted her then and laid her on their bed. He hurriedly shucked his boots and trousers and gathered her into his arms again, his hardness seeking her softness and solace.

She began to match his eagerness as his heat, hot hands touched her breasts and his tongue lapped at her eyes and face. Suddenly he erupted inside. "Too soon," he gasped, "too soon. It has been too long. Bide a moment and I'll be back." His hard body relaxed, then tensed again. "Do ye see, darling, what ye can do for a man?" He chuckled as he found her again.

She was moaning now, softly whispering, "Zeb, Zeb," as she scratched and stroked his back, his hair, his buttocks. She lifted herself for each downward thrust, matching him, feeling the heat rise below her navel, marveling at his touch and the nerves she could feel tingling as far as her toes. This time Anna tensed and sounds erupted from her throat, rising in crescendo. MacDonald clamped his hand over her mouth. "Dear Gar, woman, ye'll scare them both."

She lay gasping, almost in a stupor, then whispered, "Surely, he must know, and Mina sleeps so deeply.

He chuckled against her. "Whatever he learned, I'm sure tis wrong." He was moving again, seeking her, seeking the comfort he desperately needed.

When he slumped against her, both were wet with perspiration and breathing deeply, satisfied, yet both longing for more.

"Darling," he whispered. "I must warn ye. In my land when a laddie beds a lassie three times or more, they must wed."

It was Anna's turn to chuckle and pull him towards her. "And I must varn du. In my land, du must ved her first."

Later, as they readied for bed, they washed each other from the basin she had filled earlier. MacDonald took the basin outside, through the door that opened directly onto the porch and emptied it. He glanced at the sky lighted with stars, listened for movement near and far, and re-entered their bedroom. To him, the bedroom was their sanctuary. He smiled at his wife, now dressed in her sleeping gown and asked "Why nay leave that thing off?"

Anna smoothed her hair back and spoke in German. "Mina may have a bad dream and come running in. It has happened, or she may wake and need me. You should be wearing your nightshirt."

"'Tis too warm." He set the basin on the washstand and placed the ewer inside it and smiled broadly at his wife. "Ye twill be my shield."

It was a running argument between them. MacDonald despised wearing anything while sleeping. Within his own home, he dispensed with the clothing as often as possible. Anna would shake her head at him. Her own two years of isolation from home and cultural underpinnings allowed her to sympathize with him. For tonight she would offer no objection. He was home again, not only home, but he had returned with her middle son. Strange, to feel such gratitude for someone she loved so deeply. And love him she did, fiercely, protectively, with body and mind; this man who valued her strength, yet made her feel like a woman. He valued her as a woman, but also he valued her intelligence and asked for her opinion, her counsel as he put it. She liked lying close to him, liked the feeling of security that his strength made possible. She folded her hands for her nightly prayers and dropped immediately to sleep.

Lorenz was surprised that he had slept, but there was Mac-Donald undoing the ropes. "Did ye sleep well, laddie?" asked the deep, rumbling voice.

"Uh, yeah," he muttered in reply and rubbed at his wrists, then at his ankles. Where was his ma? Grey dawn lit some of the surroundings, but it was still mostly darkened shadows inside. He didn't hear anyone else moving. MacDonald was rocking back and forth on his heels waiting for him to put on his boots, and he dragged them on, deliberately keeping his eyes from the shotgun over the door. He could be patient.

MacDonald led the way outside and toward the outhouse. The sun threw its morning gold over the land as they walked back. MacDonald pointed to the hated pump and said, "That twill be yere task after we start the coffee for yere mither. She twill want a cup to start her day." Lorenz dutifully walked into the house. MacDonald motioned towards the chairs, and Lorenz took the one closest to the door into the dining room. He tried to look natural as he watched MacDonald fill the enameled pot with water, throw in a handful of grounds, and a small shake of salt. While MacDonald was busy starting the fire in the stove, Lorenz uncoiled from the chair. Two steps and he was through the door, two more steps and he was reaching up over the front door leading out to the porch. He pulled the shotgun down, started to twirl back towards the kitchen and the charging MacDonald when a bundle of fury hit him from the side.

"Nein, nein! Du cannot do such things! Not now, not ever again!" The words were like an echo in his head. Suddenly, his mother was in front of him, her hands holding on to the shotgun, her grey eyes cold with determination. "Du cannot so behave."

Lorenz felt his stomach sinking. "But, Mama, I just wanted to protect y'all. After he hurt y'all last night, I figured..." He'd forgotten to use his slurred speech, and his words died.

There were no bruises on her face. She was wearing what Rity had called a day shift, a gray, utilitarian dress for working:

short sleeves, shorter than clothes worn outside the home, and no need for several slips. Her arms were bare and there were no bruises there, no discoloration. This woman didn't look like she had been struck, and she was definitely protecting MacDonald.

Anna looked at her son in disbelief. "Vhat are du talking about? Mr. MacDonald has never hurt me, not even mitt vords. Vhere did you come up with such foolishness?"

Lorenz swallowed. How was he supposed to explain? He looked at his mother, took a deep breath, and tried. "I heard a noise last night that didn't sound right. I thought he was hurting y'all."

Part of the fury went out of Anna's eyes, but her grip on the shotgun did not lessen. A slight pink rose on her cheeks. "That vas my fault, but du are too old for me to explain things to du. That is Mr. MacDonald's job. He is Papa in this family." She pronounced the words with finality. "Now put my gun back up. It must be there for me if ever the Indians come again. This time I vill have more than a broom." She snapped her teeth and mouth shut.

Lorenz looked at his mother with her set face and then at the doorway into the kitchen. MacDonald stood there, watching them, his arms up against the frame. For once there was no half-smile on his face. The man was ready to jump, to bear them both to the floor if it would protect his woman. Now his eyes probed into Lorenz's. He was waiting, waiting for some movement, waiting to see if his wife's words were effective.

Lorenz suddenly realized that he wanted this man's approval. Until now Lorenz never gave a damn if someone approved of him or not, but this man was something more than all the others. Lorenz turned and slammed the shotgun back into position. He knew MacDonald would be at him this time and he turned, his head held high. He would prove he could take whatever the big man handed out.

"Now du apologize to Mr. MacDonald." Anna still barred his way with her stern eyes and commanding voice.

Lorenz's mouth dropped and his eyes didn't leave MacDonald's. MacDonald never took his eyes away from Lorenz, but the half-smile was returning to his face. This time he wasn't laughing about some secret joke he was enjoying, but he was smiling at the consternation on Lorenz's face, and his eyes held a hard, speculative look.

Anna grabbed Lorenz by the biceps. "Du vill tell him."

Helpless, Lorenz looked at MacDonald and then back at his mother. He kept his head high, but inside he was limp; as limp as his manhood dangling uselessly. Suddenly MacDonald's words returned, and Lorenz glared at the man. "Mr. MacDonald, ah just broke your rules. I sorrow."

MacDonald straightened, a tight smile was on his lips and pride and approval were in his eyes. "Aye, accepted."

Anna leaned over and kissed her son. "That is better." Anna moved towards the kitchen, looked up at her husband and smiled, stood on tiptoe to kiss him, and went outside.

"How does it feel to be whipped when she does nay even use a belt?"

Lorenz let out his breath. "She ain't scared of nothin'."

MacDonald straightened. "'Tis wrong. She fears that the Comanche twill return and break up her family again. That tis why the shotgun. She handles it well. I worry as it holds but two shots. She, however, feels secure."

"Now, tis time we went to work." The big man reached out and grasped Lorenz by the shoulder, gently propelling him towards the kitchen door. At the door they stopped long enough to grab their hats.

Lorenz offered no resistance. He was in a state of shock. Where were the expected blows or the question about whose belt would be used? Instead the man acted as if nothing of particular importance occurred, and the rhythm of ranch life continued.

"Ye can start filling the empty tubs once ye have moved them into the washhouse whilst I milk the cow. By the way, I twill be able to hear if the pumping stops too long." MacDonald smiled, handed Lorenz the pail, and then he walked to the springhouse to retrieve the clean milk bucket.

It was, Lorenz decided as the pump handle moved up and down, going to be another very long day. He really didn't know what the haying would involve, but he was certain it would not be to his liking.

Breakfast was a hurried affair. Mama plopped a big pot on the kitchen table along with cream, sugar, more milk, biscuits, apple butter, and mugs filled with hot coffee. She spooned something from the pot into a bowl, and said, "It's oatmeal. Du remember, ja?"

He shook his head and puzzlement wrinkled his brow. How was a man supposed to work eating a bowl of that stuff? Lorenz watched as the others piled on sugar and poured cream over the congealed mass. Surprisingly, it was good, and something stirred in the back of his mind. He remembered sitting up high in some kind of chair and throwing a spoonful at Daniel. He reckoned he was always good at causing trouble.

After breakfast, MacDonald and Lorenz headed for the horses and the barn. Lorenz figured once they were away from Mama's watchful eyes, he would pay for his touching the weapon. "Y'all going to use your belt when we get to the barn?"

"Nay, ye said, 'I sorrow.'" MacDonald stopped and turned towards him. This time Lorenz caught the hard glint in the man's eyes. "Did ye nay mean it?"

Somehow his words had got twisted. Lorenz figured it was MacDonald that hadn't meant he accepted the words. Lorenz felt his face sagging as he scrambled for words in his mind. "I shouldn't have upset Mama. That was wrong."

"And the shotgun aimed at my gut was nay?"

"Ah thought y'all had hurt her!"

"Hurt tis nay what a man does with his wife."

"The hell!" Lorenz broke in. "I saw what they do!" His face was flushed. "The women were screeching like something already dying."

"Aye, with good reason. Those men were brutal strangers, and using them in a brutal way ere they killed them. That tis nay the way of decent men with those they love. The object is to give each other pleasure."

Lorenz stared at the man. He was talking about his ma. "I don't want to know," he muttered and looked off toward the mountains. Was this what Mama meant when she said it was for MacDonald to explain because he was "Papa?" Did someone as brutal as Rolfe explain to Martin?

MacDonald grinned and clamped his hand on Lorenz's shoulder, aiming him towards the barn. "Ere ye have yere first bedding, ye'd best ask. Now we have work to do."

Lorenz's original surmise about the haying was correct. By the end of the day, every muscle ached from pitching the hay upward while in the field and then downward into the barn. Why had Martin complained about losing this job? To add to his misery, blisters had formed on his hands and hay had sifted down into every crinkle and crevice of his body. Yesterday's meals were but a dream. There had been nothing but beans and biscuits for the noon meal, and supper promised to be the same as his mother was still working at something, laboring over a cloth, covered board with what looked like a shirt draped over it. Lorenz began to see why towns would have a lot of young drifters looking for an easier way of life. When MacDonald suggested a different way to cleanse the hay fragments from the body, Lorenz stared at him dully. He didn't want another bath, but there sure didn't seem to be a stream handy other than the spring bubbling in the springhouse.

"We twill have to make do with cold water," said MacDonald as they filled one of the tubs with well water and carried it and a bucket behind the washhouse. It took another trip to retrieve the clean, ironed clothes, and one towel.

"Now we strip. We need nay fear the ladies twill disturb us."

They poured the cold water over their bodies, MacDonald obviously relishing the cold biting into his flesh. Lorenz felt the shock of it, and after dipping the bucket into the tub and pouring the second bucket over his head and down his body, he grabbed the towel. The itching had subsided and all he wanted was his clothes, a meal, and rest.

He should have known better. Once again he was set to milking and helping with the evening chores. Supper was a repeat of dinner as his mother was still in the kitchen devising (according to what he discerned from the conversation) something to take with them tomorrow. His rest consisted of sitting at the table with books and papers while MacDonald explained the arcane ways of reading, letters, and numbers. To his surprise, he was able to make sense of most of it, and words seem to leap off the page. He did not see the small smile of satisfaction on MacDonald's face, nor would he have understood it if he had seen.

His complete ignorance of the way people learned worked to his advantage. Since he did not know what he was doing was beyond the norm of most human beings, he did it.

Anna appeared and claimed a sleepy Mina. "I can do that, my love," offered MacDonald.

Anna smiled. "Nein, I need to be busy. I must make sure everything is tomorrow more ready. I have a while before the fire checking."

MacDonald shook his head as she walked away. The secret laughter gone from his eyes and his voice as he growled, "She does nay even ken how tired she tis."

Lorenz looked up puzzled. "How can y'all tell?"

"Whenever she tires, her English becomes more German." He shifted back into the chair. Ye are doing well. Do ye wish to take a break outside and then hit the sack? We twill be leaving early in the morn."

Lorenz stretched and realized how tired he was. "Ah reckon," he answered.

When they returned, MacDonald suggested, "Why nay strip down to your underwear? They cover ye, and your mither has seen ye naked. It would nay offend her and would be far more comfortable sleeping. Ye can hang the trousers and shirt on the chair, and they would nay wrinkle overnight."

Lorenz hesitated, and then shrugged. Why not? He rapidly stripped down. He hadn't told Mama, but he liked the crispness and smell of the clothes since she laundered them. Even the smell from the soap was different from the laundry that Rity had Theresa do. It seemed his mother possessed some secret for doing things that other women out here didn't know. He swung onto the daybed and waited for the ropes, but MacDonald reseated himself and picked up the paper Mama had read the night before. Lorenz closed his eyes. If he pretended to be asleep, he might just be able to slip off tonight. Damn, he didn't realize that haying would be such hard work. It was good to relax and lose the tightness in his muscles. He felt instinctively that he was safe, and no one would try creeping up on him tonight. The heaviness in his head overtook his intentions, and his eyes closed, and then his breathing slowed.

As Anna came into the room she stopped and looked at her sleeping son and husband reading contentedly. MacDonald looked up and smiled at her. She cocked her head and raised her eyebrows. He elaborately laid a finger to his lips, winked, and then stood. They both walked out into the kitchen where the heat still seared the lungs.

Anna quickly added two pieces of wood to her fire after checking the gauge on the oven. As she straightened, she asked, "Did he promise not to run?"

MacDonald's laughter was soft as he took her in his arms and whispered, "Nay, but I dinna think he twill wake ere morn. I worked the laddie today. Mayhap harder than I should have, but he twill sleep deeply this evening."

His words were correct. Lorenz did not hear his mother exclaim over the perfection of the pie when she pulled it from the oven. His eyes remained closed as she and MacDonald carried the food out to the springhouse to keep everything safe from rodents overnight. His body did not stir as MacDonald picked up his boots and socks before blowing out the lamp. Anna and her husband smiled at each other and then they retired for the night, gently closing the door behind them.

Chapter 7

Family Gathering

Grey, morning light was pushing against the black sky, and a grim-faced Lorenz was riding in the back of the MacDonald family cart. One arm was hooked over the board edge and his legs sprawled out in front of him. Mina was asleep on an improvised pallet and the food was stored in a basket lashed against the sideboard. Mama and Papa, no not Papa. Why was he thinking like that? Something must be wrong with his head. MacDonald might be a good man like his Ma claimed, but he sure as hell wasn't his Pa.

The grey sky became threads of rose hued gold massing towards a blood-red center as he tried to figure out how he was so easily consigned to riding in this cart like some snot-nosed kid no older than Young James. He remembered frantically searching for his boots after he'd heard a noise in the bedroom and realized he'd slept too long.

That was how it happened. He'd been a fool and slept too long. After that, there was nothing to do but get dressed and follow every direction MacDonald had given. He'd been outraged when MacDonald informed him that neither of them was riding horses into Schmidt's Corner.

"But what if we're attacked?"

"'Tis nay out there now," replied MacDonald.

Mama had appeared carrying the basket. She was dressed in some sort of grey suit, and the white hair enshrined her face like a halo in the half light of dawn. He remembered thinking she was a fine figure of a woman, and no wonder MacDonald didn't seem to care if he appeared younger. Suddenly he was glad of the darkness as he blushed. He'd clambered up into the cart when MacDonald pointed, thankful for the opportunity to hide his face. The next thing he knew they were out on the road, and Mama was talking a blue streak to MacDonald.

They had ridden, Lorenz figured, about two miles when Mac-Donald pointed off to the left and announced, "Tis the Rolfe headquarters."

It was light enough to see half-roofs, but only the barn, stable, and another outbuilding were distinguishable as separate entities. The house looked half there with the roof slanted back into the side of the high banks. "Where's the house?" asked Lorenz.

"'Tis just the front and the kitchen ye see. The rest of the living quarters are dug back into the cliff. They moved there after their house in Schmidt's Corner was burned by the Rebs."

"Drunken hoodlums from Arles, du mean, Mr. MacDonald," sniffed Anna. "Thank Gott du and Mr. Rolfe had come home. They vould have burned us all out."

"Would ye please call me Zeb or ZebZebediah till we are in town?" It was the first time Lorenz had heard any reproach in MacDonald's voice to his wife. In fact, the man sounded peeved.

"And vhat kind of example vould that set for Mina?"

"She tis asleep," MacDonald replied.

"And vhat about Lorenz? He needs to know vhat to expect from a wife," Anna retorted as though she had not been interrupted.

"Ye Gods, woman, with any luck at all, his wife twill call him by his name."

Lorenz blinked his eyes in bewilderment. Were they planning to wed him off to someone? And were they talking about now or the far future? Were they really planning on him being around that long? Nothing, nothing at all made any kind of sense. He was accustomed to getting up in the morning and somehow getting enough to eat to live until the next day. Who thought about years later?

It took another hour to arrive at Schmidt's Corner. During the trip, Mina awakened which necessitated a wagon stop, and then crackers were passed out when she complained about being hungry. "'Tis a wee bit of sustenance," was MacDonald's comment.

The road became more of a road and not just two or three ruts wearing into the soil. Lorenz could see the river here was fuller, before bending away towards the south and gradually tapering into the distance. As they approached the settlement, the road seemed to have been smoothed. He couldn't help but wonder who would bother. As he looked down, it seemed as though there were lots of fresh sign. Now what?

This town had no outlaying residences. Instead there were the remnants of a burned out hulk of a once prosperous household with a wooden finger protruding from the foundation, rising in the air as if to defy those who had tried to completely destroy it.

"That vas the Rolfe place," Anna stated. "Du should have seen Mr. MacDonald," and she stressed the formal pronunciation of his name. "The place was burning, and Olga vas crying about her mother's organ being the most precious thing she had left. He vent in and carried it out all by himself. The next time ve get together, ve vill have to go there, and she can play for us."

The rest of the town consisted of buildings lined along the river. The first was a smaller dwelling next to a blacksmith shop. The boards were still marked with bullet holes and burlap hung over the windows. "Tom Jackson's place," explained MacDonald. "He lost his leg in the war, but he's still doing the smith work for us."

Next was some kind of cantina or saloon, a small place with the door propped open. "Tis Owens that owns it," and MacDonald smiled at his use of words. "He lives out back in a small house. There's another smaller house there for the Mexican family. Cruz sometimes works for us or anyone that might need a handyman. Their lassie tis about twelve or thirteen."

Anna sniffed, but didn't elaborate on her disdain. She did, however, issue one of her few orders to Lorenz. "Du do not go there mitt out Mr. MacDonald."

On the opposite side of the road, up a small incline, there stood a rail fence with a lonely tree and headstones inside to mark the site as a graveyard. They were approaching a general store with a sign swinging between the porch posts. The sign proclaimed this bit of earth as Schmidt's Corner. Beyond the general store it looked like there might be another abandoned building or two, but Lorenz was not certain. He was looking at the signs of more recent traffic. "Hit looks like a big outfit came through here."

"Aye," answered MacDonald as he swung the team through the space between the saloon and the general store. "'Tis probably the Blue Diamond freight train. Anderson said they twere headed this way."

They were on another road-like track that ran behind the buildings. The small river lay about thirty feet beyond and part of the ground was taken by two small cabins, plus the outhouses. The ground on the other side of the general store was a garden, fenced by wire and stone and another outhouse. It looked like the owner had used any fence material he had been able to scavenge or secure. The back portion of the two story general store was obviously a home and storage area. The back of what had once been a livery stable was open to the elements. All of the buildings showed the neglect of the war years and were in need of a fresh coat of whitewash. As MacDonald had speculated, there were freight wagons in front of the open stable. The men from the freight wagons were milling in and out of the back of the saloon, and back to the wagons while giving the garden and the general store a wide berth.

At the steps of the porch, MacDonald pulled up the team. A tall, slender, grey-haired man in black trousers, collarless white shirt, and vest came running down the steps, grinning broadly and calling, "Welcome, welcome."

Lorenz stared at an older version of himself with a mustache. Damn, he thought, I might as well had a sign around my neck saying I'm his kin. The man reached up and offered his hand to Anna as she alighted from the wagon, and then he lifted a squealing Mina into his arms. At MacDonald's nod, Lorenz swung over the side.

"Kasper, this is Lorenz." Anna re-introduced her twin to her son, extracted Mina, and set her on the ground. "Lorenz, this is your Uncle Kasper, mein bruder, brother." She was smiling with pride.

Kasper put out his hand and smiled. Lorenz grasped it and noted the man's eyes were as grey as his and Anna's. There was no doubt the two were twins. They stood the same height and the shoulders were equally wide. The difference was in her feminine form and in his mustache, slightly broader chin, and a more prominent Adam's apple.

"It is so good to see you again, Lorenz. We've all prayed for this day." The man was beaming at him. "Aw, who cares?" With that the man threw his arms around Lorenz and actually hugged him. Lorenz was too startled too protest.

Kasper released the young man and continued to smile. "Do you remember playing war games with me?" His speech, unlike the others, was without an accent.

Lorenz started to shake his head no and then realized who he was looking at. "I thought y'all was a kid," he blurted.

Kasper clasped his shoulder. "That's because we both enjoyed the game so much. You were quite an opponent for a child. I still have the set packed away somewhere. I haven't looked at it for a long time." The smile faded from his face and he changed the subject.

"Come, come, Gr Gerde is waiting. There are some fresh rolls for refreshments before the service."

What did he mean *service*? Nobody said anything about a preacher man. As usual, their words had meaning for everyone but him.

MacDonald handed him the basket. "Here, ye carry this inside and greet yere Aunt. I twill put up the team."

He could think of nothing to escape, and his mother slid her arm through his. "This is so vunderbar, vonderful. Ach, Lorenz, you cannot know how I've longed for this."

They walked the short, dusty distance and up the steps. Kasper, again carrying Mina, opened the door for them. "GreGerde, they are here!"

This kitchen was large, clean, and neat; not the clean, neat of his mother's kitchen, but extraordinarily so. The windows sparkled, the floors shone, the air redolent with lingering aromas from the early morning baking, and what few dishes were still dirty from the meal preparation were stacked in a mid-sized metal tub on the counter. There was no idle potholder waiting to be used, no child's toy in a corner, no pad of paper, or book left on the huge round table occupying the center of the room. There were cabinets lining the walls and fresh linen on the table. At least this woman was normal sized. She barely came up to his shoulder. Her hair was a true, medium brown as were her eyes. The mouth seemed to be pulled into a perpetual frown, and the eyes were bitter with sorrow. She gave a tentative half-smile and extended her hand. At least here was no pretense of being overjoyed at the sight of him. Lorenz sat the basket on the counter and removed his hat. From the front came the sounds of another wagon pulling up and the shouts of greetings from the men.

Lorenz was about to go help MacDonald when young James burst into the kitchen yelling, "Tante GerGerde, hello."

She bent to hug young James, and both Mina and James began to plead with her. "Can we have some candy, Tante? Please, please," they were chanting in unison.

A look of satisfaction came over Gerde's face and she went to a large jar set on the counter by the window and unscrewed the lid. "And what do we say?" she asked.

"Danke schon," they both replied as they palmed the candy and then popped the dark, hard round into their mouths.

Lorenz stared at his aunt as though he were seeing a ghost. "Tante, yu, y'all are Tante Dirty, "he gasped. It was though he had been hit in the stomach. That last day, he and Daniel had been fighting: fighting over the last of her candy. "Mama, we wuz just fightin' over candy, that's all, just candy." Desperation laced through his voice as he remembered that long ago pain. "Why'd that make y'all so mad?"

Everyone was looking at him, including the small, young woman who had entered carrying another basket. "Lorenz," his mother admonished lightly, "du are too big to call GreGerde that now."

He turned his agonized face towards his mother, sure that she would be screaming at him again, but her face wasn't twisted in anger, puzzlement was in her eyes, and a slight frown pulled at her mouth and forehead. He swallowed and tried to think of something more to say, but no more words would come. His fight with Daniel, the screams of his mother replayed in his mind, and anguish tore at his insides. He turned and ran out of the building, bumping against the young woman and knocking her aside in his rush.

Outside he pulled in a lungful of fresh air unsullied by soap and humans and swung over the porch railing to land in front of MacDonald. He looked up, still trying to pull more air into his chest that was now too constricted to breathe either in or out.

Something in his eyes or face must have registered with the big man as he took Lorenz's arm and led him between the general store and the stable. "I think we shall go for a short stroll. There tis a graveyard across the street and up a bit. Ye twill find it a quiet spot."

By the time they reached the graveyard, Lorenz was still panting, but air was going in and out in a normal sequence. He was grateful to be away from everyone's prying eyes. How had Mac-Donald known, and why had he made such an ass of himself?

"There tis the grave of yere cousin, Wilhelm. He was but a couple of years younger than ye. The typhoid fever twas here in fifty-eight and took him; him and Mrs. Rolfe. The typhoid had started in the East the year before. If ye noticed the sadness in yere El-Uncle's eyes, or the sourness of yere Tante Gre'Gerde's, there lies the answer. For some reason the good Gar took him and left ye alive. Mayhap there tis a reason, mayhap there tis nay."

Lorenz began to settle down and he looked around as his breathing returned to normal. It was not a large graveyard, but there were a few more graves. "Someday yere mither and Uncle wish to have a Church built just to the left of here, across from the store." MacDonald's voice was soothing, talking of everyday things. He led him to the end of the graveyard and leaned his arms on the top rail of the fence. "And now, would ye like to tell me what prompted all the excitement?"

Lorenz stuck his hands in his pockets and rocked back and forth. "Ah called her Tante Dirty, just like ah used to. And then ah had to bring up that damned fight 'tween me and Daniel, and Mama being so mad she didn't even want me in the house." He clenched his jaw waiting the tongue lashing or the fist. Instead when he looked at MacDonald, the great shoulders were shaking and the man's lips were pursed as though holding back the laughter. "It ain't funny!" he protested.

"Oh, aye, laddie, tis very funny. Did ye nay notice how sanitized her kitchen tis with nay a thing out of place?" His words had no meaning to Lorenz except to illustrate how out of place he was here with these people.

"But Mama was getting upset, and it was that damn candy, and then I almost knocked Martin's sister over when I went out the door, and she's going to be mad too."

MacDonald straightened and looked at him, the amusement still gleaming in his eyes and the shoulders were still shaking, the silent laughter causing him to smile. "I am trying nay to laugh out loud for if yere mither hears me, I shall be in far more trouble than ye." He gave a nod towards the road where his mother was walking towards them in long, swift strides, the grey skirt swinging out and away from her legs in her hurry. Lorenz let out his breath and knew that his time here was over. He would no longer have to plot to run. So why would being made to leave make him sad? He hadn't cried in years. Not since he was four or five that he could remember.

Anna practically ran through the fence opening to where they were standing. Her grey eyes were puzzled at she looked at them both. "Vhat ist? Vhy did du run out of there, Lorenz?" She took his hands in hers and made him look at her.

Lorenz was struck mute. Where was the anger? Why was she acting like she couldn't remember? There was no anger in her eyes or face. There was only love and concern.

MacDonald answered for him. "It seems GreaGerde's candy has brought back his memory of a time when ye angered and made him leave the house."

It was Anna's turn to look perplexed. Then she remembered and her eyes closed for a moment and she took a deep breath. "Ach, ja, that day, that horrible, horrible day." She opened her eyes and turned to Lorenz. "I didn't vant just du out of the house. I vanted us all out of the house. I sensed there vas horrible danger, but your father had gone out and taken all the guns with him. It was so hot, and Auggie was teething and fussy. I gave the rest of du the last of GreGerde's candy to keep du quiet vhile I tried to pack up vhat I vould need for the baby. Time vas so short, and then Daniel took the candy away from du, and du two fighting vere. Ach, I lost my temper and stopped the fighting. I somehow knew time was short. I sent du with Margareatha and sent Daniel out to the field vhere his father was supposed to be. I thought he vould at least protect his child. I should have known better. By the time I finished putting the diapers in a knapsack, I had to change Auggie. Then I heard the Indians ride up, and I knew I vould have to fight for mein baby." Anna stopped. "Lorenz, I sent du out of the house to save du and Margareatha, not because I didn't vant du. I love du. Du are mein sohn!" Her voice and eyes filled with intensity and her face became as set as Lorenz could set his.

Lorenz was staring at her, his mouth open as though trying to say something to refute her, but no words emerged. Her eyes were boring into him, willing him to believe her. To relieve the tension, his mother suddenly put her arms around him. Her voice was now almost a sob, "Mein Gott, du cannot believe I don't vant du."

Just as suddenly his arms were around her and the wail he had been holding inside burst out. "Mama, I cried for y'all."

Anna looked her middle son, "Und I cried for all of du." She put her hands up on his shoulders. "Du vere a little boy then. I may have frightened du, but I vas afraid that day, but now Gott has brought du home."

Lorenz's face softened. Was it true, was he really home? He suddenly remembered the big man standing patiently at the fence and looked at him. MacDonald still looked relaxed leaning against the fence, but his eyes had narrowed as he seemed to judge the scene playing out in front of him. "I reckon your man's got his own ideas about me being home and stayin'." He looked back at his mother. The idea that MacDonald would let a kid like him stay was beyond his scope, and then there was that fake murder charge against him. Why start to believe you were home when it was going to be pulled apart again?

MacDonald straightened. "That twill nay work, laddie. I have already told ye that ye are welcome in my House. Why nay admit ye twere but a wee one when all the other happened, thank Gar that ye are home, and then start behaving like it?"

Lorenz gave the big man his full attention. "What about that poster? What if the Marshall comes after me? Y'all just going let me go with him."

"We twill cross that bridge when it happens. If need be, I'll attend ye, but if yere Red O'Neal tis an honest man, he twill set the record straight." MacDonald smiled down at him. "Do ye have any more arguments?"

"No, sir." He took a deep breath. "How do I go back in there after makin' a fool of myself?"

MacDonald grinned, "That tis easy, but first tell yere mither that there twill be no more talk of running. She needs to hear the words."

Lorenz took a half-way deep breath and looked at his mother. "Ah, ah reckon ah'll stay. Your cookin's awfully good." For the first time since he was home, he smiled at her.

Anna laid her hand on her son's face. "Danke, Lorenz."

"Now, for the words ye twill be saying," said MacDonald. "First of all ye twill call GreGerde, Tante GreGerde from now on, and ye twill tell her the smell and sight of her candy just overwhelmed your senses."

"How will that help?" Lorenz was dubious.

"A compliment to anyone twill work wonders," MacDonald assured him. "Tis why ye twill tell Olga, Miss Rolfe, that ye were too upset and did nay see such a pretty, young lassie in yere rush to leave."

"Ah don't think she'll believe me if I say lassie."

MacDonald cocked his head and pushed up at his hat. "Ye twill stop yere objections and use yere own words. Ye ken well what I mean."

This time Lorenz grinned at the big man. "Yes, sir."

They were walking the length of the graveyard and out into the dusty street. Men's voices raised and lowered as they neared the store and saloon. From the smithy came the sound of pounding. "It seems that the equipment must have been neglected during the months of the war," said MacDonald. "Tom has some nay expected work. He, too, should be able to pay on his bill at Kasper's. Tis a good day for all."

Kasper greeted them as they came in the door. "Ach, good. Now we can start the service. We're holding it in the living room."

"First the laddie has a few words to say to GreGerde and Olga," said MacDonald as he removed his hat and looked at Lorenz to make sure that Lorenz removed his hat also.

His aunt was standing by the living room door and Lorenz approached her. His tongue felt twice as thick as normal, but somehow he stammered out the words. "Tante GreGerde, ah'm sorry ah called y'all Tante, uh I mean that other name, but, well, ah smelled the candy and ah remembered. We always fought over yore candy 'cause it was so good."

GreGerde straightened and a pleased smile came onto her face. "You remembered? But you vere, were so little." For the first time, she looked glad to see him. She reached up and patted his cheek. "After prayers, you will have to tell me if it's as good as ever."

She turned to the rest. "Come, come. All is ready."

Lorenz stepped back and as Olga approached he took another deep breath. Before he could say a word, MacDonald was speaking. "Olga, ye have nay yet been introduced. May I present Lorenz, Mrs. MacDonald's laddie. Lorenz, this tis Miss Olga Rolfe."

Olga was a short, stocky woman with sun-streaked, light brown hair parted in the middle and drawn severely back into a bun. It was a style she would keep for sixty years as her hair thinned and grayed and the grave closed over her. The light brown eyes were small, set on either side of a short, straight nose, and her lips a surprisingly deep, raspberry color. She was dressed in a plain, gray dress swirling down past her shoe tops. Right now, she was regarding Lorenz as though he was some strange interloper and of small consequence in her world.

Lorenz stumbled out his words. "Miz Rolfe, ah'm sorry ah bumped into y'all. But uh, ah, uh, well, ah wuz kinda in a hurry." He stammered to a halt and then added, "Ah mean, ah wouldn't run into such a pretty woman if ah'd watched what ah wuz doin'."

Color rose in both of Olga's tanned cheeks. She decided to smile at Lorenz to forgive his gawkiness and then extended her hand. "It's nice to meet you." She stepped past them into the living room, and Lorenz pursed his lips, gently blew out his breath, and looked at MacDonald.

MacDonald smiled at him and actually winked. He then picked up Mina and nodded for Lorenz to precede him into the room where everyone was seated except Uncle Kasper.

Martin stood up and motioned to the straight chair next to him. He smiled and extended his hand. "Mr. Lawrence," he said.

Lorenz shook his hand, but couldn't figure out why Martin was acting like they just met. Was this something people like them did? And why was he calling him Mr. Lawrence? Everyone was seated once Mama settled Mina on her lap between the other two women on the sofa. The men were all sitting on straight chairs, and he wondered if MacDonald's would break under the strain. And where was the room in here for someone as big as him or anyone else should the spirit come on them like he'd seen at that camp meeting? There were lamps and some kind of fancy doodads sitting on the little tables. They didn't look like they would withstand anyone crashing against them.

Uncle Kasper cleared his throat. "Now that we have all gathered here, we're ready to begin. Since I am not ordained, our service will be brief," he explained to Lorenz. "We conduct our services in German. I understand that you have forgotten your birth language, but Anna assures me that you are beginning to understand some of the words again. It's difficult for us to change anything as it is the way we've learned the word of God and the liturgy. Our bible is Doctor Luther's translation of the oldest texts into Deutsch, much better than the English King James, and, of course, we learned the songs in German also. I'll explain everything I'm doing in English."

Kasper now addressed his congregation. "Today we are celebrating the return of my nephew and thanking God for answering our prayers." His words became unintelligible as he switched to German, and then Lorenz began to pick them out. Since everyone had their hands folded, Lorenz assumed they were praying. After what seemed the longest ten minutes of his short life, Kasper ended with the words, "und der Heiligen Geist."

Lorenz could understand the part about the name of the Father and the Son, but who or what was the Holy Ghost, and were they worshipping three Gods? He looked sideways at Martin. Martin was no help as his head was still bent and his hands clasped.

"Now we will sing the first song, *Shepherd of Tender Youth.* It reinforces how our loving Savior cares for us all, children and adults, like a good shepherd," said Uncle Kasper. Then to clarify things for Lorenz, he continued with his quick lesson. "It's one of the oldest known Christian songs, and it was written by Clement of Alexandria sometime around two hundred AD, about one thousand six hundred years ago." He pulled out a pitch pipe and blew a note. Everyone seemed to "hmm" and they launched into song.

Lorenz wasn't sure what he was listening to. This wasn't anything like that camp meeting he witnessed, but as the singing flowed in unison, he became enthralled. His mother's and Uncle's voices were soaring together and then dipping to the lowest notes: her voice a lovely, full soprano and Uncle's a matching lyric tenor. Tante's voice was a thinner soprano, while Olga was singing alto. Lorenz couldn't have named what range they were singing, he simply heard and labeled their voices as high, higher, low, lower in his mind. Young James was singing the high notes, while the elder and middle Rolfes added their baritones. Mac-Donald was singing, but it was more of a bass booming on a continuous note. Mina didn't know the words, but she added her voice by following the sounds in an "ah" that swooped along with the highest notes.

When the song ended, Uncle Kasper opened the bible in his hand. "Today's text is from Matthew 18:10-14 and Luke 15:4-7. Both of them are quoting our Lord Jesus when he explains how he cares for the lost sheep," and he began reading in German.

By this time, Lorenz was blinking his eyes. Why did Kasper keep referring to sheep when MacDonald and Rolfe were cattlemen? Before that, they had been hunters. Why would they care about sheep? He stole a glance at the two. Both seem to be listening as intently as the women. Contrary to what he had seen at the camp meeting, the children were sitting quietly. Martin had his hands on his knees leaning forward. He looked like he was afraid he was going to miss a word during the reading.

Kasper finished the reading and closed the book. "Now we will sing the second song written by our own Dr. Martin Luther. It is *Erhalt uns, Herr, bei deinenwort.* Loosely translated it means, Lord keep us steadfast in your word." Once again he used the pipe, everyone dutifully "hummed," and the voices blended again.

For the first time since he was four-years-old, Lorenz was hearing a melody in the minor key. It was both alien and familiar. He was somehow sitting on a large wooden bench with Mama and wedged in between Rity and Daniel while around him the voices swelled and fell. He could almost smell the closeness of the congregation in steamy woolens and the heavy smell of trees and grasses growing in rich soil. Just as rapidly the vision faded and he was on the straight back chair listening to nine other people singing joyously the mournful tune.

When they finished, Kasper said, "Please rise for saying the Apostle's Creed and the Lord's prayer." As one, the small congregation rose and began to recite in unison. Martin nudged Lorenz as he stood and Lorenz rose too. He figured if he remained sitting his mother would be more upset than MacDonald. He wasn't sure what a creed was, but he knew prayer was asking God for something and they all had their hands folded and their heads bowed like they were praying. He hoped God understood German better than he did.

As they lifted their heads, Kasper spoke again. "Now we will sing the last song, "*Wohl einem Haus, da Jesu Christ.*" He smiled at Lorenz. "We are asking God's blessing on this house, and of course, all other Christian houses." The pipe blew and once more the group sang.

For a change, the words were starting to make sense. This was about doing what God wanted for everyone in a home and then everything would be okay. As they finished the song and raised their heads, Kasper spoke again while making the sign of the cross and everyone sang, "Amen." At least Lorenz figured that's what the word meant. Then they all smiled, the women hugged, the men shook hands, and everyone thanked Kasper who was beaming at them all. Where, Lorenz wondered, was all the shouting that he associated with preaching?

Martin and the other men grabbed the chair they had been sitting on and carried them out to the big table. Lorenz did the same. The women all seemed to be babbling about the cooking when Tante GreGerde slipped something into his hand

and smiled at him. Lorenz looked down and his eyes widened. Without thinking, he plopped the candy into his mouth. Daniel couldn't get this one. He smiled. "Danke, Tante GreGrede." It was the same words he had used so many times long ago.

Tante smiled back at him. "Well," she demanded, "does it taste as good as before?" Her brown eyes were bright with the sadness gone.

"Yes'm!" He rolled the maple ball in his mouth, not even realizing he had switched from English to German and back to English. "Hit's no wonder we used to fight over who got the last one."

Tante GreGerde beamed at him and nodded her head in satisfaction. Martin gave him a push on the shoulder. "Come on help me get ready for horseshoes. That way we're out of the kitchen."

The horseshoe contest went as Lorenz expected. Once he learned the object of the game, he wasn't too bad, but no one, not even MacDonald could put a ringer in there every time like the elder Rolfe. Uncle Kasper's playing was erratic. He would score and then become distracted, the next shoe landing nowhere near the stake. Young James soon tired of losing and wandered off. It was a relief to hear the dinner bell. Lorenz did not like losing for any reason.

Chapter 8

Bear Cub

After the meal, the men and women excused the two younger children and brought out the sherry and brandy. Martin stood and said, "Will you all excuse me? I think I'll stretch my legs." He nodded at Lorenz.

Lorenz jumped to his feet, glad for any excuse to be away. The table had been laden with the culinary efforts of three women, and he felt he had handled that part all right. He remembered Rity's instructions about napkins and had received an approving smile from Mama. Everything seemed to go all right until the deserts. Now all he could think of was the cold, baleful look in three pairs of eyes fastened on him while being urged to select one of the deserts.

Tante GretGerdehad stood after the meal and announced, "We have a fruit pie fixed by Anna, an angel food cake by Olga, and, of course, my burnt sugar cake, Kasper's favorite." She simpered over the words burnt sugar cake.

"That's vunderbar, GreGerde. I'll have the burnt sugar cake," said Kasper.

"You must wait your turn, Kasper," GreGerde simpered back. "We want to serve the children first. Mina and James, what would you like?"

Mina looked up, gravy still clinging to one side of her mouth. "I like eine fruit art backwerk." She pointed to her mother's pie with her fork.

"She says that perfectly for a three-year-old," GreGerde ground out through lips that looked like she was attempting to smile.

Young James chimed in, "I'll have your burnt sugar cake, Tante GreGerde. I can eat Olga's cake at home any old time."

Olga glared at her younger sibling while GreGerde gave James a huge slice of cake and patted him on the head. Anna's face had become a study in stonework.

MacDonald sat back and sighed. "I twill have Anna's pie first. She kens the way to my heart. Then if there tis room, I twill have a slice of the others." He smiled at everyone.

Rolfe eyed the women. "I'll have some of each. Du can cut them smaller. Dot vay I get to finish my meal in peace."

GreGerde, Olga, and Anna busily filled their orders. Lorenz wondered how the two older men were going to hold all that food, but they fell to with relish when handed their plates. Kasper smiled happily when his cake was served. Martin made a show of wiping his lips with his napkin and like MacDonald, he smiled broadly.

"I think I'll have a piece of Olga's angel food cake now, and then come back for the other two later. James might be wrong about how much is left over when we get home. 'Sides, no one makes an angel food cake like Olga." Olga's face turned a brilliant scarlet, but she smiled at Martin.

"And now, vhat vould you like, Lorenz?" asked Tante GreGerte, her voice suddenly sugary sweet, and in her agitation, slipping into the German v for w.

It was then that all three pairs of eyes fastened on him. It was like he was being challenged to fight, but he had no idea what he was fighting, let alone how all three women could have the same stony look on their face as though no matter what he said it would be wrong. He looked at MacDonald, then Martin for some cue, but none came. He looked again at his mother, and this time she gave him a quick smile.

He took a deep breath and said, "Ah guess ah'll have some of Mama's pie. Hit sure smelled good last night."

Mama's smile was radiant and just for him. Somehow he must have made the right choice, but Tante GreGerde had tightened her lips, and Olga seemed resigned about something.

Out on the porch, Lorenz took a deep breath and began to try to figure out just exactly what had happened during the selection of a desert. He lit his cigarette, glancing at the diminishing supply of tobacco, and asked, "What the hell happened in there? Why were they all glarin' at me?"

Martin started to laugh. He had enjoyed watching Lorenz be the one squirming under the pressure of not offending one of the three women. "Those three are proud of their baking, more proud of that than their cooking. They pretty well know who's going to eat which dessert. Since y'all didn't grow up eating their desserts, your pick would say that one of them was the best. For them, it's like winning a horse race. I took Olga's cake because I want to stay on her good side when she's cooking for us at home."

Lorenz looked at Martin and shook his head. It made no sense to him. The three had given him the same type of look some of the mule skinners had been throwing at them all morning during the horseshoe game. One of the skinners went staggering back from the saloon's outhouse now, throwing a baleful glance and muttering about, "Damn Yankees."

"They sure ain't got any liken for you all," he said to Martin.

"Naw, they figure themselves Rebs. It don't make no difference here. They've just drank a lot while waiting for Tom to fix their wagon wheels. They're going on up towards the German settlements, and they need the spares to be in good order. Usually Blue Diamond does a better job of keeping their equipment in order. Uncle Kasper said they ran into a rainsquall about three days out of Arles and it was better to just keep coming here for the repairs. Tom works cheaper and there ain't any wait. He don't get too many customers anymore."

Lorenz drew in smoke and asked. "What happens now? More horseshoes?"

"Naw, they're going to sit around and talk and drink. Then everybody will have another piece of dessert, and we'll all head home. Let's go get us a beer."

Lorenz straightened and looked at Martin. "Ah don't think that's a good idea, Martin. Those men in there have been drinkin', and they don't like us. Besides, I ain't supposed to go in there without MacDonald."

Martin gave a half-smile. "Suit yourself. Me, I'm going to have a beer." He swung over the porch rail and started walking.

"Aw shit, muttered Lorenz, swung over the railing, and ground out his cigarette before catching up with Martin. "Y'all are loco. When we go in, make sure y'all pick a spot as far away from those skinners as we can find."

"They ain't gonna cause any trouble, Lorenz," Martin stated with confidence. Neither of them saw the small figure crawl out from beneath the porch, brush himself off, and dash into the house with a satisfied smirk on his face.

He burst into the kitchen shouting, "Lorenz is using all sorts of bad words 'cause Martin's going to the saloon, and Lorenz says the skinners are waiting to jump them. So Lorenz went with him."

Anna's face whitened and she spun to face MacDonald. He stood and asked, "Friend Rolfe, twill ye accompany me?"

Rolfe eyed the contents of his glass, sighed, and stood. "Ja, dumm kopfs," he snorted.

As they walked into the small saloon, Lorenz knew his assumption was correct. The ten men scattered at the small tables and bar fell silent and then started muttering, the laughter and raucous jabbering ended. Lorenz walked straight, his hands dangling at his sides, his grey eyes flickering from man to man, gauging each one's strength, agility, and ability.

Martin was still in his good mood, oblivious to the glares directed at them. "Hello, Owens," he said to the stocky, dark-haired man behind the bar. "My friend and I will have a beer."

Lorenz was about to refuse when he saw that Owens used kegs to dispense his beer and was filling heavy, glass mugs with the dark liquid. He could use the mug as a weapon. His lips tightened.

The two men at the end of the bar were shooting quick, short glances at them while they talked in low tones. He sipped at his beer as two men approached the ones at the table and began speaking in the same low tones. Martin and Owens were talking.

"Saw you folks come in. These men say this one is one of Mrs. MacDonald's lost kids. That right?"

"Ja, this is Lorenz. Lorenz, this is Jesse Owens. He's been at Schmidt's Corner since the beginning.

"How do, young feller. It's a pleasure. If I'd a been here three months sooner, this would be Owens Corner, not Schmidt's, but your Uncle had his store up when I got here. He and his missus were glad enough to turn the liquor trade over to me."

Lorenz barely clasped the man's hand. He was too intent on keeping a grip on the mug handle as the two men standing at the table started towards them. Both were about thirty or thirty-five, not too tall, and a bit rangy as skinners tended to be. The one on his side was bunching his fists, but the other one was drawing a long, bowie knife. Damn, that wasn't good. He kept his eyes forward, almost as if he hadn't noticed them and spoke out of the side of his mouth to Martin.

"Get ready to start backing towards the other door when ah do."

Martin looked up, puzzlement in his eyes, and the men were in front of them. They both reeked of the beer and chili they'd been ingesting all day.

"Well, lookie here," sneered the one in front of Lorenz. "We got us a bear cub and a wolf cub trying to drink like their daddies. Let's see if they've learned to bite." He sent his fist smashing at Lorenz.

With one swift motion, Lorenz swung the mug crashing it into the side of the man's fist, and then brought the mug up and slammed it down on top of the man's head, grabbed the man's shoulder and swung him down to the bar where he proceeded to ram the man's head up and down. He didn't bother to watch him drop to the floor; instead his flat, grey eyes watched the next man coming towards him as he started backing towards the propped, open front door. Unfortunately, Martin was standing rock still, watching the grinning man with the knife.

The man with the knife stopped long enough to make certain the other man was down and another taking his place. Then he turned back to Martin and asked, "Ain't y'all got a knife, boy? Seem's like y'all could lose a body part if y'all ain't careful."

Lorenz felt his stomach tighten as he realized the man coming towards him had pulled out a dragoon's old, long barreled Colt. Suddenly his eyes lighted as he saw the watching crowd of men in front of him being tossed aside like dried weeds in a wind storm.

The man with the gun must have heard something through his drink-addled head as he started to turn when a long arm shot out and grasped his wrist, and another huge hand clamped down on his shoulder. Then MacDonald did something that Lorenz had never seen. He somehow pulled the man towards him and then swung him away with a twisting, snapping force, dislocating the man's shoulder. Agonized screams filled the small space. MacDonald, holding the gun by the muzzle, gave Lorenz a quick glance as if to assure himself that Lorenz was okay, and stepped back towards the bar to watch Rolfe and Rolfe's back.

Rolfe had his own Bowie out and his blue eyes glinted with glee. He was smiling; the knife gripped firmly in his hand, his body crouching in a knife fighter's stance. "Du vant to do some carving? Try me."

The other man's face had gone white, but he was game, and he too went into a circling crouch and then leaped forward. The stocky body of Rolfe moved with astonishing speed for an older man, and his knife swept upward, effectively severing the man's left ear from his head. The man's screams suddenly joined the other man's, and he clapped both hands to his head, blood cascading through his fingers and spilling downward to the dirt floor.

Rolfe's eyes were still glinting, but his smile was gone as he grabbed the wounded man's shirt and cut away a swath, not caring that a line of blood appeared on the dirty skin. Rolfe then used the cloth to wipe his knife while the man looked about wild eyed and then dropped to the floor, screaming about his ear and frantically reaching around the floor trying to find his ear. Rolfe kicked the ear across the floor as the blood began running over the man's face and eyes blinding him. His screaming curses descended into moans as he tried to wipe the blood from his eyes.

Rolfe spoke to MacDonald, but his eyes looked straight at the rest of the freighting crew. "For du and your poy, I buy a drink, friend Mac." His voice was hard and steady.

Lorenz swung his eyes back to MacDonald and sucked in his breath. If there was ever any doubt of the power in the man's hands, it was gone now. MacDonald had the revolver's grip in one hand and the long muzzle in the other, his body looked relaxed, but his hands were exerting enough force to bend the muzzle.

MacDonald laid the bent firearm on the bar and seemed to eye each man standing there. "Friend Rolfe, I believe I am ready for a brew. I thank ye."

A medium built man with thinning hair pushed his way through his crew. "God damn it, MacDonald, Jackson just finished putting the wagon back into commission. What are you and Rolfe trying to do? Leave me shorthanded?" His voice was as exasperated as the look in his eyes.

MacDonald turned his head. "Do? We have done nay but finish a fight yere crew started with two laddies. As twas, two full grown men were nay enough. They had to resort to weapons. Mayhap ye should hire men that twill nay try to kill yere customers along the line."

McGregor pushed his hat back in frustration. "Hell, you all know what I mean." He turned to his crew of skinners. "Get those two back to the wagons, and I'll look after them. Then start harnessing those mules. We got miles to go."

He turned back to Rolfe and MacDonald. "No hard feelings?" he asked. "They just drank too much." He eyed Lorenz and Martin. "Laddies, huh? They both look full-grown to me." With that he stalked off.

"Dinna let such talk go to yere head," MacDonald advised Lorenz, and picked up his mug among the four that Owens had set on the bar.

Owens eyed the bent revolver. "Uh, y'all got any use for that, Mac?'

"Nay."

Owens grinned. "What about y'all, Rolfe? Y'all aim to keep that ear?" He pointed to the dismembered organ on the floor.

"No, vhat I vant that for?" asked Rolfe.

Owens came out from behind the bar and picked up the ear. "Both of them will make a nice conversation piece. I can't afford those fancy mirrors the town places have, but this will let folks know things can happen here. It'll keep folks talking and coming in to see them."

MacDonald snorted. "That ear is going to putrefy. Nay twill be able to stand the stink."

"Maybe, but I'm going to tack them both on the wall." He saw Lorenz just standing there not drinking. "Something wrong with your beer?"

Lorenz shook his head. "Naw, ah jest ain't fond of the taste."

MacDonald looked at him. "Ye had a mug before."

"Ah didn't want the beer. Ah jest wanted the mug. Ah figured ah could use it as a weapon since ah didn't have anythin' else." He stared straight ahead. He knew the big man was angry, and didn't want to give him an excuse to start on him with everyone else standing around.

MacDonald downed the contents of his mug and pushed Lorenz's beer towards Rolfe. "Here, my friend, tis best nay to waste it. The laddie and I are going for a walk now. Aren't we, Lorenz?" His voice sounded even and reasonable, but Lorenz figured it was just an act.

"Yes, suh."

Rolfe snagged the beer and drew it to him. "Mac, I'll be checking on vhere the vild horses are tomorrow." He glanced at Lorenz and added, "Du vill need to teach that poy that du don't vant to rein the vild ones too hard." He turned his attention back to his beer.

"Aye, friend Rolfe," replied MacDonald thoughtfully. He looked at Lorenz. "Are ye ready?" He nodded at the door.

Lorenz kept his back straight and his head up. No way was he going to show any signs of cringing. Clouds were scudding overhead, briefly obscuring the sunlight of earlier hours. The weather itself had cooled by several degrees, but any moisture that had been in them must have been dumped on the freighters earlier. He noticed the idle men were no longer idle, but working like fury around the three wagons. Damn, where would Mac-

Donald unleash his punishment? He'd figured the stables, but there were men all around them. Worse, his ma was standing on Uncle Kap's porch and seemed to be tapping her foot. They'd be abreast of her all too soon.

Anna's face was almost as set as Lorenz's and her lips almost as tight. She drew her breath in after studying them both. "So, du are not hurt?" she asked.

"Nay, twas the others that were damaged." MacDonald gave a quick, soft smile to his wife.

She turned her attention back to Lorenz. "I told du to stay avay from that place! Vhy didn't du listen?"

Lorenz looked at her, his face blank. How could he explain it was to protect Martin? That didn't sound right even to him. Martin was supposed to be the oldest one.

"Vell, aren't du going to answer me?" Anna's foot had not ceased tapping, and she swung back to MacDonald. "Vhat took du so long? They carried those two men by here not long after the screams."

"Herman bought us all a round of beer. Under the circumstances, I felt it would be best to bide a bit."

Unbelief flooded over Anna's face, and she stamped her foot one more time. "Bah, men! Mr. MacDonald, du vill take care of Lorenz for being disobedient." She swept around and entered the house, slamming the door behind her.

MacDonald had lost his smile and was rubbing his tongue against the inside of his mouth. "It would seem we are both in yere mither's ill graces." He shrugged. "We twill continue our walk."

Lorenz figured he was really in for it. His mother had given her stamp of approval to whatever MacDonald decided to do, and right now he couldn't be in a good mood. He stalked alongside of the ambling man wondering why MacDonald hadn't slapped his mother.

MacDonald led the way to the storage portion of the general store, opened the backdoor, and motioned Lorenz inside. "Tis quieter in here," he said as he closed the door behind them. A high placed window on the opposite side spilled light into the mostly empty place. "Yere uncle has nay been able to stock the merchandise he once did. Nay are there the people to purchase it as they once did."

Lorenz took a deep breath and waited.

"Mayhap ye can tell me why ye went into the saloon when ye were told nay, and according to young James, ye were quite aware of what those men might do."

"Young James can tattle and get away with hit. How'd it sound if ah'd come running in tellin' on Martin?" He hesitated and then looked up at MacDonald. "'Sides Martin's my friend. Ah couldn't let him go in there alone."

MacDonald allowed a slight tugging at his mouth. "It would nay have been tattling if ye had asked for help in a situation that twas beyond yere abilities."

"Y'all mean y'all would have helped me?" Lorenz stopped and then admitted, "Yeah, reckon y'all would have come to help Martin."

MacDonald shook his head. "And have I nay been helping ye ever since ye rode into Arles with that huge ball of hate in yere guts?"

The question rocked Lorenz. Help? The man had been nothing but a jailer as far as he was concerned. True, he had on clothes that fit, food in his belly, and a place to sleep, but he was a prisoner just the same. "Y'all ain't done nothin' but kept me from doin' what ah want," he exploded.

"And what twould ye be wanting to do?"

They had been staring at each other since the first question, and Lorenz felt his resolve vanish. He let out his breath, turned, and leaned up against one of the crates. "Ah dont know," he admitted aloud. Zale was dead, and he was damn tired of being alone. All those years he dreamed of being with his ma, and it sure looked like he was doing his best to throw it away.

"Ye may wish to think about it. Now, as to what ye twill do the next time ye run into a dangerous situation. Ye twill come to me and ask for assistance."

Lorenz turned and searched the face of the big man. Wasn't there going to be a whipping? Why was he talking about a next time? He squared his shoulders. No time to push things he decided. "Yes, suh." If MacDonald wanted to give him another rule instead of a whupping, he'd put up with it.

MacDonald had a tight smile on his face. "Lorenz, do ye nay ken? Ye had done everything right up until ye walked into that place. Ye correctly evaluated a situation, determined what the outcome would be, and tried to warn the person with ye. Ye could nay have done better if ye twere full-grown."

Some of the anger left Lorenz. The man wasn't beating on him, and he sure as hell wasn't yelling. If anything, it sounded like he was being praised. He straightened and faced MacDonald. "They called me bear cub." Would this make the man mad? He waited for the roar. Instead MacDonald was amused, his brown eyes dancing; his usual slight smile had become a half-smile, twisting one corner of his mouth upward.

"They called Martin wolf cub and wanted to know if we had learned to bite. So ah showed 'em what a bear cub could do." He stopped, waiting for the big man to say his words of derision, but none came.

MacDonald recognized the pleading cry in Lorenz's eyes, and removed Lorenz's hat, with one hand and ran the other through Lorenz's hair, gently enfolding his hand around the youth's neck. "And bite ye did, laddie, but ye had nay to prove to me in that manner. As for being bear's cub, I have already told ye that ye are welcome in my House and in my heart. Why have ye nay believed me?" His thumb was running up and down the side of Lorenz's neck.

Lorenz felt the heat rising within him and the air felt close. Instinctively he reached up and grabbed the forearm of the hand holding his neck. "'Cause ah cain't ever be what y'all are. Ah ain't never goin' to be as tall, or as big, or as strong."

MacDonald shook his head. "Aye, and what has that to do with it? Ye twill grow taller, though nay as tall, and ye twill put on some weight, though nay as much, but there are many things that I can teach ye about fighting and putting extra power into yere frame. None of that, however, has anything to do with the man that ye twill be."

"Yeah, and y'all are going to let someone like me call y'all paw." Derision laced his voice and covered his face.

The smile left MacDonald's face. "Ye may call me fither, as that tis my way, or ye may call me Papa as that tis your mither's way. Ye may nay call me paw as that tis the way of others."

Lorenz was left dumb for a moment and finally stammered out, "I don't know your ways."

"Ye are learning, laddie. If ye spent as much time studying our ways as ye do fighting me, ye would learn much faster."

"Ah doan fight yu'll," Lorenz protested as he reverted to the border drawl.

MacDonald shook his head. "Ye have done nay but fight me every step of the way. Even when ye say, 'yes, suh,' ye are thinking of some way to get even or to leave."

Lorenz could not respond. What the big man said was true, and yet, it wasn't true. Like when he didn't shoot him. Think about it, he had been told. He had thought, and grudgingly he had come to admit that he admired this man, wanted to be like him, but he was afraid; afraid of the things that men do to one another, and he had no strength to stop this one, and yet his eyes continued to beg the big man to tell him he was worthy of being bear cub.

MacDonald gave one of his half-smiles and used his other hand to thump Lorenz on his chest. "I could tell ye to call me fither, but until ye believe it here, it twould be another lie." He dropped his arm to Lorenz's shoulder. "And now we must go see yere uncle. I'm sure he tis in his office to escape the chatter of the ladies." He opened the door and motioned Lorenz through.

Lorenz walked into the narrow hallway, his feet moving with wooden steps. His lips were tight and his head held high. He had seen something deep in MacDonald's mind and he didn't like it. The office was tucked between the main room and storage room by a wall of boards. His uncle sat at an old desk, a book opened before him and some papers set to the side. Kasper looked up and smiled as they came in.

"Ach, there you are. I've finished going over the papers you had. There are a few points I'd like to cover." He opened another book.

MacDonald eased into one of the straight back chairs and motioned Lorenz to the other. "Mayhap ye have some paper that Lorenz can practice his letters and numbers while we do so."

"Good, you've started him on his lessons then."

"Aye, and he tis quick."

Lorenz sunk down onto the seat. The two were talking about learning, and it sounded like MacDonald was taking lessons from his Uncle. That didn't make sense.

Uncle Kasper scooted a small tablet and pencil in his direction and asked. "How soon before I can start him on his catechism lessons?"

"That twill be a while. First he needs to master English and then German."

MacDonald removed his hat and looked at Lorenz who promptly yanked his hat off. There wasn't much left of it, but it seemed nobody wore one inside unless it was the saloon.

The two men began discussing Latin, and Lorenz soon tired of listening to them. As far as he could see, his own letters and numbers looked fine. He started to doodle at horses, cows, and faces.

From the front of the house came a long knock and excited voices from the women. "Welcome, Mr. Jackson. We have saved you a goodly portion. Come in and eat."

Kasper looked up. "It seems Olga's suitor has arrived. I should go and greet our guest."

"Aye, and then we need to buy the laddie some things. His hat tis nay fit to wear."

Kasper smiled at Lorenz and then saw his drawings. "Why this is good, very good. You have drawn before, ja?"

Lorenz reddened. "Naw, just messed around with it some when ah was healin'. Rity was too busy to show me anythin' to write."

Kasper handed the tablet to MacDonald to examine. "See, he has even drawn horses. That is one of the most difficult animals to draw." He took up a pencil, "The faces, however, need more shading. See, here on the nose, if you shade like this," and he did a few quick strokes, "the nose will look more natural."

Lorenz looked down. Kasper hadn't done much, but Mina's face now seemed much more like Mina. "Huh," he said and looked up. "Do y'all draw?"

Uncle Kasper looked down with fondness in his grey eyes. "No, not really. I can draw, but the drawings have no life. Yours do. You must keep at it." He looked at MacDonald. "We can even spare another tablet as a gift if you will let him use it."

MacDonald's face was a puzzlement to Lorenz. It was as if there was some new side to Lorenz that he had not considered, but he nodded in agreement. "Aye, that I twill do. Now let us go say hello to Mr. Jackson. I still want some of that cake ere we leave."

In the kitchen, Olga was fussing over a black-suited man with a mustache twice as large as Kasper's. He stood up as they entered, and Lorenz saw that the man, about five-foot six was extremely broad shouldered and muscular. The right pant leg, however, from the knee down flopped around a wooden stump.

The men began their ritual of shaking hands and addressing everyone by their surname. It was, decided Lorenz, one more peculiar thing these people did. Bear cub or not, there was no way he was ever going to belong.

Chapter 9

Mina's Story

Darkness was fast closing over the sky when they finished the evening chores and emerged from the springhouse, MacDonald carrying about a quart of milk. "The wee lassie likes her treat ere we go to bed after a special day." He smiled at Lorenz. "Mayhap ye twill like it too."

Lorenz followed him to the kitchen where Mama was working. His belly was still full from the midday meal and the sweets they'd eaten before leaving. The hat and extra trousers that Mac-Donald had insisted on buying seemed treat enough to him, and he sure wasn't fond of milk.

Mina pounced on her father as they walked into the kitchen. "Papa, can we have some choc-o-lat?" Her tongue may have twisted over the long word, but her eyes were shining in anticipation.

"Aye, my wee one. I twill fix us all some."

Anna straightened from putting the last of the pans away. "Not for me. I vould prefer a beer tonight, but I vill the blankets and pillows put out first."

Lorenz watched with fascination as MacDonald brought out the utensils and cocoa. Mama must have known this ritual as someone had started the fire in the range. How was it, he wondered, that a man that could tear someone's arm out of joint and stand there working in a kitchen like a woman all in the same day? It made no sense.

Once the chocolate was finished, MacDonald poured the contents into three mugs. "Ye twill have to carry yere own outside," he said to Lorenz. "And, Mina, my wee one, ye must open the door for yere fither."

There was, Lorenz figured, no way out of this one. He hated to admit it, but the smell from the steaming cup was mighty tempting. Maybe he would drink it, although going outside to do so didn't make any sense either. No reason to puzzle it. Just go along and see what happens. MacDonald had said that tomorrow they'd work on the door for his room, and his mother would work on a mattress. After that he'd have his own sleeping place. Today had left him in turmoil. Should he stay and see how things went, or would it be smarter not to take a chance and just run?

Mama was already on the blanket and she hadn't been joking. She was actually drinking a bottle of beer. Lorenz felt this was completely out of the norm for the women he'd seen and heard of during his brief sojourns around white people. MacDonald handed his cups to Mama while they seated themselves on the blanket. Lorenz sat cross-legged, but MacDonald swept Mina up into his lap, and the two shared his cup amid much blowing and laughter. The other cup sat safely on the ground while it cooled.

"Papa tell me my story," coaxed Mina.

Lorenz heard the laughter rumble in MacDonald's voice. "Are ye sure ye want the same story again? Mayhap a new one?"

Mina shook her head. "No, I vant Mina's story! Lorenz vill like it too."

"Mayhap ye are right. Lorenz has nay heard this story." Since Lorenz was sitting slightly behind the big man, he could not see the smile of satisfaction on MacDonald's face.

MacDonald shifted his weight and used one hand to point upward. "Once upon a time, long, long ago, there lived a princess and prince on a fine, fair planet that circles a far star. The princess twas beautiful with her snow white hair and a magnificent build. The Prince and Princess fell deeply in love and planned to wed. Suddenly, their planet twas attacked by beings from two different far stars."

"One race twas tall and all had red hair, strange brown eyes with golden circles around the dark middle, and nay like the other beings, they had two hearts. Because they lived for long, long year spans and could control the thoughts of others with their mind, they believed they were superior to all other beings. They called themselves the Justines for they felt they ruled by a great system of justice." Sarcasm had crept into MacDonald's speech.

Lorenz thought of his extremely tall, sister Rity, her copper eyes with the golden circles around the dark pupils, her flaming red hair, and a strange disquiet began to build within. There was no way he was going to believe MacDonald's tale, but he, like Mina, was caught up in the telling, and he sat silent, trying to feature what MacDonald described, but there was nothing in his life that could evoke the images for the words his ears were hearing.

"The other beings attacking them twere shorter and squat, with brown eyes and brownish skin, and scales on their cheeks. They twere called Kreppies. They fawned over the tall, slender Justines as the master race and did their bidding. They spoke in a high, clipped way through their fangs and were quite mean-spirited."

"The Prince and Princess were mighty warriors in their land, and they fought the other beings on the land with weapons and in the sky with their flying ships, but there were too many enemies raging against them. One by one, the strongholds of the Prince and Princess were destroyed, and soon the Prince was in danger of being captured. Ere he let that happen, he took his vessel and destroyed the vessels of the Kreppies and fled the land of his birth. After traveling for many turns, he found a beautiful blue land and settled there. In his heart, he yearned for his Princess and he twas verry sad." MacDonald rolled the r sound to emphasize the seriousness of the situation.

"The battle over the lands where the Princess lived waged more fiercely. The Princess saw that they would soon be bested. She stole a large vessel from the Justines and flew her smaller craft inside. Then she drove the large vessel into the homeland of the Justines. The impact destroyed their lands, but there were still Justines in her land with their large flying vessels. The Justines found the vapor trail of the smaller vessel and searched and searched for her, but she vanished in the vastness of the heavens."

"One day, when the Prince twas riding over the new land, he looked up. There in the sky twas a craft, heading for the earth. He rushed to where it would land and saw the door open. Who do ye think he saw? Can ye name her?"

"Princess Anna," squealed Mina, clapping her hands. "It's Princess Anna!"

"Aye, and they twere together again. They hugged each other, and they both lived happily ever after."

Mina gave a huge sigh and hugged her father. Anna set her bottle aside and asked, "Vould du like to hear about Hansel and Gretel, Mina?"

Mina crawled over to her mother's lap and settled in. The story of the woodchopper's children and their encounter with the witch unfolded. Lorenz sat listening. What kind of stories were these for Mina? That the woodchopper welcomed the children back after Hans had pushed the witch into the oven to die and then taken all her fancy stones wasn't all that great either. He had just sat around cryin' after his woman had died, and had not even looked for the kids or tried to rescue them. Mina, however, seemed unmoved by the horror of it. As the tale ended with the same 'they lived happily ever after,' Mina said simply. "I have to go pee."

Anna stood. "It's time for bed, Mina. Come, ve'll go the out-house." Her smile to MacDonald showed clearly in the night-light of stars and moon. She took Mina's hand and headed for the back.

MacDonald stood. "Aye, it grows late. Lorenz, ye take the cups and rinse them at the pump. I twill shake out the blanket and gather the pillows."

Lorenz sat unmoving, gazing upward at the stars; his mind whirling, trying to sort out the logic in both tales and could find none. He had a gut feeling that MacDonald's tale had been for his benefit and told with his mother's approval. And yet, that didn't make sense because Mina asked for her story. It was something that had been told before. MacDonald nudged him with his boot.

"Lorenz, would ye take the cups and rinse them at the pump?"

He came out of his fog and looked up. "That's wimen's work," he protested.

MacDonald shook his head. "Someday, laddie, ye twill learn that work tis work." His voice changed, hardened into a com-mand. "Ye rinse them whilst I shake out the blanket and take it and the pillows inside. After that tis done, tis our turn to take the nightly jaunt ere we retire."

It was, Lorenz decided, not worth the fight. He might wind up with himself being rinsed out. He snagged the cups and headed for the pump. He would run tonight or early in the morning, taking only the clothes he was wearing. He had gained some of the weight he'd lost, and the food he'd eaten the last few days would sustain him. It would be rough at first without a gun or a knife, but he knew he could get them again.

After his mother kissed him and gave the sleep well blessing in German, Mina wrapped her arms around him and kissed him goodnight. MacDonald looked at him with approval, nodded his goodnight, and took the lamp to light the way for his wife and child.

Lorenz clenched his teeth and pulled off his boots. He'd seen what flashed in MacDonald's mind, and he knew running was his only escape. Running, however, would need to be delayed until morning when the rustlings in the bedroom proved that neither adult was sleeping. He flopped on his stomach and clapped both hands over his ears.

This time, he woke well before the first light of dawn, and moonlight flooded the room and the outside. He grabbed his boots and walked softly through the kitchen, pulled his new hat from the rung, and took care to make no sound as he closed the door.

It took but a moment to pull his boots on and head for the corral and Dandy. Before saddling Dandy, he took what MacDonald called a corn knife, but he knew it as a machete from the Mexicans that had drifted through the Comanchero camp.

It was fine to be on Dandy's back again. He kept the pace slow until over the small, rolling hill, and then he kicked Dandy and flapped the reins. He was headed away from Schmidt's Corner and away from the way he had ridden in. Whatever land lay before him would be new. He suspected MacDonald would think he went back the way they came in because it would be familiar and the money for the reward might be there. Of course, he might think different with that murder charge. It didn't matter; he was on his own again with a fine horse and a fine, new grey hat and the morning was grand for riding and elation surged through him.

And then the screaming inside his head started. It was the wail of a lost, bereaved creature, overwhelmed with grief, or in the throes of dying. As the screams built into a crescendo, he realized it was his mother screaming at the loss of her child. He pulled Dandy to a halt. For a moment the screams abated to an anguished moan and then the screeching built again. He pulled

Dandy around and headed back more rapidly than he had left the ranch. To hell with MacDonald, he'd think of something.

Grey morning light was seeping over the earth as Dandy pounded into the yard. His mother came running from the kitchen, her arms outstretched towards him. He left the saddle in one smooth jump, threw the reins on the ground, and enfolded her in his arms. "I'm sorry, Mama, I'm sorry," the words spilled out over and over again. "I won't run again, I promise. Don't cry."

Anna had thrown her arms around him and was kissing his face and stroking his arms and hands as though he were still a baby. Her words were in German and this time they made sense. She called him her heart, her lovely child, repeating the words over and over.

Lorenz heard the slap of boots behind him and tried to disentangle himself. "Uh, Mama, I'm going to have to face him," he whispered.

He turned and there was MacDonald stuffing his shirt into his britches. His face and eyes were hard. Gone was the amusement that danced in his eyes and the slight smile on the lips.

Lorenz had already decided he would do things the big man's way no matter what happened, but now he wondered if it were too late. He unbuckled his belt and held it, straight arm out, and went into a litany of his sins. "I disobeyed your rules. I ran, I touched Dandy and a weapon, and I made Mama cry and scream, and it probably scared Mina half-silly, and she's probably cryin' too." He stopped. Something was wrong. MacDonald had stopped coming at him and was looking at him with puzzlement in his eyes and his brow half-way knitted.

"Where's Mina?" asked Lorenz. "Y'all didn't leave her alone and afraid in the house? Why ain't she out here?"

"Mina tis still sleepin'," said MacDonald in a controlled voice. "Just how far did ye ride, laddie? Dandy seems to be a bit lathered."

Lorenz hesitated and realized that he should not have been able to hear his mother, yet he had. Should he lie about it? "Ah dunno," he whispered.

"A mile, mayhap two?"

Lorenz took a deep breath. "Maybe, no, uh, no more than that, maybe."

"Do ye ken why Mina still slumbers?"

Lorenz shook his head no, and MacDonald continued. "She slumbers because yere mither made no sound whilst she screamed in yere head." He swung his ire on his wife.

"Ye kenned, Anna, ye kenned that he would hear ye!"

Anna yanked her head up, moved closer to Lorenz, and answered in German, stressing each word. "I did not know. I hoped he would hear me, and prayed he would come home."

MacDonald shook his head. "And how, my sweet one, did ye ken he would hear?"

"I did not say I knew he would hear me. I said I hoped," Anna snapped back in German.

"Ye are equivocating. Ye could pray he would return because ye kenned that he would hear. Now, I ask ye again to tell me how ye kenned."

Anna drew her lips together. Lorenz wasn't sure just how he understood this conversation in both German and English, but he could hear them both, and they were arguing about him as though he wasn't there, except his mother reached out and grasped his hand as though protecting him.

Her chin lifted high, Anna replied, "Because even when he was four years old, he could use his mind. Daniel is four years older and bigger and stronger than Lorenz, but he could not win in a fight when Lorenz was mad. That's why I was screaming so loud at Lorenz that horrible day. I was afraid he would really hurt Daniel, and Daniel could not protect himself. Instead, he just lay there, prone on the floor while Lorenz kept hitting him.

When you first brought Lorenz home, he tried to enter my mind like Mr. Lawrence, and I would not let him."

MacDonald's voice filled with bewilderment. "And ye did nay warn me?"

"Why would I warn you? You are capable of defending your mind."

"I am nay thinking of myself. What of Mina, or for that matter, young James? Did ye wish to see them harmed?" His voice grew louder.

Lorenz had been listening to their exchange in wonder, but now he protested. "Y'all leave her alone. Ah wouldn't hurt Mina or James. Ah'd wait till he growed up."

MacDonald looked at Lorenz, his voice harsh. "Laddie, be still a wee bit longer." He swung his gaze back to his wife. "Ye may as well speak in English as I believe he has kenned every word ye have said."

Anna closed her eyes and moaned. Then she blinked them open, her face hard. "I did not vant him to be like his father and murder his own."

"He already has his fither's abilities. Ye canna stop him from using his mind." MacDonald half shouted. "I can, however, teach him to use it correctly."

"I vill not have du talking in your minds in my house. It vill be outside." Anna was not shouting but her voice was as hard as her face.

MacDonald took a deep breath. "Thank ye, my love." He turned his attention back to Lorenz. "And so, ye have tried walking in your mither's mind. Can ye tell me what happened when ye did?"

Lorenz wasn't sure where this was leading except to be a reason to tell him to leave. His mother hadn't relaxed her grip on his hand. It was like she was afraid he would run if she did. His looking at either face wasn't telling him much except that both were in a contentious mood. He was in a world of shit and it looked like it didn't matter whether he told the truth or lied. He decided to try truth. "It was like she slammed a door, and I ran straight into it."

MacDonald gave one of his tight smiles. "And what happened when ye tried to walk in my mind?"

"Sometimes nothin', sometimes I'd see things, and other times it was like just grey clouds."

MacDonald's eyes widened. "Ye surprise me, laddie. I shall pay more attention to what ye are doing. Now, one more thing, just why did ye run after yesterday and calling yereself a bear cub, or twas it something ye planned all along?"

Once more, Lorenz tried looking at both faces, but MacDonald's was still hard and Mama was not smiling. "Dunno," he muttered. Why didn't MacDonald just knock him down or tell him to get? What were all the questions for? And how did he tell him that?"

"I dinna believe ye," said MacDonald. "They may be wrong, or they may be devious, but ye have reasons for what ye do."

Lorenz looked straight at him and decided to hell with it. He might as well get the whole thing over with. "Ah can't tell y'all with Mama standin' right there."

"Then show me in your mind."

Lorenz brought up the scene and glared at MacDonald. "I wasn't waitin' for that to happen. I'd thought y'all was different. It was all a lie." Bitterness laced through Lorenz's words.

MacDonald stepped back as though hit. "Ye Gods, laddie. Ye have it all wrong. Did this nay happen when ye did something for a man to be proud of?"

"Yeah, that's what made it so dirty."

MacDonald shook his head. "Anna, please tell Lorenz what language ye think in."

Anna unfolded her lips which had been pursed in disapproval and answered, "Deutsch."

"Aye, yere mither thinks in German because twas her first language. Once she has formed her thoughts, she must put the words into English. So tis with me. Whilst my language tis very similar to English, my customs differ. First I think of the customs of my land and then use the customs of this land."

"That ain't making any sense. Y'all had your hand on me. Are y'all tellin' me they do things like that in Scotland?"

"And when did I say I twas from Scotland?"

"Well, y'all didn't, but Martin said folks there talk like y'all."

MacDonald's half-smile was back. "Laddie, if there tis anyone from Scotland near me, I keep my mouth shut, or run in the opposite direction. Should they ere hear me speak, they would ken I twas nay born there and they would ask questions."

"That don't change nothin'."

"Laddie, in my land, we dinna use the word adoption. We use the word, claiming. Because of my position, ere I could claim ye as part of my House, I would need to go before the Guardians of the Realm and request their permission. If the Guardians and their Counselors agree, then permission tis granted, and ye would become part of my House with all the rights of someone from the House of Don, but first, ye must go through the Claiming Rite."

"On a given date, we would both appear before the Guardians, and we would both be nude neath our capes. We would then stand before the Guardians, remove our capes and the ceremony would begin. I would put my hand on ye and claim yere seed for my House, and ye would put yere hand on me and claim my seed as yere own. Tis very moving."

Anna gasped. Lorenz shook his head in disbelief. "People are watchin?"

"Aye, but the Guardians of the Realm nay rule here so we must abide by this land's laws. To change yere name to mine and give ye the rights of inheritance, we must go before a Judge and have him say that ye are Lorenz MacDonald, but when I think of ye as my own, I think in my own way. As long as we live here, I must go by yere laws as mine have nay legality."

"Where y'all from?" Lorenz half whispered the question. He had seen enough in MacDonald's mind to know that wherever the land, it was frightening; somehow more frightening than watching a man slow skin another.

MacDonald straightened and gave a bow. "I am Llewellyn, Maca of Don, from the planet Thalia. We, that tis my world, were overrun by forces from the planet of yere biological fither. That however tis a very long tale, far longer than the one I told last night, and there were a few discrepancies in the telling."

"Is that why y'all told that story? Hell, y'all don't think ah'm goin' to believe people fly?" He swung his free hand upward.

A huge smile lit MacDonald's face. "We more than fly, laddie. We go betwixt stars. Yere mither has seen the *Golden One* that I came in, and she can attest to its existence."

Anna nodded her head when Lorenz glanced at her. "I don't believe it."

"Then ye need to go with me and see what I am speaking about. Ye can touch it, and ye twill be able to see and hear. Tis a far better way to learn. Do ye agree, my counselor?"

Anna's face had relaxed, but she was not in total agreement. In German, she said, "It puts you at risk."

MacDonald smiled at her. "Ye might as well speak in English," he reminded her. "Nay, I dinna believe the laddie twill betray me." He looked at Lorenz and said, "Ye twill nay betray me when ye find fault only with the flying and nay the two hearts."

The flush and denial vanished from Lorenz's face and he considered. Did MacDonald know? Had Mama told him, and if so why? Had MacDonald known he was a freak all this time? In desperation he looked at his mother. Why wasn't she saying something, or did she feel there was nothing to say?

The smile on MacDonald's face wasn't exactly a leer, but his eyes narrowed as he reached up and loosened the buttons of his shirt and underwear, exposing the broad, hairless chest.

"Listen, if ye dare."

This was a different challenge, and an unexpected one. He had not wanted to be that close to the man, but curiosity overrode his reluctance and he stepped nearer, sucked his breath in, removed his hat, and laid his ear against the chest. It was unmistakable: two hearts were beating inside.

His world spun and he forgot his fear, and leaned against MacDonald. Years of being called a freak, or the people in camp making a cross at the sight of him weakened his resolve. This man knew, he could understand and help him, and no one, no man, he knew could take MacDonald down.

He knew from the words that had been said, it couldn't be, but he had to ask. He looked up at the man and choked out, partially in desperation, hoping it would be true, "Are you my pa?"

"Nay, laddie. He tis a Justine by the name of Toma. He took the name Thomas Lawrence in this land. His kin did nay ken where he journeyed, and after my mither destroyed their planet and killed most of the Justines, they needed him back to replenish their shrunken gene pool." Laughter edged his words. "For all their genius, cloning, duplicating a perfect Justine tis nay possible, and they are even slower than Thalians to reproduce."

Lorenz felt his world swaying. MacDonald was running his hand up and down Lorenz's back and he was smiling gently. Lorenz could feel the tension building inside, the nerves in his right thigh twitching, and sensations he could not understand scraping at his mind.

"'Tis all right, laddie. Ye twill ken in time." He ruffled Lorenz's hair and took the hat from Lorenz's hand and placed it on Lorenz's head. "Now tis time we stilled the lowing of that cow and feed the stock whilst yere mither makes us a fine breakfast."

He smiled in his satisfied way. "And put that damned belt back on and get the buckets. I'll attend to yere beastie."

Lorenz pulled in a lungful of air as the crises had passed, and blurted out, "Uh," he began tentatively, "y'all forgot about that weapon up on my saddle, and I, well, I took this too." He dug out a small pocket knife and held it out.

MacDonald looked down at the knife and chuckled. "Dinna tell me ye twere about to attack me with that. Keep it. Ye may need it sometime." He turned, took Dandy's reins, and headed towards the barn.

Anna leaned over and kissed Lorenz's cheek. "Come, there's vork to do."

Chapter 10

The Golden One

It was a fine morning for riding and they covered the distance to the nearby foothills in less than two hours. It took another thirty minutes or so to ride up into the flat area back against one of the rocky up thrusts. Lorenz was surprised to find the ground almost barren of grass, chaparral, or trees. They left the horses in the shade of the one remaining tree. The rock rose in the form of a small mountain. MacDonald stopped at the side a huge boulder. At either side of the boulder, mountain laurel fought to survive and small trees struggled for a foothold in the rock. Mostly it looked like the vegetation had lost.

MacDonald braced his back against the boulder, set his legs, and pushed. His face began to flush, but gradually the boulder moved, scattering small rocks and dust in its wake as the opening to a wide cavern spewed out musty air.

"Now we hoof it," he announced.

The interior was cooler and the earth smell hung in the air. Several feet into the cave, MacDonald moved a rock from a ledge and extracted an implement. Lorenz couldn't see what it was until suddenly a beam of light flowed out from the front of it.

"What the hell is that?"

"Tis a small lowe for seeing our way. It works like a torch."

This was something new to puzzle on. It was no torch he had ever seen. There was no lit smoking end and no smell of oil or wood. Lorenz considered asking for the thing in MacDonald's fist, and thought the better of it. He was in awe of the thing. They walked down a wide, sloping ramp that looked like it had been gouged out to create a tunnel large enough to for two trains to pass through, but where had the debris gone? There were no huge piles of dirt outside and yet, this could be no natural thing. The earth and air seemed to close around him, and he stifled an urge to turn and run. He wouldn't let this man think him a coward.

They kept walking downward, drawing ever closer to some dim light. They finally hit level ground and entered an immense chamber filled with golden light. MacDonald pointed at the huge golden shape. "There she tis, the craft that brought me from the current Justine home to this world. What do ye think?"

Lorenz was speechless, his grey eyes were large and he almost forgot to breathe. Like MacDonald, this thing, this machine was totally alien at first sight. It also glowed in the darkness with an intensity that belied its underground existence. MacDonald threw his arm around Lorenz's shoulders and walked him closer the machine.

"Mama's seen this thing and been in it?"

"Aye."

"She's one gutsy woman."

"She tis a magnificent woman," he agreed. "Ere we enter, I shall tell ye a bit more of my tale." His voice, low and rumbling, filled the space left in the cavern. "The story I told two nights ago twas mainly true, but embellished for the wee one. There twas nay love affair betwixt a warrior Princess and a warrior Prince. My people twere threatened by the Justines and their Kreppie allies. We massed an attack against them. We thought it would be a surprise, but they twere waiting for us in their *Golden Ones*. We had over five hundred crafts. They twere nay as large as this craft, but they twere sufficient to carry almost a million of our people. Too many Thalians died that day, and my mither and elder (ye twould say uncle) twere captured."

"The Justines used their medics to wither my elder's right arm and take his seed. Twas a huge tragedy as he and his counselor had nay wee ones yet, and the current Maca of Don, though eld, had insisted on being with the fleet and his ship disintegrated under the Justine attack My elder fither (grandfither to ye) and his counselor, my elder mither (grandmither) went down with him That meant that the new Maca must come from my mither or my elder, her brither."

"Since the House of Don tis a warrior class and fought the Justines bitterly, the Justines decided to remove my mither to a place of exile where she could nay ever mingle with Thalians again. They kenned that she twas a far more dangerous opponent than her brither." Lorenz felt dizzy. Some quality of the man's voice seemed to scrape at every nerve ending in his body.

"The Justines fear the sexuality of the Thalians, so they used eight Kreppies as her guards and their eldest Justine to oversee Mither at a compound on a far asteroid. In their wisdom they felt this would contain Mither." A low chuckle came for the huge throat. "It did nay."

"In his loneliness, the Justine began to show Mither the workings of the *Golden One* on the Justine premise that an inferior race could nay learn to pilot it. Whilst he taught her, he twas nigh her. The Justines's fear of our sexual abilities tis correct. Eld as he twas, the Justine found himself in bed with Mither. Somehow she convinced him how much better it would be if he twere young once more. He took the draught that all Justines take to repair the ravages of age." MacDonald looked at Lorenz and smiled. "If I am nay wrong, tis something that ye and I shall be able to do, but I digress."

"The Justine was indeed young again, but since he twas pass the age of safe rejuvenation, it weakened him physically and mentally. Whilst on the *Golden One*, away from the prying eyes of the Kreppies, Mither bedded him. When he collapsed on her in his completion, she snapped his neck."

"She killed him?" Lorenz was awed.

"Oh, aye, that she did. She then started the *Golden One* and destroyed the asteroid and all that twas on it. Her plan twas simple; practice until she had total control over the craft, and then destroy the last of the Justines. Twas whilst she learned to maneuver the *Golden One* that it became apparent that she twas pregnant."

"To shorten, this tale, I twill condense the rest. She managed to continue learning and to birth me. She also evaded the Kreppie ships around Thalia and left me and a crystal with a trusted friend. 'Tell my brither to use his head when ye give him my wee one,' were her instructions. She then flew the *Golden One* into the Justine home world, destroying all that dwelt there and herself, as there twas nay a second craft as in last night's tale."

"For awhile this eased the restrictions on our world and that of our allies, the Brendons, and gave Mither's friend the opportunity to give me and the crystal to my elder and his counselor. My elder did use his head. He claimed I twas child of one our relatives reduced to poverty due to the occupation. Twas our misfortune that the Justines were able to regroup by calling in all the Justines from the other planets they administered and occupied a large asteroid that had served as a gathering place for the Justine League to meet with the other worlds without the inferior beings coming to their now gone world. Their rule over Thalia and Brendon grew harsher as they employed the Kreppies as their enforcers of Justine dictums. They deemed this necessary after a Justine died in the mines of Thalia's Ayran."

"My elder, Lamar and his counselor Beatrice, Lass of Betron, provided a safe haven of love and learning. When I reached the age of twenty I did nay have my full height, but I twas nearing the age for the first bedding. This could nay be arranged without revealing my heritage. Like the young here, I twas ready to rebel against authority and did so by challenging for a bedding in the arena." A swift smile came over his face. "I challenged the daughter of the Guardian of the Realm and won."

"Y'all fought a woman?"

"Aye, that tis our way, however, the Justines had instituted the rule of the Sisterhood which tis meant to castrate the males of Thalia. They truly fear us. Beauty, the lass I fought insisted I be scanned for drugs. They discovered my two hearts. I did nay even get to bed her." Bitterness laced through his voice. "And they sent me to the new Justine world to remain under their keep. I twas nay allowed to mingle with Thalians again, nay have I seen my elder since." Granite lines etched his face as his voice hardened.

"How did y'all get away?"

"When I neared fifty-five, Ricca kenned that I too could walk in minds and communicate without speaking. The Justines nay believe this possible in a mutant. That tis what they call some-one born of two different species, and twill call ye the same."

"To give them credit, they had continued my education and Ricca taught me to use my mind correctly, or I might have killed their Kreppie attendants. Thalians reach their maturity between thirty and thirty-five, although we continue to build muscle mass until we are about one hundred or more."

Lorenz's face was a study of disbelief and yet, he knew this was a true telling, but he couldn't imagine anyone larger than the man standing beside him.

"There had nay been a birthing in the Justine remnants since they lost their planet. They decided that they needed another, younger Justine. They launched a search party for Toma, yere biological fither. The searchers consisted of one adult Justine, six Kreppies, and they included me. Instinct told me this twas but a ploy to remove me to some far planet where I would nay be a tes-tament to how wrong their biological science tis. Since I should nay exist, there nay ere could be a child from my beddings. They twere so certain of their own scientific beliefs that they did nay even test my seed. Ere we wed, I had told yere mither, there would be nay wee ones." The thought of Mina brought a smile to his face.

"They just left y'all here?"

"Nay. When this planet appeared on the viewers, Ricca, the Justine, did a search for an area that may possess people of like physical appearance. Scotland and Ireland have more red-heads than elsewhere so Ricca took me as a servant and left the *Golden One* behind the dark of the moon."

"The Justine was my sole teacher on the journey, but it came in spurts. I twas about sixty-four years of age when we first went to Ireland. It twas in the year of 1842 for this planet's reckoning and there twas a great hunger in the land. Ricca foolishly went into the countryside, taking me along. A mob bent on securing food came at us. He and I had discovered our minds could nay penetrate into the minds of some of this land's people. He could nay control the mob. Ricca stood there as a superior being, pointing his finger at the oncoming men, sending out his mental command to halt. They killed him."

"What did y'all do?

MacDonald glanced down, a look of mild surprise on his face at the question. "I lifted my heels and ran. Do I look like a fool?"

Lorenz forgot that he was several feet underground, standing by a machine that couldn't exist, listening to a life story beyond belief, and smiled, his grey eyes sparkling.

"No, sir, y'all don't."

MacDonald smiled at Lorenz. "Tis now time to enter the craft. Have ye figured out how we twill do that?"

Lorenz shook his head, a head that was swimming with a tale more bizarre than any he could ever imagine, but there was one thing he had to know. "How many people died?"

"When? Where?"

"When your maw-mother blew up the other place."

"Oh, there twas about one million Justines living there. As I said, they are an eld race, and their births few." He smiled with a certain satisfaction. "Do ye have any more questions ere we go into the craft?"

Lorenz shook his head no. He did have more questions, like how did MacDonald get this machine and get rid of the Kreppies, but wasn't sure how to ask. At least his breathing was steady and he hadn't panicked.

"This tis how we open it," and MacDonald laid his hand on the side of the golden metal. What appeared to be seamless now rolled back. A huge bay area opened as a wide ramp settled to the ground.

"Can I do that?"

"Nay, it does nay ken ye, but we twill change that in time." He led the way up the ramp. Once they were inside, he leaned over and touched a panel. The entire area lighted and the ramp rolled up and the panel slid shut. Lorenz whirled and faced where the opening had been, panic clawing at his throat and guts. He swallowed it down, forcing his breathing to remain even. Behind him the big man chuckled.

"Now we are safe even though someone should discover the cave opening."

MacDonald pointed to two smaller golden crafts and another piece of machinery that Lorenz could figure no earthly use for, but it was imposing in its height and girth. "There are the machines I used to create this haven. The smallest one can be used to take us out the opening of the cave and up into the atmosphere. There ye may look down on this earth. Neither of them, however have enough power to carry us back to my world. For that we would need this one, but I canna navigate the stars."

Wonderment filled Lorenz's eyes as he looked at him. "Y'all would take me up sometime, to see what it's like?"

MacDonald's smile widened. "Oh, aye, that I twill." He led the way toward one of the walls. "We twill take the lift up to the captain's center, and I twill show ye a bit more of the craft, let ye listen to the history of my universe, and then I twill take a decent cleansing."

Lorenz followed in silence. At least he hadn't threatened to make him bath again. His curiosity and sense of wonder increased at every step. The place was cool with air coming from somewhere, and the golden walls and light blue walkways seemed to glow. He sensed no danger, but this place was unlike anything that he had words to describe. "It's big," was totally inadequate. The panic increased when the small room they entered slid a door shut behind them. He felt trapped. Was this some sort of cage? MacDonald was not concerned. He pushed a panel that Lorenz had missed seeing, and an almost inaudible hum filled his brain.

"We are going up to the top floor. This craft tis as high as a three or four story home. The lower tis for storage, the middle contains the medical and horticulture areas, the latter means vegetation for cleansing the air we are breathing, and the mechanical means of supplying the air, food, and energy to sustain the craft and life. The upper floor tis for the guidance system of the craft and contains the quarters for the crew." MacDonald touched one finger to the panel again, and the door slid open.

"How does it do that?"

"Tis run by an energy current. Yere world tis just now beginning to learn its ways, and the energy tis called electricity." MacDonald was moving with ease, a powerful body moving around the strange craft with complete confidence in his abilities. He swept his arm outward, pointing directly in front of where they entered. "There, at the front, ye can see what tis their type of desk and chair. That tis the commander's chair, and tis where ye can look outward and see all about. The screens set as 'windows' show information on your surroundings and yere capabilities.

Ye can set course to where ye go and issue commands to take out any obstacle, if ye ken the math."

Lorenz decided to say nothing. It was smarter just to listen and try to learn.

MacDonald looked down at him. "We'll visit the quarters now, and ye can listen to the crystals telling of the different beings whilst I shower. Ye can save the questions for when I finish."

They walked down a corridor and past a large open area filled with black and gold pulsing walls, tables, what were probably chairs, and huge covered daybeds with backs. The sitting furniture seemed to be covered with some sort of unrecognizable fabric. It looked soft, not like the harsh horsehair sofa in Rity's house or the stiff brocade stuff he'd seen in Red's whorehouse. He shook his head as MacDonald pressed his hand against an outline of a door and it slid open. It was hard to believe what he was seeing, and he wondered how his mother had handled it.

This room was smaller, and contained furniture much like he had seen, except there was far less of it. It looked like there was some sort of small room to the right, and as the door slid back in place he could see a ledge with one of those fancy chairs covered with lighter, blue fabric shoved underneath the ledge. The floors were a golden shimmering color like the machine. MacDonald steered him to the chair.

"Ye could have listened to this at the command station, but tis quite comfortable here, and I can take my cleansing." He pulled out the chair and flipped up part of the ledge. Something that looked like a dirty mirror was in front of his eyes and below some sort of slanted board with buttons and symbols inscribed on the buttons. MacDonald poked away at the symbols and the dirty mirror blackened. Lorenz jumped when he heard someone talking, but could not place the language nor where the speaker was located. It was as though the person doing the talking was in front of him, but no one was there.

"Steady, laddie, that tis but the beginning of the history ye are about to learn. The voice tis part of it. All has been prerecorded. I ken that this does nay make sense yet, but it twill."

The dirty mirror changed, and now there was a man's torso and face speaking that strange language. MacDonald punched at the button symbols and suddenly the voice was using Mac-Donald's inflections of speech. MacDonald held down a button and the screen stood still and the voice stopped. "We need to have the speech in yere language. Tell the screen 'this tis our alphabet' and then recite it just as ye have done at home. The words twill be in yere language, and ye twill be able to ken what tis being said."

Lorenz looked at him and shook his head. MacDonald smiled and gently pushed him into the chair. "Go ahead. Ye ken the letters, and dinna use the slurred language ye so oft do. Ye speak better than that."

It was darn hard to fool him. He might as well do as told and hear what this thing was going to say, and Lorenz obeyed. It was like the mirror started over as it changed to black and the man reappeared. It was then that Lorenz noticed the man's eyes were copper colored with golden circles around the pupils.

He looked up at MacDonald and asked, "Is that my pa?"

"Does it matter?"

"No, just wondered."

"Tis nay yere fither, but tis a Justine. They do tend to resemble each other. I twill listen with ye, and then ye may watch it again while I take that cleansing."

MacDonald removed his finger and the seated red-haired man, dressed in some sort of long, flowing material, started speaking in English. "Welcome. Since you are being allowed to hear this, our advance party has deemed you worthy of contact. This is a brief synopsis of our universe and the beings that dwell here."

"We are the Justines, a family of bipeds who have attained the highest evolved level in our quadrant. While we are able to vocalize with lesser beings, our own communications, when we reach a certain maturity, are mental. We learn speech to communicate with other beings and not frighten them."

"Physical work is no longer necessary as our science and technology sustains us. Therefore, we devote our time to meditation, study, and striving to benefit those who have not yet attained our level. The following will introduce you to the known beings in our galaxy."

"The first beings we will discuss are the Krepyons, who are our allies and administrators throughout our system." The screen showed a slight male creature with light, brown skin, brownish hair, brown eyes, and it looked like scales on both cheeks. "This is the male of the species. They usually devote their time to business, the mundane activities of living, or the military. They average about five feet six inches in height, and weigh about one hundred and thirty pounds to one hundred and seventy.

"The next is the female. Please note the double row of mammary glands." Lorenz's mouth had opened in a wide O and his grey eyes grew wide. The female, like the male, was nude except for bindings around the lower genital area, and looked much like the male with longer hair. "The Krepyons are the only biped beings with double mammary glands out of the four known groups. The females are noticeably shorter and lighter than the Krepyon males. They usually give birth to four at a time. We have been working with the Krepyons to limit the females to one birth. Their population at this time is unacceptable for their available living space. We have been moderately successful and have not had to implement harsher methods."

"While they are not capable of communicating with their minds, they are very susceptible to ours. We are hopeful that within the next one thousand years this trait will evolve into a viable ability to communicate mentally with us.

"The next beings are the Brendons. They are the best horticulturalists in the galaxy. Their entire planet, except for the Polar Regions, the areas dedicated to housing, and the necessary manufacturing sites, has been cultivated into one huge garden. Some of their advances with growing plant life aboard interstellar flights have been implemented in our space ships. Their vegetation and ours are not always compatible."

A stockier male figure filled the screen, his hair a dark, greenish color, and he wore no clothing. "Like the plant life they cultivate, the hair of the Brendons will turn to a red or an orange hue as they advance into old age. They have a medium height of five feet, seven to nine inches. Their women are usually an inch or two shorter. Both genders usually weigh about one hundred and fifty pounds."

Lorenz blinked his eyes at the woman on the screen. Some sort of cloth covered the breast area, but the breasts were not sagging and he felt himself growing hard. It seemed hair color wasn't going to make much difference in attraction. He was afraid to look at the man standing next to him, and his tongue remained still.

"When we first made contact with the Brendons, we hoped they would be able to communicate on a higher level. These are a gentler community of beings, more interested in science than warfare. They are able to communicate on a certain level with their plant life, yet they cannot mindspeak. Once again, perhaps a cultural maturing will lead them into emulating us. Unfortunately, during the last century, the Brendons allied themselves with the Thalians and rejected our teachings. They are currently under our benevolent care supervised by the Krepyons."

MacDonald could keep silent no longer. "Their arrogance is beyond belief."

On the screen, there now appeared a jock-strapped man of immense muscular proportions. His black hair was cropped close and he turned his hairless body while clenching his fists and looking upward at a group of cheering people, a wide smile slitting his craggy face below a jutting nose. Blood trickled downward from the nose, past the smiling lips, and onto the chest. "This is a representation of a Thalian male. He has just won a fight in their so-called dining arena in front of the Guardians of the Realm, the ruling elite of Thalia. Thalians revel in the strength of both men and women. The males reach a medium height of six feet, two inches, and the women are but a scant inch shorter, if that. Their weight, depending on their height and status in the hierarchy, will vary from two hundred pounds to over three hundred."

MacDonald paused the recitation. "The Thalian tis Jason, Lad of Ayran. He twas about one hundred and twenty years of age at the time. The next twill be my mither. She twas one hundred and one the day this twas recorded. The bar she tis bending tis our metal, nay the soft iron that I bent in the tavern yesterday." He released his finger.

Lorenz crossed his arms and gripped his biceps. This whole show was unbelievable, and he had a hunch it was going to become more fantastic.

The woman was as muscular as the man, and she too was clothed in a g-strap. A small strip of cloth wound around the breast area. Unlike the Brendons and the Krepyons, her breasts were minimal, hardly expanding the material. Her biceps, however, bulged as she bent and twisted the bar and then held it aloft, a wide smile showing a neat row of white teeth. Her dark hair bobbed around her ears and her flushed face was MacDonald's face.

"We once hoped the Thalians were evolving to mindspeak. Most of the Thalians have dark hair and dark eyes, but there are two of their 'Houses' that have a lighter, almost reddish-brown head of hair. Thalians can exchange emotions with their touch. This ability should be able to grow into the ability to exchange ideas mentally. Their philosophy of strength and war precludes this intellectual achievement. To prevent their ability to wage war, we have instituted a new governmental order in Thalia. It is still based on their fundamental rule of the Houses, but we have appointed the female of the Thalians to control most aspects of their day to day governing. The Krepyons insure that our precepts are followed. Thalia's manufacturing and military have been nullified.

"We are working with the Krepyons to bring order in our galaxy, and the efforts are beginning to show fruit." Here Mac-Donald snorted. "The following will show you different scenes from the different planets."

MacDonald paused the voice and images. "Do ye have any questions?" He looked down at Lorenz whose arms were crossed over his chest, and a hard, puzzled look on his young face.

"How do y'all tell the difference between Thalian men and women when they have clothes on?"

"Believe me, laddie, we can tell." MacDonald chuckled.

"Why can't I call y'all pa?" He was still looking straight ahead, but his jaw jutted outward.

MacDonald's eyes narrowed. "Why are ye quibbling over that now?"

Lorenz jerked his head around and stood. "I ain't quibbling, or whatever that means. I just want to know why it has to be your way."

"Because I am yere fither!" The big man roared back.

For a moment Lorenz forgot to speak and then asked, "But I thought y'all said Toma was."

"He tis yere biological fither. I am the fither the good Gar has seen fit to give ye, and why can ye nay accept that?"

"I dunno, Papa. I figured y'all wouldn't want me."

MacDonald shook his head in wonderment. "Dear, Gar, laddie, why?"

"Because Red wanted something from me as payment. He just didn't say what. From what y'all said before, it sounds like y'all want me because I've got two hearts and can fight the Justines when I'm grown."

"Ye twill be able to go with me because the two hearts twill enable ye to live long enough. In truth, laddie, I dinna ken when I twill ever learn to navigate this ship back. Ye are wanted because ye should have been Anna's and mine, and I canna refuse what the good Gar has given. Do ye ken ye just called me Papa?"

"Yes, sir." Lorenz's grey eyes lighted and he smiled at Mac-Donald. "And y'all didn't knock me down. Can I ask another question?"

MacDonald's eyes bulged on that one and he bent down and laid both hands on Lorenz's shoulder. "Why would ye believe I would knock ye down if ye called me fither?'

Lorenz shifted his gaze and then turned to MacDonald. "Y'all really won't be ashamed to say I'm yours?"

"Dear Gar, laddie, why else would I adopt ye?"

Lorenz wet his lips and heaved a sigh. "Maybe 'cause I wanted to believe it so damn bad. I still want to ask questions, if it's all right."

MacDonald nodded and wondered what Lorenz would ask this time. "Aye, go ahead." His voice was gruff and he straightened.

"How big was your ma-mother?"

"She stood six foot-three. She twas as tall as her brither, Lamar, and she outweighed him and twas stronger. Truly, she twas a magnificent Thalian." His face and voice hardened. "Someday, when I return, I twill stand in that arena again. I twill win the fight again, and bend the rod as Mither did."

"What happened to the, uh, Krepyons that were on this thing?"

"I killed them and let space take care of their bodies. They would have taken this ship and killed me."

Lorenz let out his breath and felt his stomach knot. He'd been mistaken. This man could kill as readily as the next when survival was at stake. "Y'all plan on getting rid of the Krepyons and the Justines, don't y'all?"

MacDonald's eyes were black obsidian. "Aye."

"Shit and I thought I was bad."

"What are ye talking about now?"

"I killed Zale and two others to get even. Y'all are planning on wiping out the whole lot just like your mother."

"Nay the whole lot. I twill only destroy their capacity to rule Thalia."

Lorenz looked up and asked, "Why don't y'all spend your time studying everything in here so that y'all can leave?"

"Because I have found my true love on this world, and we have a wee lassie, and now a laddie to raise. I canna leave till I learn to navigate between the star systems. I have nay flown a craft through the spacepath portals, nay have I the math to ken the course plotting, but I have been studying. Someday I twill need to take the *Golden One* out to practice and to re-energize its system, but it twill take years to learn what I must. Mither could command a ship like this as she had studied at our academy and twas a warrior with the title of Captain of the Fleet."

Lorenz thought for a moment. "That don't answer what I asked."

"Yere mither would nay go, and Mina would nay ever fit in my world. Ye are the only one who might travel with me and thrive on my world. So, till such time as ye and Mina are grown and my beloved Anna crosses into the Darkness, I remain here. Should I learn the handling of this craft, do ye think ye twill wish to leave this planet someday?"

A smile twisted Lorenz's face and the grey eyes lit with sparkles for he was young and adventure beckoned. "Yeah, I think I'd like that."

Chapter 11

Chalky

Anna placed the newly filled straw mattress on Lorenz's bed while MacDonald and Lorenz worked on the door jamb. From somewhere she had retrieved a wooden box and set it beside the bed. Inside it were placed the extra socks and summer underwear purchased at Uncle's store. On the top of the unpainted box, she had set a candle nestled inside an opened, cleaned, cut-off, and wallpaper decorated tin can. She surveyed the room critically after making the bed. "Ve vill buy du a proper chest vhen the money is a little better. Perhaps we can find a mirror at Kap's place. They may have an old one stuffed away somewhere."

Lorenz knew that Rity's bedroom had some kind of fancy chest and a dressing table with a chair. He wondered if Mama had one of those and then decided she probably didn't. Mama didn't look like she spent as much time as Rity in front of a mirror. Mama's hair was always pulled back in a bun, with wispy curls fighting to be free. He didn't think that would take nearly as long to fix as Rity's fancy curls.

MacDonald didn't seem to care one way or another about hair. After looking at the scenes of Thalia, Lorenz had finally been able to figure out which was male and female on Papa's planet, but you sure couldn't tell by their clothes and their builds. Most of the people had their hair short. He had more questions on their way home.

"How old did y'all say y'all were when y'all came here?"

"I twas about sixty-four."

"How old are y'all now?"

"Oh, I am about ninety of yere years. I would need to use the calibrator back at the craft to answer ye as far as an accurate year and month."

It all seemed so improbable. "I thought y'all were younger than Mama, and couldn't figure out why y'all married somebody older."

MacDonald laughed. "What would I do with a young lassie? She would prattle on about meaningless things. My Anna kens what tis important and what tis nay."

"But y'all picked somebody that is really tall, and most people can't help but notice, and they're afraid of tall women." It wasn't an argument. He was just trying to figure out why somebody like Papa would do something to draw attention to himself.

"And just what would I do with a wee lassie? I'd rip her apart or spend my nights wishing for a Thalian woman. None of which has anything to do with my feelings for yere mither. The good Gar determines who ye fall in love with."

Lorenz had spent some time dwelling on that answer. It seemed every time he asked a question it was answered, but the answer would mean more questions. He didn't even want to know why Papa would say Gar instead of Lord or God. He figured that answer would go on for a long time.

They had pounded pegs on the wall for his clean shirt and old trousers after carrying up the mattress. Now they were working on getting the hinges into the jambs. Lorenz couldn't figure out why all the fuss. A blanket hung over the door would work as well as anything. It wasn't like there was anyone else sleeping upstairs. It seemed these people were bent on working all day long. He didn't understand it.

His days with the Comancheros had seen intense bursts of activity to find meat, or break or set up camp, but pretty much the rest of the time had been spent doing nothing. His muscles were being used in ways he didn't even know they could be used.

MacDonald had set the hinge plate against the jamb and the door and now they were busy using a knife to cut out the extra wood. MacDonald had muttered something about a tool, but they'd use knives instead. It was hot up here, and water was streaking down the sides of both faces. Lorenz regretted not taking that shower at the *Golden One* when he had the chance. Besides the sweat, his hands were starting to cramp. At least he was trusted with a knife again. He stood for a moment and walked around, clenching and unclenching his hand while looking out the window. He noticed something moving way out in the distance. It looked like Rolfe, and then something switched in his brain and it wasn't Rolfe.

"Where's Daniel going to sleep when he gets here?" Lorenz shook his head. Damn, there he was talking nonsense again. "Why'd I say that? It's Rolfe coming in."

MacDonald stood and wiped his hands against his trousers, a bemused look on his face. "So ye have yere mither's kenning ability too. Ye are a surprise, laddie. According to Anna, ye, Daniel, and Margaretha twill all be here at Christmas."

He too, looked out through the window. "And yere eyes are very good. That tis friend Rolfe. Mayhap he has found the horse herd. It seems we twill finish the door another time."

MacDonald picked up the door and tools and set them against the hall wall. "Ye twill have to wait for another night to sleep in yere bed. Twill be the ground for us again this evening." He grinned. "Do ye think a new horse tis worth that?"

"I like sleeping outside, but I don't think y'all should tell Mama."

They took the stairs at a quick pace.

MacDonald explained to Anna, gave her a kiss, and then grabbed two rifles out of the cabinet set against the south wall of the main room and heaved one to Lorenz. "Dinna get too excited," he admonished as Lorenz caught the rifle with one hand and a huge smile lit his face. "Ye may need it."

He stopped at the springhouse long enough to grab a handful of dried beef before they headed to the corral for their horses. Rolfe rode in as they finished saddling the horses. He raised his eyebrows at the rifle stuck in Lorenz's scabbard, aimed a stream of tobacco at the ground, smiled, and said, "Du two got damn good eyes. The herd is above the ridge line just northeast of dot spring out on your east range. I'll get Martin and meet du two there. It looked like there vas about twenty in the herd. Ve're thinning them out."

"Aye, friend Rolfe, we'll meet ye and Martin there."

He looked back over towards the trail to the south leading to Arles. "Did ye ken what those vultures are circling?"

Rolfe glanced to the south. "Nein, too far off and out of my vay. They just started their circling the last half-hour or so. Vhatever it is, they ain't moved in. Du vant to see if it's a cow or something else?"

"Aye, we'll check it ere we strike out for the spring."

Rolfe nodded, clucked at his mount, and rode off.

"Y'all don't waste any time talking, do y'all?"

"Nay, why should we. We ken what the other tis about." They too mounted and rode out, waving at Anna and Mina as they did.

They rode slowly in the afternoon heat, heading south towards the vultures. It was strange the way the birds kept circling, but never landing. Something must be keeping them in check, or whatever they were after wasn't dead yet. They topped the rise and looked down at a mule munching at the grass, its improvised rope reins tangled in the small juniper defiantly growing in the prairie grass. A body was lying next to the stunted tree where little mounds of the grass had been pulled out. The mule looked up as they approached, backed away a couple of steps, lowered its head, and continued eating. The figure on the ground looked as gaunt as the mule, and the uncovered head sprouted sparse, straw-colored hair. MacDonald grabbed his canteen, and they both dismounted.

"Use your bandana to devise a head covering," he said to Lorenz, and then he bent and rolled the prone figure over, lifted his head and put the canteen to his lips. The face itself was flushed red, the lips cracked and drying. The youngster was maybe fourteen or a little older, and the eyebrows were as straw-colored as the hair.

"How bad is he?" asked Lorenz.

"He tis dehydrated, dried out," said MacDonald, "and he looks like he needs three squares worse than ye did."

The white eyelashes flipped upward and then closed while the boy's cracked lips sucked at the canteen. "If ye twill catch up that mule, I'll carry the lad on my saddle."

"Are we taking him back to Mama?"

"Aye, she twill tend him."

Anna's grey eyes widened at the sight of the slight, grime covered, sun burnt figure, and pointed to the daybed.

"'Twill ye need one of us to stay?"

"Nein, he vill be no trouble."

This time when they rode out, they went to the east by north-east. The ground did not rise rapidly, but seemed to swell in rolls: rolls of prairie spread with still green grass and longhorns feeding in the swales and draws. There was an occasional oak where water must flow close to the surface. It was, thought Lorenz, damn good range. The land started to rise into the foothills, and then leveled off again. Lorenz noted that there were signs of cattle and other animals browsing through here.

Someone had used a wagon coming into this area and Lorenz began to see why. The trees were thicker here and someone had logged them out creating more grass for the animals. The trail rose again, and then leveled off. They rode into a small back canyon with a spring at the base of the boulders climbing into a small mountain range. Willows and cattails flanked the spring area and small bushes fought against the rock to claim their right to live. A high fence built of oak and stone ran across the area, but the gate was wide open.

"We camp here," MacDonald announced. "We twill gather up some wood and wait for the Rolfes."

"Y'all have used this camp a lot."

"Oh, aye, that we have. This tis nay the first time we have rounded up horses and tis a great camp for hunting, branding, and cutting wood for the winter."

"Why didn't y'all just build one of your houses here?"

"Tis nay enough room for the other buildings. Even Herman saw the logic in that, though he hates the thought of a settled place. More important, during a long, rainless summer, this spring may dry out, whereas the spring at our home does nay."

They had closed the gate and were stripping the riding and camp gear from their horses. Lorenz couldn't figure it. Their houses were out there for all to see. Back in here, they could have stayed hidden. Then it came to him. They weren't hiding. They lived where they felt they would be most comfortable. "We didn't bring much in the way of eats," he said.

"Aye, but there tis coffee in my saddlebag and friend Rolfe twill bring in the rest."

MacDonald knew his friend well. The elder Rolfe threw down a huge haunch of beef when he and his oldest son arrived. Martin was grinning from ear to ear. "Good to see y'all. Now we get a chance to increase our stock."

Lorenz could think of lots of other reasons. Tonight he wasn't going to be studying or trying to read at a higher and higher level. He grinned back. It was good to be out in the open again.

They spread out early in the morning, following Rolfe's directions. Before the corals of the morning sunrise had dissipated they spotted the herd of mustangs. MacDonald used his powerful Zark to cut off the stallion while the rest bunched the remnants of the herd, and then drove them towards the spring and corral, not worrying if they lost a mare or two.

MacDonald and Rolfe worked together to close the gate behind the horses they had trapped and grinned at each other like a couple of boys. They dismounted and signaled the younger two to do the same.

"Du got the first pick this time," said Rolfe to MacDonald.

"I twill let the laddie make his choice." He turned to Lorenz. "Have ye seen one ye like? If nay, look closely."

Lorenz used his forearm to wipe the sweat off his brow and looked at the milling herd. Some were upset, some were snuffling at the water, and one mare was nuzzling her colt. The horses were in fairly good shape except for the rough, uncurried coat. These were range-hardened, agile horses, well-suited for chasing and avoiding the longhorns. None matched the picture he carried in his mind of the blooded horse he would have one day, but he picked as close as he could. "I'll take the brown mare."

"She tis a good choice. Tis your turn, friend Rolfe." Lorenz stood taller. He had Papa's approval.

Rolfe spat at the ground. "Hell, if du are spoiling your poy, might as vell do the same. Vhat won do du vant, Martin?"

Martin grinned and pointed out the roan with the white face and white stockings. "I'll take that one."

MacDonald and Rolfe chose the two they wanted and then decided they'd try to keep another two. If they found the time to rough break them, they could make a better profit in Arles when they trailed the herd in come fall. Lorenz and Martin were stationed at the gate, and the extra five horses driven out of the enclosure and shooed off to prevent any diversion for the six they meant to trail down to their ranches.

They used their ropes and voices to keep the six horses under control and kept a brisk, even pace to the MacDonald ranch. MacDonald easily swept ahead and opened the corral when they pounded in. After they watered their own mounts they headed for the house and a quick meal.

The kid that MacDonald and Lorenz rescued met them at the door carrying an empty bucket. Anna had given him Lorenz's old too-short trousers and the misshapen hat. Lorenz had discarded for his new one. His face was still sun burnt, but he seemed recovered. His pale blue eyes, however, were just as dull as when they found him and his mouth dropped at the size of MacDonald.

"What tis yere name, lad?"

The eyelids blinked furiously and no sound came from his mouth for a moment. Chalky was slight of build, slight of hair, and slight of mind, and he could but gawk at the huge form in front of him. "Hit's Chalky," he half-whispered.

"How did ye come to be out there by the wayside?"

Lorenz felt sorry for the kid. He knew the empty gut feeling Chalky must be experiencing while he was looking at the huge form asking questions when he didn't have an idea what would happen next or why they were being asked.

Mama came to Chalky's rescue. "He said he vas riding to Schmidt's Corner. His reason for doing so seemed confused, but that could be from the sun. Except for the carrying in vater, I've made him stay in most of the day." She raised her eyebrows to MacDonald, and he nodded his head.

Mina, by this time, had pulled at MacDonald's leg and was back up in his arms, hugging him. Anna reached for the child and continued talking. "There are plenty of beans and biscuits. Everything is ready."

After washing up, Lorenz got behind Chalky and guided him into the dining room. He figured that Chalky's former living conditions didn't include dining rooms, heaping tables, and people who spoke more than one language. He was feeling down-right sorry for him.

Anna practically pushed Chalky into a chair and plumped Mina into her high chair. Chalky looked at the table in total disbelief. Everyone had a plate and utensils, and the table held more than a bean pot. He sat in his chair as still as the stunned look on his face.

Like everyone else he bowed his head while grace was be-ing said and gave a low "Amen" when they finished. Then he sat there staring straight ahead. The Rolfe's ignored him, Anna looked concerned, and MacDonald's face showed no emotion, the amusement driven away.

Lorenz was sitting next to Chalky and plopped the beans and two biscuits on his plate. He wasn't sure about the milk, but poured it in the glass anyway. Anna smiled at her son, delighted at the compassion she knew he possessed and at his ability to display it.

"Ah doan want to take any food from yu all," Chalky stam-mered out. "Ah can wait until yu all are done and jest eat the leavin's." He face flamed even redder as he spoke and he bowed his head.

MacDonald looked up, completely dumbfounded, his eye-brows arching upward, and looked to his wife for a response to such a statement.

Anna smiled at her husband and answered for him. "Du don't need to vorry. There is plenty more. Eat now."

As before, the table became a jumble of people eating, talking, and passing dishes. This was not the fancy meal served when Lorenz came home, but the everyday fare for people working. Soon everyone finished, the chairs scraped back and shoved un-der the table as the men headed back to the corral to move Rolfe's horses to his ranch.

Chalky stammered out his thanks to Anna for taking him in, for Lorenz's cast off clothes, and the food. His face became a burning red and his dull, blue eyes filled with tears over her kindness.

Anna patted his shoulder. She turned to MacDonald who was setting Mina back down on the floor. "Du must make sure he gets to Schmidt's Corner without getting lost again."

MacDonald's eyebrows went skyward. "My love, have ye discovered why any would wish to go to Schmidt's Corner?"

She shook her head and replied in German. "It's something about his Ma'am told him to."

MacDonald sighed and answered in badly accented German. "That means there was no food for another mouth, and she has sent him on a pointless journey."

Trouble filled Anna's eyes. "If he makes it there, maybe he can go on to the north where there are more farms."

MacDonald shook his head. "The farmers there are as broke as the rest in this land. They are just now moving back in after the rebels chased them out. They won't have work for another, nay money to give." He saw the stubbornness settle on her face, gave in and returned to English. "Once we have the wild ones moved, I twill make sure he gets to Schmidt's Corner and has something to travel on." He followed the rest down to the corrals.

The others were busy saddling their mounts. Chalky had no saddle and was leading his aged mule out of the barn and was about to mount when MacDonald stopped him by saying, "Mrs. MacDonald tis worried that ye may become sun struck again. After we have driven the horses to the Rolfe's, we twill make sure ye get there safely."

Chalky looked confused and licked at his cracked lips. "My Ma'am said hit was real important for me to get there."

"We may need ye to help with the moving. Ye can open the gate when we have the horses caught up. Ye twill wait for my saying to open it and then ye twill ride with us. Tis a way of paying for yere vittles."

"Yes, suh." The thought of helping and paying for what he had consumed seemed to brighten Chalky's outlook.

Rolfe snorted, shot a stream of tobacco at the ground, and muttered something about, "und he'd better stay out of the damn way."

Lorenz was wondering how they were going to separate Rolfe's selection without losing the whole shebang of horses out of the corral and asked Martin. "How do y'all get just your horses?"

Martin grinned, "Y'all just watch me, Lorenz. Maybe y'all will learn something." He swung into the saddle, looked to see if the rest were ready, and shook out his rope.

The rest mounted up, and MacDonald leaned over and opened the gate. They entered the corral single file with Chalky remaining on the outside. MacDonald closed the gate and showed Chalky how the wire held the gate, bottom and top, then he turned to line up with the other two. Martin set the loop on the end of his rope into a swirling motion, kicked his heels into his horse's ribs, and set off at a slow trot.

Lorenz watched in disbelief as Martin's rope swung out and settled around the neck of the horse Mr. Rolfe had picked. Up until then, he'd figured only the vaqueros could handle a rope like that. Evidently it was something that other people did too. Rolfe had raced his horse along the roped one, and they brought it towards the corral rails. Rolfe handed over another rope and kept both his horse and the wild one under control. Lorenz saw how this would proceed and watched MacDonald pull up the rope from his saddle horn.

It was almost four in the afternoon when they had the wild horses corralled at Rolfe's and were watering their horses at the horse tank.

"Friend Mac, I buy du a drink," announced Rolfe. "Come in for a spell. Olga vill be glad to see du."

"Rest a wee bit and I twill be right back," MacDonald said to Lorenz and Chalky before the two headed for the ranch house.

Eons ago, this had been a high plain plateau gradually cut down by a deep river. The river cutting at the ground as the water sank deeper and deeper. Later the river meandered away from the first high bluffs it created and slowly shrank in size, leaving the bluffs standing guard over a flat, grass covered prairie. Rolfe had dug his home into the bluff and then built the front part from wood. The river was no longer a huge river, but a slow moving stream that occasionally rose during the seasonal rains. It was, however, deep enough to supply the household with water. A cistern augmented the supply during the dry months.

"Where did y'all learn to rope like that?" Lorenz asked Martin as they rubbed down their horses. "Can y'all teach me?"

Martin grinned. "Ja sure, but Uncle Mac can teach y'all the basics. He can rope some too. He just ain't as good as me."

Chalky was beginning to recover from seeing a second, complete homestead with a house, barn, outbuildings, and to his amazement, a chicken house with fencing around it to keep out the coyotes and other varmints. He was certain he had fallen in with the rich folks his Ma'am had talked about being one day. He felt getting rich might be harder than Ma'am made it sound, and he would not even be able to earn any money if he didn't get to Schmidt's Corner. He led his mule out of the shade of the tree and was ready to mount when Lorenz saw him and went over. "Papa said we'd take y'all into Schmidt's Corner. He ain't going to be long."

A stubborn look came over Chalky's face. "My Ma'am told me to git to Schmidt's Corner and warn that fellar about them really bad men. He might even pay me as much as a quarter for tellin' him."

Lorenz looked at him in disbelief. "Warn what feller?"

Chalky shut his mouth. "No, siree. Yu folks have been right kind, but I ain't saying, elseways yu all might git the money instead of me, and Ma'am told me to do it."

"If they're so bad, why'd they let y'all get away?"

Chalky grinned, "Cause they didn't see me. I saw 'em shoot the dawg an' ah knowed they wuz no good; 'specially when ah heard Ma'am and my little sister screaming. Ah wuz goin' to try and sneak in, but jest couldn't figure a way. Ah kept hid till Ma'am got outside to git some water. She tole me to go and warn this fellar theat built Schmidt's Corner."

"Y'all keep him here," Lorenz shouted to Martin and he ran for the house. No way could he explain to Martin what he'd seen in Chalky's mind, but he knew this was more than he could handle alone.

"Papa," he yelled as he ran across the shaded porch, "that boy, Chalky, he's talking about warning the fellow at Schmidt's Corner, and it's something bad." He was afraid to say more and sent a mental image of what he had seen and banged the flat of his hand against the door jamb.

He could see the bulk of MacDonald heaving himself up from the chair and heard the mug hit the table. "Aye, Lorenz, I hear ye. Friend Rolfe, I believe this needs my attention."

At the door, MacDonald grabbed his hat and rifle. Behind him Rolfe stood and muttered something in German, but followed his friend. He picked up his rifle as he went out.

As they hurried, MacDonald asked, "Now what tis this about?"

"Two gunmen came to wherever they live and Chalky was outside, but had sense enough not to go in after they shot the dog and his ma and sister were screaming." Lorenz was practically running to keep up with MacDonald's long strides. Rolfe followed more leisurely, but within earshot.

"When I start to question him, I dinna want ye to say a word."

Lorenz started to ask why, but thought the better of it. He knew they had to get back to Mama and couldn't see why the bother. Then he remembered Uncle, but figured, hell, he was a man full-grown, and there were other people in town.

Chalky's face had turned a deeper shade of red. Martin was blocking him from getting on the mule, and Martin didn't show any signs of letting him go until the three walked up.

"Lorenz tells me my brither-by-marriage may be endangered, and ye have information about it." MacDonald saw the blankness cover Chalky's face and he tried again. "It seems ye ken of someone who is planning to…"

"Shoot hell out of Schmidt's Corner," Rolfe finished the sentence for MacDonald.

Chalky looked from imposing man to imposing man and swallowed. "My Ma'am said hit wuz real important, but she said he might pay me a quarter."

MacDonald fished a quarter out of his hip pocket. "Here tis the quarter for the telling. If the information tis important enough, there may be more."

Chalky examined the quarter, scraped the rim, and bit down.

"What are ye doing? That tis nay gold." MacDonald was trying not to be impatient.

"Ah ain't never seed a quarter before," Chalky admitted. He pocketed the quarter and told his tale. "Well, suh, ah wuz where we get our water and ah heard two gents ride up. Ah wuz going up to see who it wuz as soon as I got the bucket filled. That's when ah heard my Ma'am scream and when ah looked they shot our dog. He warn't really our dog, but he hung around like maybe we'd have something to feed him. Doan know whar he came from, jest sorta showed up every now and then, but thar weren't no reason jest to shoot him like that, and they kept shootin' hit and laughin'. I jest knowed they'd do the same to me if ah went up thar so ah hid out. When they went back inside

207

my little sister started screamin' too. Hit wuz all ah could do to stay hid."

"That twas good thinking," said MacDonald, his lips pulled tight.

"Hit kept gettin' later and later and ah kept wonderin' what to do, and finally about dark Ma'am came out fer water. Hit was still light enough for me to see, and her face looked kinda swelled up and funny, but she said to pay no never mind. Ah wuz suppose to catch up the General, that's the mule over thar, and light out for Schmidt's Corner cause them two inside wuz gonna go there and kill the owner, and ah was to ride night and day and not stop fer anything, cause the man thar might pay me a whole quarter and even give me a job. She said they'd probably stay all night cause they wuz so drunk." Chalky took a deep breath and straightened his shoulders. It was one of the longest speeches he had ever made, and he had gone over and over everything in his mind so he wouldn't forget Ma'am's instructions.

MacDonald's face grew harder, but he kept his voice gentle. "How long twere ye on the trail?"

"Oh, ah rode all night and most of the day and rested jest a bit when General wouldn't move, and then all night and most of that day yu all found me. Ah jest got so sleepy and thirsty that ah fell off and then ah jest doan even remember."

MacDonald let out his breath. "Damn, three days." He spun to face Rolfe. "I must go to Anna and the wee one."

Rolfe's face was intent. "Ja, Indians she'd shoot mitt out asking questions, but probably not two vhite men."

MacDonald turned to head for his horse when he spun again. "Damn, I forgot, Kap and Gra Gerde."

"Don't vorry. Martin and Olga vill take care of things here. They know to look for two men. I'll go varn Kap." He spat and pointed his finger at Martin. "Du use der buffalo gun if du see two men, Olga the other Henry. Don't try to talk to them, just shoot. If vun of du is doing chores, the other stands guard, and Young James does not go out of the haus. Ja?"

"Ja, sure, Papa. We'll be all right."

Rolfe's eyes were as hard as MacDonald's and he pointed at Lorenz. "That poy goes mitt me. He shoots good."

"No, I just found Mama!"

MacDonald laid his hands on Lorenz's shoulders. "I sorrow, laddie, for I would nay put this on ye till ye are elder, but Kap tis Anna's twin. There tis a bond twixt them that nay can break. Ye are of their House, and one of us must go to protect them. Pay attention to what Mr. Rolfe says. There tis nay better man in a fight." He lowered his head and gently touched Lorenz's head with his, straightened, and turned to Rolfe.

"Bring him back to us, Herman, for he tis our laddie." He released Lorenz and grabbed his saddle.

"Ja, ve both vill come back. Dem men," he added to MacDonald's retreating form, "have vasted lots of time. Somebody hired them and they are going to have to finish the job to get paid. They probably ain't going to stop again until they get to Schmidt's Corner."

"Martin," he pointed his finger at his son, "du saddle my horse." He pointed at Lorenz. "Und du saddle yours. Ve ride as soon as I get some more cartridges."

Chapter 12

Shootout

They rode out of the yard, at a steady pace instead of the wild gallop that MacDonald had pushed Zark into. Lorenz's mind was a jumble, and Chalky's eyes were wide with wonder at seeing such a thing as Rolfe embracing and kissing his daughter and youngest son goodbye. The elder Rolfe had thrown his arms around Martin and muttered, "Auf Wiedersehen," before mounting. Neither man had shown any embarrassment. Lorenz finally decided that Rolfe must be a strange combination of white man becoming a fur trapper turning mostly Indian, but still keeping the customs of his farming people back east. Maybe people back east were that different. He didn't know. He did know he wanted this over with and nudged Dandy up alongside of Rolfe.

"Shouldn't we be going faster?"

"Vy? I think ve are ahead of them. This vay if Mac runs into them, ve hear the shots." His blue eyes swung around and drilled into Lorenz. "Du not thinking of telling me how to run things?"

"No, suh." Lorenz started to let Dandy drift back to Chalky.

"Vhen do du think they'll hit us; tonight or in the morning?"

"In the morning, I reckon."

"Ja, that's vhat I think. They'll come in first to look things over. Ve'll shoot first." Rolfe fell silent for the rest of the ride.

They rode into Schmidt's Corner about six o'clock, long before the sun was ready to set and pulled up at the back of the store. "Du poys take the horses to the stables and come on in. I'll tell everybody vhat to expect."

Chalky roused himself from his stupor. "Ah promised Ma'am that ah'd tell 'em."

"Don't vorry, du can tell Mr. and Mrs. Schmidt later." Rolfe stalked up the steps to be greeted by Gerde.

Her apron was on and her face flushed. Worry lines were pulling down her mouth as she looked at Rolfe and the unexpected visitors. "What is it?" Her tone implying that she knew something was wrong. Gerde never learned to like anything about the West. Her youth and her son had died here. The heat was intolerable in summer, the constant fear of Indians and the wild, white inhabitants, the long wait for der Pastor to ride into town, and the loss of relatives and friends who spoke German and read books written in German was a hurt too deep to articulate.

Rolfe disregardedGerde's fears as he wished to impart his news to the man, not the woman. That his daughter accepted the news with equanimity and a readiness to shoot on sight was expected. Rolfe had years ago realized that Olga was more like him than his sons. He doffed his hat and spoke in German.

"Frau Schmidt, good day. The news is not good, but I must speak with Herr Schmidt first. The three of us will need to stay for dinner, but if you prefer, we can get something from Owens."

"Come in, Mr. Rolfe. Of course, you are all welcome at our table. I'll get Mr. Schmidt."

At these words, Kasper appeared as though summoned. He had heard the horses arrive and his wife talking. "Welcome, Mr. Rolfe. How may we help you?"

Rolfe looked at him with the knowledge that the scholar would be of little help and gave his warning, still speaking in German. "There are two hired gunmen coming to kill you and

Gerde. O'Neal is probably paying them, but we don't have any proof. I've got Lorenz with me and the youngster that brought the news. Mac found him by the roadside. Be careful when you talk to him as he probably baked out what little brains he had. He'd been riding for two days without water." Rolfe shook his head at the folly and continued. "The boys are putting up the horses, and I'm going to tell Mr. Jackson and the Owens group what to expect. I don't think they'll be here before morning." He turned and stalked out of the door, leaving two white-faced adults staring after him.

Rolfe visited Tom Jackson just long enough to apprise him of the coming situation and requested that Tom simply wait and watch when the two men appeared and then join Owens in the bar if they needed to make a stand. From there he went to talk to Owens and stayed long enough for one beer. Owens, he knew, would tell Cruz and his women what to expect.

When he walked back into the Schmidt's living quarters, Chalky was telling them about the bad men that were with his Ma'am and the warning she had given him. Gedre had regained her composure, but was more tight-lipped than usual. Kasper, he decided was still far too white around the mouth. He nodded at them all and spoke.

"Ve need to check out the store and vhere ve vill be." He led the way through the short hall and stood looking at the door, the window by the counter, and the door to the left, slightly behind the counter that led to the office.

"Ve vill leave dot office door open," he decided. "I can stand behind it. They can't see me if they look in der vindow."

"I figure they'll come in the front door to check things out. If they don't, they'll be barging in the kitchen door. Vhen ve hear dem, I vant du, Gerde, to go upstairs vhile ve take our positions. Du vill be safe up there."

Gerde gave Rolfe an intractable stare and crossed her arms under her breasts. Lorenz had a hunch that Gerde was not going to allow any interloper into her domain. Rolfe, however, was oblivious to the female of the species and continued his instructions.

He had been studying the tables and shelves. The first table was really a counter with storage space underneath hidden by doors. "Dot's vere du'll be," he said to Lorenz. "Vhen they come in, stand and shoot."

Kasper started as though shot. "No, that is wrong," he spoke rapidly in German. "I will be standing behind the counter and will be able to determine if they are intent upon murder, or whether they are someone else."

Rolfe looked at him in disgust and spoke in German. "Yes, just stand there while they shoot you. This is not the time to put the best construction on everything, no matter what Dr. Luther taught."

Lorenz was looking at his uncle in horror. Did the man want to die? And why was Rolfe talking about some doctor? Chalky stood there, blinking his eyes and trying to figure out what these folks were saying.

Kasper tried again. "I cannot permit my nephew, a mere boy, to do my job; nor perhaps, murder someone unjustly."

"I ain't no kid," Lorenz protested. "And from what Chalky said, these two ain't to be fooled with. They're not the kind to leave anyone alive." He hoped like hell Chalky didn't catch that last meaning.

The adults looked at him with the realization that he understood German. Rolfe pursed his lips, and continued in German. "Good, you understand Deutsch."

He turned to Kasper. "Kap, I can't stop you from being a block head and standing at the window and making Gerde a widow, but I came here as a favor to Mac, and I'm not getting killed for it. Lorenz is here as a favor to me from Mac, and I'm not letting some fool thinking get him killed. Mac knows why Lorenz is here. It won't be the first time your nephew has killed a man; it probably isn't the second, and it won't be the last."

Rolfe turned to Lorenz. "You know what you're to do."

"Yes, sir." No use arguing. Rolfe was right: Stand and shoot.

"Good. When we hear the door open, you stand and fire. I'll step out from behind that door and fire with the shotgun."

"I should be where Lorenz has been assigned." Kasper was still protesting.

"Have you ever killed anyone?" Rolfe roared.

"No, but I will if necessary."

Rolfe cut him off. "It's different when you are looking at a man. If you see a man and not a target, you are dead. Your nephew knows how to kill a man."

Kasper stepped towards Rolfe. "I cannot allow…"

Lorenz broke in, interrupting his Uncle, the drawl he spoke with disappearing. "I don't like the idea of Tante Gerde going upstairs. What if they start s fire? They're either going to come in the front or the backdoor. If Tante and Chalky stay in the storage part they should be okay, and we can drag in a box from there for Uncle to hide behind in the kitchen. That way our backs are covered."

Lorenz turned to look at his uncle. "If y'all ain't used to shootin', then you can use the shotgun. It'll stop them long enough for us to get out there."

Rolfe's eyes lighted and he spoke in English. "I like du, poy. Ve go hunting sometime. Right now, du practice getting your aim about right, and I'll gauge my distance." He stalked into the office.

They watched as Rolfe stepped out from behind the door and pointed his shotgun. Then he walked over to the counter, measured the height with his body, shook his head, and went back behind the door. He emerged again holding the gun at a slightly higher angle and sighted. "Dot should do it. It vill hit about chest high. I'd take Lorenz's place, but my knees might creek vhen I stand. Ve take turns vatching tonight just in case. Lorenz takes first vatch, then Kap. Kap vill vake me at four o'clock if I ain't up already. Now ve go find that crate vhile Mrs. Schmidt fixes us something to eat."

Lorenz never discovered what his uncle thought of the arrangements and he didn't want to know. He was just glad he didn't have to stand there and tell him that Rolfe was right. It wouldn't be the first or the second man he had killed. Somehow he knew Uncle would be disappointed with his character. Just why this was so, Lorenz couldn't fathom. He would always feel there was something more in life to accomplish and the other person was trying to kill him or hurt someone he loved; therefore, the other man forfeited his life. He correctly assumed that Uncle Kasper was a gentle, stubborn man, while not afraid of danger, could not in his heart bring harm to another living being. In some ways, Lorenz felt, Mama was more hardened than her twin.

The sun did not go down easy that evening. Protesting fingers of fire stabbed at the sky while red coals glowed in the belly of grey clouds. Lorenz was squatting on the roof, listening for horse hoofs that might or not come this night.

He had eaten dinner and cleaned his rifle and Uncle Kap's two shotguns before heading up. Dinner had been a hurried affair of beans mixed with a stew and rolls of some kind, sourdough, Lorenz guessed. Chalky was in a state of shock. He didn't understand the speech and he couldn't begin to comprehend the scope of the food available. At first he had pushed at the mixture in his bowl and then almost inhaled it when he realized no one was going to take it away.

Gerde, sour-faced and taciturn, had gone about cleaning up the kitchen after they ate and making sure the crate was positioned for Kasper's advantage should something happen overnight. Somehow she managed to infect them all with her dour mood. Chalky had escaped to the stable to turn in early.

When Lorenz headed for the roof, Kasper said, "The clouds will keep it dark tonight. How will you see? Would you like me to come with you now?"

Lorenz thought fast. "Thanks, Uncle Kap, but I don't think they'll be here until morning. If they do come, they can't see any better than we can and I can hear their horses." He did not want to listen to Kap's admonition to not be in the storefront tomorrow. He just hoped Tante Gerde would keep Chalky out of the way in the morning.

Kasper looked troubled when he appeared at midnight with his shotgun. Lorenz headed for the stable and sleep. Later he heard Kasper appear in the barn and Rolfe bid him 'morgen,' and tried to go back to a fitful sleep. Lorenz gave up trying after one-half hour and headed toward the outhouse. Filtered sunlight was trying to break through the clouds with limited success. The air hung heavy with humidity and heat, but there was no sound of far-off thunder to offer relief in a coming rain.

He had paused long enough to shake Chalky awake and went inside. Tante Gerde had breakfast ready. Huge biscuits and gravy, the same sort of apple butter Mama served, and coffee. Lorenz headed up the stairs and boosted himself through the access door and ladder to tell Rolfe that breakfast was ready. Rolfe nodded at him and said, "Du und your uncle vill eat too. Mitt daylight they might see us up on the roof. Ve'll get into position as soon as possible. I don't think they'll vait for normal business hours."

It was not a long wait. Lorenz had sat hunkered down on his heels, figuring that if he sat cross legged he would need more space to unlimber his rifle. He had chased all worry about his mother and Martin out of his mind. He was intent on listening and he heard the two horses long before the men walked in shortly after six o'clock. He had used mindsearch to see if these two were the ones Chalky had told about. What he found made it easy to want to pull the trigger. He had to figure out some way to keep Chalky from going home.

The two men didn't bother to knock. They ignored the "Closed" sign propped in the door and walked in. One of them bellowed, "Anyone up. We need to buy some supplies."

Lorenz heard the door close behind them and he stood, his back against the wall, and brought his rifle in line with the counter by the door with one swift, sure motion. His eyes and brain registered the sight of the two men, one slightly in front of the other, and he fired. The other man brought his rifle up as Lorenz ducked down, and Rolfe stepped through the door and shot. The man bringing up his rifle also fired, but the shot went over the counter where Lorenz had been.

Lorenz heard Rolfe's shotgun hit the counter or the floor, and he duck walked his way to the front of the counter, peered around the edge, and saw that Rolfe was headed around the end of the counter, handgun in his left hand and bowie knife in the right. Rolfe was upright and fired two shots from the handgun, one into each man. Lorenz stood and saw the two bodies lying in their own fluids and wastes. A stench started filling the air spaces as Rolfe stuffed his handgun in his waistband and knocked the hat off the second man, bent, and took his scalp.

Metal scrapped against the door jamb of the hall, and Lorenz whirled to find a white-faced Kasper standing there. Kasper must have realized what Rolfe was doing and while his mouth formed a protest he sagged against the jamb, his grey eyes wide in disbelieve.

"Du vant the other von's hair, poy?"

"Ah, no thanks, Mr. Rolfe. Ah don't think Mama would let it in the house."

"Den ve pull these two out of here. Mrs. Schmidt vill fuss about der mess. Ve don't vant to hear about making vork for her." Rolfe grabbed the man by his heels and pulled him around. "Vone of du open the door."

Inwardly Lorenz was breathing a sigh of relief as he moved to the door and pulled it open. He wedged his rifle against the door and walked back to the other form, grabbed the legs, and followed Rolfe out the door; neither of them looked at Kasper leaning against the jamb of the hall opening, unable to move. Kasper's face was twisting from pain and white was outlining his mouth. He let the shotgun fall on the floor and kept trying to fight down the pain and nausea that seemed to radiate from the inside out.

They dragged the bodies into the shade of the overhangs. Rolfe dropped the legs and immediately pulled the boots off. "Du best do the same. These boots are vorth keeping or letting Kasper sell them for a cut." He stooped down and flipped off the man's hat and then the belt before going through the pockets and dumping the contents into the man's hat.

Lorenz watched for a moment, a bad taste forming in his mouth, and then he shrugged, bent down, and began the same procedure on the body in front of him. It wasn't like he hadn't stripped a dead man before.

Tom Jackson and Owens came running from the tavern, the Mexican following behind them. Jackson rested his crutch at the head of the man Lorenz was stripping and said, "Well, y'all got them."

Rolfe looked up. "Ja, that poy shoots plenty gut."

"Where's Kasper? I heard five shots."

"He's still inside; probably calming his missus." Rolfe didn't bother to add the wrong twin got the balls. Thoughts like that were better left unsaid. "Vone did get off a shot, but it vent vild. Vhat's this?"

He pulled a thin, leather folder out from under the man's shirt. Inside was a page of thin paper, stamped with a seal. Rolfe ran his eyes over the writing. "Mein Gott, O'Neal vrote out a contract for them." He waved the paper in the air, folded it, put in back in the leather folder, and handed it to Lorenz. "Here take this to Herr Schmidt. He'll get over the dead bodies quicker. I'll finish that vone for du and for Mac."

Lorenz took the folder, glad to be away from the stink of dead bodies, and hurried inside. He glanced around the empty store and continued into the kitchen. His aunt was carrying a glass of water to the living room, her face set, her brown, work shift swaying from her rapid steps. She raked Lorenz with a baleful look and disappeared into the doorway.

"Here, mein Herr, drink this," her tone was so soft Lorenz barely heard her. This was so unlike Tante's usual sharp tongue, he almost tiptoed into the room, holding the leather folder out like a peace offering.

Uncle Kasper was on the sofa; his shoes on the floor, an afghan covering his lower body and part of his torso. On his forehead was a wet washcloth, and earlier someone had placed a pillow underneath his head and shoulders. Kasper's face was still a deathly pallor and his mouth drawn in a taunt line. He opened his eyes and whispered, "I need a bucket."

Tante swung her gaze on Lorenz. "It's his heart. He's not to move. The bucket is just outside the kitchen door. Get it." She turned her attentions back to her husband.

Lorenz set the folder down on the side table and retrieved the bucket for them. He'd seen men die in lots of ways, but never in their own home. He brought the bucket and realized he still wore his new hat. He pulled it off and looked down at the two, Tante Gerde kneeling on the floor, using the glass of water to wet the washcloth which she was using to sponge Uncle's face. "Is he gonna be all right?"

"Ja," Gerde answered. "He must rest. Go away."

Lorenz backed towards the door. "There's proof there that they was being paid by O'Neal." He spun and headed back outside where the air was fresh and easier to breathe and sudden death easier to understand.

"Vat they say?" asked Rolfe.

Lorenz rapidly described the situation inside. He figured somebody ought to go tell Mama and Papa what had happened. "Maybe I should ride home and tell them what's happened," he ended.

Rolfe considered. "Nein, ve got to dig some graves." He weighed the money he'd found in one man's pocket and looked at Lorenz. "There vas money in the other guy's pocket, ja?"

"Yeah, about four two-bit pieces and a couple of bills."

"Dot's enough. Ve pay Kasper for a tarp, cut it down, and vrap them in it for a burial shroud. Let's see vhat they got on their horses."

"Uh, I'll be happy to hitch up and go tell Miss Rolfe and the MacDonald's that everything is all right here, and about Kasper," Jackson offered. "Business is kinda slow anyway."

Rolfe's blue eyes swept over Jackson and amusement tugged at the corners of his mouth. "Ve vould appreciate that, Tom. Come next veek, ve may haff some shoeing for du und du can join us for a meal."

Jackson nodded, swiveled on his crutch, and set off for the stable. Rolfe and Lorenz quickly removed the contents of the saddlebags. Each contained their camp gear, a shirt, an extra pair of trousers, and a clean bandana, but little food. "I bet they vere going to get supplies here und kill the Schmidts before paying." Rolfe spat at the ground. "Ve go get the tarp. That poy can put up the horses and guard the trappings from them on the back porch. It'll keep him out of our vay."

Lorenz followed Rolfe figuring it wouldn't be long before Rolfe found an excuse to let him do all the digging while he went for a beer. He was seriously thinking about offering Chalky money to do the digging, but realized he didn't have any. Rolfe would insist that everything they'd emptied out of the men's pockets belonged to Rolfe or MacDonald. He was thankful he'd paid attention when Martin was telling him about how everything belonged to the Papa until the Papa said otherwise.

He was half right about Rolfe. Rolfe waited until they'd dug the hole out wide enough for both men and lowered them into the ground. They started piling the dirt back in when Rolfe squinted at the sky and declared it was time for a beer. He looked at Lorenz. "Du vant vone, poy?"

Lorenz grinned. "No, suh. I don't like beer, and I ain't supposed to go in there without Papa."

Rolfe nodded and hurried off while Lorenz kept shoveling. The clouds were forming and re-forming, never dense enough for rain, but always threatening. The day was becoming hotter and stickier, the ground seemed to become heavier with each shovelful, and his stomach was growling. He heard the clops of an approaching horse and wiped the sweat from his face and eyes.

MacDonald dismounted and looped Zark's reins around the split rails of the cemetery fence and came toward him, a strained, set smile on his face. The dark eyes probed at him and as he came nearer he asked, "Are ye all right, laddie?"

Lorenz took a deep breath and felt his whole body relax. He couldn't believe he was so glad to see this huge form blocking the sun. "Yes, sir, is Mama mad?"

MacDonald glanced down at the half-filled grave and nodded. "Oh, aye, that she tis, but she tis more angry with me than with ye." He gave Lorenz a rueful smile and then surprised them both. The huge arms went out and he picked Lorenz up and hugged him. "Thank Gar, ye are well. I sorrow for what has happened."

Lorenz felt the heat from his body and heard MacDonald's tongue make a "tsk" sound in his right ear and then the left ear.

"Uh, Papa, what if somebody's watching?"

"Who cares?" MacDonald lowered him to the ground, his hands resting on his shoulders. "Now what tis this about Kasper?"

"He's on the sofa. Tante Gerde says it is his heart and she doesn't want anybody to disturb him. She's been so busy taking care of him that I don't think she's bothered to fix any lunch." He glanced skyward to confirm the sun was slightly beyond its zenith.

"Damn," MacDonald looked towards the store. "Have ye done all this work by yereself?"

Lorenz gave a quick grin. "Naw, Rolfe, Mr. Rolfe helped until it was time to shovel the dirt back in. There ain't too much left to do, but I don't know what kind of words to say once it's done."

MacDonald grabbed the other shovel. "There twill be nay words over these two." He flung the dirt in rapid motion.

They worked in silence until it was finished. Then they mopped their heads, lifted their hats to let the breeze blow through, and headed towards the store. As they passed the Schmidt plot, MacDonald spoke. "I have an idea." He smiled broadly and placed his hands on his hips and looked downward.

Then he turned to Lorenz, his eyes dancing with amusement again. "We are going to bury Kid Lawrence."

Lorenz looked at him in disbelief. "Won't that be kinda hard to believe with me walking around upright?"

MacDonald chuckled. "And just who tis going to call Mac-Donald a liar?" He clamped his hand on Lorenz's shoulder as they walked. "We twill use the money or goods that those two had on them to pay Cruz to dig an empty grave. He can throw some rocks in to make it look like someone tis buried there. I twill have Kasper or Tom carve out the tombstone. Twill be very nice." MacDonald doubled the r sound in very, so pleased with himself he did not bother trying to hide his considerable accent. "We twill tell the world that Kid Lawrence died defending his kin. Tis a fine solution should yere Mr. O'Neal nay send a telegram confirming that ye are innocent."

At the fence, MacDonald picked up Zark's reins and they headed towards the stable. He made sure Zark was watered and checked out the new horse and riding gear. "We twill let

Kasper sell the saddlebags and the contents, and we twill split the money with him."

They found Chalky on the back porch chewing on one of Tante's rolls. He stuffed the last of the roll in his mouth, and stood an eager, expecting look on his face. "Do yu all reckon what ah told wuz worth some extra money? My Ma'am sure will be needin' hit."

Lorenz swallowed, and MacDonald kept his face bland. "The information ye brought twas all that ye said. However, I would like to talk with Mr. Schmidt ere I pay ye. It may be there twill be some work for ye ere ye return home." He looked at the saddlebags and hat stuffed with the dead man's belongings and turned to Lorenz.

"Tante didn't want them in the place. She acts like they're cursed."

MacDonald shrugged and hurriedly verified the contents. "We twill leave them here for now." He walked to the door and knocked. "Hallo, the house."

"Ja, I'll be right there." After a moment, Tante Gerde appeared, drying her hands on the apron, her work shift stained with her sweat, wrinkled, and grime-streaked from being on the floor. Her face was stonier than usual and she paused to brush back a strand of hair. Lorenz wondered how that strand of hair had dared escape from her bun. "Good afternoon, Herr MacDonald," she said through tightly held lips.

"Good afternoon, Frau Schmidt. I wondered how Mr. Schmidt tis."

Gerde decided to open the door and let them in. "He is better and resting."

"Would it be possible to speak with him?"

Gerde considered and decided if she did not let the husband of Kasper's twin see him, she would have more visitors tomorrow. "Ja, but just for a little while. I do not want him to tire. He must rest."

They removed their hats and stepped into the kitchen, the heat from the woodstove radiating throughout the room. The slight breeze coming in the open window and door did little to dissipate the heat. Lorenz spotted the bowl of rolls sitting on the table and ran his tongue over his lips. Gerde softened enough to say, "You may have one or two."

He lost no time in grabbing two as he trailed along behind them, munching as he walked. At the door of the living room, Gerde barred his way. "Just one at a time, please."

Lorenz leaned against the doorjamb and continued eating. He was close enough that he could hear everything that was said.

Uncle Kasper had the afghan pulled up to his chest, but Aunt Gerde had placed another pillow under his head, effectively elevating his upper body. The leather folder lay on his stomach, his hands still grasping it. He gave them a wan smile. "It seems the spirit is willing, but the body is weak." To Lorenz his hair looked whiter than the grey shade it have been a few hours before.

"Look at this." Using one hand, Kasper raised the folder. "There is a contract in here and signed by O'Neal. It promises those men one-hundred dollars after they bring back proof of my death. It seems my life is not too highly valued." There was a slight trace of bitterness in his voice.

MacDonald opened the folder and read the contents. He returned the package to Kasper. "Ye twill, of course, keep that to show the law when they come calling for Lorenz and Mr. Rolfe."

"Of course."

"Good. I have been thinking now would be a good time to bury Kid Lawrence with today as the date of his death. I twill pay Cruz to dig the grave in our plot and throw in some large stones ere he shovels the dirt back in. If ye dinna feel like carving out a wooden marker for over the grave, perhaps Mr. Jackson would do the honors."

Tante Gerde straightened, her eyes opening wide at the thought, and said, "That is a good plan."

Kasper seemed to be thinking and then looked up. "Yes, it is a good plan. It would satisfy the law. I believe I can at least whittle out a wooden marker for over the grave. That won't require me to walk or lift anything heavy."

"How long do ye believe ye twill need to rest?"

Kasper gave a rueful smile. "Until I can move without being in agony and not become exhausted. It's Gerde I worry about. She will have to do the work of both of us."

"Ye should hire Chalky. He should nay return to his homestead. He twill find nay but death there. He can bring in the wood and water for Gerde and take care of the horses in yere stable; mayhap even some of the work in the garden. There should be space enough in the storeroom to place a cot or sleeping blankets, and room and board would be part of his pay."

Kasper closed his eyes for a moment, and Lorenz could see the weariness that folded over him. Then the grey eyes came open, dull and flat, beaten by the economics of the situation. "There is no money."

"There tis a bit left that Lorenz found on the one man, and ye can sell the saddlebags and gear that the man carried. We twill split the money. Till that time, I twill be happy to pay the laddie as it would be nay more than a quarter a week, plus his room and board that ye would supply. Gerde twill be free to tend ye and the store."

Kasper gave a slight smile and looked at his wife. "Yes, I was worried about her. Can you arrange everything?"

"Aye, twill be my pleasure."

Chapter 13

Daniel

The two men rode slowly into town, glancing at every burnt out building and the existing run-down ones. "At least there's a bar," said the smaller, older man. "I do believe that lost shoe of your horse has slowed us too much."

They pulled up in front of Schmidt's Corner and dismounted. Both were dressed in collarless working shirts, handkerchiefs tied carelessly around the neck, denim trousers, newer Stetsons, and new boots. Both wore guns belted at the lower part of the waist and tied to their thighs. They presented a picture of affluence rarely seen on the few passing, northward migrants. The younger man was taller, broad shouldered, and slim of hip. He tried to hide his pride in the black hair covering his upper lip, but he was young, and kept fingering it. His body and grey eyes seemed to convey movement even when still. The afternoon had barely begun and the street was empty; so empty that no dust hung in the air from anyone else passing by. The younger man looked to his left and the older to his right before they entered the store.

A small, middle-aged woman stood at a doorway into the back of the store, her hands firmly grasping a shotgun. "I don't know you. State your business." Her face was bitter and the brown eyes hard, when suddenly the barrel slumped downward and her eyes widened. "Mein Gott, Daniel."

Daniel, surprised by the recognition, remained speechless long enough for the older man to remove his hat. "Ma'am, you must be Mrs. Schmidt. Our employer found out that his father had sent two men here to do bodily harm to you and your husband. We've been sent to prevent that if possible. I hope we are in time and if we are, could we speak to your husband and devise a plan of action."

Gerde continued staring at the young man and barely whispered, "Du look so much like Kasper. Don't du remember me? Lorenz did."

"Ma'am," Collins broke in, "right now time could be very important."

Gerde straightened herself, the relief of seeing her nephew receded, and doubt about their intentions returned. "You are too late. Those two men are dead." Her voice was firm again, the German accent retreating.

Outside they could hear the scuffle of boots as though someone was hurrying, yet trying to hide the fact they were approaching.

It was, Collins decided, a community on edge, and the neighbors, whoever they were, were about to help out, probably with guns of their own. Damn, Daniel, why wasn't the young fool saying something.

Daniel obliged. "Mrs. Schmidt, I'm sorry we are so late, but my horse threw a shoe, and we couldn't..."

Gerde snapped at him. "I am your Tante, not Mrs. Schmidt."

Her stern tone silenced Daniel, and Collins tried again.

"Mrs. Schmidt, I can assure you, we were sent to try and stop a tragedy. I have a letter here from Mr. Jeremiah O'Neal that will explain everything. If you and your husband would be kind enough to read it before your friends and neighbors open fire,

I think another shooting can be avoided." He kept his speech mild, not wanting to frighten the woman.

Gerde, a strong, perceptive woman, realized what was at stake and decided to believe this man. "Ja, you are right. I am Mrs. Schmidt and my husband is indisposed at the moment, but I will speak to our friends." She stepped towards front door, but paused long enough to give Daniel an order. "Take off your hat. Were you too long with the savages?"

Daniel felt his body stiffen and a slight flush spread over the planes of his face. Who was this woman to call his parents savages? And what in the hell did Tante mean?

Collins suppressed a grin. He wasn't sure what or why O'Neal was paying Daniel, but it was surely too much. He knew the young man had an exaggerated notion of his own abilities. This lady had taken him down a peg and was sure to do so again. "I do recommend you remove your hat," he said in a low tone. There was a Missouri drawl to his speech cadence, not the exaggerated drawl of a Texan.

Gerde returned. "If I may see the letter, I'll take it to Mr. Schmidt. If he is feeling well enough, he will speak with you both. I know he will make an effort to talk with his nephew."

Collins reached inside his vest and pulled out the oilskin wrapped letter. "I do hope your husband wasn't wounded in any shootout."

Gerde accepted the letter. "No, they came in the front like you did, and Mr. Rolfe and Lorenz shot them." It was a simple, but chilling statement for them to mull on. She disappeared into the doorway without telling them why Kasper was laid up.

"Interesting," Collins muttered. "Do you have any idea who Mr. Rolfe is?"

"No." Daniel snapped out. Why should Lorenz get all the glory? He had a vague feeling it was always that way, but his remembrance of that long ago home was practically nil. He'd only been eight-years-old, and his father and mother had both assured him he would forget that early time with a first family. Up until now, he had believed them. He honestly could not remember his white aunt and uncle, nor could he recall with any clarity what his white mother looked like. He did remember fighting with Lorenz, and that seemed all wrong too. He couldn't have been the one on the floor.

"You need to remember that this is their household and they will have more civilized rules than what you've been around. I'd take off that gun belt when she asks. If we're lucky enough to be asked for supper, I aim to take mine off." His voice was moderate, but he spoke with authority.

Daniel swung around to regard the older man. Red had implied that he was to follow Collins orders during a fight, but he hadn't said anything about letting Collins take the lead in his personal life. "I don't trust anyone. The guns stay on."

Collins shrugged. He was tired of the trail and their campfire meals. They had pushed the horses and themselves hard to reach Schmidt's Corner before the other two, and they had ridden through or around some fair sized towns. This town did not have a hotel, bathhouse, or an eatery. It was little more than a settlement, and unless Mrs. Schmidt extended an invitation, it looked like another campfire meal and hard ground tonight. Damn the kid for his lack of feelings for meeting family. It wasn't right. He started looking around the store for supplies to take on the way back. It looked like they would need to make a stop at the MacDonald household if they were to find the other kid and convince him to ride back with them. He couldn't figure why his employer wanted another wet-behind-the ears kid, but that wasn't his problem. O'Neal paid regular and the amount was more than fair. This kid wasn't going to mess up his reputation. O'Neal would get his full report.

Gerde came back without the paper and a face softened from speaking with her husband. Her eyes, however, were still guarded and she showed no emotion as she regarded the two of them. "My husband needs to rest. He thanks you for coming and he will write to Mr. O'Neal thanking him." She drew a deep breath and looked squarely at Daniel. "You are going to go to your mother's now, is that not right?"

Daniel swallowed. "No, ma'am." He saw no reason to explain he needed to have his horse shod. Collins stepped in when he saw a look of horror on Gerde's face.

"Ma'am, we rode the horses hard to get here, too hard. Daniel needs to get his horse shod before we can go to the MacDonald's place. Until then, we need to water and feed our horses. Is there a place we can do so? If you will kindly give us directions before we leave, we'll be most grateful."

Gerde looked at him and cocked her head. "You are from Missouri." It was a statement and a question.

"Yes, ma'am, I'm Jethro Collins from Jefferson County."

Gerde nodded her head. "We're from Perry County, Missouri.

"There is a river out back which you saw and anyone can use, and we have a stable with some hay. If you stay all night it's fifty cents for each horse. Mr. Schmidt will probably let Daniel's stay for free." The implication that she would not let Daniel stay for free was clear.

Collins laid four bits on the counter, doffed his hat, and said, "Thank you, ma'am. We'll be back to buy some things for the trail before we leave."

When they were outside, Daniel looked at the graveyard. "I'm checking that out next. Something wasn't right in there."

Collins shrugged and walked along. He too felt that Gerde had not said everything, but then, he wasn't family and it must have been a shock to her to see Daniel and not get any acknowledgement. He knew how families grieved for the lost ones, and yet those "lost" who accepted the Indians didn't seem to be as lost as the ones left behind.

Like the town, the graveyard wasn't much. The Schmidt plot held a small grave for a boy that died of typhus in 1858, the Rolfe plot was marked as the grave of Mrs. Rolfe, who died in 1858, and the MacDonald plot had two graves; one a small child's grave and a new unmarked grave. There were other graves in the back; one large mound was new and unmarked. They both stared down at the new grave in the MacDonald plot. "Damn," said Daniel.

"It doesn't look like there's anyone to take back to Mr. O'Neal," said Collins. He turned back to the horses. "Standing here won't get us back, or our wages. We'll talk with one or both of the Schmidt's before we leave. Maybe that saloon will have something to eat."

They watered the horses, and then Daniel took his to have it shod while Collins put his horse in the stable. Collins noted that there were three horses and a mule out in the back yard. When they watered the horses, he'd seen the open back door to the saloon and headed that way. Mrs. Schmidt was out in the garden and he nodded to her. She kept swinging her hoe like there was something personal in her fight with the weeds. A straw-headed kid was carrying firewood up the steps. Gerde swung one more time and walked over to the fence. "Mr. Collins, are you and Daniel planning to stay for supper tonight?"

"Ma'am, nothing would give me greater pleasure."

"I do not allow guns to be worn at my table." She threw out the words like a challenge.

"Mrs. Schmidt, I would not dream of doing that in polite society. I would like to be able to place them somewhere inside of the door for any emergency, if that is all right with you and your husband."

His words seem to mollify her and she nodded her head. "We do not mind a man having a beer or two, but I do not allow drunkenness at our table either."

"Perfectly understandable, ma'am." He did not want anything to change her mind about supper. He was sure anyone as competent as Mrs. Schmidt was apt to be a more than competent cook. He tipped his hat again before continuing to the saloon.

Inside the saloon there were no lights this time of day. What light there was came in through the two opened doors and the two small front windows. A man was standing at the bar playing solitaire. If he had been edgy before, he showed no signs of it.

"Afternoon," said Collins. "What's the chance of a man getting a beer?"

"Right good, I'd say." The man smiled and took a not too clean glass mug and ran some beer in it, gradually topping the amber liquid with a small head. "That'll be five cents."

Collins laid a quarter on the counter. "My traveling partner will be in here in a bit. When that's gone, cut us off. I don't want to miss supper with the Schmidt's."

"A fine couple and a fine cook."

Collins nodded in satisfaction and took his first sip as Daniel walked in. Owens grinned and poured another beer. Daniel took off his hat long enough to brush the perspiration off and push back the hair trying to curl forward. When he looked around Owens was staring at him with open mouth.

"Something wrong?" asked Daniel.

Owens shook his head. "Are y'all the one called Daniel?"

Collins set his beer down. "How did you know that?"

"Why, it's like looking at Kasper Schmidt with twenty years wiped off his face. It ain't real hard to figure out. Mrs. MacDonald is going to be one happy lady after..." Like Gerde, Owens voice trailed off.

"We saw the grave site in the MacDonald section." Collins decided a talkative barkeep might provide some information. "We were sent here to try and stop those first two men. It looks like the folks here take care of their own."

"That's a fact," said Owens.

"It's easy to see that you've had some problems before. What caused all the fires? Indians?"

Owens leaned forward. "Nope, it was our friends and neighbors from Arles. They were going to drive out the damn Yankees, but forgot that Mr. Jackson and I are Texans. 'Course Mr. Jackson was still in Virginy fighting the damn Yankees, so his house went up in flames along with Rolfe's house, and his place of business got singed a mite before MacDonald and Rolfe got here to help drive them off. By that time everybody was shooting. Even the women folk holed up at Schmidt's. MacDonald carted the organ out of Rolfe's house, but there just wasn't any way to save that house or the rest of Mr. Jackson's old home. That little escapade left some real bitter feelings all around, particularly when young Mr. Jackson came back from Sharpsburg with that missing leg and found his home and dad gone. Then the damn Yankees even take away the name of the battleground where he lost his leg. Now they call it something else up North."

Antietam?" asked Collins.

"I reckon. They got a funny way of naming things." Owens refilled the two mugs.

Daniel sipped away and Collins tried to figure out a way to get Owens talking about yesterday's events when Daniel waved a hand at the ear and bent revolver up on the wall.

"That got a story?"

"Sure enough has," said Owens. "We usually don't get too much excitement here, but this last week has been a real go-getter. It's even been good for business." He looked approvingly at the two mugs on the counter. "There was a real crowd in here when Blue Diamond dropped off a load of freight for Schmidt's Corner. They was headed up north to some of the German settlements next. This ain't the end of the line even though it looks like it now. It used to be a real thriving community before the War. We had a wainwright along with the blacksmith shop, and they both did a fair to middling business. Malcolm Phillips was the wainwright while the Jackson's did the blacksmithing. There were some other spreads beside Rolfe and MacDonald, but since the War they're the only two of any size. I heard Tillman's still hanging on to his land, but we ain't seen him and his missus for awhile."

Owens paused to see if either man was ready for a refill, but they seemed intent on sipping. He shrugged mentally and kept the tale going. "Some of the Blue Diamond crew have kin in Arles and live there themselves when they ain't on the trail, and they were still resenting the way Rolfe and MacDonald ran them off a few years back when Rolfe's oldest kid and Mrs. MacDonald's other son walked in. Well, nothing would do but they see if the two boys got the same kind of balls the old men have."

He paused again, partly for drama, partly to see if he couldn't refill a mug. Since the latter didn't happen, he continued. "Well, sir, Lorenz might be the youngest of these two, but he sure enough was a fighter. He slammed his mug into the freighter's face and then was slamming the guy's head on the bar before I could even move. The other freighter with the knife got a little distracted by that when another freighter pulled that gun over there." He motioned at the wall. "Now, I didn't approve of that no way, but I couldn't get to my rifle without a fuss, or without taking a slug myself when MacDonald and Rolfe just sort of rolled over everybody in their way. MacDonald grabbed the revolver from behind and pulled the freighter's arm out of the socket. Then he stood there and bent the revolver while watching Rolfe with the knife. Rolfe went for the guy with the knife and left that souvenir." He waved one hand at the ear on the wall. "After that it got real quiet, and they had a beer with their boys just to prove they still run this section of Texas. Sure one of you all wouldn't like a refill?"

Daniel was staring intently at the wall. "This MacDonald, is he bigger than the average bear?"

"I ain't never seen anyone bigger, and that's a fact."

"This Rolfe, he a trapper?"

"They both were trappers 'til the fur trade went tits up. They must of have made some money at it as they came in here and bought the old Ortega ranch grant. That took a mite of doing. Folks like to say they stole the money, but that don't make sense. They just ain't that kind of men. Y'all can tell when a man's good for his word."

Daniel let out his breath and gave a low chuckle. "The wolf and the bear," he said and laughed again.

Daniel now had the attention of both men. Daniel shrugged and said, "That's what the Comanche call them: the wolf and the bear." He drained the last of his beer. "They claim MacDonald killed a grizzly with nothing but a knife."

"Ain't never heard that one," allowed Owens. "Only man I heard of doing that was Hugh Glass. 'Course, there might be another one or two. You two ready now?"

"We'll have one more and leave." There was an edge to Collin's voice.

Daniel had been around him long enough to know the man had a reason and shrugged again while Owens filled both mugs.

When they finished the beers, they walked out the back door into the sunlight, and headed towards the stables. "We are going to make ourselves presentable and then go to your Uncle and Aunt's place for supplies and supper," Collins told Daniel.

"Why eat supper there if we're buying supplies?" asked Daniel.

Collins stopped and turned to the younger man. "I do not care whether you call them family or your Indian friends your family." He held up his hand at Daniel's beginning protest. "These people consider you family. If we want a full report on what happened, we talk with them and then we stop at your Ma's place. If you didn't notice, that barkeep back there talked like Lorenz was dead in one sentence and like he was still alive in another, and he was holding back about something. A new dug grave just proves somebody moved earth around." He resumed his walk. "And you haven't taken the time to see your uncle. I don't know about Injuns, but in the white man's world it is an insult."

Daniel kept pace and tried to remember the words of the bartender. Collins was right. He had let his feelings override the job Red had assigned. Since Red was paying him more per month than most men made, he kept his mouth shut. It looked like he was going to earn his keep and pretend to be something he wasn't.

Chapter 14

Homecoming

The next morning, Daniel and Collins pulled to a halt at the top of the rise and looked down at the MacDonald headquarters. Gerde's directions had been simple and easy to follow. Since Daniel had visited with Kasper before leaving, her normally dour features were lighted by a smile. With Gerde it was difficult to tell as the lips looked stretched into an unnatural position and her eyes betrayed little in the way of emotion as she told them, "Just follow the road towards the South. The first trail to the left will be the Rolfe's and the first trail to your right runs straight to Mr. and Mrs. MacDonald's home."

They were looking down at a prosperous spread. In the corrals someone was riding a bucking horse and took a tumble as they watched. A larger man went to the one limping towards the corral and seemed to steady him as they walked to the barn. Collins nodded at Daniel and they rode on in as both men disappeared into the barn.

"I don't like this," commented Collins as they drew nearer to the house. "That horse is still out there saddle and all, acting like a wild one, and there is nobody greeting us. Stay in the saddle when we pull up."

Daniel nodded. His grey eyes swept the buildings. Surely, one of the men in the barn had seen or heard their approach.

"Hello, the house." Collins called out the standardized greeting of the West to give notice to the inhabitants that they were peaceful and no harm intended. They kept the horses still to give the people a chance to look them over.

"I say we ride on down to the stable where we saw them," Daniel suggested.

"I've a better idea. Take off your hat and let someone see your face. I think there's someone inside that can see us."

Daniel used his left hand, lifted his hat, and lowered it. Both men sat patiently.

Collin's idea worked. The door banged open and a tall, white-haired woman appeared holding a shotgun in one hand, her mouth open, and her grey eyes wide.

"Daniel, ist that du?" Her words were almost a wail.

Daniel managed a smile, "Yes, ma'am."

"Mein, Gott! I almost shot du!"

Her actions and words must have carried for the two men in the barn were now moving towards them, both of them carrying rifles. Collins noted that the shorter one was no longer limping while the other man towered over him and the landscape and then the springhouse hid them from view. His instincts had been correct. The limp had been a ploy to get into the barn as cover and retrieve their rifles.

Anna gulped air and walked to the end of the porch. "Bitte, please, step down. I your mudder am." Her Deutsch and English words mingled in one rapid, spit out sentence.

Collins caught the intent of the words before Daniel and dismounted several seconds before the younger man. He had heard the same accent during his growing up years in Missouri. He looped the reins over the railing and removed his hat. He did not want the others to believe he had any intentions other than goodwill.

Anna stepped off the porch, still holding the shotgun, her eyes searched Daniel's face, and found no welcome there. Despair edged into her voice, "Vhy did du come here if not for me?"

Collins noted that while there was sadness in her voice, her mouth line was firm as was her step. The eyes were a colder grey than Daniel's and, to his shock, the woman was several inches taller than himself. Daniel, the young fool, stood there with hat-in-hand, totally inept with words. It was a bad beginning. The boss wasn't going to like his report. He heard the crunch of approaching boots and turned to meet the two men coming around the corner of the springhouse.

The sheer size of MacDonald was almost eye-popping, mouth-dropping overwhelming, but Collins managed to keep a straight face, transfer his hat to his left hand, and extend his right hand. The features of the younger man proclaimed him to be Daniel's brother and well on his way to being Daniel's equal in height. The scar O'Neal had told him about, however, was not purple, but red. "Mr. MacDonald," he said, "my name is Jethro Collins and this is Daniel Hunter as he calls himself now. I have a letter for you from Mr. Jeremiah O'Neal. He sent us to help the Schmidt's as soon as he discovered his father's plans."

MacDonald's face was set, no emotion showing, but he extended his own hand and shook Collins's hand. On his part, Collins was relieved that his fingers were still intact. He extracted the oilskin folder from his shirt pocket, opened it, and removed the letter sealed with O'Neal's wax and ring.

MacDonald took the letter and glanced at his wife. "I think, mayhap, we should go inside and be comfortable whilst I read it."

Anna nodded and moved to open the door wider. She said not a word, but her eyes remained cold and her mouth set as the men walked in.

MacDonald took the shotgun from her, placed it above the door, and hung his hat on the pegs on the wall. His own rifle he kept with him. Lorenz hung his hat and walked over to the wall chest to put his rifle away. Anna disappeared into the bedroom to emerge with Mina in her arms. Mina looked at her father and squirmed to go to him, but quieted as Anna whispered a few words to her in German.

MacDonald and Anna took their usual seats at the ends of the table. Lorenz sat on the east side and Collins and Daniel set on the west, their backs to the door. Lorenz kept looking at his brother, searching his face for some sign of recognition, and on his face a tight, grim smile.

MacDonald began to read. "Dear Mr. and Mrs. MacDonald, Margareatha forwarded your telegram and sent me another to inform me that Lorenz is safe with you. I had returned home at my mother's request as my father had suffered a mild stroke. He was recovering when the telegram from the marshal in Arles arrived. It wasn't until a day or two later that the telegrams from Margareatha came in. Then I discovered that my father had sent two men to kill the Schmidt's. He had assumed Lorenz was with them.

I immediately dispatched Collins and Daniel to prevent murder. I pray they will be in time. If not, I offer my deepest condolences to Mrs. MacDonald. I have, of course, dispatched another telegram to Marshall Franklin advising him that my late uncle was alive when Lorenz and I left.

Lorenz was with Margareatha when he took it into his head to run away. He later did the same to me. I am aware of how headstrong he is. If he has become too much of a problem, I'm offering him a home with me. He would be safe here, and since he is large for his age, I can offer him a decent salary. If Lorenz chooses to remain with you, or you are reluctant to let him come here, I believe it is advisable that Daniel remain there also. I will hold both positions open for them when they are old enough to decide the direction their life will take.

You need not worry about another attack from my father. Shortly after he sent the two men, he suffered a debilitating stroke. He cannot move, nor speak, and requires constant attention." Here MacDonald's eyebrows rose and he smiled a wry smile. He continued with the letter.

"Again, I offer my apology for the huge wrong my father has done against you and your family. Respectfully, Jeremiah O'Neal."

MacDonald laid the missive on the table, smiled at his wife, and then turned to Collins. "As ye ken, Mr. and Mrs. Schmidt have survived. I shall write a letter to Mr. O'Neal thanking him for his concern and for sending Daniel home. As for Lorenz, he tis our laddie and he stays here."

Collins noted the mild voice and the casual slump of the shoulders and knew he would accept what MacDonald was saying. He'd spent his early years reading cards and men. He knew even without a gun, MacDonald could erupt suddenly in violence and take both him and Daniel down. The mildness was a facade. The man was waiting for him to do something stupid, yet giving him a chance to behave like a gentleman. He also wondered how MacDonald, Lorenz, and the Mrs. had been so adept at putting both Daniel and himself on one side of the table. Did they always work together in concert, or was this stupidity on his part?

Collins was sitting with his knees crossed, his hat resting on his knee. He nodded his head. "I thought as much, and Mr. O'Neal realized that this was a possibility. He wanted everyone to know that he had grown fond of Lorenz when he was in Carson City." He winced inwardly as Lorenz grinned and Mrs. MacDonald erupted in anger. "He vants to use Lorenz to kill Mr. Lawrence!" Her voice was laced with venom. "He is using Daniel as a shield to save his own skin."

Daniel was resting both hands on the table, his hat laid beside him. He looked at her and considered asking who Mr. Lawrence was, but remembered that women weren't supposed to butt in.

He addressed his response to the man of the house. "Mr. O'Neal didn't say anything about killing someone, or being a shield."

"Huh," came Lorenz's taunting voice. "Why are y'all calling him Mr. O'Neal when he's our brother, half-brother?"

Both Collins and Daniel looked at Lorenz. Daniel licked his lips. "I'd heard gossip about that, but I figured Mr. O'Neal would have said so if it were true."

"What'd he do, pay you a big whopping chunk of money, give you a horse, or let you loose in his Sporting…"

"Lorenz!" roared MacDonald, and Lorenz sat back his eyes glinting with strange lights, the corners of his lips on the scarred side of his face pulled up in an almost sneering smile.

Collins had heard enough. This was a family matter. "Mr. and Mrs. MacDonald, I can wait outside, if you prefer." He was irritated with O'Neal for not giving him more details. He had missed seeing Ms. Lawrence and Lorenz in Carson City as O'Neal had sent him to San Francisco to co-ordinate grain shipments from Mexico. Then he met O'Neal and Daniel in Texas. Now it sounded like he had been in danger from another source simply by traveling with Daniel. He started to rise, but MacDonald waved his hand, indicating he should remain seated.

"I apologize for the outburst, Mr. Collins, but Lorenz tis very good at irritating people. Tis nay secret that Thomas Lawrence tis the biological fither of Jeremiah O'Neal, particularly if any have seen the senior Lawrence. I'm sure Mr. O'Neal wished to spare his mither any further embarrassment and tis the reason the elder O'Neal had such hatred for my wife and her family. All of that, however, tis nay here, nay there. Daniel, ye are more than welcome to stay, but I have nay heard whether ye wish to stay, or whether O'Neal is paying ye to stay, and this tis another way for the younger O'Neal to keep tabs on Lorenz and the rest of the family."

Collins sat back bemused and took another look at the younger kid. Why would both O'Neal and MacDonald be willing to go to extreme lengths to have this youngster in their camp? The resemblance between the two young men should have been enough for one of them to be a decoy if that were the only reason. He realized that Lorenz was ready to spring from his chair and go into action if necessary. Daniel was wary and could react quickly, but his body was not tensed and positioned for a surprise attack. He recalled Gerde's statement. "Mr. Rolfe and Lorenz killed them."

Daniel tried to hide the surprise on his face, but he wondered how MacDonald had figured so quickly that O'Neal would be paying him whether he went back with Collins or whether he stayed here.

MacDonald's voice continued. "I canna pay ye what O'Neal pays. I can offer ye a home and hard work. There twill be a horse for ye to break, and ye can sell it when we trail a herd into Arles come fall. If ye have nay learned your letters and numbers, I can also help ye learn them. If ye have the rudiments, mayhap your Uncle Kasper would be the best teacher."

Daniel leaned back in his chair and looked at Lorenz and then at MacDonald. "I reckon I'd like to stay awhile."

MacDonald nodded. "Ye twill be sleeping in the same room as Lorenz." He turned back to Lorenz. "There tis but one problem. Twas Dandy a true gift, or twas he a bribe to keep ye there?"

Lorenz focused his eyes on the far window, swallowed and answered, "He was a bribe, I reckon. Red figured it would keep me there. I heard him and Rity talking about things at night when they thought I was asleep. They even talked about our," and he stopped, not wanting to say the word "pa" in front of his mother and MacDonald.

"Yere biological fither." MacDonald supplied the words with a smile.

"Yeah, him."

"Then, Lorenz, ye should send the beastie back with Mr. Collins."

Lorenz sat stunned. "It ain't Dandy's fault. He's just a horse, and Red is just going to get rid of him. He's passed his prime as a racer." He turned to his mother. "Mama, Dandy was my only company for 'most two years. Do I have to send him back?"

Anna pursed her lips and looked at her husband. She was undecided. Every bone in her despised the O'Neal's, but this was obviously important to Lorenz.

Collins remembered Red's instructions and broke in. "Mr. and Mrs. MacDonald, if Mr. O'Neal wanted that horse back he would have said so. It would be an inconvenience in traveling to worry about another animal."

Once again MacDonald narrowed his eyes and gave a tight smile. "I would think it would be handy for carrying extra supplies, however, if ye feel that way, I shall ask Mr. O'Neal in the letter if he wishes the horse returned." MacDonald stood. "Now I need some paper and pencil to write Mr. O'Neal." He started towards the desk.

Lorenz turned to his mother as he figured that in some things she would be more lenient than Papa. "Mama, can I write a letter too?"

Anna shifted in her chair to look at her youngest son. "Du to Mr. O'Neal are writing?"

A quick grin slashed across Lorenz's face. "No, ma'am, I want to write to Miss Antoinette. She was the only one who was kind to me when I was there."

MacDonald suppressed a chuckled. "And how eld tis Miss O'Neal?"

"I dunno. I reckon she's about my age, Papa."

Collins dutifully cataloged the word Papa. So that was how things stood here.

MacDonald looked at his wife whose grey eyes had opened wider. "'Tis up to ye, my love."

Anna shrugged. "I see no harm in his writing." She really did not expect an O'Neal to reply.

Lorenz smiled happily and followed MacDonald to the desk to retrieve his own piece of paper and pencil. Once seated he smoothed the paper in front of him, wet the pencil with his tongue, frowned, and looked at his mother again since he could hear MacDonald's pencil scratching away. "Mama, how do you start a letter?"

Anna kept a smile off her face and held tight to a squirming Mina. "Du start off with, 'Dear Miss O'Neal' and then put a comma after O'Neal. That vill be a mark like this," and she demonstrated without actually marking on the paper.

Daniel stared at his mother. It seemed all the white women were deemed competent enough to read and write. Strange.

Lorenz ducked his head, grasped the pencil, and then spoke again. "Mama, how do y'all spell dear, and why can't I say Dear Antoinette?"

This time, Anna did smile. "Du more formal must be vhen writing, and dear is spelled d e a r with a large D."

It was a very slow letter. Lorenz kept asking his mother to spell almost every word, but Collins noted the boy did know his letters. If he had been taught them in the brief time he had been here, that meant this was one sharp kid and O'Neal and MacDonald knew it.

Two weeks later, Collins was sitting in the office at the O'Neal plantation. He had given a verbal bare bones report of what they found, including the fake grave for Kid Lawrence, and slid the two letters and his written report over to his employer.

O'Neal, clothed in a brown, gabardine suit tailored to show off his wide shoulders, had MacDonald's letter spread out in front of him, his strange, copper eyes with the golden circles around the dark pupils were zigzagging back and forth as he read. There was a cigarillo clamped in his teeth, and he was frowning. Finally, O'Neal sat back and looked at Collins. "MacDonald says that they will be changing Lorenz's name to MacDonald when the judge comes through in the fall. Any chance Lorenz actually wants to leave there?"

"None that I could see," replied Collins. The kid calls MacDonald 'Papa' and he seemed right at home. I suspect Daniel will be coming back. He doesn't regard the place as home."

"What is this MacDonald like?"

"He's big, powerful, and I'd say fairly smart. He, Mrs. MacDonald, and the boy accused you of wanting the two young men as shields against their, and your, biological father. Biological is MacDonald's word." He wanted Red to know that he had found out more than what O'Neal had told him. He waited.

Red took the cigarillo out of mouth, set it in the ashtray, and looked back at Collins. His eyes had darkened and gone hard. "That information goes no farther than this room."

"Understood, that's why it isn't written down in the report." He tapped the sheaf of papers still in front of him.

"He also wants to know if I want that damn horse back, and if I do what arrangements we should make to achieve this end. He mentions that they may be in Saint Louis come summer if nothing is convenient before then. Did he say why they were heading north?"

Collins shook his head. "No, can't say that he did. They were breaking mustangs when we rode up. MacDonald had his back to us, but the kid must have seen us top the rise. He rolled off the horse to make it look like he was hurt, and MacDonald helped him back into the barn. I figured it was a ploy to get their guns, and it was. The kid was also one of them that shot the two your pa hired. No one bothered explaining why it was him rather than MacDonald."

O'Neal stubbed out his cigarillo. "I know you've been riding hard, but I've another job lined up for you after you've had a good night's sleep." He grinned at the dust covered man. "It's a hell of lot easier. I want you to go back to Carson City and run the two houses and the Player's Palace. Miss Lawrence will leave as soon as you arrive, and you decide if the bookkeeper she's hired is suitable. I just got my second telegram from her wanting to know when you'd be there. I can't leave here right now or the damn carpetbaggers will come calling. They're confiscating any property that belonged to rebels, or those who financed the War for the South. Since I didn't fight the Union, I should be able to keep the plantation; however, it looks like it's going to be more of a ranch than cotton plantation for a while." He sat back. "Any questions?"

After Collins left, Red took up the letter addressed to his sister Antoinette and weighed it in his hand. Should he give it to her? His mother would object, but it might be one way to hold on to Lorenz. He would insist Antoinette read it aloud and watch her as she did so. Then he could decide if he would permit her to write back.

Chapter 15

Margareatha

Margareatha was seated at her desk in the upper room of the Player's Palace. The previous night's receipts and orders for the coming week were spread out at the side of the open ledger. To her right sat a small tumbler of brandy and a cut glass bowl for her cigarillo. The open window let in the street noise of horses, wagons, and men from below. The light breeze that stirred the lace curtains at the window gave an illusion of air moving around the room.

Her red curls tumbled down her back. She'd swept the front hair up and back in a higher wave than what was considered stylish for now, but her hair was too curly to part in the front and smooth down in a bun. She'd used a deep green, velvet ribbon to outline the mass of curls and hold them up from her neck. She'd chosen a light, summer muslin dress of light green, sprinkled with darker green leaves. Since June brought the summer heat, her dress was without a collar and the muslin ended at the elbows to become white lace cascading down to her wrists. Her summer shawl of light green lace she had placed over one of the chairs in front of her desk. To her left sat two more ledger books holding the receipts from Red's whorehouses. Why he wanted each kept separate was his business. She dipped her pen and meticulously began the entries.

She had not sensed any outside danger and completely engrossed herself with the nice, clean numbers marching in each column. The quick rap on the door startled her, and she gave a slight jump, then frowned when a young voice chirped, "Western Union."

"One moment," she said and stood, stretched, and glanced at the ticking clock behind her. Almost noon, she'd been working for an hour. She walked across the small room and opened the door.

A slender boy of about ten in much washed clothes and hat with Western Union stuck above the brim stood there. He knew this was business and handed her the paper.

"Just a moment and I'll get my purse." She walked over to her purse and extracted a dime and gave it to the boy, who was fidgeting back and forth.

"Um, Miss Lawrence, Mr. Miller wants to know if you want to pay for forwarding the one that came in for Mr. O'Neal from the same place."

A slight frown went across her face, and she said, "Just a moment, I'll see who this is from first." She opened the telegram and stood there clutching it in both hands as her mouth opened and her copper eyes with the golden circles around the pupils widened. Silence spread over the room as she read and re-read the words, "A letter from your mother, Mrs. Anna MacDonald, nee Schmidt to follow."

"Ma'am, are you all right?" The boy finally managed to say. He had more deliveries to make, and while Miss Lawrence always tipped good and he could spare a few extra moments, he couldn't dawdle or Mr. Miller would be mad.

Rita looked up and around the room as though trying to locate the voice that had intruded on her thoughts. Finally she wet her lips, and murmured, "Yes, yes, I'll pay to forward the message, but first I want to add one for you to take back with you."

She sat down at the desk as her legs had become too wobbly to stand. She pulled a tablet from one of the drawers. The pen scratched out a quick note advising Red to return, or send someone else to run the Player's Palace and do the bookkeeping. She fully intended to leave as soon as the letter arrived with her mother's location. She also directed Miller to give the rest of the money to the boy as a tip. The note was folded and sealed to prevent someone other than Mr. Miller opening it. She opened her purse and fished out a twenty dollar gold piece.

"Here, this will pay for the two telegrams and the rest of the money is yours. I've instructed Mr. Miller to give you the difference. If you don't receive at least ten dollars, you come back here and let me know." She snapped the last sentence out to keep from getting up and throwing her arms around him. There was still enough awareness within to realize the scandal that would create.

The boy stood there staring at the two items in his hand in disbelief. Finally he raised his eyes and gulped out. "Yes, ma'am, thank you, ma'am. I'll run right back to the station." He stared at her again and then turned and ran out the door.

Rita sat bolt upright at the desk, flashbacks of her life running in her mind. The horror of losing her family, of being locked in that shed of O'Neal's, of the ordeal of a Catholic nunnery where she was branded a heretic. Dear, God, Mama was alive. Lorenz was with her. Why now, why when she had carved out a life? What words could she possibly use to tell her mother about how she made her living? And yet deep inside all she wanted was for her mother to put her arms around her and to tell her that she was Mama's beautiful daughter. She finally stood and put the receipts and money into the safe and draped the shawl around her shoulders. She had to move, leave this stuffy little room, and breathe air or she would surely scream.

She walked down the stairs and out the front, unable to focus on anyone or anything. She did not acknowledge the greeting from the cleaning woman, nor did she see the few determined card players getting an early start on the evening.

Carson City had started as a mining camp in the 1850s and boomed throughout the Civil War It had supplied the gold and silver the Union so desperately needed, and miners arrived in hordes, partly to avoid a draft and partly for the wages. Yellow-bellies, released from Yankee prisons but barred from returning to the South, migrated here where there were the amenities of civilization combined with railroads, telegraphs, a brewery, and no fervent local political challenges Carson City was new, raw, and exploding with incoming arrivals. To accommodate them, new buildings, new roads, new and bigger hotels tried to keep pace with the people who came: People determined to forge Nevada into a new and powerful force in the nation.

The War was over and the economies of the East and South were depressed, but here the building went on with the sound of hammers and the smell of raw wood filling the air. The mines ran night and day, the stamp mills adding their din to the town noises. People were arriving in large numbers on stage from the East and South, or the railroad from California to replace the few who left as their fortunes declined. The air remained dust filled and scented with sawdust and the stink of man and beast.

Rita strode unheeding through the dusty streets, past the backside of the St. Charles-Muller Hotel, and went up Curry Street. She didn't notice the women who withdrew their skirts or the young boys that gaped at her height. She wanted refuge from prying eyes and that refuge was home. Her rapid steps carried her to Proctor Street and she marched up the steps into her house, and closed the door firmly behind her.

Teresa appeared with broom in hand staring at her. "Are you sick, Senorita? Can I get you something?"

Rita tried to form words and found that her mouth and lips were dry. The blank, dumb look began to leave the copper eyes and she answered, "Yes, a glass of water. Bring it outside, please."

It took four weeks for the letter to arrive. Rita had resumed her daily life of nights at the Player's Palace and days of book-keeping and ordering. Once the incompetent fool Red had left in charge of the whorehouses had tried to withhold funds and she left him with a raging headache that incapacitated him for days. She put the Madams in charge of their respective houses, but knew it couldn't last. The one was too far gone in booze to be efficient. To compensate, she put the madam from the Sporting Palace in charge of both houses and increased her salary tem-porarily on the understanding that when Red's agent arrived, everything would return to normal.

One part of her daily routine did vary. After the second week of waiting, she started stopping at the Post Office off of Carson Street for any mail. She could not bear the thought of anyone else touching her mother's letter or intruding into her personal life.

She stopped in one morning at eleven o'clock and walked to the collection area. The men assumed their look of embarrass-ment and the women, as usual, pulled their skirts away. Rita ignored them. She knew she was faultlessly coiffured and fault-lessly dressed in more stylish, expensive clothes than they wore or could afford. Deep down, she rather enjoyed the discomfort she inflicted on them just as she had enjoyed defying the nuns. She always kept her face composed, smiled at the Postmaster whether there was mail or not, and swept out of the room leav-ing a lingering hint of expensive perfume.

The morning the letter arrived was no different except she forgot to smile. She paid the man from her bag, clutched ev-erything in her hand, and stalked out to her chaise, climbed in, snapped the reins, and turned the horse toward home. Once there, she again surprised Teresa, but this time she asked for nothing and went to her bedroom and closed the door. She wanted no one to see her face when she read it. First she sniffed at the letter, but there was no trace of her mother's smell. She smoothed it open.

My darling, beautiful, Margareatha,

Mr. MacDonald brought Lorenz home today and he has given me your address. Lorenz says hello. You must sell that place and come home immediately. I do not care what you have done. I only thank God that you are alive and my prayers have been answered. Do not delay. We are waiting for you.

I married Mr. MacDonald seven years ago, and we have a three-year-old daughter. Do not worry about a place to sleep. Our house is big enough as Mr. MacDonald is a good husband and a good provider. He will welcome you just as he has welcomed Lorenz. Our ranch is near Schmidt's Corner. The town is named after your Uncle Kasper.

Do you remember him and Gerde? They have been praying for your safekeeping also. They lost their little Hans in the typhoid plague of '57-'58 and have not had any more children. Your grandfather Schmidt is in good health. He and his wife, Johanna, have eight children.

The closest town to us of any size is Arles, Texas. Let us know when you are coming, and we will meet you there. Send any letter to Schmidt's Corner, Texas. It will take time, but it will arrive.

My darling, my heart, I cannot wait to have my arms around you again.

Your loving mother,

Anna Maria MacDonald (nee Schmidt)

Rita stared at the paper, remembering her mother's handwriting, the lessons and practice sessions. The memories of her tall, slender, dark haired, grey-eyed mother smiling at her went rolling through her mind: the cooking lessons, the care of laundry, and the help with her catechism lessons. It was a place where everything had seemed safe, warm, and loving.

She stood and mentally reviewed everything that needed to be accomplished before she left. Her mother may proclaim that MacDonald a good provider, but inwardly she wondered. The men stopping at the Player's Palace and reports from Red indicated that Texas was as beaten economically as the rest of the South.

Rita went into the dining room and opened the top drawer to the credenza and pulled out two sheets of paper. First she would answer her mother and then send Red another telegram. She would be leaving the first week of August whether a replacement was here or not.

Nature, genetics, and the year of her birth had all conspired against Margareatha. She stood six foot tall when most women were barely five foot. A century later, men would say, "She has big boobs." Now they said, "She is a fine, full figure of a woman," with the same awed look on their faces. Her height and intelligence frightened men. Few were bold enough to really talk with her, but all welcomed the chance to beat her at cards. Had they known she could also read their minds and see an image of their cards displayed in her mind, she probably would have been hounded out of town or burned as a witch. She did not care. The cards provided her with an extremely good living. It was Red's whorehouses she detested. It was impossible to fathom why the women stayed, and she felt no compassion for them.

The Postmaster looked at her in surprise when she entered the second time in one day. It was close to two o'clock, and there were few people. She handed him the letter, properly addressed and sealed. "It'll go out on the next stage, ma'am." She nodded, spun, and walked out to the railroad depot.

The depot was as empty of people as the smaller building she had just left. She saw Mr. Miller coming out of the telegraph office, hat in hand, and she stepped into his path.

"Good morning, Miss Lawrence. I was just on my way to the bank, but I'll be happy to send something for you." He opened the door and practically bowed her in. Rita tried to keep the contempt off her face and was partially successful.

The same young boy she'd tipped so lavishly the month before was seated at the key. He jumped when he saw them and almost bowed to her, and her face softened as she handed over the note for Red. Miller read it, grunted, "Humph, ten words, one dollar, please."

She paid and turned to leave as Miller spoke again. "Uh, Miss Lawrence, we truly will be sorry to see you leave."

She spun and glared at him. "That information goes no further than this room."

"Of course, ma'am, I was just voicing a personal opinion."

She nodded and hurried out of the building. It was stuffy, hot, and confining. The outside wasn't much better, but at least there was fresh air.

Chapter 16

Gerald

Marshal Franklin looked up as three men and a kid walked into his office and realized one was the huge form of MacDonald. Next to the big man were two young men wearing guns. For a moment Franklin thought he was seeing double and realized one was a tad taller and sported a trim mustache. While the two look a-likes might be considered men out here, the straw-headed one was still a kid. He didn't want MacDonald to think he'd slacked off on his job. "As y'all know there are no charges against the youngest. I see y'all gave his guns back."

MacDonald smiled. "Aye, we ken about the false charge, and he tis a responsible laddie. Marshal, this tis Mrs. MacDonald's eldest, Daniel Hunt, and a laddie named Chalky. Chalky tis trying to locate his mither, his brither, and his sister. Their place, about two days ride from here, tis burned and nay are around."

Franklin sat back. "That would be the Plank's place. We don't know who's responsible. When we got there, the woman and the little girl were dead, and the boy can't talk."

Chalky's face now matched his name in color. "Whar's my brother?" he managed to blurt out. "And he does too talk." He looked at MacDonald.

Marshal Franklin sighed. He had wondered how MacDonald would spoil his day again. "We placed him with one of the small holdings outside of town. We're not big enough for an orphanage, and there he stays. Unless, of course, you have enough money to prove you can be responsible."

Chalky wasn't quite sure what the man meant except that he had to have money to get his brother back. He pulled out the five dollars that MacDonald had paid him for being the wrangler and showed it. He might not be able to write, but he had a way with horses, and he still had his job at the Schmidt's when they went back. "Ah's got money." For once in his life, Chalky sounded belligerent. "My Ma'am 'spects me to take care of him an' ah's gots a good job, don't ah, Mr. Mac?"

Franklin doubted it as he watched MacDonald rocking back and forth on his heels and rolling his tongue around in his mouth. This could be a good day.

MacDonald looked down at Chalky's earnest face and said, "Why dinna we pay a visit to this place and see if yere brither has a good home? Then ye can decide which would be best for yere brither." He looked at Marshal Franklin.

Franklin hunched his shoulders and leaned forward. "I don't think you all need to disturb those good folks. They were kind enough to take the dummy in."

"He ain't a dummy. Ah doant know what yu all mean. He can too talk!" Chalky looked at MacDonald. "Ah gots to see him for Ma'am's sake." He had broken down at the shell that had been their home and had accepted the fact that all might be dead. Now he knew his brother needed him, and he became as stubborn as the mules he could control when no one else could.

MacDonald considered. "Marshall, I'll have to agree with Chalky. The men who murdered the woman and young girl are the same ones that tried to kill Mr. and Mrs. Schmidt. Chalky was able to get away and gave us the warning. I believe ye have my letter on that incident." When Franklin nodded, he continued. "So if ye twill be kind enough to give directions, we'll take a look. We owe that to Chalky's family."

Franklin considered and then shrugged. If they took the dummy, the county wouldn't have to pay for his keep, and Franklin would be able to take credit.

"If there's trouble, I expect you all to obey the law." He set his face and watched MacDonald. It was best to ignore the two young men. They looked like hard cases in the making.

"Aye, tis something I do."

"It's the last place on the edge of town as y'all ride out to the fort. The people there are the Quincy's. Remember, no trouble." Franklin sat back with a certain amount of satisfaction as they clanked out. He'd heard the cavalry was being moved come spring, and Rolfe and MacDonald would have nowhere to sell their beeves.

They pulled their horses up at a ramshackle place badly in need of paint. The front yard was dry and brown, but they could see a young boy busy hoeing in what was left of the garden. MacDonald put a restraining hand on Chalky's reins and bellowed out the greeting. "Hello, the house." The kid with the hoe didn't even look, just kept working.

An unkempt man with thinning, brown hair came slouching out of the house holding a shotgun in the crook of his arm. His hair was lifting in the breeze and his canvas trousers were dirty and patched. It was difficult to determine the original color of the dingy, faded, collarless shirt he wore over his skinny frame. "Yu all lookin' for someone?" His gritty voice was peevish as though he had been taken away from something more important than Yankees in his yard.

"My name tis MacDonald, and young Chalky would like a word with his brither to see how he tis faring."

The man narrowed his eyes. "That dummy cain't talk, and he's faring jest fine. Get off my property." He started to raise the shotgun when a gun exploded and the twisted metal fell from his hands.

"Lorenz, put the gun away." MacDonald's voice was calm. He had not even looked around, but kept his eyes on Quincy. "That twas a mistake. Ye should nay have raised that shotgun."

Chalky's eyes were wide, and the young boy had dropped to the ground, his back still towards them. Chalky looked at MacDonald.

"Go get your brither, Chalky. He goes to House with us." MacDonald looked at the man in front of him.

"Yu all ain't got no right!" The man was screaming, holding on to his aching arm. "Yu all jest ruined my damn gun. Yu all owes me!"

"We owe ye nay. I twill inform Marshal Franklin that ye pulled a shotgun on us. Lorenz, would ye retrieve it for us." He kept his eyes forward and saw Chalky pick up his brother. The boy wrapped his arms around Chalky's neck and his legs around Chalky's waist. MacDonald could see the gashes and old welts showing through the boy's tattered clothes. "I twill also inform the Marshal that the laddie is nay longer here, and ye canna collect from the county."

Quincy started to say something, saw the hard look on MacDonald's face, and changed his mind. He watched glumly as they rode out vowing someday to get even.

Five days later, MacDonald, Rolfe, Chalky, and Gerald clattered into the Schmidt's back yard. Rolfe was there to pick up his younger son, and MacDonald because he had promised Chalky. Gerald still hadn't said a word; not on the trip home and none to Anna. Lorenz swore he heard the child whispering one night, but no one else but Chalky believed the boy would talk again. "Sometimes it happens like dot," Rolfe opined.

James flew out of the garden and greeted his father as they dismounted. They entered the kitchen after knocking. Gerald wouldn't let go of Chalky's hand, and Chalky kept up a monotone about how good the Schmidts were and how good Mrs. Schmidt cooked. Gerde busied herself pouring coffee while the men shook hands, then she put her hands on her hips and stared at the child. Gerald immediately buried his head into Chalky's side.

"Herman, your boy has done very well on the German and Latin, but we need to keep up the lessons if he is to make it into Concordia when he's eighteen," Kasper was saying. He was trying to ignore the child, fear making his stomach turn. He could not bear the thought of Gerde dealing with a child and knew he would be turning this one away. Chalky stood patiently waiting his turn once MacDonald explained everything as he knew MacDonald could resolve all things.

Gerde took matters in hand and moved forward. "What's this?" Her face was set and grim and her eyes bored into Chalky's.

Chalky gulped and blurted out. "He's my brother, and ah'll take keer of him, and he can bunk with me, and he won't be no trouble 'cause ah'll work fer nothin' here, and Mr. Mac says ah can run the remuda when we trail cattle agin, and he doan eat much." Chalky's voice petered out. It was the speech he had memorized over and over. Then he remembered the part he left out. "And ah've got money left, and ah'm goin' to buy his clothes right here from yu all, and he won't be no trouble." Once more Chalky fell silent.

Kasper cleared his throat in preparation to speak, but Gerde asked Gerald a question first. "And what is your name, and how old are you?

Gerald kept his face buried in Chalky's side. "His name's Gerry, short fer Gerald, and he cain't talk since they kilt our Ma'am, and ah ain't sure how old he is. About seven or eight, ah reckon."

A look of horror swept over Gerde's face. "He vas there when it happened?"

"Yas, ma'am."

Gerde went down on her knees in front of the boy. "I'm so sorry, lieb. I did not mean for my words to hurt you. Of course, you may stay here. We have plenty of good food and a bedroom upstairs. We have clothes just your size and Mr. Schmidt can teach you how to read and write. Then some day we will go back and visit your mother's grave."

Gerald was staring at her, and Gerde smiled back, warmth rising in her eyes as she held out her arms. Gerald put his arms around her neck and began to cry, sobs racking the thin body. Gerde stood making crooning noises and carried him into the living room to the rocking chair, and then sat with him on her lap.

Kasper looked at the men and said, "Gerde smiled." His voice was awed. He turned and hurried after her.

Chapter 17

The Daughter

Lorenz headed towards the house carrying the evening's pail of milk. Daniel was helping Papa feed the stock. Nothing ever convinced Daniel that he should milk a cow. Lorenz was surprised to discover he didn't mind. Maybe Grandpa's Schmidt's clod buster ways were in his blood. Daniel, at least, no longer attempted to raze him about anything. Not since that first week.

It had happened one morning after they'd been working on gentling the mustangs that had left Lorenz with an aching shoulder and a cramped leg. Daniel was easily the best horseman. His years with the Comanche had given him a background with horses that most white men didn't possess. Daniel swung the saddle over the new tree and remarked, "Well, little brother, it looks like you need a few lessons on how to sit a real horse, not that dandified old nag you claim as your own."

"So you ride better than I do, so what?" Lorenz shrugged and instantly regretted the movement. He must have landed harder than what he'd thought.

Daniel grinned at him. "Lots better," he agreed. "In fact, I do it all better. I'm four years older, remember?" He looked out the open doors at MacDonald adding water to the tank. "What were you two doing early this morning? Practicing to fight?" There was almost a sneer in his tone.

"Papa was teaching me some moves."

"It looked more like you were dancing."

"It's all in how y'all control the muscles." Lorenz started to turn away. It seemed Daniel was on the prowl for some reason.

He didn't move fast enough. "Like this?" asked Daniel and stiff-armed him in the chest, grinning like he fully expected Lorenz to fall or at least stagger backwards. Lorenz felt the anger rise and the next thing he knew they were on the barn floor, and he was on top of Daniel slamming first one fist into Daniel's head and then the other.

Daniel tried to move, but his head was swimming and his arms, body, and legs felt leaden. The blows stopped as suddenly as they began. Daniel propped himself up on one elbow and shook his head. For a moment his vision blurred and he realized one eye was swelling shut. He could see MacDonald's body blocking the light coming in the open doors, and he was holding a kicking, arms and legs flailing Lorenz.

As soon as Lorenz quit struggling, MacDonald set him down. Then he knelt beside Daniel and asked, "Are ye all right?"

"Yeah." Daniel pushed himself up, and MacDonald gave him a hand, steadying him as they stood.

"Who started this?"

Lorenz was staring at them, his eyes a hard, cold grey. His mouth was open, but no sound came out. MacDonald looked at him and then at a silent Daniel. "Ye are both a wee bit large for me to take off my belt and burn yere backsides."

Daniel gave a half-smile. "I reckon I was riding him for being younger."

MacDonald turned to Lorenz. The expression on Lorenz's face hadn't changed and his breath was going in and out in sharp, angry gasps while he clenched and unclenched his fists. "Lorenz, go toss some rocks till ye calm down." He pointed to a place beyond the outhouse.

As Lorenz stalked off, MacDonald turned to Daniel. "I suggest ye nay push him into a fight again. He beat ye years ago, and he twill nay ere lose a fight."

"But he's four years younger than me. There ain't no way he can beat me. I must have slipped."

MacDonald sighed. "Daniel, ye ride better than Lorenz. Mayhap ye even shoot faster and more accurately, but nay ere pull a gun on him. Ye will die, and Lorenz twill live with the mark of Cain on his soul."

Daniel pulled in a big gulp of air. "You don't know that."

"Oh, but I do. Have ye ere killed a man."

"I may have in that last raid before the cavalry swept through and destroyed the village."

"'Tis nay what I mean. I mean stand there and kill someone whilst they are looking at ye."

"No."

"Lorenz has several times over, and those men were more than four years his elder. I mean it. Nay ere point a gun at him. I suggest ye settle any differences with words. Ye both twill live much happier." He turned and followed Lorenz. Daniel remembered those words when Lorenz bested his draw while shooting the shotgun out of Quincy's hands. He had managed to pull his gun out when Lorenz's shot rang out, yet when they just stood and practiced, he, Daniel, was faster.

Lorenz wasn't sure what Papa said to Daniel after the fight, but whatever it was, Daniel let him be. He looked up towards the road and saw a rider, leading another horse, top the rise. The day had been humid with black-blue clouds hovering in the distance. The clouds had been moving closer each hour promising a downpour to wash away the dust and brown of a too dry summer landscape. The distance from the house to the rise was close to a quarter of a mile, and the figure seated on a horse appeared grey and shrunken under the darkening sky. Even at this distance, he knew it was Rity. Like the wind, he began to move faster, not caring if he sloshed the milk out of the pail. Instead of heading for the springhouse, he ran to the front of the house, set the pail on the porch, and yelled, "Mama, Rity's coming in!" He turned and ran to meet her.

Rita flicked her crop against the horse when she saw Lorenz running towards her and then pulled up in a flourish as they met. Lorenz grasped the reins as a precaution when she dismounted, and they hugged each other. "I'm sorry I ran off, Rity, but glad I did," he said as they broke apart. He was grinning from ear to ear and his grey eyes were shining.

Rita had her hands on his shoulders and was smiling back, tears streaming down her face. "Look at you, just look. You've grown so tall and that scar has almost disappeared." They started to walk towards the house. "How's Mama?"

"She's fine. She'll be mad that y'all didn't wait in town for us to come guide y'all in."

Rita snorted. "I do not need an escort." They were walking hand in hand as they had done when Lorenz was little. "What's Mama's husband like?"

"He's the most bodacious man I ever met."

Rita stopped and stared at him. "Bodacious? Where in the world did you learn to speak like that?"

Lorenz smiled more broadly. "Mama and Papa taught me, and they're teaching me to read and write and cipher. I've even started studying Luther's Small Catechism, but since it's in Deutsch, it's taking longer. My accent ain't, isn't real good yet."

"Unbelievable," Rita murmured. They picked up their pace as they felt the first spatters of rain while thunder rolled in the background.

Anna came running out the door, and they hugged and pulled each other into the house. Lorenz shrugged and grabbed the milk pail. He knew he best get it into the springhouse or it would be wasted, and he would hear about it over and over again. He'd bring in the pitcher of milk and come back for the horses. He figured most of the things on the packhorse would go into the house anyways.

"Mein hertzan, my heart, my kinder."

Anna's words were like balm on Rita's closed heart. She let the tears flow faster and faster and did not care. The world never saw Rita cry, but Mama was different. Mama knew, Mama cared, and Mama loved her. It didn't matter that she was twenty-three and six foot tall, she was still Mama's little girl. "Oh, Mama, Mama," she kept saying over and over.

Finally they drew apart. Anna used her apron to wipe her tears and then Margareatha's tears. "Velcome home, Margareatha," she managed to say in English. "Do du remember any Deutsch?"

"Very little, Mama," and Margareatha began to cry again. Anna put her arms around her and held her tighter.

Finally the shaking body calmed, and Anna released her. "Du still have your beautiful red hair," Anna murmured. Then she felt the tugging at her skirt and looked down.

"Ach, Mina." She bent and picked her up. "This is your sister, Margareatha."

Mina was rapidly nearing her fourth birthday and losing her baby fat. Her reddish-brown curls were deepening to a darker brown with tints of red left from the sun. Her brown eyes were solemn as she gazed at her older sister, smiled shyly, said "Hullo," very softly, and buried her face on her mother's shoulder.

"Tsk, Mina," said Anna.

Lorenz came through the kitchen with the milk. "How much of your stuff comes in here?" he asked.

"Everything but the feed bags. I emptied those out last night."

"It figures." He went outside and returned with a saddlebag from Rita's riding horse and part of the packs lashed to the extra horse.

Rita bent and picked up one of the bags and opened it. "Here I have something for you." She rummaged inside and came up with a small case. "This is for you, Mama." She handed Anna a set of nacre buttons. To Mina she held out a small heart locket with the word Baby inscribed on the front. "I didn't know what else to get you until I was actually here. There's some tobacco in there for Lorenz and for Daniel, and Mr. MacDonald, if he smokes."

Anna's eyebrows were raised, and she stared at her older daughter. "Du did not need to buy for us anything." She could see the traveling suit Rita wore, while beautifully tailored from expensive fabric, the skirt was not really a skirt, but split up the middle for riding a horse astraddle like a man.

Rita shrugged and said, "Oh, Mama, I wanted to." Impulsively she hugged her mother again, Mina and all. "Let's see how this looks around your neck, Mina."

Mina raised her head and turned, her eyes opened wide at the unexpected treasure, and she smiled.

Lorenz opened the door and deposited the rest of the bundles from the packhorse. "It's really coming down out there." Water was dripping off the brim of his hat. Thunder crashed above to emphasize his words as he disappeared.

"I must to the supper see. Du can take those things into Mina's room. She'll show du."

When Rita returned, she had changed into a dull green work shift with three quarter length sleeves, a square neckline, and tied at the waist with green ribbon. "What can I do to help?"

Supper preparation became a flurry of half commands, fingers pointing at the drawer holding the silverware, the cabinet holding the dishes, and snatches of conversation to patch the holes in their lives.

"Ve vent to Saint Louis after ve vere married and saw the American Fur Company before ve vent on to see Papa and Johanna." Anna's face was flushed from stove heat and from memories.

"Some grain buyer for Red's shipping line found Daniel in a Kansas fort where he'd been taken after his village was annihilated. We'd had flyers and inquiries out."

"Your uncle is much better, but he has to take things easy."

"Are you truly happy, Mama?"

"Ach, ja, Mr. MacDonald is not like your father."

As if on cue, a very wet MacDonald walked in the door and hung up his hat. Before he had completely turned around, he was attacked by Mina. She practically leaped up into his arms, and he buried his face into her neck as she screamed in delight. He sat her down and turned to greet his wife and then Rita.

Rita had her hand to her throat, her mouth open as though mouthing the word no. Her copper eyes showed the white above and below and her tanned skin turned an underlying pallor of white.

Anna had stepped forward, pride, love, and welcome in her face and voice as she said, "Mr. MacDonald, I vant du to meet Margareatha." Her voice trailed away as she saw the look on MacDonald's face. Before he could speak Daniel and Lorenz were crowding through the door to get out of the rain.

"Lorenz, wrap Mina in a coat and go select a wine for supper tonight. Daniel, go with him. Now!" His voice cracked like a whip on the last word.

Lorenz took one look at his rigid back and Rita's white face and grabbed an extra coat, slung it around Mina, picked her up, and jostled Daniel out the door. Both of them bent their heads to deflect the force of the wind and rain.

"What was that all about?" demanded Daniel.

"I dunno, but Rity's got her back up about something. Come on, let's get under cover." They practically ran the few steps to the washhouse.

"It's getting dark in here," complained Daniel. "How are we supposed to see?"

"It isn't going to matter," replied Lorenz. "Rity likes brandy, but will drink wine. Just as long as we grab a bottle and give Papa a few minutes to settle whatever's going on in there. We'll hear about it later." He almost added *after Mina goes to bed*, but decided that would be a dumb thing to say. Mina would want to know too. "Go ahead and open up the barrel, and we'll pick something."

Anna was looking at her daughter with a slight frown on her face as her sons left the house. "It would seem," MacDonald's voice rumble out, "that yere lassie recognizes a Thalian when she sees one. That means she has been talking with her fither, and he tis alive."

"No," snapped Rita. "I've not seen the man."

"Then who have ye spoke with?"

Rita set her mouth. "That's none of your business." She turned to Anna. "Mama, why did you lie to me? You must be miserable!"

Anna took a deep breath and stepped next to her husband and grasped his hand. "I haf not lied. Mr. MacDonald ist a fine, good man."

Rita stared at the two of them. They were united against her. Her eyebrows drew together in puzzlement.

"I suggest we suspend this conversation till the wee one has gone to bed. She tis nay eld enough to comprehend what we twill be saying. There twill be a truce whilst we eat."

"Ja!" Anna agreed and looked at her daughter.

"We'll need to wait until Lorenz and Daniel go to bed." Rita's voice was firm.

"Why? Lorenz kens who his biological fither tis and were he tis from. Tis time Daniel twas aware of his heritage," said Mac-Donald. "He has heard Mina's story once so he twill have an inkling of what we speak."

Rita stared at him, a look of complete horror on her face, and she turned again to her mother, her voice condescending as though speaking to someone with less wit. "I do not know how he has deluded you, but surely you must acknowledge that Daniel cannot understand what we will be discussing."

"Vhy, because he does not have two hearts from Mr. Lawrence like du and Lorenz?" Anna snapped the words back.

This volley left Rita open mouthed again and blinking her eyes.

Amusement flooded MacDonald's voice. "Do ye think yere mither a fool? She lived with Toma for over twelve years. She birthed all of ye. She kens who has two hearts and walks in the minds of others. As I said, a truce till later. The laddies are returning, and I twill nay have Mina upset."

Rita projected her mind outward to determine if her mother was withholding something and discovered she could not enter. Anna's lips narrowed and she exclaimed, "Not in this house! I vill not permit it."

The laughter was back in MacDonald's eyes as he turned to meet the young men and took his daughter. "Did ye find a nice bottle of wine?"

Lorenz looked at him and grinned. "Yes, Papa."

MacDonald perched Mina on his shoulders and washed his hands, and then the other two took their turns. "Supper vill be on as soon as du are out of the vay," said Anna.

The meal was not exactly strained silence. There were still too many years between them and a type of family normalcy returned after saying grace and the passing of bowls and platters began. Rita closed her eyes and smiled when biting down on the yeast rolls that went with the stew. "Oh, Mama, they are as good as I remember. Did Lorenz tell you that I ran a bakery in Tucson?"

"Ach, ja, he did. Did du remember how I taught du to bake pies?"

"Yes," laughed Rita, "but it was hard at first with only dried fruit. It wasn't the fresh fruit we used from Grandpa's orchard."

"Have you heard from O'Neal lately?" asked Daniel, forgetting how that name could throw Anna into a foul mood.

"Yes, he's made accommodations with the Union and the Union Army by paying for his father's pardon, and they left him alone and the ranch intact. He doesn't think they'll get a Reconstruction Bill through congress as long as President Johnson remains so favorable to the South." Rita then addressed her remarks to Lorenz. "Why didn't you stay with Red after you went back to Wooden looking for Mama?"

Lorenz looked at his sister and answered in a flat voice. "Then Zale would still be alive."

Daniel figured something should be said to put his employer in a good light. "At least he sent the telegram telling the Marshal that you didn't kill his uncle and steal the gold."

Lorenz looked at Daniel, slightly amused. He knew Red hadn't bothered to enlighten Daniel about anything. "He had to. He knocked his uncle out and took the gold. He needed it for, uhh, some purchases." Lorenz figured Mama would have a fit if he said buy some women to ship to Carson City.

His euphemism didn't work. Anna laid her knife down and snorted. "I told du the man ist evil." She turned to Rita seated at her left. "How could du vork for such an evil man? No, vait, do not answer. Mina, eat your supper." She realized Mina was listening with rapt attention. "Little pitchers big ears have," she said to everyone in general.

Daniel figured it was time to leave O'Neal out and said to Lorenz, "You never said how you managed alone like that. Did you work some place?"

"Naw, I took some of the gold coins when I left camp." Lorenz stopped abruptly.

MacDonald looked at Lorenz. "And how do ye intend to repay Mr. O'Neal? Ye already owe him for Dandy."

Lorenz sat silent for a moment and raised his head. "When Zale's reward money gets here, I reckon." At the rate he was going, he figured he'd be an old man before he paid everyone back.

Anna was outraged. "I do not vant any money going to that man. It vas Confederate gold."

Rita glanced at MacDonald and was amazed to see him fighting a smile tugging at the corner of his mouth, and realized what a handsome man he was. The mouth line was medium with a full under lip, the nose small and well-shaped, the eyes were black-brown set underneath a high forehead, the head square and covered with deep black, straight hair combed back. His shoulders were broad and he gave off an aura of a powerful, intelligent man. Her heart thudded in her chest just looking at him. No wonder her mother had fallen for him, but why had he married someone so much older? Then she remembered the booklet had said the Thalians lived to be well over two hundred years or more. Her mother was still glaring at him. Was there a chance she could separate them? She would need to talk with Daniel.

"Mayhap tis a conversation we should save for later," said MacDonald mildly. "Is the wine any good?"

Slowly a smile went across Anna's face. "Ja, it's fine." She wiped Mina's face.

MacDonald looked at Rita. "Ye picked a good time to return. Yere mither and ye twill be able to talk with nay interruptions when we all go into Arles next week"

Rita looked at her mother and then at MacDonald. "All of you? Why"

"We're going in for my adoption," said Lorenz. My name will be MacDonald.

This time Rita's mouth fell open. "Adopted? Why?"

"Because, he's papa." Lorenz's eyes turned flinty grey and dared her to dispute him. The finality in his voice left Rita temporarily without voice. Somehow, she must talk with Daniel.

Anna stood as the others began to push their plates to the side and rise from the table. Well trained, they all picked up their plates and utensils and carried them into the kitchen.

"I'll start the laddies on their lessons since ye have someone to help ye this evening."

The dishes went quickly while Rita and Anna stayed on subjects certain to not antagonize the other. "Du may vant to get your night clothes out vhile I take Mina outside," said Anna as she retrieved the youngest from MacDonald's lap. "Or do du vant to come along and see vhere it is." There was no need to explain "it."

"I think I'll walk along." They grabbed the men's slickers and wrapped themselves and Mina against the storm.

When they returned, the women disappeared into Mina's bedroom after MacDonald had bid Mina goodnight with a hug and a kiss. Rita itched to ask if he was always like that and decided against it. She put out her nightclothes for later and hurried out to the front. Maybe there was a chance she could smoke while Mama was still in the bedroom, but the opportunity slid away and her frustration mounted until she heard Anna call for MacDonald to come and tell Mina a story. He went into the bedroom, and Rita lit and inhaled deeply on the cigarillo she'd hidden in her pocket. She looked at her two handsome brothers with their broad shoulders, straight features, grey eyes, cleft chins, and wavy, curly black hair; handsome in a lean, angular way, and tried to fish out some information.

"Do they always work together like that?" she asked.

"Always," answered Lorenz. He grinned. "I quit trying to fool them both within a week of being here."

Rita frowned and wondered how to get rid of Daniel. Surely, they could not have been serious about discussing lineage with Daniel present. She looked at his papers and saw that Daniel was practicing adding and subtracting. "I didn't know you were interested in ciphering," she admitted.

"You never asked."

Rita picked up one of Lorenz's books. It was *Luther's Small Catechism* written in German. "You are reading this?" she gurgled out.

"Some of it. Most of the time it's still just memorization, but the words start making sense after I've gone through a page." Lorenz grinned at her. "It seems I haven't forgotten everything." He stressed forgotten and looked at Daniel. Daniel ignored him.

Silence descended on the siblings until Anna and MacDonald walked out of the short hallway. "Ye might as well put up the books for now," said MacDonald. "It seems we need to cover a few misunderstandings. Did ye wish me to start?" He looked down at Anna as he asked the question.

"No," she sighed. "I'll start." She wet her lips, and MacDonald put his arm around her shoulders. They made a striking couple: both were tall, one with white hair, one with black. "I made a mistake vhen I married Mr. Lawrence so young. Having all of du vas not a mistake. Du vere, and are, everyone of one of du, beautiful, vonderous gifts from God, and I fought so hard to keep him from killing du. It vas a mistake to go with him to Texas, but I still thought I had to be the obedient frau."

Rita pushed her chair back and tried to think of some way to stop this. Was her mother as mad as the Thalian? "Mama, you cannot say anymore." Before she could stand, MacDonald broke in.

"Why? Because Daniel does nay have two hearts like ye and Lorenz have from yere biological fither?"

Rita gulped in air and stared at him, unable to rise. She had forgotten to put out the cigarillo, and smoke curled up in a lazy, scented spiral.

Daniel shook his head as if to clear it. "What are you people talking about?"

"Yere heritage, the one ye can pass down to any wee ones ye may have."

"None of us can have children," Rita said through clenched teeth.

"That may nay be true. Ye exist, and all of yere full siblings, except one, exist. I exist and Mina exists. Tis true we lost our wee laddie, but in this world who tis there to say why. I am nay medical, but there tis truly something fecund about this world."

"What the hell does that mean?" Daniel let his impatience get the better of his tongue. When he saw MacDonald's eyebrows go up, he said, "Sorry, ma'am."

MacDonald nodded his head in acknowledgement and answered, "Fertile, all things conceive and grow here."

Rita broke in. "I do not know how or why Mama had so many children, but we, her offspring aren't able to have children, and the same will hold true for Mina."

MacDonald's lips curled. "My dear, I have two hearts for my fither was a Justine. I am considered a mutant, but contrary to Justine biology and teaching, Mina exists and tis a healthy, normal Earth child."

"That can't be!" Rita was incapable of discrediting what she had learned.

"You three really have two hearts?" Daniel could not believe what he was hearing and started to rise out of his chair.

A crooked, leering smile crossed MacDonald's face. "Oh, aye, and since Lorenz and ye dinna get along and Margareatha would object to ye listening to hers, any who doubt me can listen." He unbuttoned the top three buttons on his blue, collarless shirt and summer underwear exposing his broad, muscular hairless chest. His mocking look and words were a dare to both Daniel and Rita.

Rita's face flamed red and she remained seated, but Daniel stood and took three quick steps, his lips set in a tight line, the grey eyes guarded. He turned his head as he put his ear to MacDonald's chest. The thump of two hearts was unmistakable. He looked up, wonderment in his eyes, "I don't understand."

MacDonald sighed and squeezed Anna's shoulder. "I think we should all sit down, and Anna and I twill try to clarify things.

Rita crossed her arms and composed her face as Anna and MacDonald resumed their seats. Daniel sat down gingerly, not knowing what to expect. Lorenz was sitting straight, his face and eyes somber.

"Since Daniel has heard Mina's Story, he kens the part about the stars having planets, where the Justines come from, and the Thalians. Margareatha has either spoken with yere biological fither, Toma, or someone else." Rita shook her head at the mention of speaking with their father. "It does nay matter as they both imply danger to us all." Good, thought MacDonald, that got their attention. "According to the Justines, we should nay exist. Since we do exist, they would call us mutants. Ye can equate that word with Earth beings calling a white man's mixed child a breed or a mulatto with the same amount of scorn. The Justine biology teaches mutants are like mules and can nay produce children. Toma must have realized that if the Justine teaching twas wrong in the first premise that Justines are too advanced to bring forth issue with primitives, they are wrong in the second. Ye all have the potential of producing wee ones, and they could have two hearts. That means they twill probably be long-lived and have the ability to walk in another's mind. If they have the last ability, ye twill need help in the raising, for yere mither can tell ye how difficult it is to control a child when the skill of mind control comes early. To me, she tis a wonder. She had nay kenning of the ways of mind control, but she dealt with a situation that was dangerous for both laddies."

Daniel had been staring intently at MacDonald. Now he looked quickly at Lorenz and back to MacDonald. "Mind control? That's crazy! And how is it dangerous?"

"Ye call it crazy, but did ye nay wind up on the floor of the barn even though ye had pushed Lorenz and he should have been off balance for the next assault? When ye were eight and he but four, who twas it that landed on top and continued to land the blows because the elder lay helpless?"

Daniel sat back and turned to Lorenz. Lorenz gave a slight smile and said, "Sorry, Daniel, I just did it. I didn't know y'all couldn't. It's why Papa told me to go throw rocks until I calmed down. He knew that way I wouldn't hurt y'all."

Daniel shook his head. "Does this mean O'Neal and Rita can do the same thing, and how long is long-lived?"

MacDonald answered, "I would say that Margareatha can enter a mind, though nay all. As to Mr. O'Neal, I canna answer, but it would nay surprise me. Margareatha, Lorenz, and O'Neal would need to take the 'elixir' as the Justines call it to retain their youthful looks, but they could live anywhere twixt one hundred to five thousand years, the life span of a Justine. For me tis a bit different as the Thalians live about three hundred-fifty years or more. Tis possible that I twill live to the Justine's allotted years, or longer. Tis difficult to say as the Justines must drink their rejuvenating liquid about every one hundred years to retain their youthful looks, but a Thalian does nay age once they reach one hundred and finish bulking out. We look the same till near the end of our years. Once we are near the end, a Thalian's decline tis rapid."

Daniel was shaking his head in disbelief. "How old are you? Does that mean you are going to grow taller? Heavier?"

MacDonald smiled. "Nay taller, laddie, but, aye, I twill develop more muscle and become stronger."

Rita's pursed her mouth. How would her mother take this news? Anna, however, was looking at MacDonald with loving eyes and a slight smile on her mouth.

"You still ain't said why our pa is dangerous to us," Daniel continued. "According to Mr. O'Neal, he tried using Comanche to kill us, but he didn't try outright. What has changed?"

"Tis but speculation, tis true, but he kens ye are all elder now, and he must wonder what twill yere wee ones be like? There tis nay way to ken. He, nor Margareatha, can go into every mind here. Lorenz may one day do so as he tis different." MacDonald saw Daniel's look of complete disbelief. "Look at him. He does nay have the Justine eyes, yet he has two hearts and the mind ability. Tis difficult to block him out, and he tis but a laddie. What happens when he tis full grown?"

"You're saying that Lorenz is going to be one dangerous man." Bitterness and jealousy of his younger brother began to show in Daniel's tone and his words.

MacDonald gave Daniel a slight smile and said softly. "Lorenz tis already a dangerous being. He tis learning, however, to control his temper and the gentler ways of accomplishing the same end, but, aye, he twill be a formidable opponent when he tis a man for he twill also have the strength of a Justine which lies hidden neath their scrawny appearance."

Lorenz's eyes lighted at the thought, and MacDonald continued. "This, however, does nay change the fact that any wee ones any of ye have may have some or all of these qualities. Our problem right now is how did Margareatha come by her knowledge, and how much danger lies there for all of us. Toma is nay doubt a danger for he too twill ken I am Thalian, but if ye," and he looked at Rita, "did nay learn this from Toma, the ones with such lore may decide we are too dangerous."

Rita met his steadfast gaze and shook her head. "I promised Red the source would remain hidden, and I shan't break that promise. I don't see how they are dangerous since Red is supplying them with food in his shipping business."

MacDonald asked, "Are they dependent upon him for their food?"

"I can't answer that question."

Anna stood, "I cannot believe du vould endanger all of us because of a promise to O'Neal!"

Rita laid one slender hand on her left chest and said, "I swear, Mama, I would never do anything to endanger you. I feel you are all more in danger from that man sitting there." She glared at MacDonald and swung back to face her mother. "Mama, I would rather speak when it is just you and I."

"Nein! Mr. MacDonald is my husband. There are no secrets between us."

Rita sat back, her shoulders slumping while Daniel raised his voice. "I don't believe any of this." He stood. "You all are crazy. I'm not listening to anymore of this. I'm going to bed. We're supposed to be gathering and branding beeves tomorrow." He stomped out.

MacDonald and Anna looked at each other. "Mayhap the laddie has a point. We are tired, and there tis always work that twill nay wait. See what sense ye can talk into her whilst we are gone." He bowed in Rita's direction and looked at Anna. "My love?"

"Ja." She smiled at him.

Chapter 18

Toma

Rita slept late and missed breakfast. The noise from pots and pans and the clanking from spur clad men failed to disturb her. She awoke to sunshine and Mina staring at her with accusation in her brown eyes and a set look to the baby mouth. "Mama is vorking verry hard," Mina whispered and ran out of the room.

Rita struggled upward and groaned. It couldn't be noon yet, but then she remembered this was a ranch, and it was doubtful if anyone here slept much beyond sunrise. She splashed water on her face missing the tub filled with warm water and the soft towels Teresa would have laid out for her. This would be a far more primitive way to live. She dressed rapidly in the shortened work shift and ran outside to relieve herself, noting that Mama was busy with laundry.

The morning was sheer torture; the work brutal. There was little time to talk, but while they were wringing out the men's trousers, Rita asked, "How do you stand it?"

Anna's face was blank, sweat rolling down from her forehead even in the coolness of fall. "Stand vhat?"

"The work, for one thing."

Anna tossed the pair of trousers into the basket and took the last one. "It's there, ja? There's more now with Daniel here, and

Mr. MacDonald vants to hire the vashing done, but I von't let him." She did not say and with you here there will be more work.

Rita clamped her lips as Mina appeared. It wasn't until Mina was down for a nap, and they were working on supper that she was able to suggest, "Mama, if Mr. MacDonald will not pay for a washerwoman, I'll gladly do so."

Anna whirled on her daughter. "Du vill not speak so. It is my decision. Ve need the money for other things, and I'll not have that loafer of a man following Consuela here!" She spun back to the potatoes she was peeling, her shoulders straight and rigid.

Rita was busy with floured hands shaping the rolls and lining them up in the pan. She tried again. "Mama, all I meant to say was that I found it difficult to believe that man was the one who wanted to have someone else do the washing."

Anna whirled again, pointing the knife at Rita. "Du do not call my husband 'that man' in this house. Do not make me choose between du and him." Her grey eyes were as cold and flinty as Rita had ever seen them.

Rita reddened and looked down. "Sorry, Mama," she murmured and went back to the rolls. Clearly this conversation was going to wait until she had a better understanding of the situations in this household. Was Mama that desperate to keep a man? Of course, there was Mina to consider. She desperately needed to talk with Daniel.

She finally managed to corner him alone two days later. He was not helpful as Daniel had his own concerns upper most in his mind. "When does O'Neal say I can come back?"

"When we bring Lorenz with us, that's when." She gritted the words through her teeth.

"You're going to break with your mother completely?"

Rita noted that Daniel did not think of her as his mother, but answered, "Of course not, she'll go with us: her and Mina."

Daniel snorted at the improbability. "You're as nuts as they are." He stomped off leaving Rita taking deep breaths as she walked back to the garden.

Talking with Lorenz didn't happen until they were on the way to Arles. The men weren't at the headquarters that long. They had been constantly out with the cattle, gathering small bunches and branding She had a letter started to Red about the coming cattle drive She felt it an insane scheme, but Mama brushed her objections away She had tried once more to broach the subject of leaving to Mama when they'd gone to visit Uncle Kasper and Tanta Gerde.

"Mama, aren't Mr. MacDonald's demands too much for you?"

Mama had gasped and looked back in the wagon to make sure Mina was still sleeping. "Nein, vhy such a question vould du ask? Vhat ve do is for love. Did those nuns fill you head with only bad things?"

Rita felt the pit of her stomach shrivel. Mama couldn't be one of "those women," but how else was she to phrase this? "I just meant that Thalians are said to be, uh, unusually demanding."

"Vhat does that mean?"

"I mean they treat going to bed with each other as a wonderful thing to do, time after time." She ground the words out, embarrassment flaming her cheeks almost as red as her hair.

Anna regarded her older daughter and then watched the horses, guiding them skillfully. "I vas right. Those nuns filled your head with silliness." She took a deep breath and tried to explain. "I did not have a mother to explain to me. I thought Mr. Lawrence's cold vays vere normal until I heard other married vomen talk. Some hate going to bed with their husbands, but the happiest are those that love their husbands. It is not just a chore or a vay to children have."

Rita looked at her mother, her own eyes wide as Anna continued. "It is a vonderful vay to say 'I love you, but vhen you are so tired, then, ja, it can be hard. That is vhy Mr. MacDonald always helps me, and vants to hire someone to do the laundry." Mina was stirring in the back of the wagon, and Anna finished with, "Ve talk more later."

There had been no more time to talk. Mina was always underfoot, or they were busy, and then it was mealtime. On the trail to Arles, it was worse. Rita, like the men had ridden. She knew her mother would insist on driving the team and Mina was either with Anna, on MacDonald's lap, on Lorenz's lap, or even begging rides with her, and Anna was not inclined to discuss marriage within earshot of her sons. Lorenz was dumbfounded when she suggested he should not go through with the adoption.

"He's Papa," Lorenz said and cold grey eyes looked at her. "Get it out of your mind. Whatever you were told about Thalians don't gibe with the way he's treated me." He rode off.

The adoption, Rita found out, was another matter not to be discussed with Mama, and she resigned herself to waiting for her mother to admit how horrible her life was, and the bath waiting at the hotel filled her mind.

MacDonald, Lorenz, and Daniel emerged from the Arles Stable after paying Samuels for the board of six horses for two days. They, like Rita, were planning on a bath. The trip had been made in four and one half days, and the afternoon was free until court in the morning. Lorenz and Daniel almost collided with MacDonald when he stopped short, his body rigid. He handed his hat to Lorenz and shrugged out of his coat. "Hold these, laddie, and dinna interfere."

He turned and walked in his ground-eating, rolling way towards a tall man standing besides the water trough and a blooded chestnut. His hands were curling and uncurling into fists. When he was within five feet, the man turned and stared at the approaching giant. The man raised his right hand and pointed his index finger.

MacDonald slowed, but not much. At four feet he stopped, took a deep breath, and his deep voice rumbled out, "Toma, I am Llewellyn, Maca of Don, and I challenge ye."

Lorenz was hugging the coat and hat to his chest. He had ignored MacDonald's command and thrown up a mind block against his sire. His mouth pulled tight and he was staring at the scene with an intensity that Daniel could sense. Suddenly Lorenz relaxed. "Stay out," rang in his mind. He had done what he wanted; distracted Toma. Toma was staring at him and Daniel, his mind diverted from controlling Papa's. The pain of fighting would keep Toma from controlling Papa.

Daniel was more relaxed, but his right hand was resting on his right gun butt. How had their father known to be here today or was it coincidence? Either way the fight should be a good one.

The two men were circling each other, evaluating the strengths, physical and mental, when MacDonald's left fist lashed out. Toma whirled away, but he misgauged his opponent's speed as MacDonald's right fist caught him along his right cheek. Toma threw up a mind block and used his mind to control his body movements. He swung upward into the belly area, his hand rigid, fingers cupped, aiming toward the one soft spot to disable the Thalian. When that failed, he swung hard, into the face and blood flowed from the side of MacDonald's mouth. Toma's next moves were whirls and kicks, mixed with blows that landed.

MacDonald had his own mind block in place and retaliated with blows of his own, intent on wearing down the man with his greater bulk. He wanted to inflict pain: pain that would keep the Justine's mind busy and out of his own. Suddenly his early training from his elder and the practice sessions with Lorenz returned, and he was using his fists, elbows, and knees against the enemy in front of him, hearing the blows land and then closing in and bearing the man crashing to the ground where he continued to pound away until the man was unconscious. He stood, his breath heaving in and out of the massive chest, and walked to the water trough. He submerged his head and hands, letting the cold water revive and cool him. When he raised his head, he stood there inhaling and exhaling while water ran down his face and back. He felt Lorenz beside him and looked down.

"He hurt me. I dinna expect that." He took the hat and used one hand to smooth back his hair and set the hat on at a jaunty angle. Then he put on the extended coat against the October chill and the icy water. The blood had turned pink as it mixed with water and the bleeding slowed. "Get me Zark. I must speak to Toma alone."

He didn't wait to see Lorenz enter the stable. He walked back to the prone figure, lifted the man, and slung him across the saddle. There was no rope on this gentlemen's saddle, and he led the horse back to the front of the stable doors. The small crowd that had gathered was milling into groups of two or three and gradually finding other interests.

When Lorenz appeared leading Zark, MacDonald took the rope from his saddle and used it to tie Toma by roping the hands dangling on one side to the feet on the other, and securing the rope to the saddle horn. He turned to Lorenz. "Tell yere mither I shall be there within the hour." MacDonald's r's were rolling more than usual in his words. He swung himself up and looked down, a tight smile on his lips. "We are going but a short distance, and the talk twill nay be long. She tis to have the tub for the bath ordered when I return." He clucked at Zark and headed out of town away from any houses.

Once he passed the Quincy household, he went another quarter of a mile and dismounted. By this time, Toma was stirring and MacDonald loosened the rope, pulled the man down to the ground, propped him into a sitting position against an outcrop of rock, and handed him the reins to the chestnut. He then squatted on his hunches and said, "Ye are to leave now. If ye come back and bother me and mine, I twill kill ye. Anna tis my counselor, and Lorenz tis my laddie."

He ignored the hate in the man's copper eyes and gold encircled pupils and mounted Zark. He did not bother to look back as he rode off to meet the approaching horseman.

Marshal Franklin pulled heavily on his reins as they came abreast. The marshal's face was florid as he made his accusation. "Y'all are hell-bent on disturbing my days. Where's that man going?"

"Mayhap to the next town or to Mexico. I dinna ask his destination. Nay did I kill him, this time."

Franklin sat back on his horse. "MacDonald, one of these times y'all are going to cross the line and I'll have to arrest y'all."

MacDonald grinned. "I shall consider myself warned."

Chapter 19

One Last Try

Rita strode from the house. She was dressed in a low cut gown of cream dotted with green flowers, short sleeves, and an unusually tight bodice. Mama was busy sewing, Mina napping, and Lorenz and Daniel off with Martin branding cows again. The afternoon was quiet, and she knew MacDonald was adding to the corral fencing. This time she would succeed in extracting Mama, Mina, and the boys from the clutches of the Thalian. October had changed into an Indian summer and the warm air and bright sun outlined every stone, blade of brown grass, and building in bold light. She smiled to herself as she loosened the top button of the tight bodice. She knew she was beautiful and her figure good. Men stared at her, Rolfe openly gaping when he first met her. Martin had been so tongue tied and red-faced, Lorenz started to laugh.

MacDonald was shirtless; his arms bulging as he drove the posthole digger up and down in the tough prairie sod. Perspiration soaked his summer underwear plastering it against his chest. He looked up as Rita approached, his eyes narrowing as he watched her continue to finger and loosen the buttons on her bodice.

"I have a proposal," Rita began, a smile curving her lips as she looked upward at the man.

"I twould call it a proposition if ye open one more of those buttons."

Rita's face flamed, but she kept her voice low and husky, and continued to look directly into his eyes. "If you relinquish your hold on Mama and Lorenz, I will go with you." For some reason her lower limbs trembled, and she could feel nerves working in her groin and stomach. She set her teeth. What was the matter with her?

MacDonald's face was as set as hers. "Ye are Counselor's lassie, and I am mither's Counselor. Remember that. If ye loosen one more of those buttons, or say one more thing, I twill pick ye up and carry ye to yere mither's side, and she may deal with ye."

Rita stared at him. The man was serious. Was the book she'd read truly so flawed? "How can you, a Thalian, resist when I am so young?"

He stuck the digger down and folded his arms across his chest. "Mayhap, if ye twere honest with yereself, ye twould ken ye twere told lies, and ye are suggesting this for yere benefit and nay yere mither's. Yere mither tis decades younger than I, and what ye just proposed tis as abhorred in my land as incest tis here."

Rita began buttoning the bodice and stared at him, her eyes wide. "Are you going to discuss this with Mama?"

"Oh, aye, when I return to the house. I suggest ye discuss it with her now." He picked up the posthole digger and began slamming it into the earth with renewed effort.

Rita stumbled backward for a couple of steps and turned to return to the house. What had possessed her? What had she missed about the way MacDonald regarded her mother? She wished Red had never shown her the reading materials he had acquired from his trading activities. How could a society so advanced be so wrong? And now what did she say to Mama? Her steps began to lag. Damn MacDonald. He had made her feel like a twelve-year-old child again. At the back door she hesitated a moment. The treadle on the sewing machine produced a steady whirring sound. She entered the kitchen and drank from the ladle in the water bucket.

A quick glance in the mirror above the basin revealed her face had cooled to a slight pink. Her bodice was properly buttoned again and she took a deep breath. The empty, sinking feeling in her middle, however, would not go away.

Anna was busy sewing a new flannel shirt for Lorenz's birthday present when she felt her daughter standing beside her. She stopped the treadle long enough to look up and smile. The look on Rita's face stopped the smile and in German she asked, "What is wrong?"

Rita looked at her in wonderment. Like Lorenz, she had easily picked up her first language. "How did you know?" Her words were in Deutsch.

"It is the same look you would have when you did wrong as a little girl. How could I not know?"

Rita brought one of the dining chairs over and sat down. "Mama, I—I know how you must be suffering from Mr. Mac-Donald's constant attentions."

"Margareatha, what are you talking about?"

Rita was perplexed. How could her mother keep denying that she was being used over and over? Rita tried again, but gently. "Mama, I sleep in the room directly across from yours and I—I don't mean to hear, but sometimes I can't help it. I know how frequently he bothers you, and how tired you must be, and humiliated."

Anna closed her eyes for a moment and thought. "Bah!" she exclaimed. "It was the teaching from those nuns, ja? They are the ones that gave you such ideas. God made man and woman for each other. That's why we marry. Women who are honest don't make such statements as yours. Poor Gerde and Kasper can't have what Mr. MacDonald and I have. If she gets pregnant again, she will die. Yes, it can make me tired, but that is why

Mr. MacDonald has always helped so much." She stopped at a loss for words.

Rita was staring at her dumbfounded, and Anna tried again, this time in English. "I never thought to say anything because ve vere split up before du became a woman. I just assumed du vould know things at your age." Anna's own face was growing pinker. "I vas afraid that your being around Mr. O'Neal like that meant du had, had" she paused, "committed indiscretions."

"Mama!" Rita was horrified. "I've never done anything like that." It was her turn to pause. "Except just now, I've made a fool out of myself and ruined everything." She began to rock back and forth on the seat trying to think of a way to tell Anna. Anna reached over and gently patted her hand.

"Rita, vhat are du talking about?"

"I just offered to go with Mr. MacDonald if he left you and Lorenz." She blurted it out.

Anna came out of the chair in one fluid motion, her hand sweeping backward. "How dare du! He ist my man." Anger lent swiftness and surety in her motions and her voice. Her hand descended as rapidly as she raised it and landed with a crack.

Rita rose as rapidly as her mother and stared down at her. She found herself staring into eyes that had gone a flat, grey, icy cold. There was no fear of her daughter's youth or greater height in her eyes. My God, thought Rita, Lorenz is like her.

"I told du not to make me choose between Mr. MacDonald and du. Vhy did du force this on me?"

"Mama, I'm sorry." Suddenly Rita was a little girl again, trying to placate her mother's anger. "I don't want him. I thought I was helping you, protecting you."

"And did du to Mr. MacDonald apologize?"

Once again Rita was opened mouth. "No," she whispered.

"Then du must do so. He vill decide if du stay, and I vill pray for God to forgive me my anger."

Chapter 20

Antoinette

Lorenz looked at himself in the mirror. The brown, serge suit had been ordered before he visited his grandfather's farm. The tailoring was done during his absence, and the suit fit perfectly.

"Are ye through primping? Tis time we meet with the O'Neal's for dinner. Daniel is already with them. I suspect he twill return with O'Neal." Amusement rumbled through Mac-Donald's voice.

Lorenz grinned crookedly. "I reckon." He grabbed his new hat and rubbed his new boots against the back of his calf to heighten the shine.

MacDonald was equally splendid in a new tailored suit and boots. He was looking forward to meeting O'Neal again. The first time had been all too brief. He and Rolfe had added O'Neal's herd, remuda, and hands to their drive on a handshake to pay Red when they met in Saint Louis. O'Neal then left for the coast of Texas to tend to his shipping lines and promised to meet them. Out of the eighteen hundred head of longhorns, they had arrived with almost seventeen hundred, and sold them for twenty-six dollars a head. It was a handsome profit for all.

Lorenz adjusted his new hat to a rakish angle before they left the room and locked the door behind them. They walked down the fancy stairs and headed to the hotel's dining room. It was easy to spot Red and Daniel. Both were taller than most men and being seated did little to hide the fact. Red rose to meet them, a warm smile on his face and in his eyes. Lorenz couldn't take his eyes off the young woman seated between Red and Daniel.

As they neared the table, Lorenz removed his hat and bowed. "Miss Antoinette, it's a pleasure to see y'all again." His face lighted and his eyes were gleaming like new silver dollars.

Antoinette turned her head, smiled with her perfect lips, and raised a languid right hand. Her violet-blue eyes appraised every inch of Lorenz and noted the scar was now a normal color. She knew men in the South would prize it as a mark of honor from dueling. Lorenz looked extremely handsome, and he certainly dressed far better than Daniel.

"My, don't y'all look ever so fit."

Lorenz grasped her hand, staring down into her eyes, and suddenly remembered he was supposed to kiss the hand or something. He hastily bent his head and touched her hand with his lips. He knew there was nothing substantial under his feet as he walked to the chair next to Daniel and sat down after hanging his hat on the chair. He didn't remember MacDonald shaking hands with Red, and he didn't hear Daniel's amused snort.

Antoinette was still smiling up at him, her dark, curly head bent ever so slightly. Lorenz had no idea that women assumed this pose on purpose. All he could think of was how beautiful she was, and how she would be the perfect wife.

"I do so want to complement y'all on how much y'all have changed since we last met. I do declare, y'all must have stayed up all night doing your studies. It's ever so impressive." Antoinette blinked her eyes and then looked at Red for confirmation.

Red, however, was talking with MacDonald. "The amount you were able to sell the cattle for surprised me. I'm thinking of sending a bigger herd next year. Did you have any problems bringing them through that I should be aware of?"

"Aye, Missouri does nay like us, nay the fever and scours they fear our cattle have. They may try to stop us next year or charge so much the drive twill net less; plus, there twas the grasshoppers chewing at everything. There aren't any other towns though for shipping so many head or finding a buyer. If we go through Kansas, tis a long way to water, and we would lose a fair amount of cattle. It took days to find a broker. We were almost ready to head for Omaha when I found a man. These are issues that need to be resolved, but the brokers twill come when they ken there are more Texas steers headed this way."

"Did you have any problems keeping the cattle together during the drive?"

"Nay trouble after the first day or so, except for the night stampede during a Jay Hawkers raid in Indian Territory. If the rain had nay started, we might have lost more. Twas such a heavy down pour and it helped bringing the cattle back under control. We lost a man then, and I twill need to tell his remaining family."

Red grimaced, "That's not a pleasant chore."

Two waiters approached bearing platters. "I took the liberty of ordering you all steaks. I hope that's satisfactory," said Red. "You all will have to order your own drinks."

"Oh aye, tis fine." To the waiter MacDonald said, "I twill have a brew, beer that tis."

"We have both the amber and the dark beer," said the waiter with pride and waited for the response.

"I'll have the amber, thank ye."

The waiter looked at Lorenz.

"Coffee," said Lorenz.

Antoinette turned to Lorenz after the waiter left. "Don't y'all drink?"

Lorenz gave her a quick smile. "Sometimes at home I'll have a glass of wine, but I don't care for beer."

She favored him with a smile as she unfolded her napkin.

The waiter went to fetch the drinks and the conversation returned. "Could I interest you in returning to the ranch with me?" Red asked Lorenz. "Your pay would be the same as Daniel's."

"No, thanks, I've still too much to learn, and we're building a business." He turned to MacDonald. "Right, Papa?"

"Aye, like ye, Mr. O'Neal, we twill be trailing a larger herd next year."

Red nodded. "I thought as much."

"I offered the same to Daniel, but it seems he has a wander lust and a taste for a new challenge."

"Should you change your mind, Lorenz, I'll keep the option open."

"I won't." His voice acquired a hard edge. "I like being a rancher's son and having a home. It's better than being a hired hand."

When the waiter brought more drinks, the men began to smoke. Antoinette stood. "I believe I'll return to the room now and let you all discuss business."

All the men rose, and Lorenz stepped around Daniel. "Would y'all care for a walk, Miss O'Neal?"

Red put down his napkin. "No."

Antoinette laid a hand on Red's arm. "Now, Jerimiah, I know y'all want to talk business with Mr. MacDonald and Daniel."

"It's too dangerous outside, even with an escort."

"Well, then, why doesn't Lorenz escort me to where Consuela is waiting, and he can see us to the room in a proper manner."

Red looked at her and then at Lorenz. He had let the correspondence continue as a way to tempt Lorenz to return, and now he needed Rita back too. His mind did a mental shrug and he smiled. "Yes, I would appreciate that."

Daniel's face darkened, and he was about to accompany them when O'Neal shook his head. MacDonald smiled one of his tight, half-smiles and watched the two young people walk off. He noted that Lorenz was strutting. Well, let him, for the lassie twas a beauty according to this land's standards.

"Ah do declare," said Antoinette as she took Lorenz's arm. "Red can be as annoying as a clucking hen with her chicks."

"He just wants y'all to be safe."

Antoinette giggled.

"Is Consuela your duenna?"

"Officially she is my maid, but she acts like a duenna."

"What will y'all be studying?"

"Oh, such insipid things as embroidery, but there will be another full year of French." Her southern accent was so strong, Lorenz wondered how she spoke another language fluently. "I do wish they'd have more Latin. It does so help when one studies French and speaks Spanish. Do y'all speak any other language?"

"Yes, I've pretty well mastered German, and I know border Spanish, but I reckon that's different from what y'all speak."

She smiled up at him. "Indeed it is. Why on earth did y'all learn German? No one, ah mean no one, uses it."

He returned her smile. "Because Mama is German and Lutheran. All of the Pastor's sermons are in German, and the Catechism and their Bible are in German. When I visited Grandpa Schmidt, his whole family was still using it for their language at home. Most of the people in the nearby town used it, and the church service was in German."

They were rapidly approaching the seating area near the reception desk. A middle-aged Spanish woman dressed in black stood when she saw them. Her grey hair was piled up on her head and wound in a bun in the back. Her face became stern and she frowned.

"Why are you with this man?" she asked in Spanish.

Antoinette laughed a tinkling, joyous sound. "Oh don't be silly, Consuela. Mr. MacDonald can understand every word y'all are saying. Y'all know very well Mr. O'Neal would not permit me with anyone that isn't protecting me. He will be seeing us up to our room."

Lorenz nodded at the woman, but Antoinette didn't bother to introduce them. She kept a firm hand on his arm and turned toward the stairs. "We are on the second floor in one of the two suites Jeremiah rented."

"I told y'all what I would be takin' at the school. Are y'all still doin' lessons?"

"When we get back to Texas I'll be starting a whole new session with Uncle Kasper. He's really in his element now. There's two other students besides me, and Papa will be learning Greek."

"I just can't imagine why Daniel wouldn't stay."

Lorenz felt a twinge of jealousy. Why should she care? "I don't know why he didn't. He seemed to be doing all right in his studies. He finished the multiplication tables and writes fairly decently. I guess it's just not as important to him."

"Well, ah was soo glad to hear y'all say y'all liked being a rancher's son. I surely wouldn't want to marry a poor man, or live like an Indian squaw."

He looked down at her. "I can assure you, Miss O'Neal, my wife will not live like an Indian."

She smiled at him. "What was your grandfather's farm like? Ah just can't imagine something so small can provide a good living, but the whole middle section of the country seems to be like that."

Lorenz returned the smile. "It seemed to provide a very good living. They had two barns and two granaries, plus two corn-cribs. That's not counting the washhouse, smokehouse, tool shed, and a chicken house that was bigger than a lot of cabins out in Texas. The same goes for their hog house. They don't let the pigs run wild, but keep them penned. The kitchen was larger than some of the cabins I've seen out home too, and they sure didn't want for food."

Antoinette shook her head. "My, my, ah never imagined. I thought it would be real skimpy like."

They reached the landing of the second floor, and Lorenz set his teeth. He didn't want to lose her, or this time to end. "Will y'all still write to me? I don't know what your address will be, or I'd write first."

Antoinette inclined her head. "This is our room." Then she turned and looked up at Lorenz. "Of course, I'll write to y'all. I'm not sure the school will let me see your letters though. They are dreadfully strict about the strangest things, or at least that's what I've been told." She let go of his arm and rummaged in her bag, a small, black pouch with embroidered red and pink roses. "Here's the key." She handed it to him.

Lorenz took it and unlocked the door. Evidently this was something that a gentleman did for a lady. He wasn't sure, but didn't think it a good idea to ask. She acted like he knew what to do. He handed back the key and kept her hand in his. "Ah reckon this is goodbye then. When will I see y'all again?" His eyes were desperate.

Antoinette smiled and looked up at him. It was really quite gratifying to have someone so handsome so madly in love with her. "Ah really don't know. There are two years at finishing school, and ah will be coming home for the summers. After that, ah guess ah'll have to think about getting married. Ah certainly don't want to be an old maid."

Lorenz tightened his grip on her hand and somehow the right words came to him. "Then think of me, Miss O'Neal." He bent and brought her hand to his lips again. Both young people ignored the frantic efforts of Consuela to somehow get between them.

"Why, of course, ah will, Mr. MacDonald." She smiled up into his eyes and gently removed her hand. "Come along, Consuela." The door closed behind them.

Lorenz walked down the steps, his stomach churning and his manhood protruding in front of him. His step, eyes, face, shoulders, every movement showed a determined man. He knew Antoinette would someday be his wife.

The two older men smiled as Lorenz returned. MacDonald smiled because his laddie was becoming a man. O'Neal was laughing silently at the absurdity of Lorenz's aspirations. O'Neal believed his sister would, as many of the young women of his class did, marry an older, wealthier man to support her in proper style. The fragile truce between the two brothers, however, was forever shattered. Daniel loved Antoinette and resented Lorenz's attentions.

Lorenz, however, would not wed first. Olga was ready to be Mrs. Tom Jackson, and Martin would marry by the end of next summer.

Chapter 21

Recruitment

"Who wants a drink of decent whiskey?" asked Red.

The four of them were seated in Red's hotel suite. They had adjourned there when Lorenz returned. "I believe I twill have a wee glass, and the laddie may have one too, if he wishes."

"Daniel?" At Daniel's nod Red poured the four glasses and rejoined the men at the small table. The two younger ones faced each other and he sat across from MacDonald.

MacDonald took a sip and said, "Aye, tis a grand bottling." He smiled at O'Neal. "I asked for a more private area as there are certain things we need to discuss. Ye ken who I am from Margareatha's letters, or Daniel's report. Tis this nay true?"

Red's eyes were guarded as he nodded yes.

"Have they told ye that I possess a *Golden One,* and what the *Golden One* can do?"

"They told me. It means you can leave this earth at any time." Red's face was now a set mask.

"That tis nay quite true, but I'll go into the reasons later. Have they also told ye that my biological fither twas a Justine?"

Once again Red nodded. MacDonald's voice hardened and became more Thalian as he continued. "Tis true, I do plan to leave this Earth someday, but first I need to master the craft, and I dinna wish to be attacked by whoever supplied ye with the information about Justines and Thalians. I would appreciate it if ye were honest about it as I suspect Toma kens how ye ken. I twill nay have my Anna, or our children's lives endangered by yere silence."

Red took a sip of his whiskey and sat back. It had not taken long to realize the reports from Rita, Daniel, and Collins were correct: Lorenz would side with MacDonald in any dispute. Attacking the man physically was out, and mentally was probably just as futile. Perhaps a bit of honesty would be beneficial to them both. He smiled. "Mr. MacDonald, have you ever heard of a group of people called the Ayanas?"

For a moment MacDonald sat blank-faced. Finally, he asked somewhat in awe, "Do ye mean Slavies? They are here?"

Red grinned. "Well, in a manner of speaking. They did land here, and they did try to enslave certain people. They lost so many of their own people they fled to one of the outer planets and created a world underground. How long they plan to remain there, I can't say. They refuse to do any physical work, and being underground limits their ability to grow needed grains and other food crops."

"And ye are supplying them with slaves to do their bidding." MacDonald's accusation was harsh.

"Perhaps," Red shrugged, "but I also supply them with livestock, grain, seeds, dried fruits, and other materials. They are really incompetent when it comes to physical labor. The Justines dictum about interbreeding seems to hold true for them."

"And Toma tis with them?" MacDonald was puzzled.

"Sometimes he is, but they prefer otherwise. A Justine anywhere near the Ayanas will cause them severe headaches. On the other hand, I've been told, he despises them as much as he despises this world and Thalians." Red's smile broadened. "The man really isn't pleased with any culture that is not his own. It's hard to believe he ever left his planet."

MacDonald put his head to the side and regarded the Texan. "Have ye met Toma?"

"No, he realizes if he destroys me, he is apt to lose an important food source. It seems the Ayanas' housing is more to his taste. He detests the primitive living conditions here. The Ayanas do not wish to be known. They feel someone will come looking for Toma. The more people in this world, the harder it is for the Ayanas to remain undetected. They want to keep it that way."

MacDonald allowed a small smile. "I dinna think the Justines twill send another to search for Toma as there tis nay to spare. I wish, however, ye to ken that the information ye have read about Thalians tis about two thousand years out-of-date. That is how long ago the Justines banished the Ayanas from our portion of the galaxy."

"If the Justines, for whatever reasons, aren't going to search for Toma, perhaps he would assist you in returning, or perhaps the Ayanas might simply to get rid of Toma."

"The Slavies have nay love for Thalians. At the time, we were aligned with the Justines and helped to drive them out. As for Toma, should we meet again, I am apt to finish the fight."

"Then how long do you plan to live here?"

"First I must raise my wee lassie, and study the math and the star systems. Mayhap another century, I am nay sure, but when I leave, I'd like for ye to come with us."

"Your offer extends to that time?" Red was skeptical.

"Aye, ye are a man that takes risks, and ye seem to draw a better class of adventurous men to ye."

"That's because I promise them a reasonable return for their time." Red grinned and looked at his empty glass. "Another round?"

MacDonald shook his head. "I have nay finished this one." He watched Red pour himself and Daniel a drink. Lorenz shook his head. Once Red was at the table again, MacDonald continued.

"I wish ye to keep the offer in mind. This land changes rapidly within a short time. Mayhap tis because the inhabitants of this planet have such a short life span in comparison to other known beings. Ye may find in a hundred years or so a trip to other worlds a good idea."

Red sat back. "You're right; the perspective could be different then." Amusement lighted his copper eyes. "You'd still have to make it worth my while. I'm beginning to think you want a band of mercenaries. Why? Mercenaries cost a great deal of money."

MacDonald's eyes were hard, obsidian glints. "I twill need a few fighters as I canna fight twenty Justines and the whole Krepyon nation by myself. Ye may have noticed that ye canna enter the minds of all the adults here, have ye?"

Red's eyes narrowed, and he nodded yes.

The laughter was back in MacDonald's eyes. "Nay can Toma, nay can I. Lorenz, however, may be able to do so one day. I twill need those who can block the Justine mind. I dinna care if they be man or woman."

Red felt his jaw clenched. He had been right, and now Lorenz worshipped this man across from him. It looked like he would permit the letter exchange for awhile longer. "How does that help you?" He kept his voice smooth.

"If the Justine canna enter the mind, they must fight physically with the person in front of them. A trained fighter could win."

Red slugged down his drink. "That would mean a whole planet for the taking."

"Their planet tis gone."

Red blinked his eyes. "Gone? Gone where?"

"Into oblivion. They now inhabit a large asteroid made habitable by their technology."

"Still, they would have treasures, gold, something of value."

"Tis possible. They must pay the Kreppies," MacDonald sneered out the word, "for their services, and the Kreppies planet tis still there."

Red smiled. "In that case, Mr. MacDonald, you are correct. I might well be interested in such an undertaking." The two men shook hands.

Chapter 22

A Proposal of Marriage

Late in the month of August, Olga pulled her buckboard to a stop in front of Tom Jackson's cabin. The noonday sun beat down with unrelenting heat and beads of water ran down the sides of her face. She knew the horses would announce her arrival. Tom would be in the tavern, if only for companionship. She was almost twenty and no young beau was on the horizon. The young men in Arles would have nothing to do with a Yankee girl, or one that went to a church that baptized infants and had preachers that talked in a foreign language. She pulled a small bundle from under the seat and strode into the cabin after knocking lightly. Once inside she wrinkled her nose at the smell, but set about her task. She knew Tom would be arriving shortly. They would have heard her enter town, and would soon investigate why someone hadn't gone to Schmidt's or the tavern.

Olga was right. Tom came clumping in on his crutch just as she finished her chore. The wooden leg was too painful to wear except on special days. He stood open mouth watching the bright, flowered curtains flapping at the one window. "Miss Olga, what are y'all doing?"

Olga put both hands on her hips and turned. "I have hung curtains. They are made from some left over material. Vhat do y'all think?" The 'vat' betrayed her emotions but she kept her face expectant.

"Why, why, they look fine, Miss Olga, but ain't they a little fancy for this place?" He looked around at the dish laden table, the unmade bed, and he was suddenly aware that there was far more dirt in here than in her clean kitchen.

Olga turned back to look at the curtains and slowly pivoted to look at the one room. "It would not take much to make it look different in here." She lifted her head, "I need to know your intentions, Mr. Jackson."

Tom swallowed. He felt his eyes must be twice their normal size. "Miss Olga, my intentions are truly honorable, but, well, it's been hard to earn a living just for me. I couldn't speak for y'all now."

Olga looked at the sweat appearing on his forehead with a certain satisfaction. "Mr. Jackson, the war is over, and things are getting better. There will be freighter wagons going through here at least twice a year now, maybe more often. Papa and Mr. MacDonald will be bringing in more horses to shoe, and they are going to need y'all to build a special wagon for them. Y'all can do wainwright work, ja?"

"Yes, ma'am, the tools are out in my shop."

"There, see, y'all will do much better this year. When I marry, the chickens come with me. My mother's dishes and household goods, I also bring. They are mine." She snapped the last sentence out.

Tom suddenly had visions of an egg every morning for breakfast and quickly put the thought out of mind. He made another attempt, not sure how to deflect this obviously determined, young woman.

"Miss Olga, since I came back, I, ah, if y'all haven't notice, I mean, well, look at me, woman. I'm but half a man now."

Olga straightened. "Mr. Jackson, don't du all ever say such a thing again." She quickly adjusted her English. "Y'all are a fine figure of a man, and so much more than those scraggly, bearded youngsters that come through here." She was not about to mention that she and Daniel had kissed at one of the get-togethers at the MacDonald's. He had been young and hard, but too demanding and Olga had sense enough to know that he would be riding on.

Tom stared at the short, plump woman dressed in a brown and white checkered day dress. She looked as normal as usual, but her eyes did seem brighter, and there was more color in her cheeks, but being a man he did not think of that. He saw a comely, young woman offering herself to him and he swallowed as Olga continued.

"Are y'all going to ask me to marry y'all?"

Tom was reduced to stammering. "Yes, ma'am, I surely do so intend to ask your pa for your hand, just as soon…" And Olga broke in on him.

"Do you believe in Jesus as your Savior?" Inside her stomach turned at her boldness.

"Well, yes, ma'am, of course. Who doesn't?"

Olga smiled, pleased at his response. "I will continue to be a Lutheran. Y'all may attend services with me, or go to a church you like." She did not say if there's ever one around. "I will raise our children as Lutherans. Are y'all in agreement?"

"Whatever y'all want, ma'am." Tom fervently believed in the theory that women did most of the child rearing.

Olga moved closer, and put her arms around his neck. "Den I vill marry y'all."

Tom wasn't sure how it happened, but he was kissing her and his crutch was on the floor. He straightened, and put his hands on her shoulders for balance. "I, I guess, I'd better go ask your Pa for your hand."

Olga was very flushed, and her brown eyes were sparkling. She smiled and nodded. "We can go in my buckboard."

"No, ma'am, we won't." Tom was firm on this issue. "I'll hitch up my buggy, and we'll tie your rig and horses to the back."

"Good. We'll go into Arles with Papa when they go after the material for the wagon. We'll get the license then."

Tom stared at her. At least she hadn't argued about taking his rig.

Chapter 23

New Arrivals

Lorenz and Martin were sorting through the trousers in Kasper's store when they heard the sound of approaching horses and they turned their attention to the window to watch a wagon pull to a stop. "Lookie there," said Martin his blue eyes suddenly gleaming.

The new arrival's gaunt team stood with bowed heads, half-heartedly switching their tails at the flies. Two more horses were tethered at the back of the wagon which had once been red, but was now faded like a barn on some war-deserted farm. Dirty canvas was lashed over the ribs extending from side to side. The man handling the horses looked to be of average height and possibly middle-aged when he jumped down, dust swirling around him and off of him. The next to step down was a woman clad in a cotton sweat, stained dress. She wore a sunbonnet and her figure was that of a mature woman.

Lorenz was staring at the three sunbonnet capped girls. One looked to be older than him and another at least in her teens by her figure. He really wasn't good at figuring female ages; he just knew this was better than anything else that had happened in Schmidt's Corner for awhile. He paid no attention to the smallest girl. She probably wasn't as old as Young James.

Kasper was the only adult male in the store. The others were at Jesse's, reviving themselves after raising the walls, setting and nailing the heavy roof beams, and then placing the church rafters into place. The Master Carpenter, Fredrick Richmann, from Houston and his apprentice, Frank Hegman, had secured the rafters and hurried after them. The men stopped drinking as they heard the sounds of the wagon in the street and halting at the general store. They piled outside for a look. MacDonald and Rolfe looked long enough to decide they would finish their beers before investigating the new comers.

The man strode into the store followed closely by his family. All of them blinked their eyes at the sudden lack of sunlight and the man glared at the two young men. He then made straight for the counter where Kasper had been reading while waiting for Lorenz or Martin to make a selection.

"Howdy, my name is Shelton and I was told there was good land with plenty of water here abouts. Y'all reckon y'all can direct me?"

"Good afternoon, Mr. Shelton." Kasper extended his hand and they shook. "My name is Kasper Schmidt. It's good to have a newcomer. The land around town, however, is privately owned. Mr. Tillman, one of the ranchers, may know whether the ranch across from him is available or not."

Lorenz and Martin were trying to edge closer without tripping over each other and still look like they were searching through the merchandise. The teenage girl managed to sneak a look, offer a shy smile, and show a glimpse of brown eyes peering from beneath the bonnet.

Martin was so intrigued he decided a diversion was necessary to get her attention again. He held up a pair of trousers that were obviously meant for a much larger man and asked, "Hey, Unkle, how much is this pair?"

The man at the counter stopped his questions long enough to turn his head and frown at the two. His woman and girls seemed to cluster around him, the woman not even glancing at them. The littlest girl took a quick peek before hiding her face in her mother's long skirt.

The man turned his attention back to Kasper. "Do y'all mean there's no open land? Ah wuz told there wuz plenty of free land with flowing water here. Y'all do know the land around here, don't y'all?"

"Yes, it's true that there is land with water, but you either need to go over to the saloon and ask Mr. Tillman if he has the deed to his brother's place or if the ranch is even for sale. Mr. Rolfe and Mr. MacDonald own the land on the other side of town. You would need to ask them where their boundary lines are. Another option is to continue on to Arles, the county seat, and find out where the open ranges are. The recent war has caused a great many problems in determining where the property lines are or if there are any of the owners left."

The new arrival had a puzzled look on his face and then it changed to disgust. "Y'all sound like a damn Yankee to me," and he swiveled and pointed his finger at the two young men. "And yu uns stay clear away from my girls if you all are damn Yankees." He swung back to Kasper. "Y'all hear? Keep 'em away if they're your damn nephews."

Lorenz's eyebrows went up and Martin had a definite disappointed look on his face.

Rolfe, with MacDonald behind him, opened the door to the store as the man's tirade continued. "By God, if y'all are damn Yankees, I don't know why y'all are even alive. Maybe somebody ought to form a committee."

Kasper did not see Lorenz start for the counter, but Kasper refused to be intimidated. "Sir, you are using language unsuitable for the ears of children and women. Please, leave my establishment immediately."

"By God, they're my women, and I'll talk how I want." The man was leaning forward over the counter. His women were taking small steps backward.

"Vat ist? Some sort of fight?" Rolfe had stepped in the door first.

The man swung around and was unimpressed with Rolfe's height and buckskins. "By God, a foreigner dressed like an injun. Y'all should learn to speak our language."

"Und du should learn to speak American!" Rolfe's blue eyes turned hard and glinting, his hands automatically curling into fists.

Shelton almost went for him when he realized MacDonald would probably interfere and he halted. He stood looking back and forth at the two and then shrugged. He turned back to Kasper. "Where do I find those two men y'all said would know about boundaries?"

Kasper fought to repress a smile. "They are standing right by the door. Mr. MacDonald and Mr Rolfe, this is Mr. Shelton. He came in to ask about land, but he was just about to leave."

Shelton decided to try one more time. "Is there anybody in this town that's a white man?" He glared at MacDonald as he asked the question.

"Fortunately, whether they were North or South, there tis nay like ye, and ye are beginning to annoy me. I suggest ye continue on to Arles. They twill be happy to accommodate ye."

Shelton snorted. "This Tillman he mentioned, be he a Yank or a true son of the South?"

"Mr. Tillman wore the grey, and ye twill find him in the saloon."

All sorts of emotions spread across Shelton's face. It meant leaving his women unprotected in the wagon in the midst of these, to his mind, dangerous people. "And how far out does your land go?" His question was a sneer.

"Oh, tis at least a day or two of riding in all directions." Mac-Donald's face was hard, but a small smile was tugging at the corners of his mouth and his brown eyes were hard. "And if ye err where ye set up camp, I or Mr. Rolfe twill move ye off. I suggest a ride into Arles. Mr. Schmidt twill sell ye enough supplies for five days travel if that tis what ye need for yere family."

Shelton's face became splotched with red, but he had correctly gauged the futility of attacking the giant in front of him. "By God, y'all are right. I need the county to help me against the likes of you all." He stomped out the door, his family following close behind.

"Vell, dot's dot."

Shelton, however, had other ideas. He stopped at the saloon and found Tillman. Tillman was more than happy to sell him his brother's ranch and use part of the money to buy new shoes for his girls; new shoes that Kasper just happened to have in the back, and he smoothly explained to Tillman that he hadn't had time to put them out yet.

"He's just bitter about the war," was Tillman's explanation to the others as he helped himself to the last of the food set on the outside tables. Tillman had forgotten any animosity of Yankees he might have harbored and had brought his family along when help was needed for raising the heavy timbers of the church roof. After all, Kasper had carried them through the years of fighting for the glorious cause, and MacDonald and Rolfe had hired him for the drive; plus, they let him add fifty of his own herd. "I think he just let his big flapping mouth overload his humming bird—ah—behind before he thought about what he was saying. It'll be nice for Janey having another woman within a couple of miles for a change."

Janey hid a smile behind her hand rather than let the gaping holes in her gums show. The war years had been hard, and there were few teeth left in her mouth. "There's even a girl Emily's age," she simpered. "And they're Baptists."

Janey's pleasant plans didn't work out. Whatever companionship Shelton felt for a fellow Confederate, letting his "women" visit was not something he allowed. He refused to let anyone that associated with damn Yankees to visit his place.

Tillman also left out Shelton's exchange with Jesse Owens. Shelton delivered an ultimatum before he left. "And y'all can tell those damn Yankees that they don't mess with me or come near my place. By God, if I ever find 'em alone, ah'll deal with 'em."

Jesse shook his head. "Y'all are going to have to tell them yourself."

"Y'all mean y'all are still going to serve them? Maybe I need to go into Arles and find some real men."

"Mister, the folks in Arles tried that once. I reckon they'll think twice about trying it again." Jesse began to take a strong dislike to the man.

Shelton turned on his heel and stalked out, stopping long enough at the doorway to turn and point his finger at Jesse and bellow, "Y'all tell 'em not to show up alone when I'm here. I'll show 'em why we should have won."

Even if he had heard the tirade, Rolfe would not have changed his habits. He continued to drop in at Jesse's place whenever he wasn't out branding or hunting. Part of the work load had been shifted to MacDonald's hired hand, Ramon Gonzales. Rolfe felt that by selling his cattle he had provided for his family for decades to come and he could relax. Rolfe's relaxing was interrupted one afternoon when Shelton rode in to have a horse re-shod and then headed to Jesse's for a beer while he waited.

Rolfe's presence put Shelton into a bad mood and he didn't bother to order as he asked, "Don't y'all ever air it out in here? Seems y'all would improve the air if y'all only let white men in."

Rolfe carefully set his mug down and asked, "Inside or outside?"

Shelton came at Rolfe swinging his right fist at the jaw. Too late he realized the older man had moved more swiftly than he thought the years would allow, and he took a fist to the jaw. Before he could recover, Rolfe swung again at the midsection and doubled Shelton over. When Shelton straightened, Rolfe slugged him in the jaw again. As Shelton hit the floor, Rolfe turned back to his beer and a boggled eyed Jesse. He waited patiently for Shelton to stir.

Within a few minutes Shelton pushed himself up. He sat on the floor and shook his head. When he looked up, Rolfe was standing there knife in hand. "Du come for me again und I slit du up der brisket like a scheine hund. Now get out and stay out vhenever I am here."

Shelton may not have understood the German contempt for pig dogs, but the contempt in Rolfe's voice was clear and the danger of an early death quite apparent. He slowly rose off the floor and left without a word; hate for Rolfe and anyone connected with him curling his gut and eventually curdling his mind.

Chapter 24

Martin Takes a Wife

Brigetta turned away from the window with a sick feeling in her stomach. Her pink cheeks had grown pinker, and her heart was heading upward to lodge somewhere in her throat. The man she'd seen had not looked particularly young. His hat was a strange, wide brimmed affair, his stride still loose and easy, but he was wearing animal skins and spewing a brown liquid at Mrs. Hoefmann's roses. Had she risked everything for this man?

She was twenty-two years old, a spinster by the standards of the day, and a recent immigrant from Germany. She stood barely five-feet tall, with a fully mature figure, pale blue eyes, and thick blonde hair braided and wrapped around her head. Her features were considered average, and her eyelashes were so blonde and skimpy it looked as if she had none. When her parents died, she was left with very little and her options were few as no suitor appeared on her doorstep. Working as a servant in a less than wealthy place did not appeal to her. Der Pastor had shown her the letter forwarded from an American Lutheran pastor. A young man, with the potential of becoming a wealthy rancher was looking for a good Lutheran wife between the ages of eighteen and twenty-four. He needed a strong worker who would raise their children in the old Lutheran doctrines, but there were none in his area. He was willing to pay for her passage if she agreed.

Brigetta had told the Pastor to write a favorable response, and she would leave immediately for the parsonage in America. She wasn't certain what was meant by the old doctrines, but she sold what few remaining household articles there were and booked passage. The journey had been horrifying days of being surrounded by heaving water, and wretched humans retching. Had there not been so many German speaking people in this huge land to direct her to Saint Louis, Missouri, she was certain she would have suffered an agonizing death, or been committed to a life of begging.

Pastor Hoefmann and Mrs. Hoefmann had welcomed her with warmth and with praise for the young man. It seemed he lived in a far place called Texas where few women lived, and fewer Lutherans unless you went to the large cities, or the farmlands of Texas. Brigetta did not understand. Was Texas a separate country? Brigetta willingly helped Mrs. Hoefmann, a small woman who chirped like a bird and bustled about accomplishing little. They assured her that her intended came from an honorable family and had forwarded money for her keep. Brigetta began to have visions of a fine home. Now all her hopes were dashed, but she had struck a bargain. She could hear the people below greeting each other, and Mrs. Hoefmann saying, "I'll call Frauline Rhineholdt for you." Brigetta took a deep breath, directed her footsteps towards the stairs, and descended with her head held high.

Mrs. Hoefmann met her at the stairs, her brown eyes dancing, and her plump little cheeks a rosy pink. She took Brigetta's hand and said, "Frauline Rhineholdt, may I present Mr. Herman Rolfe and his son, Martin Rolfe, your intended. Mr. Rolfe and Mr. Rolfe, Frauline Rhineholdt."

Brigetta's heart went back to her chest as Martin came forward with an extended hand. His hat was in his left hand and he was smiling. Brigetta realized this was a strong, young, bull-headed, handsome man with no tobacco stains on his teeth and no guile in his eyes, and she did not love him.

The next two days were a blur with so many details to attend to: the rings, the license, the quick ceremony by Pastor Hoefmann, the packing, and then buying tickets for a steamship. She remembered wailing, "Not another boat ride," and the two men laughing at her. "Ach, this is a steamship. You'll enjoy it."

They spent their wedding night at a hotel so fancy, Brigetta felt out of place. How could these plainly dressed men afford it? It was the table linen, food, and waiters that made more of an impression on Brigetta than the consummation of her wedding night. The letter had said the young man had the potential of becoming a wealthy man. When she gathered the courage to ask what the house was like, Martin shrugged. "Oh, it isn't much. Part of it is a dugout."

Brigetta had no idea what he was talking about as their conversations were in German, and Martin used the English word dugout. The elder Rolfe said very little. He had merely fixed his hard blue eyes on her that first day and nodded his approval. Something in his demeanor (or was it the long knife he wore at his side?) told Brigetta this was a very dangerous man. When she realized that Texas meant the West and Indian country, she became certain that she would never live to an old age.

As she walked up the gangplank to the steamship, her legs almost collapsed on her, and she could see Martin frowning as he looked down at her when suddenly he brightened. Her cheeks burned red as he said in German, "Maybe you are pregnant already."

An inspection of the cabin alleviated her fears. It was not like the steerage on the boat. "Oh, look, there's a dressing table." She was reassured her new husband could provide for her and any children they would have, and her hopes for a good life returned.

Chapter 25

Chivaree

Brigetta clung to the buckboard. Occasionally, she risked reaching up to make sure her hat was in place. Perspiration was streaming down her face and inside her clothing. Dust was billowing behind and around them, coating her heavy poplin dress, face, and hat. She had brushed and hung her one good black dress when Martin told her they were visiting the neighboring ranch to see Tante Anna and Uncle Mac. She could not imagine why they were going there first instead of into town to see his married sister and younger brother. She still hadn't recovered from the shock of the sagging roof covering a porch that stretched across a house that was a dining area and kitchen built of wood and the two bedrooms dug into the side of a cliff. Peasants didn't live that badly, did they? The pots and pans, dishware, everything was either cracked or bent. How could they have spent money on a real ring and the steamboat? Martin and the elder Mr. Rolfe, however, were oblivious to the state of the household.

Martin sat beside her, dressed in the same suit and white shirt that he'd worn on their wedding day. She knew they should have been washed and pressed, but there hadn't been time. She wasn't even sure they had laundry soap, no idea of where the tubs were, and how did one get water to the tubs? Her worst fears were coming true. Martin had warned her about snakes that had rattles on the end of their body and venom in their fangs.

Martin did not notice her distress and was in a fine mood, pointing out the good grass on either side of the dusty trail. To Brigetta the lumps, ruts, and this ground they were moving on since leaving the road heading back to Arles could not be called a road. The grass swaying toward the skyline and the distant rock and tree covered hills (that Martin called mountains) looked wilted and dry. Had she married a mad man?

They topped the rise and looked down at the MacDonald headquarters. Brigetta gasped in surprise at the sight of a two story house, a real barn and outbuildings with fences for horses and even a cow in one of the pens. A lone tree shaded a small building not far from the side of the house. She saw a rider coming from the opposite direction lift his hat and wave. Martin smiled with satisfaction. "It's my friend, Lorenz. Wait until he meets you!"

Brigetta eyed her husband with dismay. She was dusty, rumpled, hot, and completely uninterested in meeting another male in this detestable, frightening country. Martin snapped the reins and the horses broke into a brisk trot, jarring and bouncing the buckboard over the rough trail. Brigetta hung on for dear life. Within minutes, Martin drew up by the hitching rail in front of the house with a loud, "Whoa."

She opened her eyes and saw that the figure on the horse was waiting for them, grinning and holding his hat. From the porch came the sound of a woman's voice in German. "Good day and welcome!"

"Tante Anna, I've brought my wife to meet y'all!"

Brigetta looked and gulped. The woman was almost as tall as the door and she was dressed in a plain, blue chambray dress with no collar and sleeves that ended between the shoulder and elbow. It didn't look like she was wearing the required number of petticoats. Her white hair was tied up behind her head and curls had struggled loose around her handsome face. A small girl in a short dress, holding a stuffed doll stood next to her waving at them.

Martin clambered out of the buckboard, and the young man dismounted. The two shook hands solemnly intoning, "Herr MacDonald," "Herr Rolfe." Both were grinning widely, and after the handshake slugged each other in the arm. The woman on the porch came striding towards them. Martin seemed to remember her and picked up the reins to tie them to the hitching rack when the other said, I'll take care of the horses."

Martin ducked under the horses and came hurrying around to help Brigetta down. She was still flustered when her feet touched the ground, and knew her hat must be perched at an odd angle.

"Tante Anna, this is my wife, Brigetta. Brigetta, this is my honorary Tante, and this is her daughter, Wilhemina." He smiled and added to Tante Anna, "She doesn't speak English yet." The last sentence sounded like an apology, and Brigetta's cheeks grew brighter.

Anna took charge, speaking in German. "This is such a pleasure, Frau Rolfe." She grasped Brigetta's arm and pulled her toward the house. "Come in, come in, where the sun won't burn your pretty face. Mina, go fetch my fan. Would you like a glass of cool water or buttermilk?"

Brigetta's eyes opened and closed as Anna led her inside out of the blinding sun, but the words cool water roused her. "You have cool water?"

Anna laughed in a low chuckle. "Ja, we have a spring. Sit in the rocker while Mina brings the fan. I'll be right back."

Mina appeared with the fan, and Brigetta put it to good use. She heard the kitchen door close, and the horse and buggy being led away. How long, she thought, are we staying? She couldn't possibly be more uncomfortable. At least the fan helped.

Anna reappeared with a pitcher and took a glass from the cupboard. Brigetta held the glass to the side of her face and then gulped the cool liquid. How could it be cool in this heat?

"Slowly, my dear," said Anna. "There's more. Here is a wet washcloth that I dipped in the spring. Use it on your temples."

Brigetta did as commanded, and Anna continued speaking. "You'll need to buy some lighter material for dresses at Schmidt's Corner when you are there tomorrow. Our summers are much warmer than Germany's." Anna stopped when she saw the stricken look on Brigetta's face.

"You don't sew?"

"Yes, but, but I couldn't ask Mr. Rolfe to spend a lot of money, and it will take so long." She stopped in confusion when she saw the stern look on Anna's face.

"I forgot. Olga took everything with her when she married Tom Jackson. You don't have a sewing machine." Anna stopped. "Mein Gott, you don't even have decent pots and pans, do you? What about washing tubs? Dishes?"

Misery flooded Brigetta's face and eyes, and she blinked again to keep from crying. Anna bent down and folded her hands around Brigetta's. "Mrs. Rolfe, Martin would not dream of doing his work without proper tools, and you must have yours. As for money, he still has over ten thousand dollars left from the cattle drive, even with buying you the wedding ring. There's thousands left from last year's drive. I will help you make a list."

Brigetta sat dumbfounded. So much money? How could that be? It was only half a house, the rest a cave. The furniture, except for the table and the beautiful rosewood pump organ in one corner, was nothing more than sticks and bones held together with leather. She watched Anna move to the desk and bring a pad and pencil to the table.

"Now we start with the sewing machine." Anna must have seen the stricken look on Brigetta's face. "Don't worry. I'll speak to Martin."

Brigetta was fascinated. This woman was so sure, so confident. What kind of man would marry her, someone so tall and self-assured? The sound of men's voices carried into the house and the door in the kitchen could be heard opening and closing. The answer to Brigetta's unspoken question appeared, his bulk filling the doorway, and she almost fainted.

As Mrs. MacDonald had assured her, they went to Schmidt's Corner the next day. It seemed like another contradiction in reality. Small, poor buildings, certainly poor people, but there were presents and a table groaning with food.

Brigetta considered everything that happened since her arrival. She was seated beside Lorenz in the buggy as they drove home from Schmidt's Corner. How could the evening be so fair? The air so clean and sweet while the moon and stars shone so brightly and she be so miserable?

Lorenz's horse was tied to the back and Martin was wedged into the space behind the seats amid all the packages. "Sleeping it off," was their word for it. The MacDonald's buckboard followed behind them and MacDonald was riding his huge, black animal.

"Don't vorry about Young James," said her father-in-law as MacDonald supported Martin out of the Schmidt's home. "I'll bring him by in the morning. Du vill take care of things, ja, friend Mac."

Brigetta could not figure out what the big man was tending. His wife was driving their wagon team while Mina slept in the back. Lorenz was driving this vehicle, and her head was hurting and her stomach protesting. The Schmidt's had served spiced laced meat dipped from an outside pit. Everyone else claimed it was marvelous, but Brigetta's tongue still burned. The store visit had been everything Mrs. MacDonald promised. The sewing machine was on order; she had new dishes, bolts of material, spools of thread, needles, tubs, pots and pans, and a new kitchen knife. She had been the center of overwhelming attention and given linens, soap, a mirror, and scissors for wedding gifts. They called it a chiveree and all sang songs and the adults joked about married life.

They pulled into the Rolfe headquarters, and everyone helped with unloading and carrying in the packages after Brigetta lit the lamp. Lorenz supported an almost awake Martin, past Olga's closed organ, into the cave bedroom and waited for her to light the lamp. He dropped Martin onto the mattress. Brigetta marveled that the young man hadn't drunk like the others.

"Y'all want me to undress him?"

She blinked her eyes stupidly, and he repeated the question in German. Brigetta reddened. She could hear the MacDonald's carrying things into the house and she stared at the handsome youth in front of her.

"It's no bother." Lorenz began yanking the boots off. "He usually doesn't drink." He grinned at her. "He was just trying to act like his papa."

Brigetta fled to the front. Anna smiled at her. "It will be all right. Just don't let him drink. He's like his mother and can't drink beer. She died too soon. I'll be over in a couple of weeks to teach you how to make soap and drive a team of horses." A brief hug and she was gone.

Brigetta sank into the chair. This was impossible. She could never live here. These people were too strong, too overwhelming: as overwhelming as the land. If only her head would quit pounding.

Lorenz emerged from the back and asked, "Are y'all all right, ma'am?" He switched to German and asked the same question.

She rose from the chair. "Yes, thank you."

"I took off his boots, coat, and trousers. The last two things are hung on the pegs. Goodnight, Frau Rolfe." He smiled, tipped his hat and left.

Brigetta heard the horses clomping off and closed her eyes and yawned. The dishes should be unpacked and put away, but there had been no time to scrub down the cupboard. She hung the iron pots on the nails hammered into the wall by the stove. She looked at the packages of embroidered towels, needles, and thread while her shoulders sank in weariness. She removed her hat and moved into the bedroom as tears rolled down her cheeks. Papa Rolfe had ordered them a new chest with drawers as a wedding present. What was she to do? She had no funds left. How could she leave? Where could she find the strength to live in this land? Her clothes joined Martin's on the pegs. She didn't even worry about putting her nightgown on under her clothes before removing them as Martin was snoring. She simply undressed and pulled the nightgown on. Once the lamp was out, she tried praying as she had been since childhood, but her mind was blank; as blank as a night filled with November clouds. With a start, she realized the lamp in the front room was still lit. Wearily, Brigetta rose and went back to the front. As she was about to bend over and blow out the light, she heard the sound of hoofs out front. Had the MacDonald's returned?

She straightened, uncertain, frowning a bit. If it was Papa Rolfe, he usually slept in the barn, or sometimes outside. If it was the MacDonald's, she would need her robe. She turned and started towards the bedroom when the door burst open, and from somewhere she heard herself screaming at the two men rushing towards her.

Too late she tried to run as they both grabbed at her. One man held her right hand and had his arm around her waist pulling her into him, crowing, "I gets a kiss from the bride!"

The other man held her left arm and was running his hand up and down, over her hips and legs, pulling the material upwards, now rubbing up and down the inside of her thighs. The whiskey smell and sweat were horrible, and Brigetta felt the roughness of the man's skin and teeth clash against hers.

"Doan't git greedy," said the man rubbing her. "Her man's got to be around here. We got time to take what we want."

The man holding her put his hands under her hips and began forcing her backwards to her knees. The other man cursed and shouted, "Yu fool! Let's get her out of here first. Then we'll give her a real Texas chiveree."

Brigetta was screaming for Martin as the man's mouth left hers, and he pulled her upright by grabbing her arm and her right breast. Both men were laughing at her and the ease of taking her from a Yankee when Martin stumbled out of the bedroom. He was still drunk, but his rubber legs held him as he hurled himself across the room with a yell and landed on the man holding Brigetta.

The other man sidestepped and pulled out a pistol and laid it across the side of Martin's head. Martin dropped to the floor on all fours, blood pouring down his neck and ear while the two men dragged Brigetta out of the house.

"We can take her here. He ain't going to do anything." The one holding Brigetta was impatient.

"No, that ain't our orders. We're supposed to git her away from here and naked. If she makes it back all right, fine, if not, jest one more Yankee Dutchman gone. Damn shame. She's just right fer takin' care of one, maybe both of us."

They were dragging her towards their horses, when she heard more hoofs clattering in the night. As the one man mounted, the other started to lift her up to the man on the horse. The rifle bullet shattered his head. He fell, ripping her gown, and she fell with him, the horse's hooves barely missing her head as the other man kicked his horse into motion. Another shot felled him. She was scrabbling on the ground towards the house, stones cutting into her hands and knees, when suddenly Lorenz was beside her, lifting her up, and asking, "Are y'all all right, I mean, Frau Rolfe, are you all right."

His hands were strong and gentle, but she could only look at him blankly, nothing penetrated. He looked down. "We were too far out. We didn't think they would be this close and—where's Martin?"

Brigetta managed to sob out words. "He's hurt. He tried to fight."

More hooves were pounding behind them. Lorenz looked up and yelled. "Martin's inside and she says he's hurt." He turned and half-carried, half-pulled her with him as he hurried towards the door.

Martin was still on the floor, the blood pooling around him and covering his shoulder. Brigetta remembered thinking; *I'll never be able to get it out of the floor or his clothes.* Lorenz propped her in a chair, and knelt beside Martin as a man outside screamed. The scream was followed by a gurgle. Lorenz tore his shirt off and used it to stem the blood as he pushed the skin on Martin's head back together.

MacDonald barreled into the room. "How bad tis it?"

"Bad, needs sewing."

MacDonald looked at Brigetta, and she pulled her nightgown closer. She saw his eyes evaluate her, and then reject the idea of any help. He turned towards the stove and said, "I'll stir up the fire. I need some hair from a horse's mane and a needle. They must be boiled. Keep holding that together until friend Rolfe comes in."

Rolfe banged in the door as MacDonald was speaking, and he joined Lorenz on the floor. "Du go get the hair. I'll take care of my poy."

Lorenz stood and ran out the door. Brigetta stood up and took a deep breath. Were these men rejecting her as a fallen woman, or did they just assume she was useless? The gown started to sag, and she ran towards the bedroom and hid behind the curtain. She heard MacDonald at the stove and water being poured. "We twill need some bandages and a large needle."

"Ja, ve can cut off material from vone of the rolls. Maybe the voman knows vhere the needles are."

Brigetta understood not a word being said and this was her house and her husband. From somewhere strength poured back into her. Needle? Was that the word Mina had used for nadle? Were they were going to sew up Martin's head? What did men know about sewing? She heard Lorenz come back into the house. She belted on the robe she'd bought with the last of her money and walked back out to see MacDonald pawing at her gifts. "What are you looking for?"

He looked at her and must have seen the difference in her eyes. He gave a rueful smile. "A needle large enough to hold the hair from the horse's mane we are using for thread. We also need a cloth for washing the blood away." His German was decent, but the accent thick.

Brigetta moved to find what he needed.

"Friend Rolfe, I twill need some of your whiskey. Twill work as a cleanser."

"Ja, du know vhere it is."

Brigetta found the items MacDonald requested, but she held onto the needle. "How do you intend to thread it?"

The big man had removed his hat and hung it on a chair horn. His black hair was plastered against his head, and he grinned at her. "By letting you do it." He moved over by the stove, fished the bottle out of the back of the cabinet, took the basin from the washstand, and added some of the water from the pot.

Brigetta watched, fascinated at the sight of the two violent, older men bathing Martin's head. She heard Lorenz grunt as he fished a piece of hair out of the boiling water and brought it to her. There was nothing but concern in those grey eyes. She assumed the concern was for Martin as she threaded the needle and moved over to the men.

"When you're through, I'll start to sew."

The respect in MacDonald's brown eyes made her stand straighter. "Hold the needle and thread over the basin and I'll pour the whiskey over it."

She hesitated a moment and did as he directed.

MacDonald liberally dumped the alcohol over the needle and her hands. "Can you make the stitches cross over each other?"

She nodded and he continued, "If you begin to feel ill, say so. Do not be ashamed. We've seen grown men faint at the sight of blood. His father and I will hold him. Lorenz, come hold the skin together for Frau Rolfe."

Brigetta knelt and took a deep breath and began to sew. The skin was surprisingly tough to penetrate, and she ground her teeth together. Finally the bloody job was done and they were wrapping Martin's head in bandages. When they finished, MacDonald hoisted him into his arms like a baby and carried him to the bedroom.

She stood and blinked her eyes. The basin, filled with red fluid was still on the floor. She laid the needle on the table and picked up the basin to carry it outside. Suddenly Lorenz was in front of her speaking in German. "Frau Rolfe, let me do that." He smiled down at her. "You don't need to see what's out there."

She looked up at him and closed her eyes. He was right. She did not want to see those two men again. She suspected they were both dead, and without a word, she handed the basin to him.

MacDonald returned and retrieved his hat, and he spoke in Deutsch. "Mrs. MacDonald and I will be back tomorrow to see how you two are doing." He patted her shoulder. "He will be fine in the morning except for a raging headache. Martin has chosen wisely."

"Ja, gut stock." Her father-in-law was standing there, eyeing her and he too used Deutsch. "You will make him a good wife. Mac and I will take care of things outside, and Lorenz will stand guard the rest of the night." He looked at his friend and continued in English. "Ve haf a visit to make at Sheltons."

MacDonald nodded his head and they stepped outside.

As the door closed behind them, Brigetta looked at the rose-wood organ, gleaming softly in the lamplight. It sat silent in the corner, the one decent piece of furniture left by Olga. "We are starting to build the extra room," Olga had confided that afternoon. "Uncle Mac will help us move it." Like so many of Olga's dreams, the organ would remain closed and silent for another year.

Chapter 26

Ambush

Anna ignored the sweat trickling down her nose as she and Mina continued to weed in the garden. Six-year-old Mina was becoming such a help. The sun had lost its heat-of-the-day intensity, but since this was the end of August the huge dark clouds kept building and the weather became stickier and stickier, the smell of rain in the air mixing with the dust coating everything. The work was good though and would keep her from thinking. Lorenz had gone with the Rolfe's on the drive to market, and Mr. MacDonald was watching both places.

He had gone into the foothills as this was a slow time on the ranch. After breakfast, just before he left, he came in with a bemused look on his face. "Lorenz just talked to me in my mind. They twill be here this afternoon."

Anna looked at him blankly and shook her head. "How could he from so far away?"

"I dinna. He has gone beyond me. I think, mayhap, he is now the teacher." He smiled and gave her a hug. "I twill see ye ere supper."

Anna knew he was using the time to study at the "machine" as she thought of it. Lorenz should be home at any time, and then she could quit worrying. He was already late in her mind, and she knew of all the evils on the trail and in the trail towns.

She did not trust Herman Rolfe to prevent Lorenz and Martin from doing something stupid. Martin was steadier than his father, but he was young and three months away from his wife was a long time.

It was gunshots that roused her and straightened her back: First one, then two, then two more in rapid succession. The sounds came from the direction of the foothills, and Zeb would be coming home now. She dropped her hoe, grabbed Mina's hand, and ran to the gate. Her first thought was for the shotgun over the front door and they ran into the house, Mina repeating and repeating, "Mama, Mama, what's wrong."

Finally she answered, "I don't know." Her stomach was tight and so was her breathing. She knew this was bad and Zeb needed her. Pray God he was still alive. She took Mina to the cabin built for Ramon and his wife. Ramon was with Lorenz, but Armeda was there with her newborn. She shoved Mina inside and yelled, "Something has happened. Please vatch her. If Lorenz and Ramon come home, send them toward the foothills." And she raced away, not bothering to hitch the team. The shots were too close for that.

She found him just outside the pasture, walking slowly and painfully, holding onto Zark's stirrup. When he saw her, he slumped forward on his knees, and crumbled, the wound in his lower back dripping blood.

He turned his head to look at her, his mouth forming words she barely heard. "'Twas Shelton's gunnies. Tell Lorenz – to – warn Herman."

Anna ripped away his shirt and saw the bullet had taken a downward course. She used his knife to cut away her petticoat and staunch the bleeding What did she do now? She could not move him even with her strength, and help was too far away. If she left him he would die, and if she stayed he would die. It was then she heard the hoof beats, and Lorenz was riding toward her. She used the remaining part of her petticoat to tie down the material over the wound, ignoring the dirt that had collected on it as she ran it under his body.

"Ve must get him home!" she shouted at Lorenz. "Get help."

Lorenz took one look and swung his horse around. She did not know how long she sat there holding Zeb's hand, telling him not to give up when Lorenz and Ramon appeared dragging a door behind Lorenz's horse.

Somehow between the three of them they shifted MacDonald onto the door, belly down. Lorenz looped a shorter length of rope around his body and door and tied him to the improvised travois.

"Not too tight," she admonished.

"It has to hold him." Lorenz's voice was grim. He tied two longer ropes lengthwise on each side of the door and handed the end of one to Ramon. "Tie it to your saddle, por favore." He tied the other to his saddle horn.

"Mama, do you want to ride behind me?"

"Nein, I vill valk beside him. Du cannot go fast."

As predicted, the going was slow and tedious. Anna tried with every ounce of her strength to keep the make-shift travois from bouncing, but it was futile. They dragged him around to the front porch, and then Ramon and Lorenz pulled the travois up onto the porch and lengthwise up to the now empty doorway into their bedroom. Anna said not a word about the chips in the jamb.

"Mama, go inside and make sure we can lay him on the bed."

Lorenz had never gone into their room, but he suspected his mother had some sort of covering over the linens. White faced, Anna preceded them.

"Ramon, y'all take his legs and I'll get the shoulders."

"Should we turn the Patron over?"

"No, it's going to take everything just to get him inside and on the bed."

They half-lifted MacDonald and staggered into the room and over to the bed, then paused before the final lift to position him belly down. Both were breathing deeply. "Ramon, I know we've been riding hard, and the horses are worn out, and y'all have a new baby, but if y'all can ride into Arles early in the morning for Doctor Huddleson, we'll make it worth your while."

Ramon looked at the young man. "How, senor?"

"Y'all become lead hand." He grinned. "I know, right now y'all are the only hand, but we'll need more help come fall and spring. There's a ten dollar a month raise with it, starting right now."

Ramon's dark eyes were lit with excitement. "Si, Senor. I can ride. Will they believe me?"

"We'll send a note with y'all and our thanks. I can't leave Mama now."

Ramon nodded and tipped his hat at Anna who was busy getting clothes off MacDonald. Anna looked up long enough to say, "Send Mina home."

When he had gone, Lorenz asked, "Y'all need some help with those boots and trousers?" Together they finished stripping the clothes, and Anna went after the warm water from the stove reservoir and towels. He heard her telling Mina to sit and read or draw before she returned.

"Get those salves of his," she commanded. MacDonald's wound continued to seep blood.

Lorenz brought only one of the salves. "The other one closes the wounds too fast," he explained. "Mama, for him to survive, I've got to go to the *Golden One* to find the other medicines for keeping away infection, and to see if there's anything or anyway to get blood back inside of him. The doctor isn't going to make it for at least ten days. Even when he gets here, I'm not sure what he can do. I'll have to wait until Ramon leaves. Y'all can use any excuse you can think of to tell Mina and Armeda as to where I am."

Anna looked up, her eyes were hard. "He vill live." And she went back to work.

Ramon was back within six days. His horse took weeks to recover. Doctor Huddleson made it in nine and examined the huge form and the wound in the back. He was in his late forties and his training had been in the East. The route to the Texas frontier via the riverboats had been an adventure to savor a lifetime. He was no better nor any worse than most of the doctors relegated to the frontier. He didn't realize that Lorenz blocked his mind about the two hearts, and his diagnosis was simple.

"It's amazing that he has lived and there is no infection. The bullet is still in there and should come out, but I'm not the one to do it. There's a doctor in Saint Louis and one in San Francisco that might be able to. If he lives, that's who he needs to see. I can give you their names and write a letter for you."

MacDonald was conscious, but weak. "I am in this room, Doctor. Ye dinna need to refer to me in the third person."

Doctor Huddleson looked down. "You're just stubborn enough to live, Mr. MacDonald." He repacked his case and wiped his brow. "Just keep changing those bandages as needed, and don't let him get chilled."

Both Anna and Lorenz choked back the words about the unlikely possibility of a chill during the end of August and escorted him to the door after paying him. "Are du sure you von't have some coffee and rolls? I can fix a lunch if du vish to eat." Anna did not want the man to think them inhospitable.

"Thank you, Mrs. MacDonald, but a rider from Shelton's intercepted me on the way here. It sounds like Mr. Shelton's had a fit of apoplexy. He can't move or speak. I need to stop by there before I head back to Arles. I'll check back here next month." He tipped his hat, settled it on his head, and walked to the buckboard. Tipping his hat to damn Yankees was no problem. The MacDonald's were unusual in that they paid in cash instead of sundries. He doubted if the Shelton's would be so generous.

Lorenz tried to make a quick exit, but Anna blocked his way. "You did that with your mind," she accused him in German.

He set his lips and looked down at his mother. Lorenz had come into his full height of six feet in the last two years. He could hear Tilly's girl Molly working in the kitchen and he answered in German. "Mama, if I'd used a rifle, the law would have been after me. You and Papa need me right now, and Shelton still has others like the two men that attacked Papa. If Uncle Herman would have split his brisket instead of leaving him a beaten hulk after that attack on Martin and Brigetta, he wouldn't have tried to murder Papa. He won't give any more orders."

Lorenz kept all emotion out of his voice and face. He couldn't tell her how he'd been bathed in sweat afterward and how dirty he'd felt inside as he worked his way through Shelton's mind to find the way to completely disable the man. Instead, he saw Anna's grey eyes start to darken and he made a hasty retreat to his horse. He figured it would take a day or two for her to calm down. They'd hired Molly as a helper when it became apparent that Anna could not nurse MacDonald and care for Mina and the household without upsetting Papa. Daniel and Margareatha had been sent for, but Lorenz didn't expect either of them for another two weeks or more. He wondered how right Huddleson was about Papa's recovery and the need for an operation.

Chapter 27

LouElla

Mina was bored as only a seven-year-old could be after being sternly warned not to make noise or bother anyone. She had put on her winter coat and dutifully buttoned it all the way down so she could sit on the front porch while Rity slept. "There may be other boarders and you mustn't disturb them," her sister had admonished. Mina didn't think there was anyone there besides them. She hadn't seen anyone. All she had for company was Dolly, the rag doll Papa had brought from Arles. So far Dolly hadn't been much company. Mina was trying to figure out why Mama had left her with Rity when Mama and Lorenz went to the hospital with Papa to "care" for him. Maybe Papa was sicker than anyone would tell her.

When Mina first went outside there were delivery wagons making their rounds through the muddy November streets, but now they were gone, and the morning sounds had stilled. She looked at the overcast sky trying to figure out the position of the sun and what time it was. Rity would surely yawn awake soon to eat. Then they would go to Marie's place for fittings. That was also boring and tiresome what with slipping in and out of clothes made too large with room to grow, but at least it meant a trip through the streets and there were shops and other people to see. For amusement, Mina began leaning over the porch railing to see how far she could stretch before falling. If Mama or Rity saw her, they would scold and tell her such actions were unladylike.

"Du are much too tall. People think du are older. They expect much more from du." Those were Mama's words. Mama scolded a lot now since Papa had been shot this summer. Mina closed her eyes to blot out the sight of Papa lying on that door and being dragged home. She'd never told anyone that she didn't stay in the cabin with Armeda. She prayed and prayed that God would forgive her and heal Papa and the operation (whatever that was) would make Papa walk right again. Papa and Mama had told her the doctor was very smart and was supposed to be able to make Papa well.

Mina heard horses clopping through the mud, and it brought her attention back to the street. She watched a pair of smart-stepping bays pulling a utilitarian cart with an extended bed and built-up sides draw closer. She knew enough about horses to know the bays were expensive. She widened her eyes as the cart drew up by the gate, and she watched with admiration as a woman climbed down from the passenger's side. She was, in Mina's eyes, a magnificent woman dressed in fine black woolens, the head topped with a fancy hat such as even sister Rity would approve. It was her size that fixed Mina's attention. The woman must be almost as tall as Papa and she looked even broader. She easily reached over the cart boards and picked up the bulky packages, stepping high to avoid the puddles. Mina continued to stare as the woman strode up to the porch.

"Dinna yere parents tell ye tis nay polite to stare?"

Mina was awestruck and her light brown eyes grew darker and larger. The lady even talked like Papa. She gave a quick curtsy. "Yes ma'am." There, that was polite.

The woman made a "Harmph," rumbling in her throat and looked more closely at the wee one she had consented to let into her boarding house. Normally, the guests were male with their occasional female companions: discrete, of course. She had never rented to a family, but this was the off-season, and the spring and summer had been as economically dry as the rest of the country still suffering what the papers called an after-the-War depression. When a regular customer wrote her and recommended letting the rooms to this family who was paying cash, she accepted. She continued to stare at the child and found she couldn't possibly determine the age. It was odd that the child felt no fear. "I am Mrs. Gordon." How strange that name sounded after nearly fifty years. "And how are ye named?"

Mina's voice was clear and firm. "I am Wilhelmina (she pronounced it like Mama with a v sound) LouElla MacDonald."

LouElla was rocked to her core. Here she called herself Louise. How could this wee one name her? "How did such a wee lassie come by such an oversized name?" LouElla rolled the r's as rapidly as MacDonald, and Mina had no problem understanding.

"I'm named for mine grandmothers. They are in heaven, and Papa says now they live on in me."

LouElla smiled. "Tis a lovely thought." She was more disturbed than she wished to admit and started towards the door, but she wanted to know more and she turned.

"I twas about to have a wee bit of sustenance. Would ye care to join me?"

"Oh, yes, ma'am." Mina happily trailed LouElla into the house.

The Irish maid, Milly, took the packages handed to her and stopped with a blank look when Mrs. Gordon ordered cookies and a glass of milk be brought with her morning tray. LouElla led the way to the door and opened it. They stepped into her very private world.

Why am I doing this? LouElla wondered, and then she realized that this wee one, unlike all the others had no fear of her size. She twas tall for a woman, but the bulk was natural in her land, and there she twas called magnificent. Here men, women, and children looked at her as though she were one of the freaks on display at Barnum's American Museum. She laid her hat and purse on the side table and hung her coat over the chair. Mina was staring at the oversized furnishings with total fascination.

"Papa has a chair just like that one, almost. He had it 'specially made because everything is too small for him." She pointed to the chair and parlor table set near the window to catch the sunlight for reading. LouElla caught herself staring at her small visitor. The chair had been made like a Thalian chair, done in the blue of Don. There was no possibility that another existed on this world.

"Tis yere fither truly such a big man?"

"Oh yes, ma'am. He's much, much taller than you." The brown eyes were all innocence. Mina took off her head covering and revealed brownish hair twisting in small curls around her face and the rest pulled back into rebellious, turned up braids that wisped escaping pieces of hair.

"And how do ye ken that he tis much taller?"

"Because your waist is this high on me and Papa's is this high." Mina moved her hand five or more inches to indicate the difference. She then set about trying to unbutton her coat, the small fingers tugging at the large buttons.

LouElla knelt to give a hand and found her own large fingers weren't much better at the task. "Mama made the holes tight so I vouldn't run around with my coat open."

Again the wee one used the v sound for the w. Probably German, thought LouElla. She kenned that much about this world, and sometimes the Germans could be large people. "How eld are ye?"

"I just had my birthday and I am seven." Mina held up seven digits and smiled.

LouElla felt a deep sense of satisfaction. She had argued with her dour clerk and bookkeeper, Miss Walls, about the wee one's age. Miss Walls insisted that the child had to be ten to be so tall, and was probably backward since she behaved so childishly.

LouElla had felt the child behaved as a Thalian nine-year-old. Finally the last button slipped through the hole and the coat placed on the same chair as her coat when a discreet knock at the door was heard.

Milly brought the tray in and set it on the table by the window, looking sideways at Mina. She wondered how this child could be so privileged as to enter the mistress's quarters. "Anythin' else, ma'am?"

"No, thank ye." LouElla turned to Mina. "Are ye ready for some sustenance?"

The amber brown eyes sparkled. "Oh, yes, I'm very hungry."

LouElla chuckled and took Mina's hand to lead her across the room. How good it felt to hold a wee one again, if only by the hand. "How do ye ken the word sustenance?"

"That's the word Papa uses. He always tells Mama that he's ready for a wee bit of sustenance." She boosted herself up on the straight back chair and waited expectantly.

LouElla poured her brew into a large stein and picked up a hunk of cheese. "Ye may help yereself to the cookies. The milk tis already poured." Nay matter how hard she tried, her words nay sounded right in this alien land.

Mina eyed the platter of cookies and selected one. Her small teeth bit an even round and she grinned impishly. "Verry good."

LouElla found her heart leaping again. It had been at least some ninety Thalian years since a wee one had said such words in her hearing. Dear Gar, had she heard correctly, or twas the darkness reaching for her again? And what twas it the lassie had called herself? She struggled to say the name correctly. "Vil-"

"Oh, everybody calls me Mina. Only Mama calls me Wilhelmina when she's mad." Mina took a swallow of milk. "May I have another?" The brown eyes were sparkling.

"Aye, take as many as ye want."

She considered the child again. "Ye have been most well behaved during yere stay here."

Mina nodded. "Thank you. Mama said I must be good and sister doesn't like noise." Mina wrinkled her nose. "Sometimes I think she doesn't like me." The smile left her face and she pouted. "Rity never plays games with me like Lorenz, and she makes me do lessons at night. If I do them in the morning, she says I make too much noise and ask too many questions."

The staff had familiarized LouElla with Miss Lawrence's comings and goings, her late sleeping habits, and total indifference to Mina's activities in the morning. Miss Walls had sniffed during the recitation, "If it weren't for the quality of her clothes, I'd call her a fancy lady. She's too tall and independent." That Miss Walls was also describing her employer obviously didn't occur to her. Gentlewomen were small and delicate, with mincing gaits, docile manners, and relied on the men in the family. It was doubtful if Miss Walls considered LouElla a woman. Few in this land seemed to. LouElla jerked her mind back to her wee visitor.

"And who tis Lorenz?"

"He is mein brudder, no my brother. Mama says I must listen to how Rity says things."

LouElla emptied the last of the brew into her stein. "And how eld tis Lorenz?"

"He's eighteen now, but he still plays checkers with me, and he's teaching me to ride. Well, he was before Papa got shot, and he had to work harder." The soft skin wrinkled over Mina's nose as she leaned towards her new friend. "Are the doctors really, really good in Saint Louis?"

LouElla half-way gulped her beer, and dabbed at her mouth to delay an answer. In her opinion the doctors here were nay Medical at all, for they could nay cure and oft did much harm. From what she'd seen of the returning army men, most would have been better off without them. How was she to answer this wee lassie? "I have heard that the doctors are verry good here.

Tis said that one must travel to New Orleans or New York to find one better. Are ye worried about yere fither?"

"Ja." Mina nodded her head and her slight body rearranged itself on her chair. "He had a bullet by his backbone that Dr. Huddleson couldn't get out." Suddenly all of her fears came rushing out of her mouth. "Rity never answers my questions, and she thinks I'm too little to worry about things. Mama has to care for Papa in the hospital and can't watch me, so she sent me to be with Rity. And they won't let me see Papa at the hospital, and I know the doctor's done the operation, but nobody tells me why I can't go now, and why Mama has to work so hard, and I'm afraid he's going to die, and I can't even be there." The brown eyes filled with tears at the thought of never seeing Papa again.

She took a deep breath and began again. "I've been really good so that Rity would take me to see Papa, or else Mama or Lorenz would come here and tell me that Papa is all right and getting better." By now tears were rolling down Mina's face.

LouElla held out her arms to the wee one. There was no answer she could give. She considered the hospitals here little better than death houses, and she would nay want one of her own there. "Hospitals are nay places for wee ones," she managed to say as Mina ran toward her arms.

Suddenly she stopped and hung her head. Mina knew Mama would not want her to act like this, but this lady was so much like Papa. "Mama says I shouldn't bother other people. I sorrow." The last phrase was said softly as she looked up into LouElla's eyes.

"Dear Gar, where did ye learn to say 'I sorrow'?"

"Papa taught me."

How could this wee lassie stand there and say the words of Thalia? "Did he teach ye what ye do when ye say that?" Her arms were still outstretched.

Soundlessly, Mina was in her arms, the head on one side of her throat and then the next while LouElla made the clucking sound in each wee shell of an ear. Mina relaxed on her shoulder and LouElla hugged her tightly. "Ah, darling lassie, from whence have ye come? I dinna how, but I ken yere fither twill be all right. Mayhap I can make some inquiries for ye." This was madness. She had nay right to interfere in another's family's affair, but the wee lassie had brought her a measure of Thalian courtesy that she ached for. She must do something for the wee lassie.

"Does yere sister greet people in this manner and say yere words?"

"Oh, no," said Mina as LouElla set her down. Rity was grown before she came home."

The lassie did have a way of making statements that were confusing. What twas one to make of her words?

"Only Lorenz does that with Papa because he is true brother." Mina produced a hanky from her pocket and blew her nose. "I know that's not polite, but I had to."

"Is Miss Lawrence nay yere sister?"

Mina blushed. "Well, yes, but Mama was married before and she had four babies, but Papa adopted Lorenz, and so he is my real brud-brother. Rity and Daniel don't call Papa, Papa."

"And what happened to the other wee one?"

"He's with Jesus just like my other true brother that Mama and Papa had. Mama called him Gephardt Llewellyn."

LouElla felt her jaw slacken, and she lowered her huge frame into the chair. She had fought Justines, Kreppies, the emptiness of space in a battered ship, and the empty, sterile alien ways of this planet after she admitted she was stranded here, and never had she felt more defeated. "Gephardt Llewellyn?" her words came softly for she did nay wish to frighten the already upset wee one, "what tis yere fither's name?"

"Zebediah L. MacDonald." Mina said the words with pride.

"What does the L stand for?" She dare not let hope creep into her voice.

"I think it's Llewellyn. I can ask Rity."

"Nay," said LouElla. "Mayhap she tis following yere mither's wishes." The name twas preposterous and as alien sounding as any in this primitive place, still Llewellyn twas her laddie's name, and he could nay be here. Twas best just to enjoy the wee one and nay give in to fantasies.

"Mayhap on the morrow, if the weather tis fine, we could go for a ride in the wagon and take a bit of sustenance with us. That tis, if yere sister approves. In the meantime, I think it would be better if ye played in the back. There tis more room there. Have ye been to the back?"

"Oh, no. Rity says I mustn't bother anybody in the kitchen."

"Hmph, tis my kitchen. Come along."

She took the small hand in hers as they entered the main room and walked through the door leading into the kitchen. Mina carried her coat and was almost skipping with excitement.

"I don't think Rity will care if I go with you in the morning. I'll ask her first thing when she wakes up."

The kitchen was occupied by Ruth, a wide, black, efficient, jealous guardian of her realm. She looked up in surprise at LouElla. Such visits to the kitchen were a rarity since the Missus left everything to her discretion. A huge fireplace occupied one corner, a cast iron stove another, and the large, freestanding cabinet set against the wall held the kitchen's working equipment when not in use and provided a counter. Like many kitchens built in an earlier era, this room seemed an afterthought and not an integral part of the house. The rough floor planking was worn smooth from sanding and scurrying steps. Ruth was kneading a huge mass of dough for bread baking, her sleeves were rolled above her elbows, and sweat was gathering on her brow during the process. Milly, scrawny, with greenish eyes that tended to overflow on any perceived slight or accusation of wrong doing, was polishing the silverware that was Mrs. Gordon's pride. A half-filled bucket of scraps stood at the door, waiting to be filled and carried out. Charley, Ruth's man, would take it to the neighbors to empty. In return, the household was given about a dozen eggs per week.

"The wee one tis named Mina." LouElla announced. "We have become friends. She tis welcomed in my House and in my heart. When she needs to go outside and play, she may go out the back-door as tis safer out there." She waved her arm in the general direction of the door. "Whenever she needs a bit of sustenance, the cookies twill always be available." She fixed a stern eye on the two as if expecting an argument. Since the two were well paid, there was none. Milly smiled, showing weak teeth that had yellowed early, and she nodded her head. Ruth looked at the intruder and decided it could be worse. The Missus made few demands other than a plentiful table.

"'Course she can, Miz Gordon." She smiled at the child and thought it might be nice to hear a child playing in this strange household.

LouElla led Mina to the back door and picked her up, more from the desire to hold her than any necessity. She opened the door and pointed. "There tis the coach house. Charley takes care of the horses and the wagon. Ye may nay bother him, nay the beasties, but the rest of the yard tis yeres to play in."

"Thank you, Mrs. Gordon."

LouElla felt Mina squirm and set her down.

Milly finished the last of the silver and began preparing a tray. "It's jest about time for Miss Lawrence to have breakfast." If there was any resentment in such odd hours, it didn't show in her voice. Mrs. Gordon's guests were always unpredictable and some tipped well. She had no hopes that a female would tip, but she had no desire to raise her employer's ire. Working in a place that was little better than a bordello was bad enough, but few wished to hire the Irish, and fewer still could afford help. Her biggest resentment was following the black woman's orders in the kitchen. Mrs. Gordon had strange ideas about things. If one were foolish enough to remind her that black folks had their place, she would launch into a tirade about who was best qualified. Milly knew she could ill afford to lose her place, but as soon as things improved, she intended to look for a new position even if the pay was less. She put the coffee urn on the tray and followed the woman and child to the front.

LouElla relinquished Mina's hand and watched her dart up the stairs. She shook her head and entered her door. Once it was closed, her huge hands clenched and unclenched. Then she shook her head. I canna think of the eld days, she told herself, marched into the bedroom, opened the closet door, and removed the rug to reveal a trapdoor. She had nay worries about the staff interrupting her now, and she climbed down into her basement. The workmen had been here before she brought in any of the staff and her version of a gym with weights was her refuge.

Chapter 28

Heartbreak

Ruth brought her breakfast the next morning and placed it on the parlor table. "Miz Gordon, that chile is outside waiting for y'all. Do y'all want to see her early?"

"Aye, it would be nice." LouElla poured the honey over the pancakes and started chewing. Ruth almost said something, but changed her mind. She opened the door for Mina.

Mina entered almost on Ruth's vanishing heels, her brown eyes glowing, her pink cheeks scrubbed clean, and the oversized blue dress smelling faintly of lavender and mothballs. "Rity said I may go if you really want me. Miss Marie doesn't have any fittings for me 'cause she's working on Rity's clothes. Rity won't be back until almost suppertime. After that I have to do lesson, but we have all day!"

She stopped, slightly abashed at her boldness. Mina knew not to bother adults, but she knew few children. At home there weren't any children, except for Young James and Gerry. Armeda's baby was too little. Gerry lived in town with Uncle and Tante. She never saw James unless there was a gathering or celebration, and James grew progressively more annoying. He was six years older than Mina and teased and teased her. When he wasn't teasing her, he would admonish her in the ways of the Lord. Mrs. Gordon, however, was smiling broadly.

"That tis verry good news. We twill have Ruth make up a basket for us ere we leave. There tis plenty of toast and honey here. Would ye like a slice?"

"Thank you, ma'am." Mina boosted herself up in the chair. "I've already had breakfast so I'll just have one slice."

"Hmph, tis more than one ye should have. Ye need some weight on that skinny body."

Mina giggled. "That's what Papa says. He says we all have skinny bodies."

LouElla raised her eyebrows. "Who tis all?" She attacked the browned, juicy sausages.

"Mama, Lorenz, Rity, Daniel, Uncle Kasper, and me. Papa says that Grandpa Schmidt is the only one who isn't skinny.

LouElla watched the small jaws working on the toast. That Llewellyn could be her fither was nay possible. He would be about ninety-six now; in theory twas possible, but in reality nay probable. Inwardly she cried. She had missed his first steps, his schooling, his first bedding, his Maturity Ceremony, and now he would be nearing his full growth and strength. Even if he twere allowed to wed, there would be nay seed. One chance anomaly like her birthing from bedding a Justine did nay mean there would be bairns from a union. She focused on the upcoming outing.

Milly appeared to collect the breakfast items. "Will you be going out again today with the little girl?"

"Aye, have Ruth make us a nice lunch." LouElla smiled at Milly. "Ye may clean the room after we leave." This twould be a day to remember.

The day was crisp and dry, a last gasp of what the natives called Indian summer. They drove around town, exclaiming at the sights, and before swinging down towards the river to an open, grassy river bank. They put a blanket on the ground and uncovered the basket of food, Mina squealing with delight at the hunks of cheese and the apples.

Both stared with open mouths as masses of ducks rose from the river as on command, totally blanking out any sight of sky, and began to fly southward. LouElla had seen this before, but seeing it again brought back the first thrill. Thalia's wild fowl were few in number. This primitive land still possessed the charm of an unspoiled world. She mentioned that in her land, there twere few wild birds and animals left.

They began to talk of the animals on the ranch and the people that Mina knew. LouElla was left with mixed emotions for when they arrived back at her house and Charley was left in charge of the beasties.

Mina held out her arms and LouElla gladly swept her upward. Mina had laid her head on each shoulder and then touched her eyes, her nose and her lips and said, "You are in my heart and eyes forever. Can I call you, Grandma?"

It was as though a hand reached in and squeezed her heart. Where in Thalia did the child learn the proper words? She stared at the child and saw the disappointment begin to appear when there was no answer. "I sorrow."

LouElla closed her eyes and took a deep breath. She set Mina down and gently touched the upturned eyes, the nose, and the mouth. "Ye, child, are in my heart and eyes forever, and yes, ye may call me Grandma."

Mina grinned. "Can we go out again sometime?"

They walked to the house. LouElla still fighting her emotions, but she gladly asserted that they would indeed go out again. She looked up at the sky as a stiff wind suddenly struck at them.

"Aye, we shall go if the clouds stay away." She pointed at the white clouds that seemed massing over the skyline, and Mina made a face.

"I'll ask God to send them away."

"The good Gar may have other things on his mind." LouElla laughed as they entered the kitchen. Smells of chicken and apples filled the room and LouElla swelled with pride when Ruth offered them a plate of cookies. Mina took one before disappearing upstairs to wait for her sister.

"I'll start my lessons all by myself," she declared. "Good afternoon, Grandma."

Ruth had raised her eyebrows, but LouElla lifted her chin and regally departed for her own rooms. She sank onto the sofa running over the words Mina had told her about her family and life and planning the next outing.

Her plans crashed the next morning when looking out at a typical November lead, grey sky. Any leaf silly enough to have clung to a tree this long was being pulled off by the breeze. As yet there was no rain or snow, but LouElla knew the winter was closing in.

Her reverie ended when she heard the front door slam. As she looked out she saw the back of a tall, red head with green hat, dark green coated, woman dragging a child along towards the street. Mina wore her grey coat, a muffler, gloves, and some type of knitted hat. LouElla frowned. What could have stirred the lazy, Miss Lawrence out on such a day. Mayhap the fither was worse. A discreet knock came at the door, and Milly entered carrying a tray and wearing a troubled face.

"Miss Lawrence left this note for you, ma'am." She hurriedly put the envelope beside LouElla and tried to leave.

"Did the wee lassie say anything?"

"No, ma'am," Milly ducked her head and looked up. "I think she was cryin'."

"Ye think! Twas the wee one crying or nay?"

"Cryin', ma'am." Milly beat a hasty retreat.

LouElla opened the enveloped and scanned the words. Then her huge fist crumbled the letter, and she stood and paced, the words burning in her mind.

Dear Mrs. Gordon, I have been remiss in the care of my sister. My apologies for any inconvenience this has caused you and your staff. Certain information has come to my attention, and I find we must leave your establishment. As soon as I find suitable quarters we shall leave. We will, of course, expect the remainder of the fees paid returned. Respectfully, Miss Margareatha Lawrence.

Suitable quarters indeed! What information was the woman talking about? Did Mr. O'Neal nay tell them? As for the money, she had no intention of returning it. The money meant the heating, the food, and the salaries were paid for until March. Miss Walls had received inquiries from certain gentlemen as to the availability of the rooms in the spring. She could hold out until then. She would miss the wee one. That hurt. What had the woman learned? LouElla stopped in her pacing. Marie must have told her about the women that stayed here with the men. LouElla shrugged. The renting of fashionable rooms twas a good way to earn money, and this twas a discreet location for discreet people. Surely Marie had nay mentioned their liaison. LouElla did nay ken the sexual ways of these people. Sex to most of them, like to Thalians, was most enjoyable. They just didn't talk about it unless it was the opposite sex. Strange, very strange.

Then the anger consumed her again. She had lost her own laddie, and now Mina was being dragged out of her life. LouElla headed for her basement.

Chapter 29

Reunited

She emerged seven hours later, spent and sweating, and ordered water for a second bath. The servants grumbled. Twice in a day: the woman was mad.

LouElla had pulled on the last of the hated clothes when she heard the front knocker. Milly twould attend. As soon as the interloper left, she would send for Miss Walls and they would go over the books. She had planned on the MacDonald's staying through February, possibly even into April. Her physical energy was spent, but her anger burned deep. Within minutes she heard Milly's timid knock at the door.

"Mrs. Gordon," Milly's eyes were open wide in wonderment. "There's a young, Mr. MacDonald here to see you. He says that they need the large room readied for tonight and," she got no further.

"I twill see nay!" LouElla roared and was about to push Milly out the door when a slim, well dressed male wedged himself between the door and Milly.

"Y'all must pardon my sister's rashness, ma'am, but this is an emergency." Then his words stopped. The grey eyes opened with awe and his mouth dropped. LouElla could see that by this world's standards, the youth would be declared handsome.

She ground out the words. "Yere mouth tis open. Have ye nay learned politeness?"

"Yes, ma'am." The youth put his hands behind his back and bowed. "I am Lorenz, laddie of Llewellyn." He looked up at her. "I would greet y'all correctly, but we need to talk, and the others don't need to hear." The words were hurried and yet drawled.

It was LouElla's turn to stare, and he stepped inside and shut the door behind him and Milly. Her hands reached out and she grasped him by the biceps. "What right have ye to trespass?"

The grey eyes looked at her steadily, and she could nay believe they were without the fear that she could find nay in him; nay even the smell of it. He twas as strange and disconcerting as Mina.

"Because y'all are LouElla, Lass of Don, Guardian of Flight, sister of Lamar, and y'all are my grandmother. I would lay my head on your shoulders as is proper."

His words were stabbing at the foundation she had built in this world. How had the enemy found her? Milly had said O'Neal was red haired with strange eyes, but she had never asked how strange. Now she feared for her life. Why had the Justines nay taken her? Why use a wee lassie and a laddie nay full-grown? And what did this one mean? She twas nay Guardian of Flight. She twas Captain of Flight.

"So ye wish to lay yere head on my shoulders, do ye? Then do it right." The last words were snapped out.

The laddie looked up at her, his grey eyes gleaming, and his smile drawn to the right in a slash. "I'll do that, Grandma, as soon as y'all let go of me."

She was struck again by the absence of fear. She could smell the slight tinge of mothballs, the tonic on the dark, wavy hair cut short, and the male smell of him, and she released his arms.

He stood on tiptoe, put both arms over her shoulders, laid his head on the right shoulder as they both made the tsk sound with their tongues, then he laid his head on her left shoulder, and again they both used their tongues to make the sound. He left his head on her left shoulder, and LouElla reacted as though she were holding a Thalian laddie and her left arm gripped him tightly while her right hand moved from his head down his back, and she found herself shaking while the laddie murmured, "It's all right, Grandma, ssh, it's all right."

It took all her will to push him away from her. It had been so long. She stared at the man/lad in front of her and could see nay Thalian, and yet he kenned. This time she gripped him by the shoulders. "Who are ye?"

"I told y'all, I am Lorenz, laddie of Llewellyn, Maca of Don."

She looked into the grey eyes, searching for duplicity and found none. "I could break ye."

The eyes remained steady, the voice controlled. "Y'all could try, but right now I need to get Papa here. I came to get Rity's help, but she's gone so Mama and I will do it alone. I'll leave a note for her."

LouElla could nay believe his words. "Do ye mean to fight me? Do ye think ye could win?"

"Not physically, Grandma. Right now, I figure, y'all are stronger than Papa, and he's the strongest person I've ever known."

"Then how do ye think ye could win?"

"Don't even ask." He smiled. "Papa can tell y'all everything for it's his tale to tell.

"Ye canna ken my laddie!" Her voice was harsh and she was shaking him, then stopped. "Get out, and nay of ye come back!"

"We paid for that room, and I'm bringing him here tonight." He turned and headed for the door. Her next words stopped him.

Did they tell ye that Miss Lawrence is moving out and refuses to let me see the wee lassie again?"

"Yes, ma'am, and they said Mina was crying. She's probably figured out that you're our grandma, or someone that looks like her. Haven't y'all talked with my older sister?"

"Nay, I have but seen her from a distance." Her voice was harsh and bitter.

For a moment they stared at each other, each taking the other's measure. LouElla could nay help but see the determination tinged with admiration in his eyes. People in this world did nay look at her with admiration. Who had taught him? Was this some sort of elaborate scheme to ferret her out of hiding? She had remained hidden for so long from the searches she knew the Justines and the Kreppies must have instituted that she was certain this was one of their minions. While a Kreppie might use a child as a decoy, a Justine would probably nay, and she continued to search his face and could see nay but a youth from this planet.

"We'll be back in a couple of hours." He closed the door behind him and almost bumped into a red-faced, walking backwards Milly.

She's probably been listening, thought Lorenz, but he was too rushed to sweep into her mind. "I need a piece of paper and pencil to write a note to Miss Lawrence. Is either available?"

"Yes, sir." Milly led the way to Miss Walls little room that doubled as an office, her breath coming in short, little in and out puffs, her heart beating faster than it should. Her timid knock brought Miss Walls immediately. "Miss Walls takes care of all our guests and their needs." Milly explained.

Lorenz looked at the diminutive form of Miss Walls, drawn into a grotesque curve by the hump on her back. The grey hair was braided and pulled back from the no longer youthful face, the lips surprisingly full, and the brown eyes very sharp.

"Ma'am, I'm the younger Mr. MacDonald. I'll be bringing my parents here early this evening. Mr. MacDonald is still an invalid so the room will need to be heated."

Miss Walls folded her hands in front of her. "Then will you, Miss Lawrence, and the little girl need your rooms too?" She sniffed. "Miss Lawrence gave notice this morning to vacate."

"Miss Lawrence was in error." Lorenz couldn't keep the irritation out of his voice. "May I borrow a piece of note paper and a pencil? I'll pay you for them if necessary."

"Oh, my goodness, no, we don't ask for a payment for paper and pencil. Just a moment, please." He heard her shuffle back into the room, and she returned with a pad and pencil. "Give the remainder to Milly when you finish."

"The room will be warm when we get here?" Lorenz felt her resentment at the question.

"Of course, we always make our guests very comfortable."

Lorenz took the pad and pencil, went to the large table in the dining room, and rapidly scribbled out a note informing Rity of the necessity of bringing Papa here, and that Mrs. Gordon was Papa's mother. He figured the staff here would read it, so avoided any explanations. He folded the paper, wrote Margareatha Lawrence on it, and handed pad and pencil back to Milly who was looking at him with adoring eyes.

Both were surprised by LouElla banging her door behind her as she strode into the room dressed in her heavy, woolen coat and wrapping a muffler around her throat. "How do ye intend to get yere fither here?" she demanded.

"Why I'll rent a buggy when I return the horse to the stable." Lorenz's eyebrows traveled upward. The woman's eyes were hard as though she did not trust him.

LouElla was a warrior. She had decided if she were discovered, she would go down fighting. All she needed twas a chance to get close enough. "We have a conveyance that should work, and I am, nay doubt, stronger than yere mither. My man can drive. Twill that do?

"Yes, ma'am. Thank y'all, Grandma."

"I dinna say ye could call me that!"

"Yes, ma'am." Lorenz grinned. "I'll go help hitch up."

LouElla glared at him and turned to Milly. "Fetch one of the blankets off the bed and bring it to the back." Lorenz followed her to the kitchen where Ruth held court, and Charley was emptying a load of wood into the bin.

LouElla continued to snap out orders. "Charley, we are taking the cart to the hospital. Ruth, we twill be acquiring the rest of our guests. One tis nay well. Ye twill have a decent table spread when we return."

Charley shrugged. It would be a cold night. Ruth put both hands on her hips and glared at LouElla's back as the rest marched out. Decent, indeed, the Missus had her back up about something.

It was as cold as Charley expected. By the time they dropped off the rented horse and Lorenz hopped into the back of the cart, the sun was fleeing westward, and graying dusk began covering the earth while the cold, moist November air was stabbing at the bones. Lorenz was glad that Charley knew this city and where the major hospital was. He could cross miles and miles of open space out where there were no buildings, but a town was filled with twists and turns and strange pools of darkness. He wasn't sure he could have found the way back to the hospital and then the boarding house as quickly as necessary.

"We won't be long," Lorenz promised as Charley pulled the horses to a stop.

"They twill nay let us in this time of eve." LouElla was surprised that Lorenz had simply said which hospital and not directed them by streets which would have led to a trap.

"They don't have the door locked." Lorenz grinned at her as they took the steps two at a time. He pushed against the door and held it for her.

LouElla stepped in. Instead of Justines waiting for her, there were but empty chairs against one wall and a desk with one man sitting behind it. The medical, or at least a man dressed in white clothes looked at them from behind the desk and said, "We're closed. Come back tomorrow." Then he recognized Lorenz. "Oh, it's you. Is that somebody else to take care of your pa?"

"In a manner of speaking." Lorenz took LouElla's arm and led her to the stairs. Suddenly, he stopped at the foot of the stairs and then began running up them.

"Something's wrong," he muttered.

Instinct caused LouElla to pound upward behind him. From the floor above they heard a man yell and then a clanging noise. She followed him to the second door on the right. As Lorenz started to open it, the door resisted. Lorenz backed up and drew out a revolver when LouElla grasped the doorknob and pushed inward, dislodging the man leaning against it.

The man raised a knife, and LouElla grabbed his upright arm, put her left around him, and squeezed. He screamed. She saw a woman using a chair to beat on the enameled thunder mug overturned on another man's head, his shoulders covered with urine and human waste, the smell of it filling the room. Another man was over by the bed, his knife arm caught in the grip of the patient. The pressure was great enough that the knife-wielding man was slowly sinking to the floor. The man in front of her was gasping, and she heard ribs crack through his screams. She released the knife arm, lifted the man high in the air, and brought his back down across her thigh. The man quit screaming, and she threw his crumpled body against the wall and moved over to the bed. Lorenz, she noted, had gone to the woman's assistance and drove his knee in behind the man's knees, toppling man and pot to the floor. She heard a muffled yell as Lorenz tugged the pot off the man's head and rapped the exposed head with his gun. The man fell forward on the floor.

The knife wielding man by the bed was pounding at the man he was supposed to kill with his free arm, but the dark-haired patient didn't loosen his grip while he was looking up at her, staring, hoarsely whispering, "Mither."

LouElla felt her heart leap and she kenned this twas a Thalian. Not just any Thalian, but a larger duplicate of her brither, Lamar, and rage pounded through her. She could nay lose her laddie now. She moved forward and heaved the kneeling man with the knife upward by the neck and head, twisted, and heard the neck snap. She tossed him next to the other on the floor. Then she sat on the bed and gathered her Llewellyn into her arms, murmuring, "My laddie, my laddie."

MacDonald's massive arms enfolded his mother as he laid his head first on one shoulder and then the next, his tongue making the tsking sound, and he began to whisper, "Mither." Their huge forms were rocking back and forth.

Anna looked at the two forms rocking on the bed and put her hands on both their shoulders. "Stop it, stop it," she commanded in German. "You will start the bleeding again."

LouElla glared at her, but MacDonald smiled. "Mither, this tis my beloved counselor, Anna. Ye must love her as I do. Anna, this tis my mither."

"Of course she's your mother, but you must lie still. The surgery hasn't healed."

"Anna, ye are speaking Deutsch." He turned to his mother. "Ye must forgive her. Tis her first language." LouElla continued to eye Anna with disproval.

Lorenz had been standing by the window as though in a trance. Now he turned to them. "He's gone. Forget the pleasantries. Mama, get him dressed and get your coat. It's cold out there, and we've got to get Papa home."

"Du are sure he's gone?" asked Anna.

"Yeah, he's gone. He won't hang around now that his plan hasn't worked. I don't know if he figured out I was gone, or if this was just some fluke." His voice was grim.

"Who tis gone?" LouElla was frustrated and angry. She did nay wish to share her laddie.

"That twould be Toma, a Justine," answered MacDonald.

The words brought LouElla to her feet. "He tis searching for me. I'll go out and ye may rest easy."

"Nay, Mither. He tis stranded here. The ship I came in twas looking for him, nay ye."

"Y'all can explain later. Get him propped up, Mama, and get his socks and trousers on. We have to leave." Lorenz was gently guiding his mother by the shoulders. "Mama, get the things out of the trunk."

MacDonald agreed. "Aye, tis a long tale for telling later."

"And Grandma, y'all didn't do this." His arm swept toward the two bodies against the wall. "Y'all did, but y'all didn't. We don't want questions."

LouElla stared at the young, slim frame. "Ye are an annoyance."

"It seems ye are acquainted with our laddie." Pride swept through MacDonald's voice.

"He tis a scamp who thinks he tis a man." LouElla snapped the words out.

"Aye, but he tis correct. We dinna want questions."

Heavy footfalls could be heard racing up the stairs and to the door. Within seconds, two attendants and two policemen appeared. They stopped as they entered and paused to take a deep breath. All regretted the action as they noted the human excrement on the one man and the emptied enameled pot. One of the policemen knelt by the two against the wall. "They're dead." Awe was in his voice. "What about the other one?"

"He's alive," came the reply. The second police officer straightened. "But he'll be out for a while. There's a huge lump on the side of his head."

"What happened here?" demanded the first officer.

"These men attacked my father with knives. Fortunately, my mother was able to keep that one away from the bed and those two didn't realize his strength. By the time Grandma and I got here those two were incapacitated, and I knocked the other one out."

"We'll have to take everyone down to the station."

Lorenz's face hardened. "No, we're taking Papa out of here before someone else tries to kill him. I'll be down to the station tomorrow and give a statement. Where's it located?"

LouElla was gaping at the young man controlling the situation. She noted the one enforcer twas swallowing. Why would they respect such a youth?

"We need to know who these men are, and why they tried to kill your Pa."

"Ask him when he comes to." Lorenz pointed at the one man. "I suspect someone by the name of Thomas Lawrence is to blame. There's bad blood between the two since Papa ran him out of Arles, Texas. Someone hired the men who ambushed Papa and put a bullet near his spine. That's why he's here, but it's not safe, and he's supposed to stay in bed." He knew these men would infer Toma instead of the "someone" being Shelton. He knew it was close to a lie, but he wanted Papa out of here and safe.

One of the attendants broke in. "He ain't supposed to walk. How's he gonna get out of here?"

"I twill carry him."

That stilled everyone as they looked at LouElla, their mouths dropping. She put her hands on her hips and glared back, daring any of them to nay say her.

Anna had finished putting socks on MacDonald and had the trousers up to his knees. "Someone must lift him so that I can draw these on."

LouElla moved in front of her, and MacDonald put his hands on her shoulders to help. She reached under his hips, bent her knees and hefted. Quickly Anna pulled up the trousers, and LouElla lowered him.

"Leave it unbuttoned, Mama. That bandage is too big. Just get his boots on." Lorenz turned back to the four men. "You all didn't tell me where to find your station."

"No, and you ain't told us who this Thomas Lawrence is, and how you know he hired these men." This one had a lantern jaw and it jutted forward as he spoke. He turned to the attendants. "Did you two ever see these three yahoos before?"

"Never." Both attendants were quick in their response.

"Why not ask him." Lorenz jerked his thumb back at the man moaning on the floor.

The lantern jawed man moved and went to check on him, trying to evade the human waste on the floor. The man on the floor began cursing and searching for the knife. Lantern jaw decided this was a good time to put the cuffs on him. "Shut up, you. There's ladies present."

The man tried to sit up and sat back down. "Ladies, my ass. She got me with that pot."

"Keep your mouth closed except to answer me. Why did you three attack this man?"

"Ain't got nothin' to say."

"Did somebody by the name of Lawrence hire you three?"

"We ain't got nothin' to say."

"You mean you ain't. The other two aren't going to do anymore talking–ever. The big man took care of them. Maybe we should let him loose on you."

"Gawd, no." His eyes shifted from face to face. "Both of 'em are dead?" He began to look wildly around. "Get me out of here."

"Did somebody hire you?"

"I don't know nothin'. Bret said some tall, red-headed dude was payin' for it. That's all I know."

The two blue clad men hoisted the man to his feet. "It looks like you knew what you were talking about. If nothing else, we got this one for assault and attempted murder. We still need you to come with us."

"I'll be down tomorrow." Lorenz gritted the words out, staring at them intently. "My mother is worn out. I have to get her and Papa to a safe place tonight."

LouElla watched in amazement as the five men filed out after lantern jaw had recited the address. She ran every possible scenario through her mind and none provided an answer as to why they had meekly obeyed this youth. She looked at Llewellyn and raised her eyebrows. Anna finished buttoning his coat and went to the wall pegs to retrieve her own coat, muffler, and hat.

Llewellyn smiled at LouElla. "Tis a long tale, Mither, and I twill tell it to ye at yere home. Our laddie tis right. We leave now. If ye would give me a hand up, I think I can make it. I've been moving without the staff here being any wiser."

LouElla tightened her lips and moved forward. "Ye twill nay walk down those stairs." She flexed her shoulders, started a squat, and slid one arm under his legs and the other under his right arm, and lifted him as though he were a newborn babe.

Lorenz picked up the steamer trunk and hefted it up on one shoulder as Anna grabbed the carpet bag and her purse. Forty-eight hours with but four hours of sleep had taken their toll, and she was moving like a wooden figurine. Her teeth were clenched and sheer will power got her down the stairs and outside. She never saw the two attendants staring at them, once again with open mouths. The cold wind cut through her clothes and she was grateful for Lorenz's steadying hand around her bicep.

Charley was busy walking up and down the length of the wagon. When he saw them, he dropped the gate. What he thought of his employer carrying the huge form, he kept to himself. He steadied the horses as the group climbed into the back of the wagon. He heard the wagon gate being lifted and locked into position, and then Mrs. Gordon called out to him. "Take us to home, Charles." Formal she was, as always.

It was a strange, silent journey through the windy streets. Stars blinked overheard between the clouds, and Lorenz was grateful that the driver knew the way. He had a hunch that he hadn't marked the way as clearly in his mind as he would have in the wild lands of Texas. A city was unknown territory, and to him everything took on a dull sameness. Mama had immediately dropped into sleep, and he could feel her shivering. He too felt the cold as the blanket barely covered Papa, Grandma, and Mama. Throughout the ride LouElla kept making soothing sounds, and he figured she was massaging Papa underneath the cover and the darkness. Thalians were definitely different: driven by some primeval urge to touch and stroke.

"Should I drive up front, Miz Gordon?"

"Nay, use the back. Tis flat, and we can go straight in. Ye take care of the horses."

Charley pulled up by the kitchen. Before he could step down, the young man jumped from the wagon to let down the gate. Let the white man, he decided. The horses needed to be put up and rubbed down.

"I'll be back to get the trunk and help with the horses," said Lorenz, and the strange group headed inside, LouElla carrying Llewellyn again, and Lorenz carrying a sleeping Anna.

Ruth, like the men at the hospital, gawked at the sight, but she quickly closed her mouth. "I've kept the stew and biscuits warm, ma'am. Do you want them served in their room or in the dining room?"

"Bring the food and brew into the MacDonald's rooms," commanded LouElla as they trooped through. "We are all in need of some sustenance."

Ruth rolled her eyes. Milly was upstairs already, but the bell would bring her down. She and Charley would have a lot to talk about tonight. She pulled at the rope and began piling bowls and silverware onto a tray.

LouElla strode through the house and down the short hallway, turning sideways through every door. Someone must have heard them coming as the door to the separate suite opened. This was the best set of rooms in the house, kept for the well-paying guests who required private arrangements.

Mina met them at the doorway, her brown eyes wide, her mouth open, "Papa, mama?"

"Ye twill need to move back, wee one. I twill hug ye in a moment." MacDonald's voice was full of love and concern.

LouElla swept in and marched for the open door of the bedroom. The bed, made up with the finest linens and plushest blankets, was set against the far wall, and the only window on the side was heavily draped with blue velvet. A fireplace with a nicely laid fire was in the front, left corner. The bed covers were already drawn back, and LouElla set him on the bed. Anna had forced herself awake and followed behind, one groggy footstep after the other as Lorenz supported her.

"Mama, we can take care of him now. Y'all go lay down on the sofa."

"Nien, it's my duty." Her words were German and she moved over to MacDonald and bent down to unbutton his coat.

MacDonald put his hands on her face. "Anna, my love, ye have done yere part. Ye have cared for me for four days with little rest. Ye warned us that Toma twas drawing near. Let yere lassie care for ye now."

Anna was white faced, her eyelids drooping, and she slumped forward. Lorenz reached down and helped her up. Mina was watching wide-eyed, and Margareatha entered the room. Her movement caught LouElla's attention and she sucked in her breath as she saw the tall, red-haired, copper-eyed woman. "Justine," she hissed.

Margareatha lifted her head. "I am an American." Her eyes were defiant.

LouElla started for her when MacDonald spoke. "Mither, attend. She speaks true. The man kenned here as Thomas Lawrence tried to kill all of them while they were children. My Anna fought him the only way she kenned and almost won."

LouElla stared at him with disbelief, then at the retreating backs of Lorenz and Anna, and finally back at Margareatha, trying to take her measure. She saw the arrogance of a Justine in the eyes and the tight, scornful lips, but Margareatha's lips were full and her body lush and curved; a form that only Earth women seemed to possess. How, she wondered, could any of this strange trio fight an adult Justine?

Mina took advantage of the adult's lack of attention and was beside her father. "Papa, are you well now? When can we go home? If she's my grandma, why does she hate Mama, Lorenz, and Rity?"

MacDonald put his arm around her and drew her close. "My wee one, ye should nay fret. I am nay yet completely well, but Mama and yere Grandmither twill nurse me. Yere Grandmither does hate the rest of the family. She has nay had a chance to ken them." He kissed her head. "All these clothes twill over heat me, and I have grown weary and need sustenance. Ye give me and Grandmither a kiss and go help Rita with yere mither."

Mina gave him a tight hug and looked up at LouElla, her brown eyes filled with worry. "Y'all like my family, don't you Grandma?"

LouElla knelt and pulled the child to her. "We twill be one House. Now ye go with yere mither and close the door for I must take the clothes off yere fither."

She watched Mina scamper from the room and then began the task of removing the clothes. "She tis Justine. Have ye gone mad?" LouElla kept her voice low to prevent the others from hearing.

MacDonald smiled. "Mither, my Anna twas wed to Toma ere I met her, and the story tis too long for telling this eve. Ye must trust that all three of them will nay betray us."

"Ye have given me nay reason to trust them."

He raised his eyes to hers, grasped her by her arms, and his firm voice was filled with authority. "I am Maca. I need nay reason."

LouElla drew her breath in sharply. She had named him Maca in her crystals to her brither and to the Council of the Realm. His hands holding her contained the heat and the demands of a Maca. "Aye," she whispered. "So I named ye, and so ye are."

Chapter 30

When to Leave

Morning brought leaden sunshine spewing over a graying coat of white left by a cloud darkened night. The temperature remained below freezing, and the cold fought to enter any home with opened door. LouElla emerged from the sickroom to find Margareatha seated at the table playing solitaire and Anna fast asleep on the couch with the stuffed chair shoved against it to keep her from rolling off. Mina sprawled in the stuffed chair with her doll and a blanket wrapped around her. From somewhere in the house boots and a jangling noise could be heard stomping up the stairs.

"What tis that clattering?"

"I imagine it's Lorenz going back up to his room to complete his morning toilette." Rita looked up with a bland face. "He has to go into the police station to file charges."

"Ye've been up all night."

"Of course, someone had to make certain Toma wasn't out there searching for us. I'll stay on duty until Lorenz gets back or Mac wakes up." She looked at her mother and smiled. "Mama hasn't slept more than two hours a night for a week. I doubt if she'll be awake anytime soon."

LouElla nodded her head and went through the house to the outside facilities. She hated the chamber pots as inadequate in size and hated the outhouse as smelly and diseased. In the winter the outhouse was freezing cold, and in the summer one could suffocate from the heat and gasses emanating from below. Right now it was freezing cold, and she rushed back to the house and the warmth only to be assailed by Ruth and another problem.

"Miz Gordon, I need to go to the market today and buy meat, potatoes, and Lord knows what else. I didn't think all these people would be here for another week, and I'll need money for the tradesmen."

LouElla's face went blank. Miss Walls always attended to financial matters. Before she could speak, Ruth went on.

"And that young man says he's taking the horse and wagon 'cause he needs to go to the police station. Miz Gordon, is everything all right?"

It was, thought LouElla, a fair question. "It twill be," she muttered and almost ran into Lorenz. He was grinning at both of them.

"Everything is fine," his lop-sided smile appeared and disappeared. "We've sufficient funds with us to feed an army. It shouldn't take me long to file the charges against the man that attacked us, and I'll be back in time for y'all to take the wagon. I may even go along to hire a horse from a stable. Your barn is big enough."

Ruth looked doubtful. "Then we'd need more hay."

Lorenz's smile appeared again. "I'll buy more. Right now Papa's awake and hungry, and so am I, but I'll just grab one of your biscuit and eat something when I get back. Mama will wake sooner or later and when she does, she'll probably find something to do out here."

Lorenz grabbed two biscuits and ran out the door. In his hurry, he missed the horrified look on Ruth's face. "Miz Gordon, this is my kitchen."

"Aye, and nay twill take it from ye. Have Milly bring our food to the back rooms. The wee one tis there too."

LouElla hurried back to her laddie. Obviously, Lorenz was bossy and there was a good possibility his mither would be the same. She set her chin.

Cold was not all that morning brought. The entire Gordon household was thrown into an uproar. The last word from Mrs. Gordon to Milly last night had been baths for all. Even Miss Walls, with her humped back and hunched shoulder, was called to help with the linen. Ruth was presiding over the preparations and making breakfast, runnels of sweat pouring down her face and chest from the heat rising from the stove. Earlier, she had directed Lorenz to Mrs. Gordon's bath as carrying all that water upstairs this morning was out of the question. Fortunately, Mrs. MacDonald remained asleep. Ruth decided that Lorenz was entitled to the extra roll for carrying in an armload of wood after returning from the outhouse and washed his hands in the common kitchen basin. Not like other rich men's son she decided.

All but Lorenz would have been horrified at the scene in the invalid's room. The two huge Thalians undressed each other and gloried in the magnificent body in front of them. Llewellyn had lost weight, but the muscular structure was intact. They caressed each other, marveling at their strength, laid their heads on each other's shoulders, and washed every part of each other's body until every muscle gleamed pink.

"Why has the laddie nay joined us?"

"His customs are the customs here. I have promised him that. Nay he, nay my true love, twill ere join us in the bathing, and Mina kens nay of our ways. Lorenz twill be in to re-bandage me and apply the salve, but we twill nay infringe on his privacy. Ye must wait till we are in Thalia."

"Then they are all to go with us?"

"Nay, Mither, for my wee one tis Earth, and first she must grow and become a woman. There tis nay on Thalia that would wed her, and it twill take ye at least fifty or more years to train all of us. By then my Anna twill have passed into the Darkness."

LouElla considered as she redressed him for the bed. She had been resigned to living out her years here, forever an exile with nay the comfort of another Thalian next to her, nay ever kenning whether her laddie lived, or her revenge complete. Now her magnificent laddie twas here and telling her that still the Justines and Kreppies overran her world. Her desire for vengeance was stroked with each tale of the Sisterhood rule and the raped earth of Thalian. She could nay remain here. Llewellyn had the means, and they could accomplish what she started. The wee ones (for such she classified Lorenz) would go with them.

They heard tapping at the door and LouElla answered, impatient at the interruption. Mina wandered sleepily into the room, lifted her arms, and said, "Good morning, grandmother." It was too much. She picked the child up and sat down in the rocker. Discussions could wait, and wait they did until Lorenz came running back in an hour later.

"Sorry, Papa, but it took longer than I thought. Did y'all get too tired?"

Llewellyn smiled. He hadn't felt so vital in weeks. "Nay, laddie, and I have been telling Mither about our ranch and our way of life. Yere mither tis still sound asleep, and we have all had our baths but her. He paused. "Ye had best dig out some of those greenbacks for the one in the kitchen. Mither tells me sustenance needs to be purchased."

Lorenz nodded and dug into the steamer trunk. LouElla watched with interest. Obviously the laddie obeyed without question and twas trusted with the funds. She filed the information away Lorenz was ready to step out of the bedroom door when Anna appeared, her hair more disheveled than he had ever seen it. She had a befuddled look on her face, and sleep still sagged at the lines of her jowls. Her eyes met Llewellyn's and relief flooded over her face and she spoke in German. "I could not remember where I was. How silly of me. Are you all right, Mr. MacDonald?"

He smiled broadly. "Aye, my love, I am fine. Tis a lovely morning and so are ye. Come and I twill introduce ye properly to my mither."

Anna advanced into the room, her head held high. LouElla stood and put Mina down. In her mind, her height would intimidate the interloper, but no fear showed in Anna's grey eyes when she turned to face her.

"Mother MacDonald, I'm so happy to know you are alive. Now our children vill know their grandmother."

It was enough to stop LouElla, and the two women stared at each other. Neither of the women moved towards the other to greet in the formal Thalian manner, and vexation clouded MacDonald's eyes.

Lorenz moved towards them. "Come on, Mina, let's go see if Auntie Ruth has any cookies while I tell them to get the bathwater ready for Mama."

Mina's brown eyes lit up at the prospect of eating cookies. Such a thing would not happen at home in the morning. It had not occurred to her that the two most important women in her life would not like each other. "Shall I bring some back for everybody?" She smiled at her mother.

"Nein, Mina, and it's time for your lessons." She kept her eyes on LouElla while the two left the room.

Llewellyn swung his legs over the bed, making a slight grimace, and reached out and took Anna's hand. "Mither," he said, "Anna tis my true love, and she and I are one."

LouElla took a step backward and looked at him. She had no intention of backing down. "Ye have nay Walked the Circle."

"There tis nay Council of Guardians to approve a Walk the Circle here." His voice rose. "I twill nay go back to Thalia till I can win all that tis mine."

LouElla looked at him and then Anna. They were as one, and she kenned she had lost.

Anna turned to MacDonald, her head held high. She might have withdrawn her hand, but his grasp was too strong. "Vhen do du plan to leave us?" Her grey eyes were hard.

His deep voice gentled. "I canna leave ye, Anna, nay our wee one. We are wed till death do us part. When I leave, Mina twill be a woman grown, mayhap even a grandmither."

Anna took a deep breath and turned back to LouElla. "Mr. MacDonald has taught me how Thalians greet one another. I vould lay my head on your shoulder."

LouElla nodded yes. The word twas 'shoulders,' but it did nay matter. She opened her arms. A warrior always waited for the right opportunity to change the battlefield and outcome.

Llewellyn watched with satisfaction. "Now attend, both of ye so there tis nay miskenning. Lorenz tis our laddie, and he twill be a great help when we return to Thalia, so twill Margareatha. Mither, ye twill teach us all to fly the *Golden One* and the math for navigating. The third person ye twill teach tis Jeremiah 'Red' O'Neal. He tis also Toma's laddie, but except for his eyes and his mind, he tis more Earth than Justine."

LouElla shook her head in disbelief. She regretted remaining secluded from her guests and never meeting them. "Ye have met him?"

LouElla listened in disbelief as Anna said, "He is a bad man."

"He tis an adventurer and a pirate at heart, but he has agreed to go with us. He twill also provide the band of Earth adventurers that twill go with us."

"Why would we take these people?" Scorn was added to her disbelief.

"There are many of them that the minds of the Justines canna enter. My Anna has such a mind, and so does my friend, Herman Rolfe. When we meet the Justines on their own ground, the Justines canna control them. These beings can fight the Justines physically and twill make a difference in the outcome. The important thing is that we now have the nucleus of our group, and the means to regain Thalia. The training means we twill succeed." A tight smile crossed his face and his dark eyes gleamed at thought of reclaiming his inheritance and destroying the power of the Sisterhood.

LouElla was more practical and thought of logistics. "And how far have ye progressed in yere math and flight control. How far has the laddie? What shape tis the *Golden One* in?"

Before MacDonald could answer, Milly's slight knock was heard. "Beg pardon, Miz Gordon, but Mrs. MacDonald bath is set up in the bathroom, and we almost have lunch ready."

Anna leaned down and kissed MacDonald's cheek. "One moment, I must my clothes get." She rummaged in the trunk and pulled out her skirt which she carefully laid to the side of the trunk. Then she placed her undergarments, hosiery, and blouse on the skirt, and carefully folded the skirt over the items the public should not view them. "I vill be back as soon as possible."

Llewellyn swung his legs back over the bed and leaned back against the pillows as LouElla drew the blanket back over him. "Where do I start? The *Golden One* tis in fine shape." He launched into a description of the *Golden One* and his efforts to maintain it while hidden from the beings of this planet. From there they began to explain their lives during their separation, and finally Llewellyn could explain the math that he and Lorenz had learned.

"Ye twill need to come to the ranch with us."

"I am nay sure that twill please yere counselor."

"Anna twill be honored."

LouElla did not believe him. She decided to let events unfold to prove her point rather than argue. "There tis, however, a major problem with attending ye. What do I do with this property and the paying guests that have already requested accommodations this spring and summer? I am in some measure responsible for Miss Walls and the staff here."

Llewellyn smiled at his mother. "Ye can sell this place, or if ye believe yere Miss Walls to be a responsible person, she can run it in yere absence. This solution twill provide for them and possibly bring ye an income."

LouElla considered. Miss Walls had been her friend since their days in the mills of the northeast. She had nay said a word to others about LouElla remaining young while she had aged. It would be best to let her manage the place. She handled all the funds anyway. Why change things and embitter someone into causing trouble?

"I shall speak to Miss Walls. There tis another problem."

"And that tis?"

"Yere laddie has nay enough math for me to begin teaching him the ways of space navigation. It would be better if he attended a school here. Do they nay have the basis for all math?"

"Aye, there are some outstanding schools in this land and in Europe." They both looked at the door that opened to admit a refreshed Anna and a happy Mina.

Her white hair gleamed, her skin glowed pink, and her step was firm. She looked, thought LouElla sourly, the very picture of the Mistress of Don clothed in the alien garments of this world.

"Did I hear du talking about schools?"

"Aye, what do ye think of sending our laddie to a university to acquire the education he needs?"

Anna stopped mid-stride, her grey eyes widening. "Ach, I've always dreamed of it." She hesitated, and her eyes grew troubled, "Lorenz may not like the idea."

"He tis our laddie," Llewellyn said firmly. "He twill follow our guidance. I twill broach the subject when he returns."

The "broaching" did not go quite as planned when Lorenz returned from renting a riding horse and purchasing the necessary feed. He had discarded the more formal clothes of the city and was in his usual ranch wear of denim trousers, collarless flannel shirt, and a blue bandana knotted around his neck. The woolen winter underwear made his body appear wider than his "skinny" frame. The cheeks were reddened from the winter cold and his grey eyes were excited at the thought of riding again; excitement that died at the mention of schooling.

"I'm not going. There are other things more important." His eye narrowed and his mouth set tight.

"And what would be more important?" asked MacDonald mildly.

"The ranch is, Papa. Y'all still haven't recovered, and we'll have to work twice as hard to make up for lost time."

"Daniel tis there and can remain."

"He'll go back to Red just as soon as he can. He doesn't care about the ranch like we do. Frankly, he doesn't want to be around us; any of us. Rity will go back too. She much prefers account books and numbers to hard, physical work."

LouElla was shocked at his disobedience. Her laddie twas the fither and Maca of this skinny male. How dare Lorenz defy him?

MacDonald's shoulders were straightening and his mouth growing harder. "Ye're mither and I have decided."

"I'm sorry, Mama, Papa, but after we get back from selling the beeves next fall, Antoinette and I will be married."

He heard the gasped "nein" from his mother and continued on, his voice flat, broking no opposition. "She's agreed to be my wife."

"Ye are too young to wed. All ye need tis a First Bedding!" LouElla snapped.

Lorenz saw his mother's lips tighten and she started to turn her ire on her mother-in-law. "That is a sin," Anna glared at her and then turn back to face Lorenz. "Vhy can't du vait at least von year?"

"We've already postponed it for this year. We were able to keep our letters from Red's prying eyes by posting through Rity, and we'll have to wait until Rity's back there to plan more, but we won't delay the wedding again."

Lorenz noted his father's eyes were starting to bulge, while the huge fists clenching and unclenching. It was time to let them cool off and argue it out among themselves. He spun on his heel and headed back to the carriage house and the horses, grabbing his jacket from the peg by the kitchen door. Outside, he buttoned his jacket against the wind chilling cold. They could talk about schooling all they liked. They weren't fooling him. Schooling was to help him prepare for leaving Earth once Mina was raised and Mama had passed away. He wasn't going anywhere. He was going to marry Antoinette. The thought of her as his wife lightened his mood, and he began to whistle a trail tune.

The End

About the Author

Mari Collier was born on a farm in Iowa, and has lived in Arizona, Washington, and Southern California. She and her husband, Lanny, met in high school and were married for forty-five years. She is Co-Coordinator of the Desert Writers Guild of Twentynine Palms and serves on the Board of Directors for the Twentynine Palms Historical Society. She has worked as a collector, bookkeeper, receptionist, and Advanced Super Agent for Nintendo of America. Several of her short stories have appeared in print and electronically, plus three anthologies. Twisted Tales From The Desert, Twisted Tales From The Northwest, and Twisted Tales From The Universe. Earthbound is the first of the Chronicles of the Maca series.

Mari Collier's website can be found at
http://www.maricollier.com/

Lightning Source UK Ltd.
Milton Keynes UK
UKHW020708311220
376171UK00009B/466/J